the sweetest thing
a River Bend novel

Lilian Darcy

TULE
PUBLISHING

What others are saying...

"Lilian Darcy's writing is wonderful, and the characterizations are rapier sharp."
-*New York Times* bestselling author Mary Jo Putney

"It's the writing that grabbed me... reading [*Cafe du Jour*] is like talking with a friend."
-Jayne at DearAuthor.com

"[*Saving Gerda*] was dark and yet it drew me in, pulled back, made me long to get back to it... My eyes are filling up as I type this... Stunning, stunning book. I am totally in awe."
-Liz Fielding, multi-award-winning author of *Liz Fielding's Little Book of Writing Romance*, from Amazon

"Lilian Darcy really brings the town of Marietta, Montana, to life with vivid descriptions that will have readers kicking up dirt, smelling the food from the concession stands and enjoying the beautiful scenery. *Marry Me, Cowboy* is a fresh and fun novella that makes for a quick and satisfying read."
-Chris Read of Romance Junkies

"Darcy handles serious subjects with heartrending humor and laugh-out-loud wit. Her characters are a rare and refreshing mix of honesty and sincerity, and their love scenes are powerfully emotional."
-Debbie Haupt in *RT Book Reviews* on *It Began With a Crush*

"Excellent storytelling and a strong conflict will keep readers turning the pages..."
-Melanie Bates in *RT Book Reviews* on *A Marriage Worth Fighting For*

"I totally loved this book! Whether you're a first time Lilian Darcy fan or a returning reader you will be pleasantly surprised at just how powerful her writing can be."
-Sara of Harlequin Junkie on *A Marriage Worth Fighting For*

"[*Café du Jour* is]... warm and witty, an excellent read."
-Dianne Dempsey in the *Melbourne Age* newspaper

"I would give [*Café du Jour*] six or seven stars if I could."
-Amazon UK reviewer

"Captivating novella. *Marry Me, Cowboy* had me hooked from start to finish."
-Amazon reviewer

the sweetest thing

© Copyright 2014 Lilian Darcy

The Tule Publishing Group, LLC
ALL RIGHTS RESERVED

No part of this book may be used or reproduced in any manner whatsoever without written permission except in the case of brief quotations embodied in critical articles and reviews.

This is a work of fiction. Names, characters, places, and incidents are products of the author's imagination or are used fictitiously. Any resemblance to actual events, locales, organizations or persons, living or dead, is entirely coincidental.

ISBN 978-1-940296-22-7

For my brother

Dear Reader:

What do you think about the importance of timing in a relationship? Is it make-or-break? If the timing is bad, should you accept that the relationship wasn't meant to be, or should you fight to overcome what's working against you?

This was a real question for me and my husband before we married. I'd come over to the US for a stay of several months and we met toward the beginning of that. But partway through, I had to cut the trip short and fly home. We'd only known each other for ten weeks at that point. We could so easily have shrugged, cried a bit, and let things go. After all, Australia and the US are an awful long way apart. But we didn't. Instead, we decided to make the relationship work and we wanted marriage to cement that.

A few months ago, we celebrated our 25th wedding anniversary, so clearly it was the right decision. But how do you know, in that kind of situation?

There are issues of timing in this book, and in the spin-off novella I'm planning to write next. If you like Charlie in this book, and are curious about him, you'll get some answers in the novella. Unfortunately I can't tell you the title of it yet, as I haven't come up with a good one!

In the meantime, I hope The Sweetest Thing makes you laugh and cry, and that it doesn't make you crave chocolate *too* much.

All the best,

Lilian Darcy

Contents

Chapter One	9
Chapter Two	13
Chapter Three	19
Chapter Four	27
Chapter Five	40
Chapter Six	45
Chapter Seven	62
Chapter Eight	75
Chapter Nine	85
Chapter Ten	98
Chapter Eleven	115
Chapter Twelve	128
Chapter Thirteen	142
Chapter Fourteen	153
Chapter Fifteen	162
Chapter Sixteen	176
Chapter Seventeen	191
Chapter Eighteen	205
Chapter Nineteen	218
Chapter Twenty	230
Chapter Twenty-One	237
Chapter Twenty-Two	257
Chapter Twenty-Three	270
Chapter Twenty-Four	278
Chapter Twenty-Five	289
Chapter Twenty-Six	295
Chapter Twenty-Seven	301

LILIAN DARCY

Chapter One

May, 2014

"You're still holding that photo?" Tully asked her birth mother gently. She took the thin hand and pried the damp fingers open, revealing a fragile rectangle of shiny photographic paper. It was a spare passport photo, formal and unemotional, showing a very good-looking young man against a blank white background. "Look, you're crushing it. It's getting soggy around the edges."

"I'm so nervous. I hate this. I'm afraid I won't recognize him. I'm afraid he'll hate everything he sees." She sounded as if she was on the verge of tears, which made Tully want to cry too.

"He won't," she said.

"How can you know that?"

"*I* don't hate everything I see, when I look at you. C'mon!" Tully squeezed the frail hands and felt a welling of love that she wouldn't have believed possible a few months ago.

"Thank you. Thank you so much for saying that. Thank you for saying it *now*." The tears came, fogging her mother's voice.

"Hey, you're welcome. And as for not recognizing him, you must have looked at that picture a thousand times since he sent it, and the other photos. You don't think his face is grafted onto your memory, by now?" Still she spoke gently.

Really, she was almost as nervous as her mother about the meeting with her brother—her long-lost half-brother, the one she hadn't even known about three months ago and had never met—and she understood the anxiety. There would be other passengers getting off the plane. Standing here, she and her mother were surrounded by people waiting to greet the incoming flight. Tully didn't know the size of the aircraft, or whether the flight was full. It might get crowded and confusing when people started appearing, especially when she and her mother were both already so emotional.

Ren was here with them, like a rock in a stormy sea. Or like a lighthouse, maybe, guiding them faithfully. Thinking about Ren made Tully's stomach kick with the prospect of loss. Not much longer and she'd have to say goodbye, and that would be that.

Done.

Over.

It was only a fling, could only ever have been a fling.

But his presence here at the airport was perfect and wonderful, despite everything. She would have found all of this so much harder without him.

"My memory isn't all that great, sometimes," her birth mother said, voice faltering in regret. Tully already knew the truth of this, and wasn't surprised to see her sneak yet another look at the photo barely surviving in her hand. "What's the time? Has the plane landed yet?"

"It's about two minutes later than it was when we last checked, silly." Tully pulled the bony shoulders close against her and kept the contact, feeling her mother leaning on her for support. She wasn't strong.

Beside her twenty seconds later, Ren said, "Flight's landed. Look, the board just changed."

He reached for Tully's hand and squeezed it, because he understood about the nerves and the reason for them, then he unlaced his fingers and put his arm around Tully instead, so that the three of them stood close together. His body was big and sturdy against her side, strong and warm and familiar, smelling of sandalwood and clean skin. Tully's heart and stomach did their usual lurching movements at the contact, and her bones wanted to melt with longing and fulfilment if she would let them.

She didn't let them.

She'd had a big lecture last night from David—her uncle—about going home to Los Angeles, back to her job, back to her life.

"You have to bite the bullet, Tully, make a decision, or the decision will be made for you," David had said.

"I have made a decision. I'm going back."

"Have you told the studio?"

"Uh, not yet."

"If you haven't told them, it's not a decision. Lock it in. Make it real. I'm astonished they've let you have four months. You need to signal your commitment."

"To the studio?"

"To yourself. Your life is in Southern California, not here."

But she didn't want to think about her decision, or what David had said.

Not right now.

If Sugar—

If Ren—

But Tully knew she couldn't hope for anything from Ren. She knew exactly where he was coming from, and where she wanted to go, and their directions were so completely different.

It was a fling, and it could only last a few more weeks. She'd begun to hide from him how much she minded about that, which didn't feel good. It felt dishonest and uncomfortable and she didn't know what to do.

"How long between when it says Landed and when they start coming through?" her mother asked, although she didn't seem to expect an answer. She was muttering, half talking to herself. Tully answered her anyhow.

"Soon," she said. "Should be pretty soon."

"I hate this."

"I know. It'll get better when we see him."

"You don't know that."

"It will," Ren answered, and her mother seemed to believe him more than she believed Tully—another reason Tully felt thankful that he was here. He was the kind of man you did believe, always. He was competent and trustworthy and knowledgeable and rock solid.

The three of them stood together, waiting, arms still around each other, counting down the seconds until the plane taxied to the gate, opened its doors, began to let passengers stream onto the jet-way and along the concourse to the arrival doors.

After ten endless minutes, finally here were the passengers from the flight. A woman in a business suit, then two men striding together. Next came a family of four, and a string of three men on their own, consulting their phones as they walked.

Then Tully's mother cried out, "That's him. This is him. Oh, I do recognize him! I didn't need the photo. That's him."

She burst into tears, and Tully folded her into a tight embrace and saw Ren watching her with something in his dark eyes that she knew was care... or even love... but that still didn't count in the way she needed it to.

Because it can't last.

"Let's go meet him," she said, her voice thick. She felt one last touch of support from Ren against her back as she walked forward.

Chapter Two

February, 2014

"I want you to help me find my son."

The woman sitting in the rust-colored leather armchair opposite Ren Fletcher's desk was blinking back tears as she spoke, and her voice had gone foggy and thick on the last two words. She was thin and large-eyed, neatly dressed in black pants, suede boots and a cream top, with a rather nice gray wool coat hung over the back of the adjacent chair, because it was only the second week in February—the eleventh—and there was snow in the forecast.

Beyond the neat appearance, though, she'd lived a hard life, and it showed. She had long, thin and slightly snarly straight hair, inky dark with gray roots, and a fine network of wrinkles on her skin. Her eyes were a watery blue. She had nicotine-stained teeth, and a couple of missing ones showed at the back when she opened her mouth too wide. She looked around sixty, but something about her told Ren she was younger than this by some years. She might only be fifty, which would make her just fourteen years older than he was.

"Your son. Is he missing, or—?"

"Not missing. I gave him up for adoption a long time

ago. And I want to make contact, with your help."

It wasn't the kind of task a small-town Montana lawyer was often asked to perform, Ren thought.

He sat back and invited her with practiced professional courtesy to give him more detail. How old was her son now?

Thirty, he learned.

Born in Montana?

No, California, she said. San Diego.

So when had she given him up? How? Why? What details did she have that might help him find her child?

When she'd answered most of this, and he'd taken a few token notes to show he was listening, he said gently, "This isn't my usual area. And in fact it's not the usual process, to go through a lawyer. There are systems set up to help people locate their birth parents after adoption, and vice versa. It does vary from state to state, but not much. My office manager can put together some Internet links for you, if you want, to get you started."

"I know there are systems, but I don't want to do it that way," Suzanne Morgan said.

"No?" He was doubtful. He wasn't convinced she had a lot of money, and those other systems cost quite a bit less than involving a lawyer. She had to know that, surely. This was why his notes had only been token ones. He'd honestly thought she would stand up, say thank you very much, take some information from Nina on her way out, and that would be that.

But no.

"I—I just don't," she said. The last two words were very firm and certain. "I want a barrier, you know?" She seemed a little shaky and he began to worry about her. There was something about her, fragility coupled with pride, a frayed and hard-won dignity and determination. "A go-between," she went on. "For as long as needed. My son might not want to have anything to do with me. I want him to know that this is..." She groped for a word that worked for her, one she could live with, "...respectable." She added after a moment, "Safe for him."

Safe. Okay. It seemed like an odd word to choose.

"Well, yes, I can help you with this, if it's what you really want," Ren said. "But you do need to know—"

She cut in, polite and proud, "If you're going to say that it'll be more expensive this way, I do know that. I understand. You have to charge your usual rate. And you're a lawyer, the best in town, so I know your usual rate is not going to be, like, twelve dollars an hour. That's okay. I want this to be..." Once again, she searched for a word, "...classy. And neat. And right. I have some money saved." Her chin jutted out for a moment, and she narrowed her eyes. "This is a high priority for me, and I need help with it. I need someone like you. Someone discreet."

"Of course."

"If you have to call me, please, I don't want you leaving any message other than your name."

"That's understood." He wondered about the way she emphasized this. She was frowning at him, looking a little hunted and haunted suddenly, and he strongly sensed her need for secrecy.

"I want someone serious and qualified and trustworthy," she was saying. "Someone professional. So that my son will know it's safe."

That word again.

Ren nodded, and picked up his pen. "In that case, let's go through it again in more detail, shall we?"

He understood why this woman, Suzanne, seemed reassured by the prospect of his help, and he would do his best for her. He noted down in greater detail the facts she had given him before, and she remembered a couple of extra bits of information she'd forgotten to give him the first time he'd asked his questions. It was a dry, stumbling account on her part, with a few evasions and euphemisms that told him more than she probably knew.

She hadn't been a good person.

Or, no, he revised, she hadn't lived a good life.

The two didn't necessarily mean the same thing.

"My family doesn't know about him," she said at one point.

"They don't know...?"

"That he exists. That I ever had a son. And I'm not ready to tell them about him, or that I'm doing this. Not yet. That's why I don't want you leaving messages, okay? Just your name, and I'll call back."

"Okay."

He thought he knew her family, here in Marietta, but wasn't completely sure. Morgan was a fairly common last name, one that resonated with his own past in a way he didn't think about very often any more. When he did think about it, the thoughts were complex ones, tinged with regret and tragedy and questions. He'd have to check later in the file that Nina would have made for her, to confirm one way or the other if they were the same people.

When they'd finished, he told her, "I'm optimistic. You have quite a few strong leads, here. This may not take all that long."

"Thank you." She stood and smiled with a glow of genuine gratitude in her face, and he saw those gaps in her back teeth again. "Thank you so much!" There was a kind of warmth and courage to her that he couldn't put his finger on. She seemed like someone that, on paper, he shouldn't like very much.

Yet somehow he did.

He couldn't explain it.

"You're very welcome," he said, "and I'll be in touch as soon as I have any information for you. My office manager has all your details? Address and phone number?"

"Yes, she has all of that."

"Good." He reached out and shook her hand, that was dry and as thin as the rest of her. "Take care," he added, because he knew now that she hadn't, for most of her life. She hadn't taken good care of herself at all.

♡

Sugar stopped in the Java Café on her way home, after the visit to the lawyer. She sat by the window looking out on Main Street and watched a woman in the florist store across the street re-arranging her window display in preparation for Valentine's Day on Friday, three days away. It was going to be pretty.

She looked at the even prettier window display in the adjacent candy store, too, while she sipped on a tall latte laced with two packets of sweetener, and thought about buying a little candy store treat for herself afterward, to take home.

But the high quality items at Copper Mountain Chocolates were expensive, and she had to watch her pennies if she was going to be able to pay the lawyer, and pay her own way at home, for her mother's sake. Mom had already covered most of her medical bills and would be covering more. She decided not to blow any money on candy today. This coffee was extravagance enough.

Sugar had only done two good things in her life.

One, she'd gotten clean, finally—clean, drug-free, independent, and healthy.

And, two, she'd given away her son, when he was still small enough to have been undamaged—or so she hoped and prayed.

Two things.

Pretty short list.

She didn't know what order of importance to put the list in, but she thought about it often. Two good things. Not very impressive. Better than nothing.

Mr. Fletcher, the lawyer, seemed confident that he could help her find Zack.

Well, she always called him Zack, in her head, even though she knew his name was Charles now. She'd given him Charles as a middle name—Zachary Charles, she'd called him—and she was grateful to his adoptive parents for keeping it. She wondered if there would ever be a way she could thank them for that.

When Mr. Fletcher had seemed skeptical about helping her at first, she'd thought about flirting with him to close the deal, but she was glad now that she hadn't, even though he was a mighty good-looking man, with those whisky brown eyes and that strong mouth—but it had laugh lines all around it, she'd noticed—plus the olive skin, the full head of dark hair, the well-worked body, the expensive tailored suit with its jacket hung over the back of his chair.

His office building looked expensive, too, with its Nineteenth Century brick façade, and its quiet, high quality décor—the clean cream walls, the built-in bookcases, the art photography prints on the walls. A different world.

Ugh, she was very glad she hadn't come on to him. She would only have embarrassed herself, ruined everything. Thank heavens she'd learned a little about how to look before you leap.

She had no assets to flirt with any more. Her looks were long gone. René Fletcher had to be ten years younger than she was—no, even younger than that, still in his middle thirties. And she was out of practice, compared to those years when she'd known exactly how to provoke a response in any man who was looking.

Of course, the kind of men who'd been looking, back then, hadn't had much to recommend them, and what they'd been looking for was about as sordid as could be.

So maybe she'd done three good things in her life, she decided.

Gotten clean, given away her son, and stopped selling her body.

Huh.

Three things.

That was fifty percent better than two.

She sipped her coffee some more, and then prayed inside her head. She'd been doing this since her final, successful decision to get clean seven years ago, and it helped.

Please let René Fletcher find Zack. Please let him want to meet me. Please let them all forgive me for everything. Please let Patty and Tully forgive me, so we can have some good time together for a while.

She took her time over the coffee, recouping her strength, and then hugged Patty's thick, beautiful coat around her, put on the hat and gloves she'd tucked into the sleeve, and walked slowly, slowly home.

Chapter Three

Tully hadn't brought a gift.

She only thought of it as she was driving into town, after a grinding day and a half and one sleepless night in a bad motel on the road from Los Angeles—seriously, what did they do to those mattresses?—and she realized at once that she had to do something about it.

How could she claim she was ready to forgive and forge a better relationship, if she hadn't even brought a gift?

She stopped in Main Street, where the winter snow had been plowed into dirty heaps and then covered by a three-inch layer of fresh fall so that it almost looked pretty in the thin February sunshine. Behind the town, Copper Mountain was in some places as white as a pile of powdered sugar and in others as blue as mist, and there was a strong wind blowing up there. She could see the way it scoured the snow into shiny ice sheets and thick, feathery drifts.

Farther down the street from where she'd parked, Marietta's stores looked quiet today. No one wanted to be out in the cold for long. It was almost lunch-time, but Tully only saw one person outside the Main Street Diner. Just beyond her own parking spot, though, an expensive-looking SUV was pulling out of a slushy space at the curb and there was another vehicle waiting to take its place, while two or three pedestrians were passing by. This seemed to be the active end of town.

Okay, a gift... a gift.

There was the florist, a few doors down, with a customer entering and another one leaving as Tully watched. She gave the idea of flowers some serious consideration, but then decided against it.

She was all too familiar with flowers—not their physical presence, but as a line item on the lengthy budgets of the major movie studio where she worked as a senior accountant in the finance department. No, it wasn't as glamorous as it sounded. No, she hadn't ever met... fill in the blank with the name of your favorite star.

But yes, she was familiar with flowers.

Flowers for the dressing rooms of pampered A-listers. Flowers to make the lower level female staff feel valued and important, after a major box office success. Flowers sent to her boss's discarded mistresses.

The budgets weren't always honest about those particular flowers.

Besides, Suzanne was ill, and nothing said illness like a tasteful arrangement of blooms in a cellophane-stuffed, pastel-painted box full of brittle green foam. Why draw attention to Suzanne's state of health in such a way?

With a spurt of her mother's contrary spirit, Tully decided to go in a different direction. To the next door beyond the florist, to be exact—the candy store. To Copper Mountain Chocolates, where all three of the nearby pedestrians seemed to have come from, judging by the gleaming, copper-colored candy boxes tucked under their arms.

Wait a minute, the florist was busy, the candy store was busy, this was a Friday in February, and what was the date?

Tully laughed out loud.

Valentine's Day.

She hadn't even thought of it until now, but as she

climbed out of the car and hurried coatless through the cold air, with the wind blowing right through her, she saw another man enter the florist and yet another coming out of the candy store. The lunchtime rush of little-finger-wrapped boyfriends, guilty husbands, and wildly over-optimistic secret admirers had begun.

Yes, it was February 14, and Tully had been so busy getting her life sorted out in LA so she could make this open-ended visit back home to Marietta, she'd totally forgotten.

The likelihood of any red envelopes or pink packages being forwarded here from her home address, over the coming days, seemed rather slim. If anyone had a crush on her, it was a very secret crush indeed, and her work for the studio kept her far too busy to notice. She was single, and she would quite like *not* to be single, so she laughed about the whole thing for self-protection, and right now her status didn't seem likely to change.

Chocolates weren't just for Valentine's Day, however. Suzanne had always had a weakness for them. Most of her life, she'd disdained her given name and called herself Sugar, and it wasn't because she herself was especially sweet. In fact, she wasn't sweet at all, and never had been. Sugar was what she *liked*, not who she *was*.

Tully went into the store, thinking about all the other things Sugar had a weakness for, and wondering if this forgiveness idea was completely crazy. Mom's idea, not hers. A quest for forgiveness wasn't the reason she'd taken indefinite unpaid leave from her high-powered job and come home.

She'd come for Mom, not for Sugar.

But Sugar was the one who liked candy.

Sugar and me, both.

It was possibly the only thing they'd ever had in common.

The candy shop was utterly, gorgeously wonderful. Tully hadn't been home to Marietta since it opened a couple of years ago, so she had no idea. Mom hadn't mentioned it. As soon as she walked through the door, the store's glowing warmth bathed her all over and the smell of chocolate filled the air, not just in boxes or even in the piles displayed behind the pristine glass that fronted the counter, but fresh.

Chocolate being made... created... *crafted*... right now, right here, in this very building.

Chocolate still warm and liquid and thick.

Chocolate mingled with other flavors like caramel and hazelnut and vanilla and coffee.

Chocolate being *born*.

This wasn't a store, it was a temple, and Tully felt a seventy-percent cocoa butter hallelujah coming on.

There was no one in the front of the store after the recent rush of three customers, but Tully could hear female voices in back. They sounded harried.

"... crazy to be testing this today, when we're so busy," said one voice, "but Margery's here for the weekend and she absolutely insisted on having samples of all six options to look at. She says she'll go to a place in Bozeman if we can't deliver, and it's a big order, so we don't want to lose it."

"When's she coming in?" said a different woman.

"Four o'clock this afternoon."

"And when did she call you about it?"

"Seven-thirty this morning. On my cell phone. I wish I'd never given her the number."

"Summer people and a high maintenance bride, what a perfect combination!"

They hadn't heard Tully come in. She rang the little bell on the counter, and heard an exclamation. A woman hurried out, a pretty and slightly freckled redhead five or six years younger than Tully herself, who looked vaguely familiar. "I'm so sorry to keep you waiting," she said. Her cheeks were flushed from the warmth of the melting chocolate and her jazzy red and white apron was streaked with it.

"It's fine. I haven't even begun to decide yet." Tully felt drunk and dizzy with the power of glorious choice. She needed a little time for silent worship before she began the cacao hymn-singing out loud.

There was so much to consider and it all looked so perfect and delectable. Nut clusters covered in gleaming rich darkness. Chocolate in the shapes of shells and flowers and hearts and animals. Exquisite truffles peppered with coconut or crushed almond. Round chocolates with a tiny sugar rose in the center or heart-shaped ones covered in shiny foil the color of prom dresses or bridesmaids' gowns.

Tucked between two banks of shelves stacked with gorgeous pre-packed candy boxes, there was a little alcove containing three small café tables. A chalkboard on the wall behind the counter told Tully that she could sit at one of them and have tea, coffee, or hot chocolate if she wanted. Iced chocolate, too, in summer, she guessed. The row of pretty mugs hanging on hooks just below the chalkboard looked so inviting that she would have stopped and sat and sipped for a while, if this had been any other day.

Any day other than the one on which she was arriving home, ready to forgive.

"Take your time," said the younger woman, as if she understood the silent worship thing.

Who was she? Tully was sure she ought to know, but she had come home to Marietta so rarely since she'd left so suddenly at eighteen, and never when Sugar was in residence. Mom understood Tully's reasons for staying away, and since David was in LA too and also preferred to keep his distance, Mom and Dad...

Oh, Dad, I still miss you so much!

... Mom and Dad had mostly made the long drive to California for family time.

Sugar had never been any good at family time.

She'd destroyed most of it.

She hadn't even made it to Dad's funeral, four years ago. He'd died suddenly of heart failure, and Sugar had said she was coming, had given her flight details, but then she'd supposedly had a fender bender on the way to the airport and she'd called and said through soggy tears that she wasn't going to get here in time.

Tully hadn't believed the fender bender story back then, and didn't know if she believed it now. Mom insisted it was true. Sugar had finally made it home two days later, after Tully herself had already left again. Not long afterward, Mom had come to California for a long, nurturing stay, half of it with David and half of it with Tully, but she herself hadn't been home to Marietta since.

Until today.

"I'll try to be quick," she said. This was not about her own worshipful love affair with all things chocolate, it was about finding a gift for Sugar, and she might as well be generous if this forgiveness thing was going to get off the ground.

"Really, it's fine," the woman insisted. Hm, that tumble of copper-red hair...

"You're... one of the Carrigans," Tully realized out loud, although she couldn't come up with a name. There'd been Mattie, and—

"Yes. I'm Sage." She looked surprised at being recognized—well, half-recognized—and clearly didn't know Tully at all.

"Sage. Right. Your sister Mattie was a couple of years ahead of me in school," Tully explained. It began to come back to her. "And then Danielle was a couple of years behind me. And then there's you, and...?" But she couldn't remember.

"Callan. Callie. She's the youngest."

Sage still clearly didn't know who she was talking to, so Tully quickly continued, "I'm Tully Morgan, Patty and Walter Morgan's daughter."

It never *felt* like a lie.

Sage's face cleared. "Oh, of course! I know Patty, and I knew your dad, Walter, a little."

It never felt like a lie, even when she was telling it to people who knew the family.

"You have a brother, too, right?" Sage went on. "David?"

"Yes, in LA. We both live there, so Mom and Dad tend... tended... to come there to visit. I don't feel like much of a Marietta native any more, I'm afraid. And then there's my-"

A distressed exclamation sounded from the back room, saving Tully from her next familiar lie.

My sister.

"Sage?" the other female voice called. "Help! I can't get

this one out of the mold."

"Please browse all you want," Sage said hurriedly. "And I'll be back in a minute."

"Oh, no rush." Tully was quite sure she'd be able to browse for a good fifteen minutes in here before she grew too bored... or too hungry.

In fact, there were some slivers of chocolate to sample in a little dish on the counter. She took one, and glimpsed a paradise made of dark sweetness and a tang of fig and pistachio, as it melted on her tongue. Did Sugar have the kind of palate that would appreciate chocolate like this? Mom said she'd given up smoking, finally, but less than a year ago.

Maybe one of these pre-packaged and gorgeously gift-wrapped boxes, instead? They came in so many sizes, the choice confronted Tully with the murky ambivalence of her own feelings.

How much are you worth to me, Sugar?

The $250 Deluxe Copper Mountain Gift Stack?

The $180 Limited Edition Single Source Truffle Assortment?

Or just the Milk Chocolate Gift Mix, with twelve pieces, for ten bucks.

What price did you put on forgiveness? As an accountant, should she know?

Someone came into the shop while she was still very busy feeling appalled at herself. Out of the corner of her eye, she could see that he was male, dark-haired, built like an athlete, wearing a brown leather jacket on top of dark pants, and not in an especially patient or happy mood, judging from the rhythm of his footsteps.

There could be a lot of emotional blackmail in the air on Valentine's Day.

He went directly to the shelves containing the pre-packaged gift boxes, and she eased out of his way without really looking at him, back to the main counter where all the expensive gourmet specialties bathed themselves in soft golden lighting behind the glass.

Wow, spicy mango? Candied lime? Cornflake and chili?

Inspirational!

I'll get some of these for her.

It was a decision that made Tully feel a little giddy and scared.

What, she was actually going to choose a candy assortment for Sugar piece by piece, as if it *mattered?* As if they might find some common ground together, in exploring the exotic flavors? She was going to make a choice based not on her inner emotional balance sheet of anger and pity and, yes, shame, but on the hope of something *meaningful?*

Wow.

Way to go, Tully.

The new customer plunked a medium-sized copper-wrapped box down on the counter to Tully's left, adjacent to the cash register. After her attempt to quantify love and forgiveness in candy form just a minute or two earlier, she pegged his choice as a very ambiguous one.

Neither stingy nor generous, neither token nor wholehearted.

This was either a boss with a valued secretary that he genuinely wasn't trying to hit on, or a long-married husband who was very much over the whole thing.

Then Sage came hurrying back to the front of the store, and said, "Ren! Hi!" and Tully's feelings about chocolate and Valentine's Day suddenly became a whole lot more complicated.

This man right next to her, with the seriously buff body filling his jacket and the aura of professional confidence all over him was *Ren?* Ren *Fletcher?*

Chapter Four

She looked at him with shock in her face, and Ren recognized her at once, and said her name without even a long enough pause to blink. "Tully?"

She had a stylish bob haircut that swung around her face in a dark, syrupy, streaky brown, and professionally arched brows above her blue eyes. Over very nice designer jeans, she wore a soft, draped top in a dark green that hugged her figure and hinted at it and showed off the soft smoothness of her skin at the neckline.

In short, she looked fantastic in a way that kicked at him at once and that he had to work to ignore.

"Ren Fletcher," she said. "Is it?"

Apparently she wasn't sure. Might not even have recognized him, Ren thought, if Sage hadn't greeted him by name. That was probably a compliment, since he'd been every inch the weedy nerd, last time they'd met, complete with studious and unflattering spectacles. Now he wore contacts most of the time, and his six-foot frame had filled out a lot since—a side benefit to the serious working out he'd done more as an escape than for any other reason.

Lord, it was nearly eighteen years since they'd seen each other.

Long time.

Suddenly, though, eighteen years felt like nothing at all.

"Yes, it's Ren," he said to Tully, turning to face her a little more directly.

"Wow." She stepped back, looked him up and down so fast he wasn't even sure he'd seen her eyes move, and then gave him a smile. Her teeth were whiter and straighter than they used to be, he thought. She looked... citified, very urban, very self-contained, not a small-town Montana girl any more. Energetic and healthy, too. "It's—you look like you've—Wow," she said again. "It's great to see you."

"Likewise," he answered, then thought this had sounded way too pompous, a remnant of the youthful shyness he thought he'd gotten rid of long ago.

Why should it rear its ugly head now, in such a form? He softened the pomposity with a smile, and she gave another smile in reply, and there was too much in the air.

More than there should have been, after so long.

More than there should be, given his marital status.

More memories.

More disappointment and regret.

More of a bite of curiosity.

It *was* a relative of hers who'd come to see him the other day, about finding her son. He'd looked up Suzanne Morgan's address. It matched, as did the last names, so a cousin or a sister seemed likely, he didn't know which.

Sister, he thought, trying to dredge up the town gossip to which he never paid much attention, despite his wife's taste for it. There'd been talk about an older Morgan girl who'd given the family a lot of trouble and heartache over the years, but wasn't around much. It fit with the impression he'd had of Suzanne on Tuesday.

The connection had put Tully into his mind and kept her there, and now here she was, as large as life and much, much prettier.

It seemed like a coincidence, but really it wasn't. He joined the dots. Suzanne Morgan was clearly ill, so Tully

Morgan had come back for some kind of family visit and quality time. It fit.

Sage was looking at him and Tully, masking a degree of impatience pretty well, considering. Since Ren's law office was three doors up from her store—*René Fletcher, Attorney at Law* said the very nice professional sign out front—he knew how busy she always was on Valentine's Day. She didn't have time for any fraught, meaningful exchanges between him and Tully Morgan, the girl—now very much a woman—who'd ditched him on prom night, eighteen years ago, the girl he'd shyly and self-consciously wanted to date back then.

Meanwhile, the box of candy he was waiting to pay for looked smug, sitting there on the counter, as if it already knew that Ruthie wouldn't like what he'd chosen.

Well, he already knew this, too, which was why he'd selected it so quickly and with so little thought. It really didn't matter what he picked.

And yet Ruth would like it even less if he didn't get her anything at all.

He thought she honestly didn't realize she was like this, so impossible to please. They'd been married for twelve years, and had dated on and off since the end of high school six years before that, so this was his eighteenth Valentine's Day failure. Her parents thought he was wonderful. Her father had told him more than once, "Ruth isn't strong, emotionally." Her mother had said even more often, "Ruth needs you more than she would ever say."

But if Libby Wilson was right, Ruth didn't let her need for him show in kindness, or in appreciation of his gifts. Red roses were a cliché, she said. Household items meant he saw her as a drudge. Anything for the garden was too out of season, and where was she supposed to store it until it could be planted? Jewelry or a luxury clothing item was good in theory, but she never liked what he chose.

By this point in their marriage, he ricocheted back and forth between doubting his own taste in those areas and just feeling wearied and worn out by the automatic trip back to whatever jewelry or fashion store it was, so that Ruth could present the receipt, return the item, and exchange it for something else.

Last year, he'd bought the biggest box of candy in Sage's store and Ruth had told him it was extravagant, and he must *want* her to get fat, and didn't he care that she was trying to eat healthy to help with getting pregnant?

This year, she wasn't trying to get pregnant anymore, because she "needed a break from it"—well, they both did. He shouldn't criticize her for that, *trying* to get pregnant was a miserable way to have sex—so maybe she'd be okay with this medium-sized box.

She wouldn't, he revised to himself.

He knew this, but to be honest, he'd given up. He didn't care anymore. Her pickiness would wash over him the way it always did and he'd find an escape somehow.

"Can I take these?" he asked Sage quickly, because he liked her and didn't want to keep her waiting. He handed over his credit card, and she rang up the purchase and put it in a bag.

"Happy Valentine's Day," she told him. "Say hi to Ruthie for me."

"I will." He gave a brief nod to Tully, then spent a moment wondering if she knew that he'd married one of her high school friends. She must, he decided. Of course she must. The chain of town gossip in Marietta was pretty short and very efficient, even if chance hadn't brought them together face to face in all this time.

Uncomfortable, he got himself out of the store, thinking that for a first meeting after eighteen years, it hadn't been nearly dramatic enough, or long enough, or significant enough, and might it be another eighteen years before they saw each other again?

As he opened the door to leave, he heard Tully say, "I'm going to hand pick some of these, Sage. All the really special, unusual ones. They look amazing. Like chocolate jewelry. I don't care how much they cost. Can you put them in the nicest gift-wrapping you have?" Her voice sounded just a tiny bit higher in pitch than it should have, he thought, and a little flustered, too.

Like him, she'd been shy back in high school. Like him, was she experiencing an unwarranted flashback to those years?

Then the door closed behind him, and he and his token box of Valentine chocolates stepped out into the February cold and he had to forget about Tully Morgan and face the issue of lunch.

Ruthie wasn't working today, so she might easily be at home. Her job at the town drugstore was only part-time, but she was thick as thieves with the owner Carol Bingley. Mrs. Bingley was one of the nastiest women in Marietta, and Ren used to admire Ruth for managing to get along with her. Now, he wasn't so sure. Maybe their smooth working relationship had more to do with their being sisters under the skin, than the result of any tact and graciousness on Ruth's part.

At any rate, her hours at the pharmacy never seemed to have much of a pattern to them. He sometimes felt she would spring the changes on him in a way that deliberately pulled the rug from under his feet, but this might have been yet another area in which he was being unfair.

Ruth wasn't a bad person. She really wasn't. She'd never been openly rude to a client or a neighbor, never stolen so much as a flower from someone else's garden, never cheated on him or spent too much of his money or kicked a dog or slapped a child. She cooed over babies. She was good to her mother.

The two of them had been thrown together by tragedy and at first the idea of himself as the strong one in the relationship had done him good, helped him to become a better man. Hearing, "I need you," so often had turned him into someone who *could* be needed—someone steady and strong and reliable and forgiving.

But in his heart he knew their marriage had been an easy way out for both of them, something they'd fallen into rather than actively choosing. It had been wallpaper over a gaping crack, and now it was like death by a thousand cuts. Each moment of discord or criticism between them, each grating action in itself was so tiny, but over time they added up and added up, and he felt so raw that he hurt in places that shouldn't have been possible. His teeth. His eyeballs. The hinge of his jaw.

He could have anesthetized himself with alcohol or other women—a few had made offers or sent signals over the years—but instead he'd chosen fitness as an escape. The hours and hours he spent jogging or cycling or working weights or horseback riding on Mom and Dad's retirement ranch had given him the body he'd despaired of ever having, back in his teens, but these hours weren't anywhere near enough to deal with the strain.

Ironically, too, Ruth wasn't a fan of the buff body. She took it as a personal insult and a criticism because she'd gained some weight herself. She wasn't fond of exercise and thought he only did it to show her up.

His car was parked in the street, giving him too much choice about where he went next. He could eat in the diner or grab a sandwich from the Java Café to take back to the office. He could sneak upstairs to the minimally furnished apartment above the office that was in theory vacant and for rent, only he never did anything to find a tenant.

Hm, why was that, actually?

Or he could go home and give Ruthie the candy box, if she was there.

He ought to go home.

Okay, he would.

Get it over with.

The house at the east end of Crawford Avenue was less than five minutes' drive from his office. In good weather, he walked or ran. Today, the journey by car seemed too short, and Ruth was in the kitchen, leaning her heavier-than-it-used-to-be chest over the kitchen countertop while she thumbed through a magazine, catching up on the celebrity news she loved.

"Can you believe how bad these women look on the red carpet, when they supposedly have the world's best stylists working on them?" was her sour greeting. "It's ridiculous! This thing, you can't even call it a dress."

"So don't look at the pictures," he suggested, even

though he knew it was the wrong answer. This was why she loved celebrities, he thought—so she could be mean and nasty about them without needing to watch her mouth, because they were high-profile targets so they deserved all the bitchiness she had in her.

And maybe that was a pretty harmless way to vent life's stress. Ruthie vented it on Twitter and Facebook and in the comments sections of fan blogs and celebrity watch websites nearly every day.

Ren tried to imagine himself doing it too—blasting a TV star for gaining weight when she had all that expensive help from personal trainers and nutritionists, speculating on the sinister sexual tastes of certain Hollywood A-listers who wore a different woman on their arm every week.

But no, he didn't think it would help with the tension that was balling tighter and tighter inside him. He thought the jogging and the weight lifting were healthier.

"Happy Valentine's Day," he said to Ruth, and brought the candy box out of the carry bag Sage had put it in.

Ruth threw her arms around his neck, and for one moment of cynical astonishment he thought he'd gotten it right and they were going to avoid an ugly scene, but then she took the box and looked at it and said sniffily, "Oh, from Sage's, I might have known," as if he should have driven to Bozeman for them.

"She makes great candy," he said lightly.

"And conveniently, she's almost next door to your office."

Last year, there'd been a couple of accusations that he was having an affair with Sage, but since she was now happily engaged to Crawford County's new sheriff Dawson O'Dell, becoming a mother to his little daughter Savannah, and living in a very pretty house on Bramble Lane, Ruth had at least dropped that particular line of complaint.

Death by a thousand cuts, he thought again.

"I'm going to drop in to see Mom and Dad," he said.

"Well, I wasn't expecting you for lunch." Ruth waved a hand around the pristine kitchen. She was a good housekeeper, never letting a dirty coffee mug sit on the sink for more than thirty seconds, or his sweats stay draped over the back of a bedroom chair, vacuuming almost every day. It was one of the things he tried to appreciate about her... *did* appreciate.

Everyone said marriage was hard work. Was this really what they meant?

"But I'm home for dinner," he said.

"Oh, I'm supposed to cook on Valentine's Day?"

He said with steely patience, "I can cook if you want."

"That's not what I meant. If you want to say I'm lazy, just say it, Ren."

"I didn't say you were lazy."

"Then what was it *supposed* to mean?"

"I'm not doing this," he muttered, and got himself out of there. She followed him, her silence hitting his back like a rough, repeated shove all the way to the front door, and when he reversed back down the driveway, she was still in the open doorway, looking speechless with indignation at his crass inability to understand anything at all.

He wanted to hit something, and he wanted it to hurt his hand. He wanted to yell or run, or just head north to Interstate 90 and drive East until he hit ocean somewhere in Massachusetts, around two thousand miles away.

Instead, he drove to his parents' hobby ranch, fifteen minutes from town, and felt the tension slowly ease, although it didn't ease nearly enough. How had this happened to him? How had he let it happen? To both of them?

He remembered how Ruth used to say to him early in their marriage, when he was paying attention to anything that wasn't her, "Is it the book or me, Ren?" "Is it the game or me?" He used to put the book down, stop watching the football game, give her the attention and lavish romance that she wanted, but it had grated. And then one day he'd said it, without knowing in advance that he was going to.

"Is it the book or me, Ren?"

"It's the book." And he'd kept on reading.

Was that the moment?

No, there was no single moment. There were countless

moments, and the kindness between them had long gone. It was his fault, too, not just hers.

Like Ruth, Mom was at home, in the beautiful place she and Dad had bought about four years ago, when he'd retired. Unlike Ruth, she'd made lunch. She heard his car, and came to the mud room door to greet him, her trim figure looking neat and casual in jeans and a fluffy black sweater, accented around the neck by a scarf glowing with color.

He smelled something delicious as soon as he stepped inside, and asked her in French if there was enough for three, because he could hear country music coming from Dad's study, so he knew Dad was home, too.

On paper, his parents' marriage shouldn't have worked. Dad was a plain-spoken, practical Montana businessman from an ordinary family, and Mom was a creative, intuitive, emotional artist from France with an aristocratic last name. Yet they'd been together and happy since meeting in Europe when Dad was stationed there with the military in the early seventies.

Right now, Ren could see twin Valentine cards on the sideboard in the dining room, next to a nice pile of wrapped gifts that he knew would have been carefully chosen by each of them and would be warmly appreciated by each of them once they were open. They probably had a whole evening planned, with food and wine and a good movie to watch on DVD, snuggled up together on the couch with the wood fire burning in the potbellied stove.

Mom answered him in English, her accent still strong even after nearly forty years in the USA. "Of course there eez enough for free."

Her inability to pronounce the "th" sound and therefore her daughter-in-law's name was one of the many things that Ruth complained about. "Does she *have* to call me Roofie? I know she does it deliberately."

"She doesn't," Ren had told her more than once. "She can't say "th", that's all. It's your choice, if you don't like Roofie. You can be Rootie or Roosie or Root or Roof. She really can't do Ruth. She has tried."

But Ruth wouldn't accept this, although she didn't

speak a word of French herself, and wouldn't even say "*merci*" for "thank you" or "*salut*" for "hello" the two times they'd been to France together, to see Mom's family.

"What is it?" he asked his mother, still in French.

"French onion soup," she answered, still in English.

It was the opposite of what they'd done when he was in his teens. Then, he'd refused to speak French to her, and she'd wanted him to practice, so she'd *only* spoken French to him. He'd hated being different, back then—it had been a major source for his shyness—and had wanted to be a proper, normal American guy like everyone else, with an apple-pie mom.

But he valued his French heritage now, was proud of the mix of fourth generation Montana and classic Europe, and he really, really liked French onion soup. "Yum."

"I'm so glad you came!" his mother said.

"Me, too."

"You never get enough of a break."

"No?"

"Well, my opinion, of course." She gave him a sideways glance, as if worried about him, and he wondered whether the tight jaw and the ache behind his eyeballs showed.

He rubbed his eyes with a thumb and forefinger. He had some complicated contracts to look through this afternoon, and someone coming in to talk about their will at two-thirty, as well as his first steps to take on the quest for Suzanne Morgan's son. It was grassroots, small-town legal stuff and he liked it much better than he'd ever liked corporate or criminal law, when he'd studied them in college.

If he had a specialty, it was real estate and property law, and Montana offered a lot in this area—drafting inheritance plans for huge ranches when one sibling wanted the land and another wanted the money, resolving disputes between neighbors when there was a traditional rancher on one side of the fence and a rich celebrity or business tycoon owner on the other.

Ruth had said she wanted to stay in Marietta, and this was one of the important things they'd agreed on before they got married—one of the things that had made Ren believe the marriage was possible, and a good idea. Lately, though, he'd noticed Ruth had been sighing about the climate and wondering what it would be like to live somewhere warm, like Florida or Southern California.

Was she hinting about a move? He didn't want to. No matter how often her parents told him that Ruth needed his strength, that Ruth would be lost without him, he wasn't going to put her desires ahead of his own to that extent. To go somewhere new where they had no friends or family support? No. That would only make everything worse.

Yes, he was glad he'd chosen small-town law, and he was happy in his work, and yet his life wasn't right. In fact it was seriously wrong, and he knew it, and—

"How eez Roofie?" Mom said.

"Oh, she's—she's—Yeah. She's good."

"Zat's great." Mom took out some black and white patterned Japanese bowls for the soup, which sat in a thick ceramic crock pot in the oven, the layer of cheese on top going bubbly and golden above a savory pool of rich, dark liquid and rounds of sliced and toasted French bread.

His mother had never, ever, in nearly eighteen years, uttered one word of criticism about Ruth. She always asked warmly about how she was, even read all the magazines so she could talk to Ruth about the celebrity gossip Ruth loved. Ren was under no illusions about this. Mom couldn't give a flying fig about celebrity diets and divorces and outrageous baby names, she did it purely to create common ground with her daughter-in-law. He'd never seen any evidence that Ruth tried to reciprocate.

"You should 'ave brought her for lunch. Oh, is she working?"

"No, she's home. I dropped in there, gave her some candy for Valentine's Day, but she seemed happy to stay in the house, so..."

"Well, it's cold today," Mom said lightly. "She wanted to stay in the warm." Ren knew in his heart of hearts that Mom didn't love Ruth and that she worried about their marriage, and he valued her tactful dishonesty and silence on the issue more than he could say.

Dad ambled into the room and gave him a bear hug and a slap on the arm. "Good to see you, son."

"You, too, Dad."

"Mm, honey, that smells so good," Dad said to his wife.

Mom had taken out the crock pot and was ladling the soup into the bowls. It was the perfect dish for a winter lunch, with the weather clouding over outside. Mom was like this. She had what you could only describe as a talent for daily living. She'd set the dining table with bamboo placemats, and on the wall Ren saw a new piece of her art, an elegant scroll of a thing in dusty yellows and greens and blues, whose construction and materials he could only guess at. Wool fiber and copper wire and thin strips of cane?

She was a weaver, represented by a major Bozeman gallery and regularly commissioned to make unique pieces for buyers all through the West. Ren thought that if Ruthie knew the names of some of the celebrity clients with whom Mom had built good friendships, she would be clamoring to meet them, but Mom wisely kept her clients' details very vague.

"Hey, we had the vet out here," Dad said as they ate, "and he says Coco is definitely in foal, probably going to deliver in April."

"Do you think the sellers knew she was in foal when you bought her?" Ren asked.

"Well, she would only just have been, last June. Maybe they didn't."

"You going to call them and ask about it?"

"I'd better. She's a pretty nice horse even if we don't know much about her breeding. If she's in foal to a good stallion, we should know about it. First foal for me, though. I'm going to get a foaling alarm and read up on caring for foals, might breed from her again if we like what we get." He had a keen light in his eye and Ren sensed the start of a new passion. After forty years in business, Dad was loving every second of his retirement.

After the meal, he wanted Ren to go see the mare, which Ren dutifully did, because there was still nearly another hour before he needed to be back in his office for the appointment about the client's will.

"Coming out for a ride on the weekend?" Dad asked after their visit to the pungent-smelling barn.

"If I can. If the weather cooperates."

Dad slapped him on the back again. "Good." There was a little too much significance in the simple word. "It does you good. The open air. Getting out and away..."

"Yeah, I know it does."

"... from, you know, the domestic detail."

"Yeah, I know." Suddenly, Ren felt emotional, wondering exactly how much his parents saw about his life, and what they said about him and Ruth to each other in private.

They worried about his younger brother Laurent, too, after the tragedy two years ago, when Laurent had lost his beloved wife Brooke in childbirth—the kind of loss that belonged in a Nineteenth Century novel and really shouldn't happen anymore. The whole family was still in shock over it, in many ways, and Laurent was struggling to raise two young children on his own. There was a horrible guilt-making irony in the fact that Laurent had lost the wife he'd loved so much, while Ren's wife was hale and hearty and it was the marriage itself that was struggling to survive.

"Go inside and say goodbye to your mother, won't you," Dad said, "before you leave?"

"Sure, I have time for that." He pretended he hadn't noticed the loaded undercurrent in Dad's suggestion.

"I'm going to grab some hay for the horses. See you on the weekend, I hope."

"Yeah." He headed for the house, aware that Dad hadn't gone back into the barn yet, but was watching him. He had the uneasy feeling that this was a relay race and he was the baton, and Dad had just passed that baton back to Mom for the next leg of the course.

Chapter Five

After all the thought and guilt and significance Tully had put into choosing the candy gift for Suzanne, she wasn't home when Tully pulled up outside the house. Mom heard the car and came out at once, moving more stiffly and slowly than Tully wanted to see, and they engulfed each other in a huge, warm hug, with tears on both sides.

"It's so good to see you, Tully." She looked tired and too thin. She was such a giving person, she'd had a lot to deal with over the years, she was seventy-five years old now, and Tully worried about her. The hands patting her back had finger joints knobby with arthritis, and Mom had needed to balance herself against one of the porch columns before starting down the steps.

"Good to be here," Tully said, holding onto the hug. "But where's—?"

"She went for a walk. She'll probably stop in somewhere for a snack, or something, or maybe just sit in the library." This wasn't far away, since they lived at the western end of Church Avenue. "You're earlier than we thought you'd be."

"I got as far as Pocatello, yesterday. It's a pretty easy

drive from there, and the roads were nice and clear."

Because of the long and open-ended nature of her stay, she'd brought several bags and boxes, and Mom insisted on helping her unload and carry everything up to her old room on the top floor of the hundred-year-old Queen Anne style house.

Mom had redecorated the room years ago, and it was so much prettier with its soft yellow walls, antique furnishings, and Native American patterned quilt, than the former teenage girl-cave papered in movie star posters and—because Tully had been a nerd back then and probably still was—the charts showing the Periodic Table and the anatomy of the human body.

Thinking of the teenage cave made her think of Sugar and her erratic periods of residence during those years, when Tully would spend most of her time in this bedroom, hiding from the chaos and misery Sugar created.

Next door, the atmosphere at the Shepherd house had been similar. Neve, in the same year at school as Tully, had been beautiful and arrogant, precociously mature, sexually aware, rebellious, charismatic, and wild. She'd sneaked out a lot at night, and sometimes Tully would hear her sneaking back in at almost dawn, climbing up to her open bedroom window on the old treehouse rope ladder that had never been removed from the big oak tree in the Shepherds' back yard. Handy, that.

Kira, Neve's younger sister, had been more like Tully, studious and nerdy and very much lost in Neve's flamboyant shadow. Pushed to the margins, just like Tully was whenever Sugar was around, if for different reasons.

"How is she?" she asked Mom abruptly, then added even more abruptly, before Mom could answer, "This is going to be hard, I'm not going to pretend."

"I know it is. Thank you. You can't know how glad I am that you've come." She brushed at her eyes with the edge of her sleeve, and sat down on the bed, perching with stiff hips on the edge of the mattress.

"Mom, honestly, don't say that as if I'm generous in being here. I'm not."

"You are. I know how you've felt all these years. Anyhow, she's... good, right now. They've adjusted her pain meds and she's trying to keep as strong as she can. But I know she'll start to go downhill and need more care, and the doctors have said that might happen quite fast. She abused her body for so long, it's damaged, and that won't go away. She's trying now, eating healthy, not smoking, but..." She finished on a sigh.

"You're tired, Mom."

She smiled through the tears she was still blinking back. "I am. And Sugar feels bad about that."

"She's developed quite a conscience, then, at this late stage," Tully drawled.

"Don't."

"Sorry." She looked at Mom again—the gray hair, the tired face, the determined cheerfulness and energy, and knew she was in the wrong. She sat down beside her on the bed and once more put her arms around the woman she'd called Mom her whole life, the woman who smelled and sounded and felt like she should be Tully's mother but who actually wasn't. "I *am* sorry. Always, this has been harder on you than on anyone else, even Dad. My whole life. Suzanne's whole life. I have no right to be angry with you, like I was at eighteen."

"Maybe I should have been tougher on her. I gave her so many chances, and she blew them all."

"Don't question that now. That's the last thing you need, isn't it, to beat yourself up? You did an amazing job."

"After all, she's my daughter."

"Yes, she is."

And I'm not.

"Tully, thank you."

"Now, stop!" she cajoled.

"You've been pretty angry with her, over the years..."

"Yes, but I'm not here in that spirit. I'm here to forgive and understand. I stopped on the way through town and bought her the most beautiful assortment of hand-crafted chocolates. I know it's not much... "

"Oh, from Sage Carrigan's store?"

"That's the one. It's amazing! I wanted to *inhale* that store. I wanted to bring a camp bed and move in." And she'd seen Ren Fletcher there, and he'd looked pretty damned good, lucky Ruth.

A kind of aftershock ran through her—self-consciousness and sadness and questions. She'd known for years that he and Ruth Wilson were married. You heard that kind of news in a town like Marietta, even if you barely visited.

She and Ruth hadn't kept in touch after high school. Tully had left town too suddenly, even before her senior year was officially over. They'd been friends, she and Ruth, but it was the kind of friendship that only lasts when you see each other every day.

All they'd really had in common was the fact that they were well-behaved in class and not in the popular group. Ruth had a finely-honed talent for bitching behind their backs about the popular girls—Neve Shepherd, Gemma Clayton, Lorelai Grey—and when you weren't popular yourself, that kind of clever bitching was *soooo* satisfying, at seventeen. Tully had long outgrown it now, though. She didn't like the taste it left in her mouth any more.

She and Ren hadn't kept in touch, either. Hardly surprising. He must have been so angry with her on prom night, when he'd come to collect her from this very house and she was gone without a word.

Not the kind of memory she had time for right now.

She finished, about the candy, "It's a small thing, I know, bringing her a gift."

"But it's a first step." Mom patted her back warmly with those knobby hands. "Thank you for trying."

"Well, of course I'm going to try! Having me here would hardly help you if I didn't. And you know I want to help you. I'm not going to leave you in the lurch."

"Is that the only reason?" There was a lot of appeal in Mom's voice, but Tully hardened her heart.

"I don't know. Sometimes I think so."

Mom controlled a sigh, then said, "That sounds like her, now."

They both heard the front door rattle, downstairs, and Tully packaged up a whole lifetime of anger and dislike and pity and shame, and tried to leave them behind as she went down to greet the woman who wasn't really her sister, the way everyone thought.

Chapter Six

Back at the house, Ren's mother had finished clearing away the lunch things and had wandered into her weaving studio. Ren found her standing in front of her latest work on the huge loom, testing colored wools against an abstract pattern of grays and whites and blues that reminded him of the winter colors on Copper Mountain.

She was so absorbed in her creative process that she didn't hear him come in, and gave a little yelp of shock and put her hand on her heart when he spoke. "It's nice," he said.

"Nice is not worth a heart attack!"

"I didn't think I was walking that quietly."

"You know me, I don't hear anything when I am thinking about colors and patterns." She smiled, and it wrinkled up her face, reminding Ren that she was sixty-one, feeling her age a little sometimes, and that he and Ruth had been trying to give her and Dad a grandchild on and off—mostly off—for nearly ten years without success.

And this wasn't counting the accidental grandchild they'd failed to give her when they were twenty-three, the one they'd hastened their wedding for, only to have the pregnancy end in miscarriage.

Ruth had suggested more than once, since then, that Ren wouldn't have married her if she hadn't been pregnant, but he thought he could easily have made the same accusation back to her.

Would she have married him without the prospect of a baby? Really? Would she have married him if they hadn't leaned on each other so much after the tragedy of prom night, back in 1996? If they hadn't been together that night, at River Bend Park? Would she have married him if someone better had come along? Troy Sheenan, say, who'd been one of their classmates and was a multi-millionaire now.

Why was he thinking about this stuff so much today?

Well, Valentine's...

And maybe seeing Tully in Sage's candy store, even though that little scene had only lasted a minute, which should hardly have been enough to catapult him back eighteen years.

"What's wrong?" Mom asked, and he realized how narrowed and tight his face must look.

"Nothing. I should go."

"Come for dinner on the weekend, the two of you. Laurent is bringing the children over on Sunday."

"Let me check our calendar." Although he knew Ruth found Laurent's kids way too noisy and active, now that they were beyond the cute baby stage, and would probably say no to the idea, blank calendar or not.

Mom was still studying his face with the same searching depth as Dad had done, out by the barn. Ren blinked and swallowed. His fist suddenly tingled with the need to punch something, and he wanted to yell or roar or run howling into the wind.

And whether it was Valentine's Day, or his mood, or a conversation Mom must have had with Dad—more than one conversation, probably—or the fact that Ruthie had told Mom a few weeks ago that they were "taking another break" from the burdensome task of trying to conceive, or some other reason he couldn't guess at...

Whatever it was, for the very first time ever, Mom said

it.

Very gentle.
Very tentative.
In French.
With the skeins of bright wool still in her hands.

"Why don't you separate, René? Why don't you get a divorce?"

"What?"

"Get a divorce. You're not happy, either of you. Why don't you do something about it?"

Yes, why didn't he?

His mind went into a helpless, sputtering whirl.

Well, because he believed in commitment and responsibility and hard work and honor—all the things his parents had been the very people to teach him. He'd seen them as such a good example. He'd wanted what they had. He'd wanted what Laurent and Brooke had, too, and after the tragedy of Brooke's death and Laurent's grief, how could he disdain his own marriage?

Ruth's parents had moved to Bozeman to be close to their other two daughters—Ruth was the middle one—but they still saw each other often, and Ray and Libby Wilson still pep-talked him constantly. "She needs you... She depends on you... You're her rock." They spoiled him in all the ways that Ruth failed to. They introduced him with pride to friends and neighbors. "This is our wonderful son-in-law, Ren."

Added to all of this, Mom had been raised Catholic and wasn't a huge fan of divorce. The fact that she was actually *suggesting* it was a tribute to the level of misery she perceived—a misery that Ray and Libby seemed determined to be blind to.

Maybe Mom was thinking about Valentine's Day, too, and the contrast between the private celebration she and Dad were clearly looking forward to, and the absence of any similar plan made by Ruth and Ren.

"Wh—I'm amazed that you're saying this."

"Have you never considered it?"

"I—Maybe I don't let myself, because—Does Dad think

the same as you?" he asked.

"Yes, he does." Still gentle. "We've talked about it."

Another shock. His parents were the ones who'd modeled all those things he valued, the honor and commitment and enduring love, and now they were the ones, both of them, who thought he should *bail*?

He blinked and swallowed again, balling his fists ready for the wall-punching he knew he'd never actually carry out, even though punching a wall was probably the right response. He really did feel this bad.

Hopeless.

Miserable.

Angry.

Wrong.

He really did hate his marriage this much, and had for too long.

"You've never said anything—" he managed, then stopped.

She made a very French gesture and sound. "Well, because it wouldn't have helped, early on, when you thought you were in love. And because there were those two times when we thought there was a baby coming." There had been a second miscarriage, five years ago. "And then because of Laurent losing Brooke. And then there were the times you were trying and we thought maybe there might be a baby coming and you just hadn't given us the news yet. But if you're taking a break again... why does Ruth always want to take breaks?"

"She needs time to regroup when it doesn't happen. After the miscarriages, too, it was the same."

"You only try for a few months, then there's another doctor visit, and then you don't try for two years. That's not how to get pregnant!" She made an impatient sound. "Listen to me, this isn't what I want to say. It's not the real issue. I'm sorry."

"It's okay. You've been pretty restrained, over the years," he drawled, "about a whole lot of things."

"René, I have to ask... You have to ask yourself... and tell me... are you happy?" she said quietly.

"You know I'm not." He barely let his mouth move.
"Is Roofie?"
"I don't think so. Not really. She never acts happy, anyhow."

"And yet when it comes to a decision like this, she is maybe not the kind of person who would take the first step to make a change..." Mom suggested carefully.

Hell, she knows her damned well...

Ruth indeed wasn't that kind of person.

It was suddenly clear to him.

Ruth would never make the first move on any separation, because if she did, she would lose her right to act as the injured party. Montana had no-fault divorce laws, so it wasn't a matter of legalities, but on a personal level, Ruth would never, *ever* want to relinquish the chance to make Ren feel that the whole sorry thing was his fault because he had been the one to say it first, just like it was always his fault when he got her the wrong thing for Christmas or Valentine's Day. Didn't Ray and Libby see any of that? Didn't they *want* to see it?

His temples tightened and his jaw started its familiar ache.

I want a divorce.

Mom was right. How could he stay married to a woman he could be so cynical and negative about? It was cruel to both of them, a pointless prison.

"... so you will have to be the one to do it," Mom said, as if she was suggesting he was the one who would have to take an elderly cat to the vet to have it put down.

He nodded.

An elderly cat. That was his marriage. Deserving only to be put out of its misery with as little pain as possible, something a colder, more practical, less idealistic person might have done years ago. And he was the one who had to do it.

Maybe this was the one act of kindness toward Ruth that he had left in him, to be the one to take the blame.

Mom was silent for a moment, looking at him with her big brown eyes, then she shifted focus and said in English,

"Do you 'ave an appointment? I fink you said so."

"Yes." He looked at his watch. "You're right, I probably need to go." He could have stayed longer, but he felt an intense need to be on his own so he could think things through.

"We can talk about this some more, if you want."

"Probably not."

"You both should be 'appy. Free."

"Yes. Yes."

She touched him on the arm, clearly not daring to hug him in case he... collapsed, or something. Wept. Moaned. They said a brief goodbye, then he drove away out of sight down the road, and pulled over because he needed to breathe for a while, even if it meant he was late getting back.

The turnoff to River Bend Park was just a hundred yards ahead, he saw. He pulled back onto the road and then took it, driving the quarter-mile down to the parking lot that overlooked the big curve in the Marietta River. He had exactly twenty-one minutes until his appointment, which meant he could sit here for ten.

The water was flowing rather than frozen, but snow crusted the coarse sand of the beach that lay in the elbow of the curve. Farther from the water, ice hung in the trees and coated the grass stems and branches, transparent and glistening.

There was a footbridge over the river now that hadn't been here eighteen years ago. It led to a short boardwalk loop on the far bank, with built-in wooden benches and interpretive plaques detailing the local plant and animal life, and the geology that had formed the landscape and the river.

On this side, over to the right, there were picnic tables shaded by healthy young trees and a purpose-built stone and concrete hearth with a set-in metal grill plate for barbecues. The county parks department kept it supplied with firewood in summer.

Everything looked very different here in the winter snow from how it looked in spring and summer, but there was a sparkling beauty in the cold air and he just sat there at the wheel of his SUV, watching the rush of the deep, icy river and thinking about his life.

He wondered why his mother essentially *giving him permission* to seek a divorce had created such a cataclysm in his own thinking. She wasn't a tyrant, and he wasn't tied to her apron strings. He'd never felt he needed her permission for anything. He certainly didn't need it over something like this.

"It's because she and Dad have never said a word before," he realized out loud. Inside the car or out of it, there was no one to hear.

If his parents had hinted or nagged or criticized all these years, he wouldn't have taken any notice. He was too used to hinting and nagging and criticizing at home. If Mom had been the same as Ruth in that area, her words wouldn't have been such a shock, and such a trigger. He would have been numb to them.

It was the very fact that Mom had never said a thing, not one single thing, and then had worded her question so quietly and gently today, like breaking the news to someone that they were fatally ill, when at heart they'd known it all along, only no one would say it.

Why don't you separate?

Hearing the question spoken out loud by someone else, someone who cared about him, made a difference.

Made all the difference.

His thoughts tracked back through all the studied silences and petty sniping and cryptic arguments, the two pregnancy losses that had brought him and Ruth a deceptive sense of closeness and sharing each time they'd happened, the worries over her health and fertility and the announcements she would make about her decisions on the subject—decisions he tried to support, because he remembered their shared grief. "I think if I only worked part-time, Ren, then I'd relax more." "I think if we take a break for a few years, really work on our marriage, before we try again."

He tracked back farther, to the years they'd half-heartedly dated when they were both in college, each seeing other people from time to time, waiting for a thunderbolt with someone else—it had never happened, for either of them—then rekindling the relationship that had begun in such tragic circumstances, the night of the 1996 Marietta High School Senior Prom.

The prom.

Would they ever have gotten together in the first place, if it hadn't been for the prom?

Sweet Jesus, the prom, and its aftermath, right here at River Bend Park...

May, 1996

As a general thing, Ren was incredibly glad he lived in Montana, not California or Florida, or anywhere else beachy and warm. Specifically, today, he was incredibly glad that a high school prom involved dressing in a tux, which had pretty good camouflage value.

He did *not* have the kind of body he wanted any girl seeing bare on top. His mother said he was only this skinny and weedy because he'd grown so fast in height that he hadn't yet had time to fill out sideways. Over the next few years he would, she promised him. He might be six feet tall and as wide as a piece of spaghetti now, but he would have an excellent body by the time he was twenty-five or so.

He wasn't sure if he believed her, and she reassured him about it too often, which made him feel worse, as if his body really must be freakishly bad, since she had to keep on insisting to him all the time that it would get better.

Meanwhile, by putting two identical undershirts on beneath the white dress shirt and formal black jacket he'd deliberately rented one size too large from a store in Bozeman, he hoped to give his torso just a little more bulk.

Tully Morgan, his prom date tonight, was so pretty he didn't want to look like a gangly idiot beside her. She wasn't sexy model beautiful, she was what Ren and his friends privately called "nerdy cute."

Being nerds themselves, they knew this was the best

they could aspire to, in the dating department, and secretly they found this kind of girl a lot less scary and threatening than they found girls like Neve Shepherd and Gemma Clayton, who had such a knowing, adult confidence in their sexuality and desirability that Ren's whole body went like a sweaty ham every time he saw them.

"You look bee-yu-tee-*fool*," Mom said, when he showed himself to her in the front hallway, ten minutes before the car was due to arrive.

Her French accent was as thick as a slab of Normandy butter, even after nearly twenty years in America, and Ren found her exotic appearance and exotic attitudes and exotic way of talking deeply embarrassing. He'd said to her a couple of years ago, "Can't you even *try* to be more American?" but apparently she couldn't, and didn't even want to, and Dad seemed to like her that way.

She straightened his already-straight tie. Fixed his already-perfect collar and best-he-could-manage hair. His incredibly annoying younger brother Laurie abandoned the TV long enough to stand in the living room doorway and guffaw at him, newly-broken voice cracking on the sound.

"*Chut, Laurent!*" Mom told Laurie with an irritated frown. "It'll be your turn in a few years."

The car came. It was a 1957 Buick Super, in dark blue and cream, dent-free and chrome-covered and polished till it gleamed, driven by none other than Marietta's new sheriff, Harrison Pearce. Sheriff Pearce's brother owned the car and was driving its garage-mate, a black and silver Oldsmobile 98, and even though Ren was part of the posse of nerds, they were going to be the coolest nerds at Marietta High, tonight.

Barely anyone came to prom in a limo, the way they did in California or on the East Coast. Most kids came in their own pickup trucks, or in the fanciest car owned by anyone in their extended family who was willing to lend it.

He couldn't wait to see Tully's face when they pulled up outside her house, because even though his buddy Andy Pearce had promised that the cars would be incredible, Ren hadn't completely believed him, so he'd played it down to his date. "Vintage cars okay? Don't know what they'll be like..."

Tully's bright, clever blue eyes had shone. "Oh, I would *love* to arrive in vintage cars!" She'd clapped her hands together. "That is so cool!"

Andy and his date Louise were in the car driven by his dad, along with another two couples. Everyone was already on board, but Andy's dad was taking the same roundabout route as Sheriff Pearce's vehicle, so that both cars would arrive at the high school at the same time, for maximum impact. Ren was the second-to-last passenger to be picked up, and Tully would be the last. It wasn't a long trip between his house and hers. Three minutes, and they were there.

He jumped out to go up to the front door of the pretty dwelling, hoping he might see her peeking around the edge of a window curtain and doing an excited double-take at the sight of the two awesome vehicles. He couldn't see her, though.

He rang the bell.

After a moment, her mom answered. She was an older lady, probably a good ten or twelve years older than his own mother, but real nice. Ren had only met her a couple of times, but she was so American and ordinary compared to his mother, and this scored Mrs. Morgan instant points, as far as he was concerned.

"Ren... " she said. She had a weird look on her face. Not comfortable. Not happy.

He hoped some old relative hadn't taken ill, or something, or Tully might be all mopey and down. Worse, she might not even want to go. Because where was she? Not visible yet.

He cleared his throat, and stated the obvious. "Um, I'm here for Tully."

"Ren, I'm sorry. She's gone."

"Gone?"

"You'd better come in."

"I can't." He gestured to the curb, where both of the beautiful cars sat, engines idling like tigers purring. Ruthie and Sam were arguing about something already, he could tell by the way they were sitting with their shoulders turned away from each other. The other two were just bored.

"Everyone's waiting."

And Tully was "gone." What did that mean?

"Is she... is she coming back in time for prom?" he asked stupidly.

"No, she's not. I'm sorry. Something's happened. She was upset, and she... just didn't feel she could face the prom tonight."

It's me, he thought at once. *She's sorry she said yes when I asked her. She didn't want to go with me. Mrs. Morgan is just being nice.*

He'd spent weeks gathering his courage to ask Tully in the first place, and when she'd said yes, he hadn't known what to do next.

Did this mean she wanted to date him in an ongoing way, or was he just a convenience for the one night?

He hadn't dared to find out the hard way, because if he asked her on an actual date before the prom and she turned him down or they had a horrible time, prom night itself would be a disaster.

He'd been pinning himself totally on tonight, and now it wasn't happening.

It's me, I know it.

"Oh, okay," was what he said out loud. "Never mind, then."

"I'm so sorry, Ren." Mrs. Morgan looked distracted, and the words were kind of tossed out there, as if she didn't have the energy to make them any more convincing.

It's definitely me, and she doesn't want to tell me that, and hurt my feelings.

He went back to the car, and saved face as best he could. "Something came up. Tully's had to cancel."

Nobody knew what to say, so they didn't say anything. Ren climbed awkwardly into the car, where there was now plenty of room in the back seat with only three of them, instead of four. Ruthie picked up the argument she and Sam had been having before, and said to him, "Well, I just don't understand how you could think that," then turned away from him in a huff.

This meant she was facing Ren, and she would have

looked pretty with her petite build and pixie face and salon-styled caramel-brown hair, if her eyes hadn't been all narrowed and tight.

He didn't know what the fight had been about, except that Sam always seemed to be doing or saying or thinking the wrong thing, as far as Ruthie was concerned. Since teenage girls seemed to have a better handle on these things than teenage boys did, Sam usually ducked his head and apologized, because it seemed all too likely that he was indeed the one in the wrong.

Tonight, he wasn't doing that, he was staring stubbornly out of the window, refusing to back down. Ruthie gave Ren a wan smile, and he gave one back to her, and felt a tentative link, as if they appreciated each other's suffering. He was dateless, while she was paired with someone who didn't understand her.

They arrived at prom and drew some gratifying looks because of the vintage cars. The moment of arrival was soon over, however, and it turned out to be the high point of the event. Mom was there, taking pictures of their arrival, and she asked about Tully's whereabouts, and he felt his cheeks turn red with embarrassment. He hurried inside, knowing that barely anyone would remember a week from now, that he, Ren Fletcher, had been one of the kids in the cool vintage cars.

Marietta High School didn't draw its students from a rich or flashy community, so the prom was a lot more basic than what you might get elsewhere. It was held in the gym at school, which was all decorated with mirrors and stuff. The theme was, "Shine on!" and it really did look pretty good. There was a buffet supper, followed by the dancing, and then most people would make the night last as long as they could, by going on to various after parties later on, some of them organized in advance, some of them basically just drinking.

Tully's mom had said she could bring her friends back to her place, but that wouldn't be happening now. Ren realized how much he'd been counting on his date to navigate their way through the evening, socially. He felt lost without her, and pretty miserable, too, no idea how to behave or what to do, let alone how to enjoy himself.

Supper came and went. His mom's food was way better. The dancing started.

Ruthie and Sam still weren't speaking to each other.

No, weren't speaking to each other *again*. They'd managed a truce through supper and halfway into the first dance, but then something else had gone wrong. "Will *you* dance with me, Ren?" Ruthie said, in a confiding and long-suffering tone, as if he was the only person she had a hope of being able to rely on.

"Sure. Sure I will." He reached out his arms for her, his palms slithering over her pale blue bead-encrusted gown. She looked nice. She felt nice, and smelled nice. She had a slighter and smaller shape than Tully did, and her body held an immediate appeal, this close, because he felt so big and manly in comparison. They began to move together, shuffling their weight back and forth from side to side. It wasn't much like dancing, but apparently it satisfied her.

She stuck to him the rest of the evening, and he was glad because it made him look like he had a clue, and with a girl on his arm it wasn't quite so hard to pretend that his heart wasn't hurting about Tully.

He liked Tully.

A lot, to be honest.

Those hopes he'd had for tonight—that it would be the start of real dating for them—seemed so stupid, now. He would have crawled under a rock if anyone had guessed.

At the end of the night, Ruthie came back from the bathroom and whispered in his ear, "River Bend Park. That's where everyone is going, after." She had her mouth too close, but she smelled good, so he didn't mind.

"Everyone?"

"All the people who matter. The Sheenan twins, Gemma and Neve."

"Sam..."

"Not Sam. Don't tell him about it. We're just going to disappear. Lorelai Grey says we can go in their truck."

"Whose truck?"

"Does it matter? Just don't tell Sam."

"How come?"

"C'mon, Ren! After the way he treated me tonight? After he's been such a jerk?"

He wanted it spelled out. What had Sam done? He felt he needed to know, because it might be so easy to do the same jerky thing himself, without realizing.

Some people, girls especially, always seemed so clear on what constituted jerk behavior, or lame behavior. Ren felt totally at sea about it, most of the time. Things he thought were total jerk moves, other guys considered cool. The rules his mother had about such things seemed so European and irrelevant.

"Okay, then," he said, then felt bad inside, yet again, because he was going to River Bend Park with Ruthie, and she was acting as if she liked him, and he liked her delicate body and her pixie face, but really he still wished she was Tully.

Numbers in the gym were starting to thin out. He looked around for the girls who'd drawn lustful and envious eyes all evening, Neve Shepherd in a hot pink dress that left her back completely bare, Lorelai Grey in scarlet, Gemma Clayton in bold dark red. They'd all gone.

Ruthie dragged him out to the parking lot and they just had time to pile into a pickup driven by Jason Hamilton. Jason began to gun it out of the lot before Ren even had the door shut. There were too many people in the back seat and he knew they'd be stopped by the highway patrol, if they were seen.

But they weren't seen.

At River Bend Park, there were fifteen or twenty people already gathered. Some of them hadn't been at the prom at all, like Judd Newell. He was the older brother of Gemma's date Garth, and he was twenty-two or twenty-three now, dangerously adult it seemed to Ren. He and Trey Sheenan and a couple of others had brought alcohol, lots of it, beer and spirits and mixers. Right after Ren and Ruth got there, the Newell brothers roared off again, saying they'd be back later.

It was a warm night for the end of May, and everyone

was hot from dancing in an overheated gym and being crowded in cars. The snowmelt-filled Marietta River rushed right beside the crescent of coarse sand where they'd set up, beyond the untidy mess of parked vehicles in the official parking lot. Just a few miles downstream from town, the Marietta joined with the Yellowstone, which would be even fuller.

Somebody had kept their headlights on, to shine light on the sand, and had their truck doors open so that the sound system could carry. The music was so loud it shook the vehicle. There was a fire already lit and blazing in a circle of rocks, and the girls in their thin party dresses stretched their hands out to the flames, or danced in the fire-light.

Neve Shepherd looked amazing when she danced, unearthly in the firelight, a hot pink flame. She'd pulled her hair out of its prom do and it rolled around her head like a halo of white-gold glinting waves. Her back was as thin and perfect as a model's, and her whole body language said, "You can look but you can't touch." She'd clearly been drinking and maybe more, and she was coming on so outrageously to her date, Jay Brown, teasing him and frustrating him so much that he was starting to get mad at her.

Lorelai Grey laughed at everything anyone said. She had a bottle of liquor in her hand and drank directly from it. Trey Sheenan had a hand on her breast and his shirt was open to the waist. He was dressed like Elvis, with sideburns he'd been growing for two months and a blue velvet suit.

Looking around at the faces, Ren was struck by the blinding understanding that he shouldn't be here. They would take one look at him and know he didn't belong. Could he possibly fake his way through? What was Ruthie thinking? Had Sam's behavior really been that bad?

"Are you sure you're happy about this?" he said to her.

"It's going to be the best night of our lives," she said, as if saying it would make it so. She found a bottle of cola and drank a big swig of it, then poured bourbon into the bottle to fill it again.

Ren started drinking too, grabbing a beer and putting money into an empty bottle someone said was the kitty to pay for it all. Trey Sheenan saw it was a fifty he'd put in and laughed at him. "You really gonna drink that much, Fletcher, or you're gonna to pay for the rest of us? Generous guy..."

"I'm gonna drink that much," he said.

And then of course he had to prove it.

Which must have been why he ended up an hour and a half later, lying half-wrapped in a blanket on the sand by the fire, with a near-empty beer bottle still in his hand, kissing Ruthie in a fume-filled blur until he thought his face might fall off.

When Neve disappeared down in the water and didn't come back up, everyone started yelling and screaming and he had to fight to swim up out of the haze of sexual need and vague, lingering pain about Tully, fight to work out what was going on.

Jay Brown was yelling himself hoarse, wading like a crazy man in the rushing current. "Neve! Neve! For God's sake answer! Somebody get the headlights shining on the water so we can fucking see!"

The girls were crying and crying, Ruth clung to Ren, and Jay's prom tux was plastered wet all over his body. He kept calling and calling, yelling for people to help him look for her, but the water rushed and roared in the darkness and Neve was gone.

Prom night had been such a horrible night.

Ren still remembered it in way too much detail for someone who'd drunk that much when he wasn't used to it. Kate MacCreadie, who'd been their English teacher and was now Marietta High's vice principal, had driven him and Ruthie home in the early hours of the morning, along with a couple of other people, and then the next day he'd called Ruth as soon as he was confident she'd be awake, to ask, "Are you okay?"

"Can I see you?" she'd answered, starting to cry. "I need you so much, Ren."

A fellow student's death was the kind of thing that

linked you together. Neve's body had been found downstream two hours after the search for her resumed in the morning. They'd all felt changed by that night, everyone who was there. Still, even now, when Ren saw someone like Gemma Clayton or Trey Sheenan or Lorelai Grey, there was an awareness in the back of his head.

You were there that night.

He and Ruth had felt the link especially strongly, because of the way they'd been locked in each other's arms when Neve went under.

Even when Ren went off to Northwestern, twenty hours' drive away in Chicago, and Ruth went to UMT in Missoula, they'd managed to stay together, on and off, and Ren thought it was prom night that had kept a thread of need in place between them when really it should have broken long ago.

It should have.

And now it was going to.

Mom had only said what he'd known in his heart for a long time, no matter what Ray and Libby always told him. He had to bite the bullet on this. He had to make the hard decision, because Ruth never would.

He would tell her tomorrow that he wanted a divorce.

You really couldn't say something like that on Valentine's Day.

Chapter Seven

Sugar looked exhausted and on the point of collapse. Ahead of Tully, going downstairs, Mom reached her first and gave an exclamation. "For heaven's sake, how far did you walk?" She shepherded Sugar into the house and sat her down on the couch in the living room while Tully was still on the stairs. Delaying, if she was honest.

"Too far," Sugar said.

"Silly girl!"

It was almost comical, Tully decided, one frail woman scolding an even frailer woman for walking too much.

"I went to Main Street." Sugar slumped back on the couch with her eyes closed.

She looked so thin and fragile and prematurely aged, and yet in many ways better than she had the last time Tully had seen her, which was one horrible occasion in Los Angeles about ten years ago when Sugar had been using heavily and practically living on the streets. Then, her thinness had come from choosing drugs over food, and she'd been twitchy and shaky, with a face covered in half-healed lesions and fungal infections in the beds of her fingernails.

When Tully thought about that time, she knew that her mistrust of Sugar's fender bender excuse after Dad's death was an understandable response, even if Mom was right in saying it was the truth.

Sugar really did look better now. Her skin was tired but clear, her clothes were neat and clean, her nails clipped and healthy and coated in clear polish. For the first time, Tully found herself able to believe that Sugar really was clean and drug-free, apart from the prescription pain medication she needed. Mom had said she was clean, and that she had been for seven years, but until now Tully had stayed stubborn and cynical.

Clean. Yeah. Sure. How long would it last?

Apparently she'd been wrong.

"Why didn't you stop for a break in the café, or somewhere?" Mom was saying to Sugar.

"I was going to, but then I realized I'd forgotten my purse."

"Sit."

"Patty, I am." She still had her eyes closed. She'd called Mom and Dad by their first names ever since Tully could remember. Tully used to hate that, but she found it didn't bother her now.

"Let me get you something," Mom said.

"I bought candy," said Tully from the bottom step.

Sugar opened her eyes. "Oh. Hi." She gave a tentative smile.

"Hi." Tully's smile was more like a wince.

"If you're offering the candy..."

"Well, I bought it for you."

"You did? Thanks. That's... That would be great. Would help." She smiled again. "And you know how much I love chocolate. Is it all chocolate?"

"It is."

"Yum."

"Let me grab it right now, then."

As a mother-daughter reunion, it left a lot to be desired, Tully thought as she headed back up the stairs. As a reunion between this particular mother and daughter, though, it had gone much better than it might have done. She'd felt less angry than she'd expected.

Sugar really was clean.

And calm.

And ordinary.

Nothing like the erratic, frightening "sister" who had periodically blown into Tully's quiet life with Mom and Dad and David and then disappeared again for years at a time. Nothing like the "sister" who had given so much grief, failed on her promises to all of them so many times, and ruined so much for Tully.

♡

May, 1996

Ren Fletcher had asked Tully to the prom.

It gave her a good feeling every time she thought about it. She'd been terrified that no one would ask. Or—possibly worse—that creepy Hobey Anderson might, and she wouldn't be able to think of a good excuse not to accept, and it would all go downhill from there. And in fact Hobey *did* ask, but Ren had asked first, so she was able to say truthfully and without being unkind, "Oh, I'm sorry, Hobey, I'm going with Ren Fletcher."

The confirmation that Hobey considered her to be at such a low rung on Marietta High School's coolness ladder that she might actually have accepted his offer was disappointing but not surprising. A lot of people probably thought she wouldn't feel that much better about going to the prom with Ren, but she... carefully... liked Ren.

He was skinny and shy and nerdy, but he was bright and nice, and when he said something in class it actually made sense. Tully was shy and nerdy and bright herself, and she'd reached the conclusion that guys just didn't come with the complete package of looks, brains *and* a moral code.

Or not in high school, anyhow.

You got two out of three at best. Good-looking, bright, and a complete scumbag, like Garth Newell and his older brother Judd. Handsome, kind, and so dumb they didn't know English and American were the same language, like Shane Peak. Decent, clever, and plain as a fence-rail like Ren.

If she'd been a normal teenage girl like Neve Shepherd next door, she probably would have chosen looks over either of the other two qualities, but she wasn't a normal teenage girl, so she was really looking forward to going to prom with Ren.

She had a gorgeous dress in a soft sea green, with shoes and bag to match. She was going in a group with friends like Louise Meissen and Ruthie Wilson. She was excited about the vintage cars. And Mom had said they could all come back to the house afterward for a party. They had drinks and snacks and music all set up in the basement rec room. There would be twelve of them—the six couples who were arriving at prom in Andy Pearce's dad's two cars—and that seemed like the perfect number. Enough to be fun, not enough to overwhelm.

Right up until the day before, she was looking forward to the whole thing without a cloud on her horizon, but then Sugar turned up and Tully knew the moment she heard her older sister's voice coming from the kitchen when she let herself in the front door after school that prom was spoiled now.

She hated Sugar.

Yes, and don't try to tell her that hate was too strong a word. Just don't, because it wasn't. She *did* hate her.

Tully dumped her school-bag in the hall.

Sugar! Her name was really Suzanne but she refused to go by that, and Mom played along, always called her Sugar, despite it being a stupid name.

Sugar, indeed. Should be Vinegar, because that would better represent the effect she had on the Morgan family. Tully's older brother David had gone away to college six years ago and only came home to visit once or twice a year, and she knew it was because of Sugar. Because of his anger toward their parents for putting up with her. Because of the mess she made any time she was around. Tully still missed her brother like crazy and hated Sugar all the more for driving him away.

"Hiiiii, Sweetie!" Sugar said when Tully came into the kitchen.

"I'm not your sweetie, Suzanne."

"Oh, and I love you, too, baby." Her voice had that quavering quality that said she was either high right now, or wanting to be.

Tully didn't say anything in reply. Mom was making herbal tea. She put a steaming cup in front of Suzanne, and said, "Try it, go on, maybe you'll like it," and Tully knew it was yet another attempt in Mom's endless, hopeless struggle to break Suzanne of her addictions.

As if herbal tea could substitute for heroin and methamphetamine and cocaine and who knew what.

Right now, Sugar didn't look as if she was remotely clean. She was skinny, with breakouts and blemishes not just on her face but on her hands and arms as well. She was only thirty-two and she could have been pretty, but her bleached hair looked cheap and her eyes had circles of dark gray underneath. She was repulsive, and if she'd come here for some of Mom's endlessly patient detox, then it was going to be a long road for all of them.

Tully knew this from experience, because Sugar had come back home to try to clean herself up many times before. Occasionally it seemed to work for a while, but mostly there'd be an admission of failure. They'd wake up one morning and Sugar would be gone again and there'd be a note. Sometimes it would at least be honest and say, "Sorry, I can't do this." More often it would be a lie. "A lead came up about a job. I'll call when I have news."

Tully honestly didn't know if Sugar believed her own stories or what. She'd been difficult from the moment she was born, apparently, which was why Mom and Dad hadn't had David until Sugar was eight years old, and Tully six years after that. Sugar had taken all their energy and more, from babyhood to grade school and beyond. Things hadn't gotten much better since.

"Would you like some tea, too, honey?" Mom asked her.

"I'm going to grab a snack and start some work."

"Aren't you about done with school by now?" Sugar asked. She herself had dropped out at sixteen, and skipped school most of the time long before that.

"I have thank-you letters to write to everyone who helped with my college applications, and there are quite a few of them so, no, I'm not *about done*."

"No need to bite my head off."

"If you say so."

"What's that supposed to mean?"

"Well, you tell me. Are you here for the usual reason?"

"Don't be like that."

"Okay, I'll go upstairs to my desk and then I won't have to be like anything."

"Tully, you're going too far," Mom said. "Give Sugar the benefit of the doubt, okay?"

"Think I'll let you do that, Mom."

Which was bratty of her. She'd been bratty the whole conversation and if it had been anyone other than Sugar she was being this rude to, Mom wouldn't have let her get away with it, but Mom knew.

Knew that Sugar should have been called Vinegar instead.

Dad knew it, too.

Tully made herself a bowl of cereal and went upstairs to work on her thank-you letters. Miz MacCreadie was such a great teacher, she'd been so fantastic, and seemed genuinely thrilled that Tully was going to UCLA. For her, Tully chose the nicest of the cards she'd bought.

Writing the letters was almost fun, until Sugar went outside to chain-smoke—because, you know, it would be a shame to try to break all your addictions at once, right?—and the smoke rose up through Tully's open bedroom window, along with a bout of tar-filled coughing that did not sound very healthy at all.

She closed the windows, turned on the radio, put on her headphones, and tuned her sister out. If she could tune her out tomorrow, during her preparations for the prom...

There, she could only hope.

But hope failed her.

She and Ruthie and Louise and the other girls had a big group appointment the next afternoon at Trudi's Hair, a cozy little salon above Trudi Gallagher's garage in North Marietta, then they were separating to dress at home before Andy Pearce's dad and uncle came to collect each of them, one at a time. It would make for a roundabout route, but Andy wanted to make sure the vintage cars were seen by as many people as possible. Tully's house was the final stop on the pickup route, which was kind of a pity because she would get the least time in the vehicle, but never mind.

She brought out her dress to iron it one final time, two hours before she needed to put it on. It was so beautiful, real silk. Mom had said she could have a home-made gown in expensive silk or a bought one in some cheaper synthetic fabric and since Mom sewed so well, and Tully loved quality things, she'd chosen the luxurious natural fiber.

It felt so sensuous and swishy and rich and beautiful against her skin. Quality counted. You could tell it was silk. But it did crease...

She decided to protect it beneath the iron by using a damp but pristine dishtowel on top of the fabric and went to the kitchen to get one, and on her way back, she heard Sugar swearing. When she came back into the room with her damp cloth—

There weren't words. There just weren't.

Sugar had put a mug of coffee down on the ironing board, right on the silk, and then she'd bumped the feet of the ironing board and the coffee had spilled. She'd clearly been using.

Using what, Tully didn't know. Maybe just alcohol and pot or weed, or whatever was the latest cool thing to call the stuff. It didn't matter. What mattered was the result. Tully's beautiful dress ruined, because her hazy, crazy, strung-out sister hadn't even looked to see what she was putting her mug on.

Tully screamed at her. This was hate. It really was. Her whole life. All those other times. And now this. Mom came running. "My God, what's happened?"

"She has ruined... *ruined*..." She couldn't breathe, she had so much feeling lumped up inside her. She was crying, gasping, lungs frozen with anger. Coffee was still pooling on the dress, running off the edge of the ironing board in a brown stream, dripping onto the carpet.

Sugar began to cry, too—soggy, alcohol-laced sobs of remorse and self-pity. "Oh my god, sweetie, I didn't see, I didn't know." Mascara blotted her eyelids, making the gray circles beneath them look even worse. Her mouth shook, and her hands. Her fingers looked as if they were grasping for a cigarette out of thin air. "I didn't notice it was the dress. I've come all this way to see my baby girl going to her prom and—"

"Sugar!" Mom said, sharp as a blade.

And maybe if she hadn't spoken, Tully wouldn't even have noticed the slip.

"What did you just say?" She shot a dagger of a look at her sister.

"Nothing." Sugar shook her head and closed her eyes. "I meant... I just meant..."

Tully turned to Mom. "She said *my baby girl.*"

"Suzanne, I swear one of these days..." Mom began.

There were bands of iron tightening around Tully's head. "What does she mean? Why did you yell at her? She said *my baby girl* and you yelled at her, and she's trying to come up with a lie and she can't."

"It's okay, Tully. We'll hand wash the dress."

"I don't care about the dress. You can't come up with a lie, either. She was only fourteen when I was born. But she said *my baby girl.*"

They admitted it, after that. There wasn't much choice. They'd been caught and she wasn't stupid. She wondered, in fact, if she *had* been extremely stupid over the years, not to have guessed before. But there had been all those blocks of time when Sugar disappeared for months or even years on end, and when she was here, Tully worked so hard at avoiding her, tuning her out. Maybe Sugar had made slips before and Tully had never noticed.

But, yes, it was all true.

Sugar wasn't her sister, she was... *I'm going to throw up...* her mother.

They'd been living in San Diego before Tully was born, and Sugar had been sneaking out, in all sorts of trouble, abusing her body already. Turned out she couldn't even say for sure which guy the father was. She thought it was most likely guy number one, but it could have been guy number two. She couldn't remember either of their names.

So Tully's mom and dad were actually her grandparents, and her father was some horrible sleazy shit of a guy who'd slept with Sugar when she was thirteen years old. And even though both of the guys themselves apparently hadn't been that much older, still in their teens, it was still unspeakable.

She hated Mom and Dad for lying to her, even though they said they'd done it for her and for Sugar, and okay, Sugar had been a child herself then, but she wasn't a child now, and she'd turned Tully's whole life story inside out with one spilled mug of coffee on a precious dress that Tully knew now she would never wear.

At least Mom did seem to understand the extent of her outrage and pain. "Go, Sugar, okay, for a while?" she said, through dry white lips. She scrabbled in her purse and pulled out a bill. "Here's a twenty. Go sit in the diner. Do whatever you want. Tully and I need to sort this out."

"How can we sort it out?" Tully demanded, without even waiting till Sugar had gone, although she was already on the way. Tully could only wonder what Sugar would spend the money on. She never had any of her own. "You lied to me my whole life. I know, to protect Sugar, to give her a second chance, that's obvious, but what about protecting me?"

The front door closed with a loud rattle, and Sugar's uneven footsteps thudded across the porch

"We weren't thinking that far ahead," Mom said. "We were taking it one day at a time. She was fourteen."

"That's why you moved here, after I was born? So that people wouldn't have to know?"

"Yes. And it was a protection for you, too, Tully, you

have to see that."

"How are you going to protect me now?"

"Tell me what you want. Tell me what you need. Do you want me to kick Sugar out? I'll do it."

Tully tried to imagine that. Mom and Dad would have to give Suzanne more money. She would disappear like she always did, sporadic contact at best, until the next time she was broke or desperate and landed on them again.

And if they do kick her out, where will that leave me?

Still here. In Marietta, Montana. It seemed unbearable.

She knew that nothing could go on as before. Nothing would be the same. She couldn't *erase* this, and just go put on her dress for prom and wait for Ren and the vintage car, even if the stain did come out.

She couldn't.

She was a different person now. She needed days and weeks and months to think about this and deal with it. She needed a different place. She needed someone who knew her and someone who was on her side, not people with the conflicted loyalties and love that Mom and Dad felt.

Because Sugar was their daughter, and Tully was their grand-daughter, one generation removed.

"I want to go stay with David," she said. She spoke the idea as soon as it formed in her head, and it was the only thing that seemed possible.

Maybe, just maybe, if she and Ren had really been dating, she might have felt differently. She might have stayed and gone to prom. She might have trusted him enough to talk to him about it. She imagined a bittersweet heart-to-heart, imagined him holding her and whispering all the right words, with his body warm against her and his neck all clean and male when she buried her face against his shoulder.

It's okay, Tully. I'm here for you. None of this changes how I feel about you.

It would make so much difference if she had someone in her life like that—someone who cared about her and whom she trusted enough to spill her guts to, someone who'd tell her everything was going to be okay.

But she didn't know why he'd asked her to the prom. If this was only one date, if he'd only asked because he'd thought she was a safe bet, likely to say yes, then how could she stay? There'd be no bittersweet heart-to-heart. The double humiliation was too much of a risk.

"With David?" Mom said.

"Yes. My *uncle,* remember?" As she said it, she felt a stab of shock and hurt that he wasn't her lovely brother any more, he was only her uncle. She'd always loved having a brother.

My brother. My older brother.

She liked saying it. She liked that he was steady and clever and responsible and good, nothing like Sugar. *My uncle* didn't feel the same.

"With David," Mom repeated.

"He knows, right?" It suddenly struck her.

"Yes, he knows. He was old enough to understand what was happening, enough that we couldn't pretend to him."

"And you must have talked about it with him behind my back about a thousand times since. What did he think?"

"The same as you, once he was grown up. That you should be told."

"Were you ever *planning* to tell me?"

"Years ago. We planned to tell you years ago. But Sugar never got clean. We put it off."

"So that she could break the news at the worst moment."

"I can understand how it seems that way." Mom reached a hand out to the ironing board as if for support. The dress was still draped over it, the pool of coffee spread as wide as it was going to go, by this time, beginning to darken and stiffen around the edges as it dried.

Poor Mom. Tully suddenly found a tiny space for empathy to seep in. Mom—*my grandmother*—looked pale and shaken and old. Sugar had worn her down. Worn the whole family down.

"Hindsight is easy, I guess," she said reluctantly, to the woman who was her *grandmother.*

Gratitude flashed onto Mom's face. "Thank you for

saying that." She didn't speak for a moment. "You really want to go to David? I think that's a good idea."

"You do?"

"Of course I do! He'll have you, I know he will. He'll understand why you need a... a change of scene." She made a face, as if she knew the words sounded impossibly insipid and inadequate for what had happened. "And you're going to UCLA anyhow, in the fall. This is just pushing it forward a few months."

"Today," Tully said. "I want to go today."

She felt as if she was suffocating, screaming inside. She couldn't go to prom, but she couldn't hide in the house, either, while Mom broke the news to Ren that she was standing him up. She needed to be *gone* by then, *away,* even if that meant standing beside the interstate with her thumb stuck out and a duffel bag slung on her shoulder. She wasn't the same person she'd been fifteen minutes ago.

"Today?"

"You do not *honestly* think I am going to prom now, do you? I will explode. I will just *leave* if you won't support this, Mom. I have a credit card. I'll buy a bus ticket."

"Plane ticket," Mom said instantly. "Okay. You're right. If you mean this, if you want to go, we'll make it happen. I'll call Dad and he'll drive you to Bozeman for a flight. You can stay in a hotel near the airport tonight if we can't get you anything this evening. I'll call David and tell him you're coming. I do know that this is a serious thing to have happened, Tully, and I want to make it right for you if I can."

"David won't want me for the whole summer."

Mom looked at her. "He will. He'll tell me we're finally seeing sense about you, and he'll be only too happy to do something to prove his point."

"You're mad at him?"

Mom sighed. "No, I'm mad at Sugar. Mad at myself. How did I go so wrong with her? How could I have a daughter who went off the rails so bad? Was it my fault?"

Tully had no answer to those questions, and her teeth were chattering together when she picked up the phone to call around the airlines to see if there was a flight. It was probably the craziest two hours of her life. There was a flight tonight, with seats still available. She packed a bag, with too many books and not enough clothes. Dad... her *grandfather*... came home early from the hardware store—he was the manager, he could do that—and she said goodbye to Mom, and Dad drove her to the airport in time for them to grab a burger there, in the airport bar, before she had to board.

They left the house forty minutes before the vintage cars were due to show, and it was eighteen months before she even came home for a visit. Sugar was long gone again by then, of course.

Chapter Eight

"Oh, wow," said Sugar. "It looks like good candy."

"It's locally made. Sage Carrigan is a real artist with chocolate." Tully carefully took the chocolates out of the prettily patterned copper-colored gift bag Sage had placed them in.

She'd bought three of each kind she'd chosen, and Sage had wrapped each kind separately in a clear cellophane bag, attaching a tiny sticker to each bag so that Tully would know which was which. The stickers said things like, "Dark chocolate with lemon zest splinters," "Cornflake chili bombs," and "Mocha espresso cream."

"Where shall we start?" Mom asked.

"Are those hazelnut clusters?" Sugar pointed to a bag containing three chunky shapes.

Tully read the label just to make sure. "Yes, they are."

"Let's have those."

"You're only having one kind?" Mom said.

She didn't have a very sweet tooth. That particular weakness—and joy—came down through the Morgan line, Dad's side of the family. Sometimes Mom even claimed not to like chocolate, but what she really meant was that she wasn't greedy for it. She always stopped at one piece of candy, and often said no to wedges of mud cake or slabs of brownie.

For Mom, a little chocolate went a long way. Tully and Sugar usually felt differently, and Mom knew it.

"We might," Sugar said, in answer to the "one kind" question. "Or we might have more."

She and Tully still hadn't made any attempt at body contact, not a hug or an air kiss or even a touch of the hand. For so many years, Tully had felt only revulsion for Suzanne and never touched her if she could help it.

I grew inside that body.

The old, messed up, wired high Sugar wouldn't have picked up on the revulsion, or wouldn't have cared. She would have tried to hug Tully anyhow. This new, clean, worn-out Sugar knew a little about wanting and holding back, and kept clear of Tully's space.

Finally.

It had taken her long enough.

Tully handed the candy around and Mom shook her head at first, but then Sugar said, "Join us. Or Tully and I will fight over the third piece." She bit into the knobbly shape, then slumped back on the couch again. Tully heard the crunch of the small round nuts in her mouth, then silence. She bit into her own piece.

There was a pyramid of four hazelnuts inside each candy, resting like a miniature sculpture on a plinth of brittle, splintery caramelized sugar. The whole thing was covered in a sleek flow of rich, dark chocolate. Tully didn't know which was better, the taste or the texture—the mix of nutty and sweet, or the crunch and silkiness.

"Those are good," Mom said, after they'd all communed in silence with their pieces of candy for a good minute.

"Good?" Sugar said. "They're amazing!" She had her eyes closed again. "But Patty, could I have some soup or a grilled cheese sandwich, or something as well?"

"You don't want more candy?"

"Not right now. Just a mug of that creamy chicken and

vegetable soup you made yesterday, with maybe a piece of toast on the side? There's some of the soup left, isn't there? Just in a mug, heated in the microwave. Would that be okay?"

"Of course it would." Mom rose stiffly to her feet.

Tully said quickly, "Let me, Mom."

"You don't know where everything is. And you've had a long drive. Tomorrow I'll start letting you help." She was already halfway to the kitchen.

Which left Tully and Sugar alone in a room together for the first time in nearly eighteen years.

This is when I start hissing at her about how much I hate her. This is when I tell her all those home truths I've screamed at her in my fantasies since before I even knew she was my mother.

But this tired, fragile, broken yet oddly peaceful person wasn't someone you could scream or hiss at. "Have more candy," Tully said instead.

"Nope." Sugar grinned suddenly, opening her eyes.

"Nope?"

"I don't do things that way anymore."

"What way?"

"Have more. Get greedy."

"You forbid yourself?" When had that kind of self-discipline ever worked for Sugar before? She'd had no willpower at all.

"Opposite, really. I tell myself I can have as much as I want, whenever I want. Tell myself there's no hurry, and if I don't have it this minute, I can have it the next. I'm real gentle with myself about it. And maybe I don't want it at all. Some things I'm very clear I don't want at all."

"And that works for you?"

Sugar shrugged. "I'd be dead by now if it didn't. I got close."

"I can't believe that was what worked." Tully meant it as a barb, but Sugar didn't hear it that way.

Or else pretended not to.

"'Cuz I'm a stubborn, contrary bee-yatch, I've worked out," she said, "and if one half of me tells the other half that she can't have something, then that other half rushes out the next minute to get it. I learned finally. So I don't make it a battle with myself anymore."

Sugar had taken the conversation in this direction on purpose, Tully thought. She was trying to explain a few things, or apologize, or something. Tully didn't want to buy into it. Not now. But she appreciated the effort.

Mom came back a few minutes later, with the soup in a mug and the toast on a plate. "I can make more," she said. "And should I put away the candy?"

"No, you should leave it right here on the table where we can see it," Sugar said. She smiled again.

♡

Pascale lay beside Robert in bed, still nestled in his arms, feeling replete and lazy and relaxed. It would have been such a good Valentine's Day if she hadn't been so worried about Ren.

"I said somefing to him," she murmured to Robert.

"You what?"

"To Ren. About Roofie."

"So you cracked, then?"

"I don't know why. Why today?"

"Valentine's Day. And because you and I were talking about it before he came, remember?"

"Well, we've been talking about it a lot."

He sighed. "Let me go get some scissors."

"What?" She stretched away from him a little and peered at him in the darkness.

"You don't remember?" He was teasing her. She picked up on the tone, now. It never took her long. They enjoyed each other's sense of humor. "You told me to cut out your tongue if you ever said to him how you really felt about Ruth."

"So I did." She was the one to sigh this time. "I'm going to miss my tongue."

"You could probably bribe me, somehow, into leaving it alone."

"Bribe you? The traditional way? Already?"

"We can take a rain check."

"Okay." She nestled back against him, palm on his chest, head on his shoulder. They fit together so well that way. "But Robert, I'm scared now."

"Why, honey?"

She switched to French, which Robert understood very well, even though his accent and grammar were shocking. He spoke her native language fast and fearless and full of mistakes, got his point across when they visited France through sheer American bravado, and loved it when she spoke French to him, especially in bed. "That it wasn't the right thing," she said. "All this time I've held myself back and today I blew it. Completely."

"I don't think you blew it."

"Nobody tells you how hard it is to see your child in an unhappy marriage. When you hold your first baby in your arms, you want to protect them, you worry about sickness and pain, and later about studies and careers, but to watch a child in a bad marriage... It's almost as hard as watching Laurent after he lost Brooke."

"I know."

"It's such a powerless kind of hurt. When they're small and you see they're about to fall, you swoop down and snatch them up and they're safe at once. You can't do that with your son when he is six feet tall and thirty-six years old."

"Don't beat yourself up, honey. You've tried so hard with Ruth. With both of them. I've been proud of you. You're right, though. It's hard to see a grown child unhappy, and we've had a lot of it with our sons these past few years, haven't we?"

"I'm holding my breath, now. I'm afraid that he'll close up, now that I've said it. That he won't come over to see us so much."

"I know," he said again.

"Nothing will happen," she predicted, superstitious about it. She should never, never have spoken. "It will all go on between him and Ruth as before. They'll stay together, both of them unhappy. It hurts me."

"I know," Robert said for the third time, then they lay together silently in the dark, worrying about it.

♡

"You say this to me the day after *Valentine's* Day?" Ruthie's eyes had narrowed and her cheeks were red. She wasn't crying. Hadn't cried yet, but Ren thought she was like a toddler—like his little niece Evie, when she had fallen and grazed her knees. Sometimes the shock was so great, the tears didn't come right away.

Or maybe Ruth wouldn't cry at all. Maybe anger and affront and indignation were the only emotions she was planning to feel.

Ren wondered what the statute of limitations was, on the Valentine's thing. Clearly in Ruthie's eyes, the day *after* was as bad as the day *of*. What about the week after? The month after? How long should he have left his announcement for it to not be an insult to Saint V? Or would another holiday blackout window have kicked in by then, with no break in between? The day after *Easter*. The *Fourth of July*.

This isn't me, he thought in sudden disgust. This cynical man. This isn't who I am, or who I want to be.

So maybe the narrow-eyed, sour-mouthed, resentful and prickly creature who sat opposite him wasn't who Ruth was, either. They'd done it to each other, through being wrong together.

Was that possible?

"I suppose you've thought it all out," she said huffily.

You say that like it's a bad thing...

"Uh, yes. I have." It was Saturday. His law office kept Saturday morning hours, and after his last appointment at noon he'd stayed on there for most of this afternoon, making calculations about their assets and what he could afford to offer her. "Not all of it. But I'm a lawyer, Ruthie. That's a plus, isn't it?"

They were sitting at the kitchen table finishing their Saturday evening meal of meatloaf and vegetables—Ruth was a decent cook who favored traditional homey recipes—and he thought it was probably the last time he would ever eat in this house.

She narrowed her eyes again, suspicious. "Why would you say that?"

"Because I know the best way to proceed. Of course I've thought through the legalities and the finances. Don't you want to make this as easy as we can?"

She sniffed. "I haven't even said that I want a divorce, yet."

He didn't tell her that the decision wasn't up to her. He'd decided, and he was moving out, and in a hundred and eighty days this would qualify him to seek a divorce whether she wanted it or not.

But there was an easier way. He hoped they could go that route, for both their sakes.

"*Do* you want one?" he asked quietly.

"Do you think I want to stay married to someone who doesn't want to stay married to me?" Her narrowed eyes glittered. With tears or anger? He couldn't tell. Probably both.

"That's not an answer," he pointed out.

She shrugged.

"I'll take that as a yes," he said.

"Is there someone else?" The hot color burned brighter on her cheeks as she spoke.

"No, not at all. There isn't, Ruth. That isn't what this is about."

"Why should I believe that?" She stood up from the table and began to roam the kitchen, instinctively tidying the mess from their meal.

"Because you've been married to me for long enough to know that I'm not a liar, I would think."

"*I* think anyone can manage to lie about an affair," she drawled, "when they want to."

He repeated steadily, "I'm not having an affair."

"So it's just me? You're saying it's all me. My fault. I'm unbearable. You can't stand to be with me any longer. That's—that's—" She burst into noisy, indignant tears, and wouldn't let him touch her, even though he only tried to put a hand on her arm.

He tried to talk her into a better place, but she resisted at every step.

Just ride it out, he thought. *Just get through it. You knew it would go like this. You knew it would be horrible.*

They went round and round. She stopped crying and yelled at him instead, then demanded that he get angry, too, because she knew, she said, that he was staying calm on purpose to show her up.

Must have taken twenty minutes before things began to grow more peaceful, and already he had no memory of what they'd actually said to each other. The whole conversation had been full of senseless recrimination and pettiness, going round and round and round, and he hadn't stayed as quiet and honest and rational as he'd wanted to, in the end.

Seriously, they were so bad for each other. It was toxic on both sides. She had to see it.

"Don't do this, Ruth," he finally said, his voice cracking on the words. "Are you honestly saying you think we're happy together? That this is working?"

Suddenly, she dropped the aura of martyrdom, gave a big sigh and said in a plainer, less petulant way, "Tell me, Ren. What have you worked out?"

There was no concession in words that he was right about their marriage, because she wasn't like that. She never conceded an argument straight up. She hated to lose face that way. After some more pointless back and forth that took longer than he wanted, she agreed to it all. It was pretty generous in her favor, so there was no reason not to.

The house was already in her name, because the law office was in his. They'd decided on this balance years ago—one piece of property each. He owned the whole building, over on Main Street, and there was no mortgage either on it or the house. He'd inherited a little money from Mom's parents in France, and if he took out a mortgage on the law office building now, he could afford to give Ruthie enough of a lump sum to match the IRAs that were in his name, and compensate for any disparity in their future earning power.

She would be left in a pretty healthy situation, financially, with a house she owned free and clear, and good money in the bank.

"You don't want this house?" Ruth asked, looking around.

"I'll move into the apartment over the office. I'll go tonight, if you like. It's best, don't you think?"

He saw something change in her face, a dawning realization that she would have this place all to herself.

No more of his damp towels hung untidily on the rail in the bathroom. No more coffee mugs left on the drain board instead of put directly away. No more polite... or sometimes irritable... tussles over what to watch on TV—tussles that usually ended with Ruth sitting up in bed watching reality shows on the bedroom TV while Ren watched crime dramas or sitcoms or documentaries on the big flat-screen in the living room, while wishing she would let him keep his exercise bike up here instead of in the basement, so he could cycle and watch TV at the same time. Down in the basement, he always felt banished.

"There's no need to go tonight," she said stiffly.

"I will, though."

"Where will you sleep?"

"There's a couch in the apartment I can sleep on for a night or two. We can make a time tomorrow or during the week for me to come back for the rest of my stuff."

"What do you want to take?" A steely look appeared in her eyes, but the house was furnished and decorated mainly to her taste not his, so he wasn't planning on claiming much.

He glimpsed a shopping spree in his future, a really efficient one where he furnished the whole of the one-bedroom apartment in one expensive hit. He *hated* trailing around stores taking weeks and multiple trips to decide on one blender and a coffee table. "Apart from clothing and papers and personal items, just the exercise bike and the rest of the gym equipment," he said. "Maybe the TV, although I can easily buy a new one if you want. Some of the CDs and DVDs."

"That's *all*?" She got ready to feel snippy again, as if he was insulting her taste.

Which he was, truth be told.

Then her tone changed again, and she gave another sigh. "You really are making this very easy, Ren. Take the TV. It's too big for this room, anyhow."

"No point making it hard. If we close out our joint account and I transfer the lump sum to you, then we can go the "dissolution of marriage" route and it'll only take a few weeks."

"A few weeks, and the divorce will be through? Finalized? Done?"

"That's right."

She pressed her lips together and nodded. "That sounds like the best way," and he thought that even if she never said it to him in words, she was actually relieved and glad that the decision had been made. He felt a rush of tenderness for her, suddenly.

Wouldn't it be great if she could end up happy? Wouldn't it be great if they *both* could?

Chapter Nine

Sugar was laughing.

Tully let herself into the house after a brisk walk and the strangled, gasping sound came to meet her. Sugar wasn't just laughing, she was *crying* with laughter and struggling to breathe, holding her stomach. She had tears streaming from her eyes. On the TV in front of her several evil-looking South American drug lords had just been reduced to fawning fan-boys by discovering that Kathleen Turner was their favorite novelist.

"Are you okay, Sugar?"

She recovered herself enough to speak, at last. "Oh, that felt so good, laughing like that. I thought I was going to die. This movie is hilarious."

"*Romancing the Stone?* That has to be thirty years old, by now. You've never seen it?"

Sugar shrugged and offered a wry, apologetic smile. "There are a lot of movies I haven't seen, over the years. I'm still catching up."

"Oh." Understanding began to dawn.

"It's great." Sugar grinned this time, and there was

something gallant about it, something defiant and brave and admirable.

Tully's heart kicked a little. Her birth mother had missed out on so much, through her addictions. Not just the big things like happy motherhood and solid friendships and a rewarding career, but life's sweet, small pleasures as well. Picnics in the park, shopping for shoes, seeing a good movie. When you spent all your time scrounging money for your habit, jonesing for your next fix, or lying in a stupor as it washed over you, you missed out on all of that.

"Want to watch with me?" Sugar asked. She patted the empty space on the couch beside her and there was an eagerness in her voice that she couldn't hide.

Tully gave in to it. "That would be nice. It's years since I last caught it on cable."

"Oh, you've probably seen it a million times." Sugar sounded disappointed, as if she thought she was forcing Tully into something she didn't want.

Which was only a little bit true.

"Only twice. And you're right, it's a pretty good movie."

She sat where Sugar had indicated and they both kicked off their shoes and scrunched their legs up. Sugar's laugh—smoky yet melodious like a jazz club singer—broke out occasionally, but mostly she sat quietly, and it was peaceful. She smelled good. She seemed content.

They sat through the rest of the movie together, laughing in the same places, and when it was over they both agreed that they should watch movies together more often, and that now it was candy time.

"Which one are we trying today?" Tully asked, when they'd called Mom to join them. She'd been sitting dutifully on the chaise longue in the sun room with a book, after Tully had nearly yelled at her earlier about taking a break.

"Mom, there's no need for you to be on your feet all day," she'd said. "We have this covered, now. I know you love to read and yet you've been reading the same book since I got here, because you never get time."

"I finished it," she announced now, as she came into the room.

By now, the tasting of chocolate had become a kind of game, a rite of renewal or family celebration. Every day—not always at the same time of day, and occasionally twice—the three of them gathered around the coffee table to try another piece of Sage Carrigan O'Dell's hand-crafted treasure.

Tully had been in Marietta for nearly a week, and there were only a few pieces of candy left.

"I gotta admit I'm curious about the cornflake and chili," Mom said. "It sounds awful, but Sage hasn't let us down yet."

Tully opened the cellophane bag. The dark chocolates with cornflake and chili were square in shape, with smoothly rounded corners. As always, Sage was generous in her sizing. You could bite into each candy, let a nice mouthful melt against your tongue and still have enough left for a good second bite.

"Mm, there's a crunch," Sugar said, the words blurred by chocolate.

"And a kick," added Mom, after a moment. "Ouch, spicy!"

The subtle heat of the chili didn't hit right away. It lurked, letting you feel the satiny swirl of dark chocolate and the scratchy texture of the crushed cornflakes first.

"I like it," Tully decided.

"I love it. Score another point for Sage," said Sugar. "We are going to have to make another trip to that store." She gave a grin, and Mom smiled back at her and blinked a little, and Tully found that she was grinning, too.

What again? Actually enjoying Sugar's company? It had lasted half the afternoon, now. They were such simple things, watching an old movie and tasting chocolate together, but she never would have believed even those things were possible, back when Sugar was such a crazy, delinquent mess.

But maybe any new connection between them needed to be made from small and simple things like these. The forgiveness was still very fragile, the trust still on high alert. It wouldn't take much for it to shatter as it had shattered so many times before. One lie or one piece of manipulative behavior could kill it off in a heartbeat.

For now, focus on the tiny successes, Tully decided, not the possibility of huge future failure.

I'm so glad I stopped at Copper Mountain Chocolates. Who knew that a few mouthfuls of candy could help us so much?

"Well, we have the doctor tomorrow," she said. "Maybe on the way home we could stop in there?"

"If she's not too tired," Mom pointed out.

"I can rest in the car, Patty," Sugar said.

The specialist oncologist was in Bozeman, forty-five minutes away.

"I think you need to rest now, honey," Mom said.

"So do you, Mom," Tully suggested gently. "Don't just read, take a proper nap."

Mom had put a bell by Sugar's bed, because sometimes Sugar needed to get up in the night and it was too painful for both Tully and Mom to hear her moving so slowly, trying to manage her pain medication on her own without waking anyone else. "Wake me!" Mom had ordered.

Tully had then ordered Sugar to wake *her* instead, so Mom could sleep, but she suspected that the bell woke Mom anyhow, and she probably didn't manage to get back to sleep for a long time. Tully had heard her going to the bathroom in odd hours of the night.

Now, Sugar lay back on the couch and closed her eyes, and Tully thought Mom would go directly upstairs and lie on her bed for a while, but instead she headed for the basement. "What are you doing, Mom? Didn't we agree you were taking a nap?"

"Laundry, first."

"Let me."

"Well, you can help."

"And then you *promise* you'll take a nap? And that you'll let me cook?"

Cooking was another thing Mom did too much of, for a woman of seventy-five—a woman of seventy-five worn out by years of raising a grand-daughter... Tully... when sometimes for months or years at a time she hadn't even known where the child's mother was, or whether Sugar was even still alive.

It took its toll. Even though Sugar was doing so much better now, and was so much less dangerous to Mom's well-being, you couldn't get the years or the energy back. Now there was a new source of weariness, because of Sugar's cancer, which had spread to her bones.

Mom wanted to build up Sugar's weight and nourishment and strength with homemade meals, to help her quality of life, and this was an admirable goal, but not if it left Mom looking the way she'd been looking this past week, bone-deep weary and old.

"Okay, missie, I'll take a nap," she said to Tully in mock annoyance. "I'll let you cook."

"You're so good to me," Tully drawled.

"Even when you're as much of a brat as your mother," Mom drawled back.

Down in the basement a few minutes later, with the dryer rattling away and a load of sheets chugging around in the washing machine, she told Tully, "It was great to hear her laughing at that movie."

"I know."

"But she has something on her mind."

"Sugar does?"

"I'm pretty sure."

"Not just her pain and tiredness?"

"Every time the phone rings, she goes on high alert. She's waiting for a call."

"How do you know?"

"I've seen what she looks like when she's waiting that way. For a call from her dealer, it used to be."

"Is this—? Is she—?"

"No, she's not. But I'm not sure who it is instead, or what it might be about, and she hasn't said, and when I asked her about it, she just shook her head."

"From David, maybe?"

He was planning a visit, Tully's brother-uncle, and he was the other member of the family who still held a lot of anger, was still suspicious of Sugar and the changes she'd apparently made.

"No, it's not David. We've talked about that. He's not sure when he'll be able to get away, what with his job and the kids. He doesn't like leaving Rachel with them too much on her own."

"And he won't bring them with him," Tully guessed, "Because he and Rachel don't trust Sugar."

"That," Mom conceded, "and he doesn't want to introduce them to an aunt they've never met, only to have them lose her again, in however long it takes." She paused for a moment, struggling. They all knew they were going to lose Sugar. It was just a matter of when. "She's been clean for seven years. I think he could have brought them together before this, and then the prospect of loss wouldn't be such a factor. They could have built a relationship. It would have been good for her." She sounded angry.

"Has Sugar earned that? Really, Mom? All those other times she claimed to be clean, or she was clean for a while, and then she fell in deeper than before. How could David have known her being clean this time would last? Hannah and Mitchell are only ten and twelve. If I had kids, I would have kept them well away from her. Maybe I still would, even now."

Mom shrugged in half-hearted agreement. "Okay. Maybe. But I don't think it's David who's on her mind right now. She's hiding something. I know what Sugar looks like when she's hiding something."

"Yes." There, Tully had to agree. "Upstairs now, okay, Mom? I'll take care of this when it's done."

Mom went, her movements still suggesting anger, and Tully thought she wasn't really angry with David for not wanting to bring Rachel and the kids, or with Sugar for hiding something. She was angry because anger was easier than sadness, and kept her stronger.

The house went quiet, apart from the muffled sounds of washer and dryer in the basement, after Tully had gone upstairs too. She puttered around in the kitchen, carefully and amateurishly following the recipes Mom had left out for her.

Lightly fry finely chopped onion in butter and olive oil.

She never cooked in LA. She was the classic single professional thirty-something woman, living on takeout and deli meals, and when she'd had a big working lunch in a restaurant, she ate cereal or toast for dinner that night, in front of the TV.

Of course she had some private vices. That went without saying. You were allowed to, when you lived alone. It was pretty much compulsory. Private vices were the whole point of living alone, in fact. They were the things that made it bearable when really you were starting to wonder about your future, and if this was all there was going to be.

Tully loved sitting on the couch in front of movies that made her cry, with a plate of sushi and a glass of white wine set out on the coffee table. She loved putting on sweats on a Saturday morning, not to go jogging or to the gym—because there were only rare periods when made it to the gym as often as she wanted—but to raid the newsstand for a big pile of weekend reading and the French bakery on the corner for a chocolate croissant, sometimes two. She loved turning up a CD until the sound of the music filled her whole apartment and she loved dancing in the dark to the music with her eyes closed while she sang the lyrics out loud and off key.

Those were the ways you had to celebrate being single and living on your own, instead of feeling the regret. Thirty-six years old, no kids, no soul mate, no growing bank of shared memories, no carefully stored-away wedding gown.

"Go ahead, say it's a cliché," she threatened her reflection in the smudgy glass of the oven door, on a fierce mutter. "Things get to be clichés because they're true, don't you know that?"

Her life in LA was so different from being back here in Montana, living with two other women, her mother and her grandmother—or her mother and her sister, she could never really settle on what to call the relationship. What it felt like, in her heart, wasn't what it was in reality.

So different, and she didn't know how long it would last. "A matter of months," the doctor had said.

Four? Eight? No one knew.

Suzanne woke from her nap when the evening meal was almost ready. It was a dish of chicken and pasta and vegetables, flavored with a can of cream of celery soup in true nineteen-sixties style, and Tully hoped she hadn't overcooked the pasta or undercooked the broccoli before putting the whole thing in a big lasagna dish and finishing it off in the oven with a layer of grated cheese on top. Mom hadn't come down yet. If she was still asleep, so much the better. The meal could sit in the oven for a while without too much danger of being ruined.

The sound of the TV started up again. Suzanne must have had the remote within reach, because Tully hadn't heard her getting up from the couch. The news was on. Tully felt out of touch, here in Montana. This was another of her private vices, caring about certain quirky little news stories that would run their course for a few days and then reach a happy outcome. Missing hikers found alive and well. A stricken cruise ship evacuated in time.

She went to watch for a while, thinking that she would tiptoe upstairs in twenty minutes or so if Mom still hadn't appeared.

"Here, I'll make room," Sugar said.

"No need, I can sit on the other couch."

But Sugar had already moved, so Tully sat down beside her the way they had earlier and they watched the screen together, while a stream of local and national and international events washed over them, seeming largely unimportant right now. Tully barely took any of it in. This felt too strange, for the second time today, sitting here with the woman she'd called her sister for half her life.

She never would have shared a couch with Sugar in her teens, because Sugar would either have been half-unconscious and snoring in a drug-induced sleep or bouncing around erratic and wired and not making any sense, stinking of tobacco smoke and worse.

"Clean" wasn't just about being addiction-free. Sugar kept herself so nicely groomed now, no makeup, just clean skin and fresh-smelling soap and shampoo. It felt good to sit beside her without hating her, the way Tully would have years ago. It felt like a relief, like the arrival of calm after a storm. She would look at the TV guide soon and find some other classic movies they could watch together over the next couple of weeks, romantic comedies for preference, because she wanted more of the feeling in the room while they'd watched *Romancing the Stone*.

The news was back on local Montana stories now. "Next up after the break," said the male anchor. "Who failed Bae-Deen Smith? We reveal the secret horror behind the toddler's shocking death."

Sugar stood up from the couch and swayed.

"Hey, don't move so fast," Tully scolded her. "If you need something, tell me and I can get it."

"I'm fine." But she didn't seem to be. She leaned a hand heavily on the arm of the couch, then stepped away, reaching for the next piece of furniture that she could rest on. She made for the front door. "Just need some air."

"You'll freeze."

"My coat's here on the stand." She took it and shrugged into it, her movements awkward and not strong. Really, it was Mom's coat, but it looked good on her, hid the thinness a little.

"Want some company?"

"No, it's okay. Just... you know."

But Tully *didn't* know, and she thought Sugar didn't really expect her to.

Or want her to.

Mom was right. She had something on her mind—a secret something that she wasn't hiding all that well.

Speaking of Mom, here she was now, coming down the stairs looking a lot fresher than when she went up. "Was that the front door?"

"Sugar's gone out for some air." Through the front window, blurred by gauzy white drapes, Tully could see the rhythmic, shadowy movement of the porch swing going to and fro beneath the faint gold of the porch lighting.

"Air? In February? It's dark out and the ground is half-frozen!"

"She put on a coat."

They both stood there and looked for a few moments, while the shadow moved and the chains of the swing went creak, creak, creak.

♡

Sugar didn't know who Bae-Deen Smith was. It was a local story, from Billings, about a toddler who'd been handed back to his abusive mother and step-father despite having documented injuries on file. The result had been tragedy.

She didn't know who he was, beyond that.

But she knew who he could have been.

He could have been Zack, her own son, and she couldn't stay to watch the details on TV, even when that other child was a stranger.

She sat on the porch swing and its movement soothed her, although not nearly as much as a cigarette would have done.

I can have a cigarette if I want, went the mantra she'd repeated to herself thousands of times, *but I really really do not want.*

So she swung instead, using one shoe heel to push and pull gently to and fro, with Mom's coat collar turned up and a woolly hat jammed down on her head and her hands jammed in her pockets, and just her legs cold in their sweat pants where they stuck out below the edge of the coat.

Best thing she'd ever done, of the three good things in her life.

Getting clean of drugs and alcohol and getting her tricked-up body off the streets didn't even rate, by comparison.

By far the best thing she'd ever done, the only remotely decent thing she'd ever done, was to give up her child.

She hadn't done it soon enough, this was the only thing that haunted her. Maybe the damage was already in place. Maybe if the lawyer, Ren Fletcher, tracked her son down he would be in as much of a mess as she'd been at that age, as much of a mess as that little Smith boy would probably have been, if he'd lived.

Zack Morgan, a.k.a. Charles Barnett, would be thirty now.

He'd been three years old when she'd given him up, and he'd already been to the ER four times—different hospitals, and different stories given about how he had "hurt himself"—and that final time when Merc hit him, even though it wasn't as violent as the time before... well, it gave her a warning and a scare that for once she'd been lucid enough and honest enough with herself to listen to. Merc wasn't Zack's father, he was Sugar's dealer and pimp and boyfriend, and he was a dirty, evil man and he wasn't going to change.

She couldn't keep Zack safe unless she got him out of her life.

Got *Zack* out of her life.

She couldn't have gotten rid of Merc. Not then. She hadn't been strong enough for that. She'd needed him too much.

She'd cried for months after she'd given up her little boy, any time she was lucid. Her heart had broken. Giving Zack up hadn't inspired her to stop using, it had made her use more for a long while. She probably would have died during that time, if she hadn't eventually called home after a near-death trip to the ER, and gotten Walter, her father, to come pick her up and take her back to Montana for some detox, so she could break herself from the ugly, destructive relationship with Merc and make a fresh start.

Well, a fresh start of sorts.

Tully had been nine years old at that time, while Sugar herself had been twenty-three. She'd been horrible to Tully, she remembered. Tully wasn't cute anymore, by then, and anyhow Sugar barely knew her. She was just another obnoxious grade-school-aged kid with an unflattering haircut and a tendency to hide in her room and giggle too much with her friends.

And Tully had never, *ever* felt like Sugar's daughter. Hell's bells, she'd been fourteen when she'd given birth, and she hadn't cared, hadn't wanted a baby, and had taken several months to even realize it was happening. Tully had meant less to her than a mangy kitten. Patty had reached out for the tiny little preemie-born creature and taken away all Sugar's responsibility, and—

Well, if she hadn't, Tully might easily have died.

Twenty-seven years ago, though, Sugar had ached and ached and ached for Zack, who still *had* been cute, at three, and whom she missed like breathing—or, no, like *heroin*—but she couldn't confess to Patty or Walter or anyone that she'd had another child.

They must not, *must not* know, she'd thought, because she'd known how angry they would be.

Angry that she'd had another baby.

That he'd been born addicted.

That she'd kept him without telling them, hadn't given them a chance to rescue him or intervene.

That she'd given him up to go to strangers.

She'd had to bear her pain of loss secretly, not letting it show, and she'd resented Tully for being there, and for being her child, too—although so few people knew that. For being her child but not being Zack.

She couldn't stand Tully, but she'd hated herself worse, because deep down, when she wasn't scrambling to anesthetize herself with the help of a local sleazebag by the name of Warren Newell and his fourteen-year-old son Judd... she always knew how to track down the dope dealers pretty fast, anywhere she went... deep down, she knew she was the worst person in the world.

"But I did it," she reminded herself now. "I gave him up. I did the right thing for him in the end, even if it took me too long. I didn't keep him till he got too damaged or turned into the kid on the news. At least there's that."

At least there was that.

She clung to the hope and the tiny parcel of self-forgiveness. She hoped. She *hoped*, and wondered if she had any right at all to be trying to find him now, any right to even *ask* to have him back in her life, any right to tell Patty and Tully and expect them to understand.

Every time the phone rang, she thought it might be

Fletcher, the lawyer, to tell her he had some news. Every time it wasn't him, she thought she probably deserved to wait and wait and wait for that phone call until the day she died.

Chapter Ten

"How did it go?" Tully asked, as she and Sugar walked slowly from the doctor's office to the car. Tully had stayed in the waiting room during the appointment, because Sugar had said she preferred to see the oncologist on her own.

"Good," she answered now. "He says I'm doing okay. He tweaked my medication a little, that's about all. He had a couple of ideas about taking care of myself. And I've put on weight."

"That's great!" It felt so good to be genuinely pleased for her.

Sugar smiled. "That's Patty's cooking. And yours."

"I'm just the apprentice."

"No, you're good. Only a couple of pounds, but he was real pleased about it. It's much easier here than in Colorado when I was trying to take care of myself. It's much easier now that you're here, too, so Mom isn't trying to do it all. Thank you. Thank you."

"Hey, it's okay," Tully said, her voice scratchy. She put her arms around her mother... her birth mother... and they had a clumsy hug.

Half a minute later they reached the car and began the drive home, under a watery blue sky that made the wind-scraped snow on the ground look even colder, but it was cozy and warm in the vehicle and Tully felt a tentative kind of happiness. Sugar had thanked her. They'd hugged. It was... good.

Halfway home, her cell phone played Blake Shelton's "Austin" and Sugar gave one of her dark, jazz singer laughs. "That's your ring tone?"

"Do you hate it?"

"No, I love it! It's adorable."

"Can you get it for me?" The phone sat in a cup holder below the dash.

"Sure... Oh, Patty?" Sugar listened, then said, "I know. I'm the last woman in America with no cell phone." Another bout of listening, then in a very different tone, tight and blank and controlled, "Okay, thanks. I'll call back right now. Can you give me the number?"

When she'd disconnected Mom, she asked Tully, "Is it okay if I...?"

"Of course! You don't have to ask."

Sugar put in the number on the touch screen. She seemed tense and jittery about it and cursed a couple of times under her breath as she got it wrong and had to start over, then she said in a shaky voice, into the phone, "Uh, this is Suzanne Morgan, returning Mr. Fletcher's call."

At the sound of the name, Tully didn't even *try* not to prick up her ears, but Sugar finished the call very quickly without her short phrases giving anything away, leaving Tully still in the dark.

Silence in the car. Thick, thick silence.

Tully could almost feel Sugar thinking, feel her like a coiled spring. Finally, she prompted her, "So, are we still going to stop in at Copper Mountain Chocolates on our way home?"

"What? Oh, no. Maybe tomorrow." More silence, then, "But could you drop me in town?"

"Drop you in town," Tully repeated.

"There's someone I have to see." She sounded jittery and scared.

"You mean Ren Fletcher."

"I said his name on the phone," Sugar realized.

"You did."

"I forget what it's like in a small town." She'd been living in Denver before she moved back home, working at a garden center for a number of years until she'd gotten too ill. "I guess you'd know that Fletcher's the lawyer."

"He was my prom date, too," Tully said lightly, with an edge, "but I wouldn't expect you to remember that."

"No, well, I don't. Guess I wasn't around."

"You were, actually."

Silence. Not from any profound realization on Sugar's part about that day, because apparently she'd totally forgotten the spilled coffee and the spilled history, the stained dress and the ruined night. Silence, instead, because she'd sunk back into the state of preoccupation that had been coming and going all week. The "something on her mind" that Mom was clearly right about.

From the corner of her eye, Tully could see her working her fingers, picking at the hem of her sweater, the way she always used to when she was in the grip of drug withdrawal, and the old anger came flooding back. "I'm not dropping you at Ren Fletcher's, Sugar," she said.

"But—"

"It is completely obvious to both Mom and me that you have something going on. Don't you think you owe it to us to talk about it? To let us in on it? Is it money? Are you in trouble with the law? You have ground Mom into the dirt with worry about you over the years, and now there's something else, and let me tell you, with your history, our imagination might turn out to be more of a torture than the reality. She's killing herself trying to take care of you. I'm here to make sure that doesn't happen. So you can damn well—*jeez*—at least tell *me* what this is about, so I can make an intelligent decision about whether Mom needs to hear it, too."

More silence, then Sugar said in a strained voice,

"Okay, you're right."

"What?"

"You're right. What, you think I'm still so stubborn that I can't see a good argument when it hits me in the face? You can come to the lawyer's with me."

"Good. Thanks."

"He says he has space for me in his schedule now. He knows I... yeah. But if you come, it's on the condition that you do not tell Patty. Please?"

Tully glanced across at her and saw her lips pressed together as if she was fighting not to lose complete control. "Sugar, sheesh, you're putting a condition on this? Do you have any right to do that?"

"Probably not," Sugar answered meekly. "Okay, don't call it a condition. I'm just asking, okay?"

"Okay. I'll accept your condition. For now."

"So we're good?"

"Yeah. We're good. I guess. But remind me to tell you about prom night, some other time."

"Okay," Sugar repeated meekly.

"And I'm reserving my judgment about what Mom might need to know, and when she might need to know it."

♡

Sugar hadn't dared to ask on the phone what Ren Fletcher's news was. She'd reached the office manager, not Mr. Fletcher himself, and the woman—Nina, was it?—had been formal and courteous and hadn't given anything away.

If she even knew.

It had been the same during all those doctors' appointments eighteen months ago. "The doctor wants to see you as soon as you can come in," and that was it.

Today, it had been, "Mr. Fletcher has some news for you and he's wondering if you can come in to talk about it this afternoon."

Did those people not have *any* idea how it felt to have to wait in a situation like this?

They didn't.

To have to wait for even a millisecond?

Or maybe they didn't want to get caught on the phone answering question after question from some hysterical woman ready to throw up from fear and dread.

Sugar felt ready to throw up from fear right now. There was no place to go, no way to find relief. You just had to wait out the minutes. Tully was a good, steady driver who kept to the speed limit and did all the right things such as looking in her mirrors before she changed lanes, but right now Sugar wanted to scream at her or grab the wheel.

Go faster! Get around *this guy!*

It was like waiting to score. It was hell.

Waiting to die was so much easier. Waiting to die was actually very peaceful and lovely, so far, apart from the times when her pain meds didn't quite cope.

They weren't quite coping right now, but it wasn't their fault.

Relax, Sugar told herself.

Time did pass. It was incredibly predictable and reliable in that respect. A minute lasted exactly sixty seconds, every single time, even when it felt like it was stretching out to twice that.

It seemed appropriate that Tully was here. It seemed right that she'd gotten angry and forced the issue. Sometimes Sugar knew that she needed to be forced into things.

Tully might have a younger brother, although Sugar didn't want to spill this particular bombshell of information just yet.

In case Tully *didn't* have a brother.

In case the news was bad.

Oh shoot, oh damn.

Tick tock, tick tock. Another sixty seconds crawled by like a glacier creeping down a valley.

Sugar sat in the passenger seat, praying in her head and picking at her hem, the same way she used to pick at the seams of her nightgown in bed when she was four years old.

Main Street was quiet, and there was space for parking right out front.

"Listen, if I came on too strong back there," Tully said, because Sugar had seemed so quiet and fragile for the rest of the journey. "We can go back on our agreement. I can wait in the car if you want. We can talk later, after you've seen Ren Fletcher."

But Sugar said, "No. You were right." She firmed her mouth. "It's time. I want you there. Please."

"Okay," Tully said. The earlier anger left her and she had a weird rush of something that felt tender and protective and almost maternal. If this mysterious visit to Ren was going to involve bad news, then she wanted to make it better for Sugar, with her own support. If it involved good news, was she actually starting to feel as if Sugar deserved it?

Mentally, she took out the enormous box of negative feelings that she carried about this woman and examined it. Had it shrunk a little, helped by her outburst in the car just now? It felt emptier, lighter, the way it had yesterday when they'd watched Michael Douglas and Kathleen Turner in South America and then eaten chili cornflake chocolate.

Sugar was shaky on her feet, and then they had to wait a few minutes in the very attractive reception area, and she looked so tired and strung out and nervous that Tully almost ducked down to Copper Mountain Chocolates to buy a whole bag of hazelnut clusters, since they'd succeeded in bringing Sugar's energy level back up, last week.

She was on the point of asking the office manager how long the wait might be, and if it was going to be more than two minutes she really would go to the candy store, and then force-feed Sugar like a mother bird feeding a shut-eyed, featherless baby.

But then, "Mr. Fletcher can see you now," the office manager announced.

Sugar stood abruptly and swayed, which always happened when she tried to get to her feet too fast. Tully grabbed onto her to keep her steady, and Sugar grabbed back and they hugged.

Hugged.
Again.
Jeesh.
Warmly. Tightly.
As if they cared about each other.

Sugar felt so bony and frail, ribs like a birdcage, shoulders like a coat hanger. She smelled good, the way she always did now, but she was trembling, and Tully didn't think that chocolate would have been enough to help the trembling to ease, this time. She was really nervous and scared about this appointment with Ren.

Join the club.

Only Tully wasn't thinking purely about Sugar's news.

Those short moments in the candy store last week didn't count, but this... this would be a real meeting with him. First time in eighteen years. First time since Tully had vanished on prom night and left him in the lurch, and... if he ever bothered to think about it, which was doubtful... he still wouldn't know why, because Mom had always kept that stuff very private.

He wouldn't know that it was because of this fragile, frightened woman in Tully's arms, clinging tight. This woman who didn't know—because she didn't remember—about prom night, either.

"Come in," he said in the doorway of his office. He gave a professional smile, as Tully and Sugar let each other go, and he looked shockingly good. Better than she remembered from that short glimpse last week.

Happier, somehow.

Less harried.

He'd been so goofy and nerdy in his teens, with reading glasses that didn't suit him and limbs he didn't know what to do with, and a way of speaking that was a little different from everyone else in school, because his mom was French. Now, he was solid and comfortable in his own frame, and he looked super fit and strong, with just the right kind of lines beginning to form around his eyes and mouth.

They walked forward, and he shook Sugar's hand, then Tully's. She felt calluses, instead of the soft pinkness she was used to. She shook hands with a lot of corporate types in LA, and none of them had skin that felt like this. Just the right amount of dry. Just the right amount of rough. What did he do to get it? Ride rodeo as a hobby in his time off?

The idea seemed ridiculous, and yet she could imagine him on horseback, with the leather of a western saddle creaking as he moved, his legs wide and the horse and his balance perfect. He must do *something*. No man acquired a body like that from sitting at a desk.

He shook Sugar's hand, too, but she apologized for the damp of her palm, holding it out. "Sorry. I'm so nervous."

"You don't need to be nervous," he said seriously. "The news is good."

"Oh, it is? It is..." She sagged suddenly, as if her legs wouldn't hold her, and Tully had to hold her up again. "The news is good," she repeated, then added on a mutter that Ren probably couldn't hear. "Oh, Tully, this is going to hit you like a brick. I—I couldn't explain in the car. I don't even *know* how I'm going to tell Mom. How can I possibly? I'm so scared. So scared!"

"We'll handle it," Tully soothed her, although she had no idea what was coming. Her heart began to beat even faster.

She kept Sugar leaning on her arm as they walked through, and settled her into the closest chair. There were two matching armchairs, and she took the second one. It seemed as if a lot of people came for legal appointments in pairs.

Sugar said in her cigarette-damaged voice, "Mr. Fletcher, this is Tully." Then she gave a panicky look across at her, and added abruptly, "My s-sister," before giving another look that sought permission and reassurance.

Sister? We're still going with that, Tully? Not daughter?

Tully returned the look with a tiny nod. *Sister, please.* Mom and Dad had never spilled the truth to the town, and she didn't intend to spill it now.

"We've met." Ren gave a very small smile. To Sugar, not to Tully, although he was talking about her. "Long time ago.

We were at high school together."

"Oh, right," Sugar said. "Tully mentioned it just now. Well, I want her here for this." She sounded a little more sure of herself now.

"Of course," Ren nodded. He touched a paper on his desk, with the hand that looked... and felt... as if it spent as much time outdoors as it did in a clean, cushy office. Even in winter, the skin was tan, and Tully saw the two-inch-long pink slash of a healing scar near the base of his thumb, as if he'd cut himself stretching barbed wire fence, or something similarly ranch-like. "Well, as I said, the news is good, Miz Morgan. I've located your son."

Tully's whole world shifted sideways.

♡

Uh-oh, Ren thought, as he looked at Tully's face.

It happened, sometimes, in a law practice. What was to him a simple piece of factual information turned out to be a massive and emotional revelation to someone sitting on the other side of his desk.

Tully had no idea about this.

In the past, he'd had to spill the news that an old man's will left everything to his housekeeper instead of to his children. He'd had to show proof that a very polite and charming woman was trying to sell to a nice young couple a property which she didn't actually own. He'd once told a woman that the man she thought she'd been married to for thirty years was in fact still married to someone else. He'd told a sister that her own brother had scammed her out of everything she had.

Today, he was clearly informing Tully Morgan of the existence of a nephew she'd never known about, and her reaction left him in no doubt that there was drama involved. "Your son?" she said to her sister. She started to stand, then sat back down. "Your *son*, Sugar?"

Ren noted the nickname, as Suzanne Morgan chewed on her lip and winced in apology. "I didn't know what Mr. Fletcher was going to say, Tully. I should have told you about

Zack in the car, I probably should, I know I should, after you yelled at me, but I was too scared. We'll—we'll need to talk about this more later. Obviously."

"Yes. Please!"

"Not right now. Not to Patty, yet."

"No?" Tully's eyes were very bright.

"No. Please."

"Why?"

"Just... please." Sugar turned back to Ren. "Can—can you tell me anything about him? Where is he? Is he okay? Is he far away? You said the news was good," she repeated once more, as if she was begging him to make it even better.

Ren cleared his throat, to buy himself a little time. He could do better than telling, but would these two women handle it? He hoped so. Even good news could be shattering, sometimes.

"I can show him to you." He turned his computer monitor around to face them and brought up the screen he'd minimized earlier. It showed a New York Park Hospital website page with a photo of a good-looking man in a white doctor's coat smiling at the camera, against a backdrop of what seemed to be very serious medical literature. "There you are."

"That's Zack," Suzanne Morgan said blankly. "You're telling me this is Zack."

"Dr. Charlie Barnett," he confirmed. Suzanne had given him the first and last names herself, as a starting point for his search, courtesy of a previous search she'd made almost twenty years ago but hadn't followed through on.

Hadn't followed through on because she'd relapsed back into addiction, he'd concluded, reading between the lines. He added, "He's a final year resident in Orthopedic Surgery."

"That's Zack." Suzanne muttered a string of curse-words half under her breath and sank down in the chair until her chin was almost against her chest. She was crying silent tears that she wiped away with the heel of her hand as she sniffed.

"It's okay, isn't it? It's good. If you're doubtful, I can

promise you I've done all the necessary checks."

"I'm sorry. I'm so sorry." She tried to sit higher again, but she couldn't. Her strength had gone. She was clearly ill. Cancer, he suspected. She was so thin. "I'm sorry," she said again. "I thought he could easily be dead, with the start he had in life. Or maybe in prison. Or off the grid, on the streets. But he's a doctor. A *doctor?* I can't—I can't—"

Tully seemed to put her own very apparent shock and emotion on hold in the face of her sister's distress. She scrambled over to Suzanne's chair, kneeling beside it on the floor. Her hair bounced around her face as she moved, shiny and clean. She wore a neat skirt and top in shades of blue and gray, and her knees and calves were smooth and soft.

An image flashed through Ren's mind, product of pure imagination and fantasy—running his hands lightly over that dewy skin. His groin stirred, and high school felt like yesterday. All the things he'd wanted with Tully back then and never had… They felt as if they were beckoning to him, and he was eighteen again.

Very appropriate, Ren, very professional.

Through sheer will, he forced himself to think about Suzanne Morgan's son instead—the nice, clinical coat and stethoscope, and the capable-looking man who wore them.

"Are you okay, Sugar?" Tully said. She was white, herself, almost as pale as her sister. "It's good, isn't it? Isn't this good news?" Her voice was strained. "He's not dead or in prison. He's doing great. He looks great. He looks like you, and like… like Dad, actually." Her voice went husky. "We'll have a lot to talk about later," she tried to joke, but Suzanne… Sugar… had really fallen apart. She had her eyes closed, and they ran with tears, while she breathed in and out in a shaky way that suggested breathing was the only thing she could handle, right now.

"I can't deal with this," she said. "I'm sorry, Mr. Fletcher. I was waiting to hear he was dead, steeling myself for it."

"I'm the one who should apologize," he realized out loud. "I should have told Nina to make it clear on the phone that it was good news."

"I can't believe he's the boy... the little boy..." She couldn't go on.

"Look, I don't have anyone else to see this afternoon," he offered, moved as much by Tully's crouching, questioning, supportive position on the floor beside her sister's chair as by Suzanne Morgan's emotion. "Maybe we should go upstairs."

"Upstairs?" Tully echoed blankly, looking up at him.

This was the weirdest way for them to meet up again. No chance to talk. He wanted to ask her, straight up, why she'd ditched him on prom night, but that was crazy. It was so long ago, eighteen years, even if it felt like last week every time he looked at her.

What would she think if she knew he still thought about it? She must have kept up on the Marietta news, even though she'd barely been back. She must know about Neve Shepherd's shocking death, and his marriage to Ruth.

Something kicked inside him. Soon, he wouldn't be married to Ruth any more. He would be a free agent. Arguably, since the separation, he already was.

Don't let that thought go too far, Ren.

"I have an apartment," he told Tully. "We can make your sister more comfortable and private, while we talk about where she wants to go next. It's obvious this is important and overwhelming for both of you." He met her gaze, which was troubled and upset and—

Something else.

They exchanged almost the same look they'd shared last week in the candy store, the kind of helpless connection and clash of two people about to be torn apart by floodwaters, seeing each other for the very last time. It didn't make sense.

Together, they took Suzanne up to the apartment, reached by a set of back stairs near the office bathroom that took a while to negotiate because Suzanne still had no strength and couldn't stop crying.

When Ren flung open the door at the top of the stairs, he was hit by the same sense of ease and relief that he'd been having all week in this place. Even last Saturday night, when he'd come here in the cold and dark with a makeshift load of bedding and clothes in a big carry-bag, he'd felt it.

Alone at last.

It felt so good to be alone!

Moving on.

Still raw, but with a chance of finally healing instead of reopening the same old wounds time and time again.

Sunday morning he'd called Ruth to arrange a time to collect his things, and she'd told him she'd be out Sunday afternoon at a quilt show in Bozeman, and could he please come then. She didn't want to see him, thanks very much, if that was okay.

It was.

By Sunday night he'd had his TV set up here with the exercise bike right in front of it and the rest of his gym equipment in the bedroom. Monday lunch-time he'd shopped for basic groceries. Wednesday afternoon, when he usually closed the office and went horseback riding, babysat his niece and nephew or helped Dad with chores out at his parents' ranch, he instead drove into Bozeman and ran his credit card red hot. A proper queen-sized bed with a puffy comforter in dark cotton, a better couch and two matching armchairs, a bigger refrigerator, a coffee table, a lamp...

That same day he called his parents, reached his father and told him, "Ruthie and I have separated. I thought you should know. I've moved into the apartment over the office. Things are going okay with it so far, better than I thought they might. Ruth is coming around to seeing it as the right decision."

Her parents had called, too. "How could you do this to my daughter?" Libby Wilson had said. But then later Ruth's dad Ray had called back to apologize on his wife's behalf. He'd sounded tired. "Look, she'll come around," he'd said. "You're a good man, Ren. I know that. You wouldn't be doing this if you both hadn't gotten to the end of the road."

"Thanks, Ray. I appreciate it," Ren had told him, because it was true.

"You'll always have my good wishes. And Libby's too, when she settles down."

"Thank you. And the same from me."

Thursday—yesterday—when he returned from his lunch break, Nina showed him a huge, carefully wrapped bundle sitting on the floor behind her desk. "Your mom dropped this off."

It was one of Mom's weavings, one she'd had in her studio for a while. He'd admired it before and thought it was one of the best pieces she'd ever done. For the whole of their marriage, he and Ruthie had never displayed any of his mother's artworks on their walls. Ruth had never said anything about wanting one, and Mom wouldn't have given one as a gift without some indication that it would find favor.

Ruth favored pastels and lace. She loved Victorian-era décor. Mom's work was too bold and raw for her. Ren had never minded the pastels and lace, they were cute and warm and homey, but one room with a more masculine look would have been nice.

Now he had only his own taste to consult.

Alone. I'm alone.

He'd hung the weaving on the blank wall near the stairs last night, and so far it was the only piece of decoration in the whole place—unless you counted his gym clothes flung over the handlebars of the exercise bike, and the three stacks of books piled like a modernist sculpture in the corner of the room because he didn't have any bookshelves yet.

He was *happy* here.

Weirdly happy.

Happy in a way he'd forgotten about, or possibly never known. At eighteen he'd gone direct from his parents' place—they'd lived here in town back then—to a college dorm, and then direct from the dorm to living with Ruthie, even before their wedding.

This was the first time in his life he'd ever lived on his own.

"Sorry, I haven't been here that long," he apologized as he ushered the two women inside. "It's a mess, and not as inviting as I'd like. It needs a rug, for a start." The hardwood floorboards of the Nineteenth Century building were nicely polished but cold and echoing underfoot. "And pictures."

"It's fine." Tully smiled at him, but he caught a fleeting expression of uncertainty.

"Ruth and I have separated," he explained simply. Even after less than a week, the words were becoming familiar. He'd said them to Dad, and to Nina, to the bank manager and a couple of acquaintances and friends.

People didn't know how to react. He tried to give them a cue by making it matter-of-fact. Not smiling. Not frowning. Just saying it.

Even so, everyone usually said automatically that they were sorry. Sorry about the ending of a marriage. Sorry for Ruth. Sorry to have made things awkward by not knowing whether to be sorry or not. He wasn't sure which.

Sure enough, Tully said it, too. "Oh, I'm sorry."

"It's okay. It's good. Things hadn't been going well for us for a while."

"Right."

Another little zing of a look.

Alarmed.

Aware.

And so quick and subtle he wasn't even sure if he'd seen it. Or felt it. Could you *feel* a look? This was bad. He didn't want anything like this. He wasn't ready for it. Not at all. He made his own face into a mask that he hoped neither woman could read.

Suzanne sat down, using a bony hand to balance herself on the arm of the couch so that her feeble weight lowered gradually. She was so thin. Her legs didn't fill out the black trousers she wore. "Does Zack... Charlie... want to meet me?" she asked.

Tully sat down beside her, clearly keeping tabs on every nuance of emotion in Suzanne Morgan's face and every shaky movement of her body.

"That's getting ahead of ourselves," Ren said carefully. "I haven't made contact with him, I've just tracked him down and confirmed his details. I didn't know if you would still want me involved, from this point on."

"I do want you involved. I want to do it all through you." Suzanne sounded very firm about it, even when she was still so shaky he could see the movement of it. Tully had taken her hand. "For his sake. And—and maybe my mother's."

"Would you like something to eat or drink?" he offered.

"Oh... no... I don't want to—"

"It's no trouble." He blessed Monday's grocery shopping trip. He'd only gone to the store because the idea of eating a very large bowl of ice cream with chocolate sauce and sliced banana while sprawled on the couch in his gym gear watching noisy sports held such a huge, rebellious, and very masculine appeal, but then he'd ended up picking up half a cartload. "I have tea, coffee, cookies, crackers, and fruit."

"Coffee and cookies?" Sugar suggested.

"Coming right up. For you, too, Tully?" It felt weird saying her name. After prom, he'd said it in his head so many times, usually in anger. For the shy, nerdy guy he'd been back then, he'd come up with an impressive series of cutting, witty, straight-talking lines in his imagination, even while knowing he would never utter a single one of them, even if they did meet.

And they never had.

Plunging into college life four months later, he'd let the whole thing go. He still ran into some of the people from that night occasionally. Troy Sheenan, who had business interests in town and occasionally came home. Gemma Clayton, who taught at the high school. Not Jay Brown, though. He'd moved away soon after, with his family. Not the Newell brothers. No one really knew what had happened to them. Stints in prison in another state, he'd heard, but it was only a rumor.

And never Tully. Not until Valentine's Day, a week ago.

"Coffee would be great," she said. She came over as if she wanted to help, but then stood there uncertainly and he was far too aware of her—of the way the three-quarter sleeve of her top slipped against the skin of her forearms as she leaned for a moment on his countertop, of the way one strand of hair was tucked in crooked behind her ear. He kept his face as still and unreadable as he could.

The kitchen was just an alcove off the living room,

which meant they could keep talking while he ran the coffee machine and shook the cookies from a packet onto a plate. "So Suzanne, you'd like me to make contact with him and let him know you're interested in a meeting?"

"Only if he wants. That's—that's really important. It's completely up to him, and he needs to know what my situation is. Tell him—be honest about me. What he'll find. What he'll see." She gestured down at herself, and Ren felt a growing respect for her honesty. At this point in her life, she knew who she was. "And if he doesn't want to meet me I don't blame him one bit. He might remember things from when—" She broke off, then began again. "I really don't blame him if he doesn't want to meet up, or even talk, or have anything to do with me, and I need him to know that." Her husky voice cracked and she covered her eyes with the back of one hand.

"Sugar, why do you think he won't want to meet you?" Tully asked gently. Her eyes were fixed, wide and troubled and beautiful, on Suzanne's face. She left her position by the kitchen counter and went back to the couch where Suzanne was sitting, easing herself down beside her.

"I can't tell you," Sugar whispered.

"You have to. Or how can you expect me to protect your secret from Mom, the way you're asking me to?"

There was a long pause before Suzanne answered, but then she said it very simply. "Because I let him get hurt."

Chapter Eleven

There was shame in Sugar's face, and silence in the room.

"You let him get hurt?" Tully said.

She was still reeling from the revelation that he existed in the first place, this younger brother of hers. And yet Sugar still didn't want Mom to know.

Neither Ren nor Sugar had mentioned how old he was, but if he was a final year surgical resident she guessed he must be about thirty or thirty-one, five or six years her junior. At some point during those turbulent years when Sugar had come and gone from the Morgan family home, she'd given birth to another child, one she'd never mentioned, not one word, and whom she'd given up. How old had he been, then?

Tully tried to work out the timing, based on when Sugar had been around and when she hadn't, but the dates were hazy in her head. She'd only been a child herself, after all.

"I—I wasn't in a good situation, back then. Can we talk about it later?" Sugar said.

"Of course."

"I do want to tell you about it, Tully, about all of it. I can see that I have to. And Patty, too, at some point. But not now."

"I understand." She wasn't totally sure that she did, especially the reluctance about telling Mom. Wouldn't Mom be overjoyed to discover a long-lost grandson?

Ren was pouring the coffee, over in the kitchen area. Tully wished they were still down in his office so they could just make a polite excuse and go home, but really Sugar wasn't in a fit state for that, anyhow. She needed to sit and rest a little longer and have some nourishment, even if it was just the empty calories in sugar-laced coffee and cookies.

"Here." Ren had come over now, bringing mugs on a tray, along with a small carton of milk and sugar poured hastily from a packet into a glass tumbler. There was a plastic spoon sitting beside it.

He really hadn't been in this apartment for very long. Tully recognized the telltale signs of that very *single* phenomenon called "having only yourself to please." Her LA condo betrayed some of the same signs. The exercise bike right in front of the TV. The stack of DVDs on the floor, and the two pizza boxes tucked neatly between the trash pail and the side of the fridge. The underlying cleanliness overlaid with a few untidy touches, like the gym gear draped on the bike, and a couple of dirty mugs on the sink.

You really had to be clean and relatively tidy if you lived on your own, she knew from experience. It was about self-respect and control and celebration. If you let things get too messy and dirty, your space became a prison rather than a haven. Occasionally, when she'd had her soft, cream-colored carpet professionally cleaned, she lay down on it and made snow angels in the freshly fluffed up, fragrant pile, stretching her bare toes.

If Ren had been in this place longer, she would have had a better idea, she thought, as to how he really felt about the ending of his marriage to Ruth.

Right now, this apartment could go in one of three different directions. It could turn into a very enticing and attractive celebration of the freedom of living alone, as was her apartment in LA. It could become a sleazy love-nest for a man eager to make up for lost time in the dating department. Or it could end up a mopey, miserable bolt-hole where Ren only came to sit on the couch and brood about his unhappiness, or stumble off to bed to drown it in sleep.

More than she should, Tully wanted to know which was the truth. What was Ren looking for? Independence and peace? A series of one-night stands? Or a reconciliation with Ruth?

She wanted to know how Ruthie felt about it, too. What was she like now? How had she changed? Eighteen years since high school... in a town like Marietta, they were bound to run into each other soon.

I could even call her and suggest we get together...

Sugar drank her coffee, holding her hands around the mug as if clinging to it for support. She dipped a vanilla cookie in to soften it, and ended up eating four of them, which Mom would be pleased about. "He was three," she said, out of the blue, when the silence had lasted a while.

"Charlie?" Tully asked. Sugar had to mean Charlie.

"Zack... Charlie... He was Zack when he was mine. Do—do kids remember anything from when they were three? Almost three and a half, I guess."

It wasn't clear who she was talking to.

"I don't know," said Tully, while Ren said nothing.

"I don't want him to remember me, because if he does, it'll be bad. If he remembers me at all, he won't want a meeting. I'm sure he won't." She shook her head sadly.

"You can't know that." Tully threw a glance at Ren, a frightened glance. She hadn't intended to, it just happened. She was out of her depth, and she needed to know if he was, too.

He didn't seem to be.

"Suzanne," he said, "I know this is probably impossible advice, but maybe you should try not to think too much about all of this until we've made contact. Is there a particular way you'd like me to do that? A phone call? A letter? I wouldn't suggest email."

"You mean he wouldn't read as far as the offer to split

eighteen million dollars in funds smuggled out of a war-torn country?" The joke was a surprise. It wasn't the first evidence this past week that Sugar had a sense of humor now that she was clean, but still it was unexpected.

"Exactly," Ren said. "With all the spam and scam offers people get, email is so easy to delete unread, if the address is unfamiliar."

"A phone call, then," Sugar decided. Her eyes were narrowed and papery around the edges, showing her tension. "Could you do it?"

"You want me to make the call?" Ren clarified.

"I don't know if I can wait for a letter. I've... never been hugely good at waiting for things."

"We can make a call now, if you like."

"No. No." She looked alarmed. "I don't want to be there for it. The waiting kills me." She gave a shaky laugh. "But I think listening to you make a call to him might kill me worse. I—I still need the distance. For his sake. For my mother's."

"I'll call him after you leave, then."

"Might take a few more minutes before I can do that. I—I'm still feeling a little shaky."

"No hurry," Tully assured her quickly, but then realized that Ren might not agree. "That is..."

"It's fine." His gaze met hers again, and it had the same masked quality to it as she'd seen in his expression before.

A very large part of Tully wanted to be alone with him so they could talk. So she could tell him why she'd stood him up eighteen years ago, what had happened since, and who Sugar really was.

Would she really spill such a secret to him, when so few other people knew?

No, of course not. That would be crazy.

She had questions about him, too, and maybe if they were alone, he might answer them. He could tell her why he'd married Ruthie Wilson, of all people, and why they were getting a divorce, and whose idea it had been to split up.

In Tully's world, the financial behind-the-scenes of Hollywood, there was only one reason why most men sought a divorce—they'd found a newer and younger model—but this was Marietta, Montana, not beautiful downtown Burbank, and this apartment over Ren Fletcher's law office didn't look like the place a man moved to when he was having a hot, ongoing affair. Still, you couldn't jump to conclusions.

As if she'd be likely to find out the truth in casual conversation, anyhow, she scoffed at herself inwardly.

She and Sugar sipped their coffee, and Ren finally broke a soon-to-be-awkward silence by asking, "Are you in town for long, Tully?"

"Open-ended. I'm needed here, right now, and it seemed like a good idea not to make firm dates for when I'll leave."

She had a brother in New York, six years younger than she was.

It hit her once again. If she hadn't responded to Mom's need for help with Sugar, how long would it have been before she would have heard this startling piece of news? The Morgan family had a thirty-six-year history of successful secret-keeping, after all.

"You're in California, I think I heard?" Ren said.

"That's right. I'm an accountant in the finance department at a major movie studio."

"Wow!" He grinned.

She headed him off fast, with her usual line, "Not as glamorous as it sounds."

The grin faded and he grimaced instead. "Sorry, I bet you get that all the time. People probably ask if you can introduce them to George Clooney, right?"

"I have a spreadsheet listing all the celebrities I've met," she joked. "I can show you if you want. It has column headers according to whether I've only shaken their hand, or whether we've been seen together in a compromising situation at the Beverly Hills Hotel."

"Aha, that *was* you in the grainy footage I saw last week."

"Sigh. I knew the wig wouldn't fool anyone. But how about you? Are you—?"

"I don't think my wig would fool anyone, either."

Another look flashed between them. The lame humor was fun, but he'd closed a door with that last comeback line. How about you, she'd asked, meaning *How's your life?* But he clearly didn't want to give her anything in return.

Or not now, anyhow.

"I think we can go," Sugar said after a moment or two. "I'd like to get home. Can we stop in at Copper Mountain Chocolates on the way, Tully?"

"Just try to stop me!"

"You'll call, won't you?" Sugar turned to Ren. "Even if you don't get through to him, you'll call to tell me that?"

"Of course. I'll update you on every step."

♡

Out in the street, Sugar needed to hang on to Tully's arm as they walked the few doors down to the candy store. Sage wasn't serving at the front counter today. Tully didn't know if she was working in her mystical and sacred chocolate laboratory in back, or just wasn't around.

Either way, being served by an unfamiliar and much younger girl was a lot easier. Even though Tully and Sage didn't know each other very well, the Carrigans were an established local ranching family, thoroughly plugged into the back and forth of Marietta town gossip. Sage would be bound to ask a few friendly questions, which Sugar might blurt out hasty answers to, and Tully wasn't ready to let anyone else in town know about her birth mother's long lost son, or any other Morgan family secret.

"Do you want to try something new, or some of the same ones we had before?" she asked Sugar now.

"I loved those hazelnut clusters. And the dark raspberry ones, and the ones with the lemon shavings."

"Mind if we try the coconut clusters, too?"

"Well, you know, we wouldn't want to get too much. Only two or three pieces, I think."

"Two or three—!" Tully turned a shocked look in Sugar's direction, then saw her slightly gap-toothed grin. "Oh, you're kidding."

"Of course I'm kidding. If you want to buy out the whole store, it's good with me. I can probably chip in for the purchase. Say thirty dollars?"

"Now that really might be too much, buying out the store and depriving our fellow Mariettans of chocolate until Sage has time to make more."

"Does she make it all?"

"No, I think some of it she buys in, but all these in the display here are hers."

"I think we should support the local industry," Sugar said very seriously, looking down at the immaculate offerings. "You know, for the economy."

"I think you're right."

"Not because we like these the best, or anything."

"No, of course not. Purely for the economy."

"We're good that way."

"There should be a medal for people like us," Tully said. "After all, eating candy is the supreme sacrifice."

"Oh, it is!"

The girl behind the counter was looking at them as if they were slightly crazy. Apparently she didn't think their family-style humor was very funny. They made their choices and went away with a nice weighty bag that rustled enticingly with individually wrapped treats.

As soon as they'd left the store, Sugar said in a pained way, "You must have a thousand questions, Tully."

"When are you going to tell Mom? That's the first one."

"Not yet. Please don't tell her, Tully! Please!" She looked so frail, standing there on the sidewalk wrapped in Mom's coat, with her arms hugged around herself.

"I won't, yet, if it's that important to you. But why? Why do you think she'll be angry?" Mom so rarely was.

Sugar closed her eyes and shook her head. "She will be angry. And I just... I'm not ready for it, okay?"

"Okay," Tully said obediently.

What was happening, here? Sugar looked... not strong... in a way Tully remembered from years ago. Like she was looking for a place to hide from things she didn't want to face.

"You wouldn't know about him yet either," she said, "if we hadn't been coming home from the doctor when Mr. Fletcher's office called."

"Then I'm glad we were. I'm glad I pushed."

"I know. Me, too. With you beside me in the car, it was bound to come to that. I bit the damned bullet and it feels good. I've wanted to. I've been wanting to talk about it ever since I decided I was going to try to find him. But it's been too hard to find the right words. And not to Patty. Not yet. Keep my secret for me?" She put a pleading hand on Tully's arm, and Tully felt a spurt of suspicion and mistrust from long ago.

What was her birth mother drawing her into, here? For a strung-out addict, she'd often been incredibly good at manipulating other people into giving in to her needs, in the past. Maybe she still was, even if her goals and reasons were different now.

Or was that too cynical?

Tully pushed the mistrust aside, and said instead, "Tell me about him. Tell me..." then she stopped.

But Sugar heard the words, even though Tully hadn't said them. "... tell you what I meant about hurting him?"

"Yes. That."

"I can't talk about this at home, where Patty might hear."

"No, okay," Tully said, going along with it once again.

"I want to talk to someone else first, someone other than Patty. To practice. Saying it. To someone who might... hurt less about it. Be less angry. I talked to the lawyer the first time I saw him, but that's not the same. Tully, tell me if it's safe for me to talk to you," she begged.

Tully didn't have an answer. She was astonished, really. All her life, she'd given nothing back to Sugar. They'd punished each other at every interaction, Sugar with her confronting and dangerous lifestyle, Tully with her blank wall of open hostility and dislike.

Now Sugar was reaching out.

Creating a closeness.

Telling Tully she trusted her, was what it came down to.

Tully didn't feel she deserved the trust. Even now, there was the lingering suspicion that she was being manipulated in some way, and she was afraid, too, of how angry she might be with this fragile woman, her mother, if Sugar told her too much. She could feel the potential for it hovering at the edge of her awareness like a storm that might pass nearby, or might hit direct.

"Can we go somewhere?" Sugar asked again on a pleading note.

"You mean, the Java Café, or..."

"No, not somewhere public. Just sit in the car. Drive and park somewhere. And just sit. Like in our own little cocoon."

"River Bend Park?" Tully suggested.

Back in the nineties it had been *the* teen hangout. Half the kids at Marietta High had had their first kiss or lost their virginity there in the dark of a summer night, and families on picnics had been confronted by broken beer bottles glinting on the sand the next morning.

But Mom said the place had been cleaned up after Neve Shepherd's shocking death all those years ago. It was neat and pretty now, she'd told Tully, with a boardwalk and picnic tables and landscaping. Annette and Gary Shepherd had poured their hearts into fundraising for it and contributed a substantial amount to the cost from their own pockets. There was a plaque in Neve's memory on one of the tables.

"Wherever," Sugar said. "As long as it's quiet."

"River Bend Park will be quiet."

So they drove there, and Sugar didn't really talk, which gave Tully ten minutes to think about Neve and Kira Shepherd and their parents. Annette and Gary still lived next door to Mom, and Tully had waved and said hello a couple of times since she'd been back, and had promised to drop in for coffee with them soon. Kira was married in Bozeman, she thought. With a daughter? A son? She couldn't remember. Step-children too, though. She remembered that. Kira's husband was quite a lot older, and had been married before.

Wait, though. Was her information out of date? She vaguely thought Mom might have mentioned a divorce, and that Kira and her child were back in Marietta now.

Mom was right about the changes to the park. It was much prettier and better cared for than Tully remembered. Neve Shepherd had been incredibly wild and not especially nice in high school, but this positive legacy was good, all the same.

Tully parked at one end of the lot and turned to Sugar. "Want to eat some of that candy?"

"Let's wait until Patty can have her share."

"I hate to break it to you," Tully said, "but she really doesn't love it like we do."

"I know. How weird is that? Seriously. Not to love chocolate."

"It should be against the law, a criminal offense."

Sugar burst into tears.

Tully thought she was laughing at first, the sound was so sudden and it came out of another moment of shared humor, but no, this wasn't laughter, it was sobbing, rough and raw. Kind of rusty, as if Sugar had forgotten how to cry.

"I'm sorry," she said. "When you said against the law, and I'm thinking about Zack..."

"It's okay. It is. It will be." Tully reached an arm across. It was awkward in the car. They were shut away together in the warm little cocoon that Sugar had wanted, but the gearshift lever kept them separate and got in the way. Sugar didn't cry for long. She shut off the tears like a faucet, as if through sheer willpower.

She'd never had any of that in earlier years, but somehow she'd developed it now, the way some people never did a scrap of exercise in their youth then suddenly took up marathon running at the age of forty.

Willpower was a kind of muscle, it seemed.

"I kept him until he was three and a half," Sugar said. Her voice sank to a monotone, too wooden for the words, stripped of emotion because the emotion was too strong and deep to fit into human language. "I should have never done that. Should have never thought I could do it, raise a child. I was a terrible mother. Ninety-five percent of the time, I was the worst mother, but just the five percent that was better made me think I could do it, on a good day. I loved him so much, Tully. When I hugged him I wanted to squeeze him so hard... I just couldn't squeeze him hard enough to express what I felt. With you, I was too young and Patty took you—thank the Lord—and you never felt like mine, but Zack, that five percent of the time..."

"It's the other ninety-five percent that's upsetting you."

"When he was like a buzzing fly, I just wanted to swat him out of the way, when I was using or needing to. He made me crazy. I gave him cold medication to make him sleep. I stuck cola in a bottle for him if I didn't have formula or milk." Still she spoke in the same dead, bone-tired way, as if she'd relived these guilty memories so often that they'd simply worn her away, worn her into the ground.

Had they given her cancer? Tully wondered. Could memories do that? Could guilt? She rebelled against this idea, on Sugar's behalf. People didn't get cancer because they *deserved* it. Good people got cancer all the time.

"If I didn't have a clean diaper," Sugar was saying, while the Marietta River rushed in front of them, "I left him in the same one for two or three days, or else I fished an old one out of the trash and put it back on, if it was better than the one he was already wearing. I told myself the old one would have dried out by then. He always had a rash. He fell asleep on the floor at night, on our filthy rug, and most of the time he was still there in the morning. Sometimes he was in his crib and I never even remembered if it was me that put him there, or if he woke up and climbed in there himself, when he got bigger. He cried a lot, especially if he was hungry. He was pretty thin and small for his age, back then. I had this guy—" But she stopped and shook her head.

Tully couldn't speak. The cough syrup. The dirty diapers. The cola. The perpetual rash.

That would have been me, if she'd kept me.

She wondered if she should feel angry, the way Sugar was convinced Mom was going to be. Should she let the storm of anger she'd sensed in herself earlier break over their heads?

But, no, she couldn't, somehow. You couldn't. Not

when Sugar herself was so broken by the memories of the things she'd done.

"When I saw him in that picture on Ren Fletcher's computer... I can't even believe it's him. Is it really him?" She sounded eager now, and pleading. "He really survived? Survived how I treated him? Grew into a good man, after that terrible start? He's really okay, and healthy, and happy? He looked happy, didn't he? Don't you think?"

"He did." And he'd looked like a Morgan. Tully had seen Dad in his smile, in the way it made his chin jut forward. It was four years since Dad's death, and to find that his smile lived on in someone she hadn't even known existed was amazing. It was unutterably precious, a miracle.

"The people who adopted him, the Barnetts, they are going to heaven, those people," Sugar said. "They will have the best place in heaven, with a VIP ticket. To turn my bruised little boy into that man, after what I did to him, after I let Merc hurt him those times."

"Who is Merc, Sugar?"

Sugar told her.

Told her about the low-rent good looks and the wads of cash, the people coming to their apartment night and day, only going away happy if they'd arrived with enough money to pay for what they wanted. Told her about the way Merc would say he loved her right after he'd hit her, or cursed at her, or both. Told her the things she'd had to do, and how Merc had paid her with drugs.

"He's not Zack's... Charlie's... father. But he wouldn't have been any better with him if he had been."

"So who—?"

Sugar covered her face. "I don't know. A guy. A john." She was silent for a moment, then said, "I know why you hate me. When I hear these things coming out of my mouth, I know why you hate me."

"But I don't," Tully said. Her throat had thickened and tears came suddenly. She leaned across again and put her arms around those painfully thin shoulders, smelling the clean, nutty fragrance of shampoo as she pressed her face against her birth mother's fine hair. "Sugar, I don't hate you.

Really."

It was true. For the very first time in her whole life, she knew for certain that it was true.

Chapter Twelve

"My name is René Fletcher," Ren said into the phone. "I'm an attorney in Marietta, Montana, and I'm calling on behalf of a client."

"Yeah, hi, okay," said the male voice at the other end of the line. It belonged to Dr. Charlie Barnett, finally. Ren had been calling since Monday, but the man was incredibly hard to reach. He clearly kept long and demanding hours, a mix of surgery, outpatients, appointment hours, hospital rounds. Ren felt as if he'd been chasing him all over the hospital and knew the guy's schedule over the past few days almost as well as Charlie Barnett must know it himself.

"Do you have access to a computer at the moment?" he asked.

"Uh, yes, right in front of me. Can I ask what this is—?"

"I'd like you to confirm my credentials first, before we talk any further. If you could search for the State Bar of Montana website and click on I Need a Lawyer, you'll find a referral service." He guided Dr. Barnett through the search criteria until his own name came up. "What I'd like you to do now, Dr. Barnett, if you wouldn't mind, is to hang up the phone and call me back on the number you see listed there, so that you've confirmed whom you're talking to."

"Look, if this is legal stuff, shouldn't we be doing it in writing?"

"My client preferred me to make contact by telephone first. But I can report back to her that you'd like a more formal approach. And of course I will follow up this call with a letter."

"Hey, no, it's fine." A tired sigh came across the line. "Let me do it the way you've suggested." The voice was friendly but distant. Charlie was reserving his judgment. Ren didn't blame him for that.

The line disconnected and he waited, wondering if Charlie would really call back. After a minute or two, the phone rang and he picked it up and heard Nina's voice. "I have the call you were hoping for, Mr. Fletcher, from Dr. Barnett."

"Thanks, Nina. Put him through."

"Look, I'm still not sure about this," Charlie said. "What is it that you want? Why have you contacted me?"

"As I said, I'll follow everything up in writing, in more detail," Ren said. "But what you need to know now is that I'm acting on behalf of Suzanne Elizabeth Morgan." He gave her age and her address in Marietta. "She has reason to believe that she is your birth mother and she's interested in making contact."

There was a heavy beat of silence. "What?"

Ren explained again.

"My *mother?* My birth mother!" Charlie Barnett swore under his breath.

The call lasted quite a while.

♡

"I don't want to go to a salon," Sugar told her mother. They were both sitting on the couch in front of daytime TV.

"It would be my treat," Patty answered at once. "We don't have to go to the Cut 'n Curl if you think Nell is too hard to take. Trudi works from home, above her garage and it's such a sweet little place. She has a beautician on staff, now. There's usually two or three women there at once. She brings everyone coffee and cookies and has music playing, it's like going for a girls' day out."

"But you're good with hair." The description of the salon hadn't made her mother's case. The last thing Sugar wanted was to sit somewhere like that, listening to a lot of cozy gossip that would shift, as soon as she left the place, into gossip about her.

My lord, she almost looks older than her own mother!

Patty barely talked about her until suddenly she was back here. I think she's ashamed of her.

She's obviously not well.

No, thank you!

"Couldn't you, please?" Sugar said. "Just cut it short?"

"You'll be gray," Patty threatened gently.

"It's time I stopped with the black. I went that way when my hair grew in after the chemo, but I looked at myself in the mirror this morning. I'm like a moth-eaten crow."

"You could choose something softer, color-wise. A golden mahogany, maybe."

"Would you do it for me? We could make a whole afternoon of it."

"Well, since it would *take* the whole afternoon, we'd better do that."

"So you will?"

"Oh, you have backed me right into a corner as usual, Sugar."

"C'mon it would be nice," she cajoled, and wondered if this was manipulation, the way it once would have been. "Mother and daughter. We could put on some music, have coffee and cake..."

Was it manipulation when it was honest?

The phone rang. René Fletcher had called a couple of times since last week, but only to report that he hadn't yet been able to reach Charlie. As always when she heard its long, insistent pealing, Sugar's heart jumped in her chest and she felt sick. She stood up, but she was too slow and

Patty got there first, despite her stiff hips. She listened for a moment, then passed the cordless handset over, with a brief, "For you."

Sugar lost her breath and could only nod as she sat back down. A shallow heave of air gave her just enough wind to say a thin, "Hello?" into the phone.

"It's Ren Fletcher," she heard.

"Oh, hi." *Don't say his name, because Patty's right here.*

"I'm sorry this has taken a few days," the lawyer said. "As you know, I've called Dr. Barnett several times with no luck, but I got through to him just now."

"And?"

Patty was listening, although trying to pretend she wasn't. She fussed around, neat and well-meaning in the way she tidied the magazines on the coffee table that Sugar had been reading this morning. Her behavior reminded Sugar of all the reasons she'd rebelled the second she'd hit puberty at twelve. Earlier, really.

She'd craved excitement and glamour and a dark, shady kind of glitter to life that was the polar opposite of the way Patty and Walter lived and felt and thought. Her parents were too neat, too sweet, too good. Patty still drove her crazy that way sometimes, no matter how much Sugar understood now that this kind of life was worth a million times more than the life she'd actually lived, with her quest for the dark glitter.

"It came as a shock to him," the lawyer was saying. "I offered to follow up in writing, and he would like me to do that before he makes any commitment to a meeting."

"But... um... you think that's going to work out? The idea of a meeting?"

Patty, go away!

"In principle," said the lawyer. "The practicalities may be a little difficult."

He kept talking, but Sugar barely took it in. She made herself keep a blank face, and she would have to tell Patty some story about her bank account, or something. Maybe the doctor. Test results from last week.

She knew exactly why she was scared of telling Patty about Charlie, and she knew she couldn't put it off forever, but she'd been so strong lately, about so many things. Being strong had worn her out, honestly. She let herself be weak about this. Put it off as long as possible, Sugar. Pretend it would be better if she left it. Hey, maybe it even would.

"Who was that?" Patty asked, when she'd ended the call.

"Oh, just the doctor's office to say my blood work was good."

Patty wanted the detail, and Sugar straight up lied about it, which she was pretty good at, after years of practice. She didn't need to lie very often these days, but it was like riding a bicycle. You remembered how.

♡

"Tully? Tully Morgan?"

Tully looked away from the drugstore shelf she'd been browsing in search of some items for Sugar. She had a list. Calcium supplements, moisturizer, an herbal menopause tonic, vitamin E cream, lip balm, hair dye, leg compression stockings.

In each category, there seemed to be multiple options, and Sugar hadn't given her any detail about preferred brands, apart from saying that Mom had suggested golden mahogany for the hair color. She'd been apologetic about even asking if Tully could run such an errand, but Tully didn't mind.

She'd been back in Marietta almost two weeks now, and even though she was needed on a daily basis and her nights were broken by getting up to help Sugar with her medication, she was accustomed to a much busier and more active life, and she was in danger of growing bored. She needed to find more to do, but meanwhile even a simple shopping errand broke up the day.

The woman who'd spoken Tully's name wore a pale yellow uniform with the drugstore logo embroidered on the breast pocket and she looked very familiar, like someone's sister, yet Tully couldn't place her. "Hi... you're—we were at—" Marietta High. A safe enough bet, even though she was only guessing.

"At high school together," the other woman confirmed, and a fraction of a second before she said her name, Tully knew what it would be. This was Ren's wife, and one of her own friends from high school.

Sure enough, "Ruthie," said the lemon-clad blonde. "Ruth Wilson."

"Oh. Oh, wow, Ruthie, it is you! Of course." She manufactured pleasure and apology in roughly equal amounts, while noting the last name Ruth had used. Wilson, not Fletcher. How significant was that? "I'm so sorry." She reached out her arms and they gave each other an awkward hug that ended with them each stepping back a pace. Tully's beautifully cut black wool coat was really too thick for hugging. "I knew you as soon as I saw you. So well. But my mind went blank."

Ruth was still smiling warmly. "You haven't changed a bit!"

"Neither have you."

They were lying, both of them.

Polite lies with good intentions behind them. Well, on Tully's side, anyhow. She couldn't speak for Ruth.

Ruth had changed a lot. She had been so petite back in high school, a wisp of a thing with natural light caramel brown hair, a nervous touch with makeup, and the same skin breakouts that had plagued Tully during her teens. Now she was a lot more solid and a lot blonder and her skin and her makeup looked fantastic.

Even though she'd been on Tully's mind lately—something that it shamed Tully to admit to, even in her own head—recognition had been slow. She'd been imagining Ren married to the nervous wisp with the spiky mascara and slightly crooked lip-liner, not to this fuller-figured, beautifully made-up and much more socially adept woman.

"Wow, how long since you've been back home?" Ruthie asked.

"Oh, it's four years." Dad's funeral. She'd only stayed a

couple of days.

"And before that?"

"Probably another four years, and then only for a night or two. I—I really don't come back all that often. Mom likes—and Dad did, too, before he died—to come to California for some beach and sun, and my brother's there, too, so it makes more sense."

"I was sorry about your dad. I was away when it happened, so I couldn't get to the funeral. I hear news about you from your mom when she comes in here. Such a glamorous life! I'm not surprised you haven't bothered to keep in touch." The smile was still in place, but it didn't seem so warm now, and Tully wasn't sure what lay behind it. A criticism, she thought. An implication that Ruth thought Tully considered herself to be too important for her former Marietta High School friends.

And it was true that she hadn't kept in touch with any of them, even a couple of girls whom she'd been closer to than she'd been to Ruth. She'd felt back then as if her whole life was a fraud, her perspective had changed so fast and so completely that day, and it had taken her years to adjust to the idea that Suzanne was her birth mother.

"It's not glamorous," she said to Ruth.

"Oh, you're kidding me! Stars, and parties, and—"

"Honestly, the kinds of parties we have in the finance department aren't the ones that make it onto Entertainment Tonight. You should see us all standing stiffly around in uncomfortable clothes, wishing we were at home in our sweats eating takeout in front of the TV."

"Well, of course you'd have to say that. You wouldn't want people hounding you for detail on all the celebrities."

"Honestly, Ruth."

"Don't worry, I'm not expecting any dirt. Or not right away, anyhow." She gave a wink. "Now, can I help you with anything, Tully? We'll get you fixed up, and then we'll work out when we can go for coffee. It's so great to see you!"

"Yes, it is. I'd love to have coffee." The words felt stilted.

Ruth was very helpful about the hair dye, the herbal supplements, the moisturizer and the compression stockings. "These are for your Mom?"

"For my sister, Suzanne. She has trouble with fluid retention in her legs."

"Oh, right, of course." Ruth nodded. "She and your mom have been in a couple of times." The nod and the words exuded both tact and knowingness. Anyone who worked in a pharmacy in a town like Marietta knew a lot about everyone else's health issues.

"She has cervical cancer, spread all over," Tully said bluntly, and Ruth looked first shocked at the bluntness, then sympathetic.

"I know," she said. "I know all about it." Tully wasn't sure how comfortable she felt about that. "It must be hard."

"It is. She's not strong, and Mom's not young, and they both needed help."

"So you're here for a while?"

"Open-ended. Till June, at least."

"Maybe we could grab that coffee right now. I'm due for a break."

"I'd like that," Tully said, as she'd said before.

She honestly didn't know if it was true. Ruth's line about her not having changed one bit still rang in her head.

If it was accurate, it wasn't a compliment, she decided. Like Ruth herself, she'd been awkward and uncertain about her personal style back then, inclined toward cheap and conservative outfits that did nothing to show off her figure or her coloring. Unlike Ruth's, her figure had stayed much the same, and she thought she'd improved out of sight when it came to style.

So maybe they were both at fault in delivering the old cliché that high school classmates used the world over. Maybe they were both capable of using a two-edged sword.

Ruth put her purchases through and handed over a white paper bag that bulged at the seams. "Let me go check with Carol. We're pretty quiet." She disappeared between the aisles toward the prescription counter at the back of the store, and returned a minute or two later to announce, "We have an hour! Isn't that great? I never took a proper lunch break today, and it's not like people are waiting in line."

She rolled her eyes. She always used to do that in high school, any time a teacher or someone she and her friends didn't like said something she considered clueless. She'd had a knack of being acutely perceptive about other people's faults and weaknesses, although she'd possibly been less aware of her own.

She was married to Ren.

The fact hit Tully once again, like a slap on the face.

Still married to him, her life interwoven with his, deeply familiar with everything about him, his tastes, his habits, his flaws... although apparently for not much longer. They were separated, and Ren was living above his office.

Did Ruth have any idea that her soon-to-be-ex-husband was helping Sugar to track down her long-lost son?

It was six days since Tully and Sugar had seen Dad's smile in the face of the nice-looking young man on the Park Hospital website on Ren's computer, and Ren had called yesterday afternoon with some news, while Tully was out running. Sugar had updated her after she got back, while Mom was in the kitchen, a mumbled account with gaze kept firmly on the kitchen doorway. It made Tully feel uncomfortable about the fact that Mom still didn't know.

"The lawyer says he'll call again when he's heard back from Charlie about possible dates for a visit," Sugar had said, "but I want to go to New York. I don't want to wait a long time if Charlie can't get away. I want to see him."

This was a problem they hadn't yet resolved. Tully really didn't think that Sugar was strong enough to go, but she understood the fear that time might be short.

"Where would you like to go, Tully?" Ruth said now. "The diner? The Java Café? The saloon?"

"Java sounds good."

"Ooh, she's from LA, she's too good for Grey's or the diner now!" Ruth said to an invisible audience. Mocking or teasing?

Tully chose to laugh, then said quickly, "I didn't mean— We can go wherever you like. Don't they do hot chocolate and coffee at Copper Mountain Chocolates? I've been meaning to—"

"Not there," Ruth said. "Sage Carrigan and I do *not* get along."

"Oh, okay," Tully answered politely.

Ruth put her hands on her hips. "Well, would you get along with the woman who tried to steal your husband?"

This was a shock.

"I'm sorry, I had no idea."

"I mean, she's engaged now, and all," Ruth added in a confiding way, "so that particular storm blew over, but if Dawson O'Dell hadn't come back into her life, you can bet she would have had Ren if she could have got him."

"I'm sorry."

"It broke up our marriage. Well, it was *one* of the things that broke up our marriage."

"I—I heard about that, your separation. I'm sorry," Tully repeated yet again.

"I'm not," Ruth drawled. "It was overdue. We'd grown too far apart. We just didn't want the same things anymore."

"That's hard."

"Hey, we still haven't decided where we're going for this coffee."

"Let's just go across the road to Java."

"It is *so great* to see you, Tully! I can't even tell you!"

A minute or two later, they were sitting at a table in the café window, and the awkwardness had eased. They both ordered mochaccinos, then Ruth leaned into the rim of the table and said, "Tell me all about Southern California, because I've been thinking of making a move to somewhere warmer now that Ren and I have split."

"I'm glad you're okay about that," Tully said. "The separation, I mean. I'm sure it can't have been easy."

Ruth sighed. "Oh. Yeah. Well. We got together in high school. That's a recipe for disaster, isn't it?"

"In high school?"

"On prom night, if you want the exact timing." She smiled suddenly, and there was a knowing glint in her eye. "That's right, he was your prom date, wasn't he, and then you stood him up? I'd almost forgotten."

Had she?

Tully supposed that could be true. After eighteen years, the start of a relationship was probably overlaid with so many other memories, good and bad, that it stopped being significant. For her, the memories of that night still felt far too fresh.

"What happened that night, by the way?" Ruth was saying. "I don't think anyone ever knew why you didn't show."

"Family stuff," Tully said. "I went to live with my brother. It was all decided pretty fast, after a bit of a crisis, and I never had a chance to let Ren know. By the time things settled down, I thought an apology would be too late to be meaningful."

"A crisis?"

"Yes. Long over with, now. Not important." She didn't want to talk to Ruth about Sugar.

"It was a horrible, horrible night, after the prom." Ruth shivered self-importantly. "We clung to each other, Ren and I. No one who was there at River Bend Park stayed the same. It changed us. We needed each other. We were good together for a while, but we had too many ups and downs. It all turned sour. I don't blame him, really, for looking elsewhere. I knew in my heart that I needed something different... something better. For me, that's not going to be in Marietta. I'm looking for wider horizons, now."

She sounded very firm and determined about it—putting on a brave front maybe. There was a discordant note to her words that made Tully question her honesty, and the suggestion that Ren had cheated on her—whether with Sage Carrigan or someone else—hung in the air like a lingering odor that you couldn't quite place.

"Do you have definite plans for a move?" Tully asked.

"The divorce has to come through first. Ren says that should only take a few weeks, since we're not contesting anything, and we don't have kids. I don't think I'm cut out to be a mom, I've decided! Then I'll need to sell the house—that's mine, free and clear, as well as the contents." She looked satisfied about this. "I'm looking at the Oceanside area. Carlsbad, or Vista. I'm dreaming about the sun on my skin, and the hibiscus and bougainvillea in flower."

"Yes, Southern California is beautiful if you love the warmth and sun."

"But tell me more about you."

"Well, there's not much to tell. I work pretty hard. I like to keep fit. I love to read. I volunteer at a charity book fair that's held four times a year, in my local area."

I sound boring. I can't talk to this woman. Why not? She used to be a friend. We sat together in English and Science classes for four years, but now we're both so stilted about it.

"You're single, obviously," Ruth said. "You never got married?" The implication was clear—if it hadn't happened by now, then it wasn't going to.

"No, I never did."

"You never wanted to, or...?"

"Just didn't happen. Hasn't happened." She wanted to add "yet" but held it back. Somehow, she didn't want to give Ruth very much of herself. No secrets. No speaking from the heart. No wistfulness or regrets.

Her reasons were complex, and she didn't have time to work out whether they were justified, or important.

It was a mix of memories about the kind of gossip they'd enjoyed in school, an ingrained privacy on the subject of Sugar, and an awareness of Ren's presence in the background of her life that Tully wasn't letting herself think about very much. She felt that in many ways she would have preferred the same open dislike she'd felt for Sugar, back in her teens, rather than this more veiled version that both she and Ruth were pretending not to feel.

They talked a little more. Tully told Ruth about the downsides of So Cal. The blasting summer heat, the smog and traffic, and real estate prices. Ruth told Tully about people from their class. Gemma Clayton had settled down so fast after high school, you wouldn't believe. You'd never guess, now, how wild she'd been back then. Gemma had never, ever let on the smallest detail about the father of her child, but Ruth had her suspicions.

"In fact, I know for sure," she said. "It was Garth

Newell." To Tully this didn't seem like much of a revelation. Everyone knew Garth and Gemma had been going out together back then, and had been each other's dates at prom. "No wonder she doesn't want people to know," Ruth finished. "She always acts as if it was some mysterious stranger, but it was Garth."

"What happened to Garth? Is he still around?" Tully remembered him as a reasonably good-looking but not very bright guy under the thumb of his older brother.

"He disappeared for a while, came back a few years later when his Mom died, then disappeared again. Never took the slightest notice of his daughter."

"His—? Oh, you mean Gemma's daughter."

"Wouldn't even have said hello to her in the street. And didn't even come home for his father's funeral. Neither did his brother. Well, Judd Newell was always bad news, despite those incredible looks."

"Yes, he was definitely the better-looking one, wasn't he?"

"Judd Newell and Jay Brown, best-looking guys in Marietta, back then. Oh, and those Sheenan boys, too."

"What are they up to these days, Troy and Trey?"

"Oh, Troy is a huge success story! I always knew he would be. He lives in San Francisco, a multi-millionaire. It's his company that's just reopened the Graff Hotel. Have you seen it? It's amazing!"

"I've walked by it. I haven't seen inside."

"You should. My only issue with Troy is that he hasn't come back to town to marry a local girl so he can spread the good fortune." She giggled comfortably. "Trey is still a troublemaker, of course, but that's another story."

They stretched out the conversation with this kind of stuff until Ruth's hour was up and she had to get back. Tully took her drugstore bag and walked home, taking a roundabout route for the sake of exercise and so she could get rid of the slightly sour taste in her mouth that catching up with Ruth had given her.

It definitely wasn't the coffee.

So what was it?

It's me.

She could have blamed Ruth—Ruth's inclination to gossip, and the little undercurrents of upside-down meaning—but that was too easy. Tully knew she couldn't let herself off the hook by dismissing the sour taste as all coming from Ruth.

"It's me," she said to herself as she neared home. "Because I have Ren on my mind and Ruth has no idea."

Chapter Thirteen

"It would be best if she could come here," Charlie Barnett said to Ren on the phone on Friday, two days after he'd first made contact. "My schedule is so full right now. I have zero time for a personal life, and trust me, I'm feeling the strain of that."

Charlie himself had been the one to call, this time. Ren had express-mailed him copies of the paperwork that Sugar had, including her own birth certificate and one for Zachary Charles Morgan. The formal documents had made a difference. Dr. Barnett sounded less distant and suspicious, although still cautious in the extreme. As a lawyer, Ren approved of that.

"I understand about your workload. The only problem is, I'm not sure if it will be physically possible for her to come to you," he said.

"I'm a little confused that she doesn't want to talk to me directly. I'd really like to hear from her. This is a very weird situation for me. My parents... my adoptive parents... are incredibly important to me. They've been fantastic. My birth—your client—"

"Suzanne," Ren suggested, to help him out.

"Suzanne, yes. She needs to know that I'm not going to do anything to jeopardize the relationship I've grown up with, and I'd rather talk to her about that directly before either of us commits to anything."

"I think she'd understand that. She's feeling a strong need to protect you," Ren said. "And I think to protect herself. She's concerned about how you might feel, and not sure about how well she'd be able to connect with you over the phone. She's afraid that a direct contact might not help, at this stage. She wonders what you remember about the years you were with her."

"I have remembered a couple of things, actually. I thought I didn't, but then after you and I talked on Wednesday, some of it came back."

"She was a little concerned about that possibility," Ren said carefully. "She's aware that any memories might not be pleasant ones."

"Yeah, I understand that now." There was a silence. In the background, Ren could hear the strident rush of city traffic and, oddly, something that sounded like flamenco guitar. "I remember a guy... but it wasn't all bad. Tell her that. Tell her I really would like to talk to her directly."

"I will."

There was another silence from Charlie, then the sound of the guitar grew louder, as if he was moving toward it. The music was beautiful despite the background of traffic. Ren thought he heard the clink of coins and realized he was hearing a street musician busking for money. Was it Charlie who'd just dropped coins into the musician's guitar case? It must have been, if he'd been able to hear it on the phone.

"Where are you, can I ask?"

"Oh, yeah, sorry. It's noisy. I'm on the sidewalk outside the hospital."

"Right, that makes sense." They were such big city sounds, traffic and music mixed, not the kind of thing you heard on a Marietta street.

"Look, give her my number," Charlie said. "I'm not enjoying this barrier you're providing, even if I do accept her reasons for it."

"I'll tell her that, too."

"I need to go now, but I'll be waiting for her call."

Ren put down the phone and rubbed his eyes, then picked it up again and called Suzanne Morgan, to report what Charlie had said. He didn't mention the flamenco guitar.

♡

"Sugar, don't you seriously think it's time to talk to Mom about all of this? *Before* you try calling him?"

Sugar sat in the bathroom on the same ancient swivel desk chair that Tully had had in her bedroom in high school. She had towels draped around her neck and hair dye creamed through her roughly cut hair, and Mom had gone to bring up coffee and cake as if this was the kind of hair salon where they pampered you with a snack while you waited for the timer to announce you were ready to rinse.

"Yes. Of course it's time I told her." Sugar added tightly, "Doesn't mean I want to."

In a throaty conspirator's whisper she'd gabbled a summary of Ren's latest phone call the moment Mom's footsteps announced that she was on her way down the stairs, a few minutes ago.

"So you'll say something? Today? Now? When she comes back."

Sugar laughed her ex-smoker laugh. "Gee, you know how to nag, don't you?" She added mockingly. "Who are you? My mother?"

"Yeah, you'd think," Tully drawled.

It wasn't their first secretive disagreement of the day. Sugar still insisted that she wanted to go to New York, since Charlie apparently didn't know when he might manage to get out here, and Tully not only thought that Sugar wasn't well enough to go, she thought that any plan for a visit was putting the cart way before the horse, with Mom still completely in the dark.

Mom had said again to Tully just after lunch, while Sugar was taking a nap, "What is it that's on her mind? Do you have any idea? She's had a couple of phone calls this week, Tully, and she says they're from the doctor, but I don't think I believe her. I know when she's lying."

"Well, you've had the practice at spotting it," Tully had answered lightly.

And I'm lying, too. By omission. I know exactly what's on Sugar's mind.

"I want you to tell her, Sugar," she repeated now, more forcefully. "You're putting me in a position that's really uncomfortable and wrong, and if you don't say it, I will."

Sugar tucked her chin down to her chest, closed her eyes and muttered, "It's not your story to tell."

"Then tell it."

"I'm going to, Tully. Let me time it right, okay?"

As if Sugar had ever done that!

The kitchen timer clicked its way down from thirty minutes toward zero and Tully went to help Mom bring up the coffee and cake. The latter was fresh-baked, a springy vanilla butter cake base with a German-style streusel topping, and the coffee was made with a rich Arabica blend and hot milk.

"You're killing yourself, Mom," Tully scolded her, not for the first time, as she carried the tray upstairs in her mother's wake, watching the stiff way she moved.

"If I don't tempt her appetite, she doesn't eat."

Tully sighed. "Yeah, I know." She'd become a slave to this thinking, also, shopping for delectable ingredients and planning inviting meals. She'd made the streusel topping for the cake this morning, while Mom had made the base.

In the bathroom, she put the tray down on the antique wooden vanity and went to bring in two more chairs.

As a substitute hair salon, the bathroom worked surprisingly well. Mom and Dad had remodeled it six years ago, taking its decor back to something more in keeping with the house's hundred-year-old Queen Anne roots.

Above waist-high cream-painted wood paneling, there was a pretty wallpaper in dusky pink, cream, sage green, and beige. The metal radiator and mirror frames and faucets were all in gold, and the claw-foot tub had a simple gauzy white curtain all around it. There was plenty of room for the three of them to sit, the antique light fittings created a warm glow on a dull late winter afternoon, and it felt so pretty and warm, not like a bathroom at all.

Like a hair salon, right now, all gossipy and slightly pungent from the chemicals in the dye.

"This is fun, the three of us," Mom said. "Your eyes aren't stinging, Sugar?"

"No, it's fine. This paper band thing you put on is keeping the cream in place. You can't see any drips running down can you?"

"No, nothing. I wish I didn't have to hack your hair off like that first, but it didn't make sense to dye all of it when it was so long and we're cutting it short in a minute. I'm itching to get the proper cut done once we've rinsed and conditioned. I've had a few ideas about the style."

"As long as it's short."

"There may some ends of the black left in a couple of places."

"Hey, that might look interesting."

"Black was a terrible color for you, honey, I don't know why you ever did it. This is going to look much nicer." Mom herself had accepted her gray hair for the past twenty years or more.

Sugar sipped her coffee and nibbled her cake and didn't say a word about Charlie, and Tully felt her anger growing. She met Sugar's gaze in the mirror and glared at her. Wasn't this a good opportunity? Mom seemed happier today and not so tired. The hair project had energized her.

But Sugar made a face that said, *In my own time, okay?*

"You've got nine more minutes," Tully answered her out loud, her voice heavy with irony, and they both knew she wasn't talking about the timer.

Mom knew it, too. She'd seen the way they glared at each other. "What's this?" she said. "What do you two have going on that you're not telling me about?"

Sugar started to cry.

The tears were genuine, but they were convenient, too. Sugar let them come, knowing they would soften Patty up and maybe make this a little easier, make her less angry.

The last time she'd told her mother about a baby, she'd been thirteen years old, in San Diego, with two different eighteen-year-old boyfriends who lived in two different, dispiriting neighborhoods along the commuter rail line that went all the way down to the Mexican border at Tijuana. She'd met both guys on the streets somewhere. One of them was Tully's father. She'd forgotten both of their names. Impressive, Sugar.

I'm knocked up, okay? I'm pregnant.

She'd screamed it that time, using her voice like a weapon of rebellion, and a much, much younger Patty had gone white and silent with anger. Thirty-seven years later, Sugar didn't think Patty's reaction would be much different, even if the anger had a different source.

I. Do. Not. Want. To. Do. This.

Shoot, she was such a coward!

Those quizzes in women's magazines always seemed to assume that people were consistent—like plain chocolate bars, the same all the way through. Those quizzes assumed that if people were brave in one situation, they'd be brave in another, but Sugar didn't think this was true.

Or maybe it was just her. Maybe this was yet another of the ways in which she was flawed and different, and always had been.

If she was a chocolate bar, she was made of rocky road, not smooth caramel.

She could be brave sometimes. She'd faced the symptoms of drug withdrawal bravely in the end. She'd been brave about her cancer diagnosis. She thought she'd been pretty brave so far, too, when the pain meds weren't strong enough.

But she couldn't be brave about this—telling Patty about Charlie, because she knew what Patty's reaction would be.

Through her tears she said, "You know when I disappeared off back to San Diego that time, back in the eighties, and you didn't hear from me for... I don't even know how long it was. Do you remember?"

"Back when Tully was just starting grade school?" Patty was on high alert. She sat up in her chair and put her coffee mug back on the tray on the vanity, even though it was still half-filled.

"Yes," Sugar said. "Would have been then."

"Do I *remember*? It was almost four years that we didn't hear from you. Of course I remember. We were beside ourselves. My heart still hurts when I think about it, Suzanne."

Shee-iiit, she's calling me Suzanne, I know what that means.

"Something happened, back then."

"Yes, I'm certainly getting that impression," Patty said crisply. She was such a sweet, good person, but she could be roused to anger, Sugar knew all too well. Cold, quiet anger, powerful, simmering below the surface and seeming scarier for that. She wasn't someone who shouted. She went silent, instead.

Sugar knew she should just straight out *say* it, now. She knew that putting it off and skirting around it like this, while Patty grew more and more suspicious, wasn't going to help, but she couldn't bring the words out of her mouth.

Which words? How did she even say it?

Having forbidden Tully to take the initiative, she now looked pleadingly at her, through the big, shiny, gold-framed mirror, but Tully just shook her head.

Dig you own grave, Sugar, the gesture might have said.

Sugar dug, feeling her stomach churn. "I had another baby back then." A smear of dye had worked its way into her left eye and it was stinging. "I never told you about him." She blinked and ignored the stinging, and hoped her tears weren't going to make it worse. She waited a moment, but apart from a tiny, strangled cry Patty was silent, as she'd expected her to be, so she kept going. "I kept him until he was three... almost three and a half... and then I gave him up, because—I was using too much, I couldn't handle him, I just... gave him up. And now I've tracked him down. Well, the lawyer did. René Fletcher, here in town."

She waited again, then watched as Patty's face dropped like a rock and her mouth pressed shut and she simply stood up and walked stiffly and slowly out of the bathroom without saying a word.

Six minutes left on the timer.

"Go after her," Sugar begged Tully.

"No. Not going to do that."

"Okay, then *I* will," she retorted. See, there was a difference between bravery and bravado. Maybe it had only ever been bravado Sugar was any good at. This was bravado, for sure. Not real courage.

She stood up, and felt one of the towels around her neck begin to slip, while her other eye started to sting like the first one. She ignored both towel and stinging. Patty was in her bedroom, sitting on the edge of the bed like sitting on the edge of an open grave. As soon as she saw Sugar she said with deceptive calm, "Get back in the bathroom." Her voice cracked, sounding old.

"So you're mad."

"You've dropped your towel. You're going to get dye on your clothes. I'm still processing this, Sugar, and yes I'm mad. My brain is on ice. I don't even know how mad I am. I don't have the slightest idea how I feel, except that I know this is wrong. This is a scene we shouldn't be having." She turned away, then added abruptly in a strangled voice, "How old is he?"

"Thirty."

"Thirty! We should have had this conversation thirty years ago and you're asking if I'm mad."

"I'm not asking. I know you are."

"Get back to the bathroom. That timer must be about clicked off."

"Probably still four or five minutes."

"Get back there."

"Why? Don't you want to talk?"

"Get back there before I start screaming."

"You never scream."

"This might be the day I do. I—I can't believe this. I cannot. You kept him. You were using. He was born addicted."

"Yes."

"You didn't tell me about him. I didn't even know where you were, all that time. We were waiting for the police to knock at our door, half the time, your father and I. You kept him, then you gave him up to strangers, and you said nothing. That little baby. That little boy. My grandson. Did you hate me that much for taking Tully?" She added on a harsh whisper, "Don't answer. Don't. I can't bear to hear what you'd say."

"I didn't hate you."

"Did you hate yourself?"

"Not about Tully. I was too young. About Zack, yes. And I still do."

"Good!"

"Okay, Patty. Okay, Mom."

Sugar crept back to the bathroom, full of a guilty, despicable relief that the worst was probably over. The words were out. Any news she had for Patty from now on would be good news in comparison, once Patty let her talk some more.

The timer went off.

"I suppose you want that rinsed," Tully said.

"Yay, you're mad at me, too," Sugar sang back at her.

"But at least we'll have your hair looking nice," Tully drawled. "So it's not all bad."

♡

Mom didn't come back. Tully went looking for her in the end, while Sugar's hair gleamed with the thick, goopy conditioner that would counteract the drying effect of the dye. There were some drops of golden mahogany staining the white porcelain of the basin and she wondered if and how she would manage to get those out.

Could you use bleach, or powdered cleanser?

She found Mom down in the kitchen starting the homemade pizza she was making for dinner. Correction, starting the dough, going the whole hog, using granulated yeast, because if the dough was fresh and yeasty and good, Sugar would eat more than she would eat if it was only a frozen base, and if Sugar ate more, then she'd keep some weight on, and be stronger, and live longer.

And even when Mom and Tully were both mad at her, they wanted her to live longer, so they spoiled her.

"We'll get over it," Tully said.

"Oh, you think?" Mom glared at her.

"Says the woman kneading homemade pizza dough for her terrible, unforgivable daughter."

Mom just closed her eyes and shook her head.

"Did you let her talk more about it?" Tully pressed.

"No. And I can't believe you knew. And said nothing."

"She wouldn't let me. She wanted to be the one to tell you. But she kept putting it off."

"When did you know? Not long. It had just better not have been long."

"Last week, coming home from the doctor, when you were surprised we'd been gone the whole afternoon. It's time to rinse off the conditioner. Are you going to come up and do the cutting?"

"I might hack it all off and leave her bald."

"Well, if that's on the agenda, I can do it. My talent as a hair stylist would about rise to hacking and baldness."

Mom pushed the ball of dough away from her hands, suddenly. "This has killed me, Tully. This has been one step too far. I'm so tired. So unbelievably tired."

"I know you're mad at her."

"You say that, but you don't. You have no idea. I have had a lifetime of this with her. Things are going along, and I think I've heard everything there is to hear, and then there'll be something else. Oh, by the way, I'm having treatment for Hep C, and can you pay for my medication? Oh, I didn't tell you, I'm on parole at the moment and I have to drive to Denver to check in with my parole officer. Oh, I have cancer and not long to live, and please can I come home so you can take care of me?"

"Oh, Mom!"

"And she's my daughter, so what else do I do? It's taken seven years of her living a more or less normal life for me to *start* to believe that she had no more surprises for me, that she really is over that lifestyle, and now this. Oh, I had another baby, sorry, did I forget to mention?"

"It's good news," Tully ventured.

But Mom wasn't ready to see that yet. "How do we know that? How do we know how nasty this could get? What's he like? He must be a mess. I don't have room in my life, in my heart, in my aching bones, for another person who's a mess, Tully. I really don't. Maybe I don't even have room in my heart for someone who's *not* a mess."

Tully reached out and Mom slumped into her arms like a bony rag doll. "We don't know what he's like. The only person who's even spoken to him is Ren."

"Ren, your prom date."

"Yes, Mom, my prom date. The way Aunt Barbara in San Diego is still your bridesmaid, even though it's fifty-something years since you were married."

"You know what I mean."

"My prom date showed us a picture."

"A picture."

"Your grandson is a doctor, turns out. So if he's a mess, he's a pretty successful one, a final year resident in orthopedic surgery in New York."

"You're kidding me!" Mom said blankly. "I have a thirty-year-old grandson who's a doctor in New York and I never knew he even existed." If she'd been the kind of person who cursed and swore, she would have cursed and sworn then. But she wasn't, so she didn't. "You are kidding me!" She began to laugh, a weak, helpless laugh that sounded more like crying and said she was at the end of her rope, too far gone for good news.

Then she pulled herself together and went upstairs to the bathroom to cut Sugar's hair.

Chapter Fourteen

"Sweetheart, it's beautiful!" Pascale told her three-and-a-half-year-old granddaughter.

She and the two little ones were in her studio doing some arts and crafts, during a session of afternoon babysitting. She had only recently grown brave enough to invite them into her precious work space, knowing all too well how much mischief these two pairs of hands could find for themselves in a remarkably short space of time.

She still couldn't let two-year-old Jerome out of her sight for so much as a second, but Evie loved art and she was growing so sweet and focused and careful, lately. Today, as often, she'd drawn a fairy princess with a tiny, misshapen circle for a head, a scribble for hair, stick-figure arms, and the most enormous dress filling almost the whole sheet of paper. It was like a triangle-shaped mountain, which she was now coloring in vivid and untidy yet oddly pleasing patterns.

Pascale was sure that Evie had some serious artistic talent, but then she and Robert both laughed at herself for this. "I don't say it because I'm an artist," she'd told him, "I say it because I'm her grandmother and I love her in tiny little pieces."

"You're cute," was Robert's verdict.

"No, *they* are cute, both of them, the little darlings."

Handfuls, though. Running a little wild. Laurent had struggled so much.

Scooping Jerome up from his arrow-like trajectory toward her biggest loom, Pascale heard a vehicle outside. "Shall we go to see who this is?" she asked her grandson.

"Tar tumming," he said.

He was perhaps a little behind in his language skills for his age, although there had been a noticeable improvement lately. Laurent had finally hired a nanny, after running himself into the ground through grief and stress and hard work since Brooke's death.

Emma Peabody was from England, she was extremely well-qualified, and Pascale saw Jerome's speech as a sign that the new nanny had been the right idea.

She was very, very careful, however, not to hope for anything more than increased signs of confidence and contentment in her grandchildren. Laurent had growled at her one day that Mary Poppins was a *fictional character* in the same tone he might have said *serial killer,* and once more she'd had to beg Robert to cut out her tongue if she opened her mouth too much and said the wrong thing.

Because Emma was *pretty*, and that could be a danger in so many ways.

"If I live to a hundred and five, I'll still worry about them," she'd told him.

"For sure you will! Ren will be eighty by then. That's an age where men can go right off the rails, so I've heard," Robert had teased her back. "You'd be right to worry."

She believed this was the point where she'd hit him on the arm with the back of a spoon.

In her arms, on the way outside to see who was here, Jerome wriggled with a wordless demand to be put down. She complied, taking his hand and then seeing a familiar silhouette against the glass beside the front door. "It's Uncle Ren."

"Untle Wen!" Both children loved him, and he was very good with them, one minute speaking to them very seriously about bugs and horses as if they were quite grown up, and then next doing silly walks or singing Wiggles songs.

"Oh, the kids are here?" he said, in the front hall, when he saw Jerome.

For once he didn't sound happy about it, and for a man who had his serious lawyer look down to a fine art, he seemed even more sober and solemn than usual. Pascale went on the alert at once.

"Yes, for another couple of hours," she said. "And Jerome has already taken his nap, I'm afraid. Should I start up the electronic baby-sitting?"

"Yes... no... this won't take long, I guess," Ren said. "I wanted to come and tell you in person. And Dad, if he's here."

"He's not. He's gone to Bozeman to buy a foaling alarm." She threw up her hands.

"Oh, yeah?" Ren laughed. "Well, then, it'll have to be just you. The divorce is through."

It was only the middle of March. "Already?"

Oh, dear, she must not cry with relief! She must not! Or sing, or dance, or clap, or scream. She wanted to do all of those things, but René looked so very earnest and quiet and tired.

"With a dissolution of marriage, it doesn't take long," he said, "and there were a couple of ways I could push things through faster, being familiar with the system."

"So why are you not seeming more happy?" she cried out, then bit her tongue—since she didn't have scissors at hand.

"Because it's a kind of failure, Mom, you know it is."

"Ren, two wrongs don't make a right. You made a mistake, both of you, and you corrected it."

"And look how long it took us to do that."

Jerome was wriggling again, in his uncle's arms, this time. She said quickly, "Would you like a snack, little boy? A cookie and milk?"

He jumped up and down, clapping his hands, and ran

eagerly ahead of them to the kitchen.

"It took you a long time, because you are not a man who gives up easily," she told her firstborn. "You give everything your best shot, always. Anyhow, it's never too late to change, or strike out in a new direction. Never! I believe that!"

"I know you do, Mom. Thanks for... thanks."

"I'm not going to say anything about Ruth. I can't. It's not fair. But I won't have you feeling you've done the wrong thing, in any way. In getting married. In getting divorced."

"How much am I paying you to say this, just remind me?" he drawled.

If she'd had a spoon in her hand, she would have hit him with the back of it. "Tell me you're really not feeling good about it!"

"Getting the papers was a... milestone, I guess, that's all. A place to pause for thought."

"Have you seen Ruth?"

"She called. Her papers came, too. We actually haven't yelled at each other since the day I told her I wanted the separation. She's already talking about putting the house on the market and moving to California."

Forgive me Lord, I'll be even more relieved if she's not in Marietta any more...

"Well, that is a positive step for her," Pascale said aloud, very carefully. "I wish your father was home."

"Tell him for me," Ren answered her. He didn't want to turn the official end of his marriage into a big announcement.

Mom was trying so hard to hide how much she wanted to celebrate, it was almost comical. A part of him wanted to tease her about it, and he suspected that Dad would do exactly that, but Ren couldn't, not today.

"Are you staying for cookies and milk, too?" Mom asked.

"No, I won't." He wanted to go for a run. As befitting D for Divorce Day, the March weather was dull and gray and he would probably come home after four or five miles of pavement-pounding with his ears aching from the cold and his lungs on fire, but he needed to run anyhow.

An unhappy marriage and the end of an unhappy marriage were both good for your cardiovascular fitness, it turned out. All those years of seeking an escape with gym and cycling. He'd been running a lot since the separation, too, and the exercise bike in front of the TV received way more of a workout each night now than it used to get when it had been banished to the basement of the house he'd shared with Ruth.

"Are you sure?" Mom said.

He turned his mouth upside down because he didn't have the right words for a reply, and she nodded. "Okay, I won't push. I'm sorry the kids were here."

"I'm not. In fact, I'll go give Evie a hug before I leave."

"She's in my studio, and actually she's been alone there for long enough! Tell her to come for cookies and milk, too?"

"I'll bring her."

Somehow, with the kids in the equation, he didn't leave for another fifteen minutes, but they lifted his spirits and nourished his heart, and at home he changed into his running gear with a sense of anticipation. Run and run and run and get rid of this sense of sadness that he shouldn't be feeling, when he knew he'd done the right thing and even Ruth had almost admitted it, when they'd talked today. "I hate you for being right, Ren," she'd said in a drawl. "I hope you know that."

"Yeah, I do..."

She'd given a big sigh on the phone, the hiss of it hurting his ear.

Running.

Running felt good.

He went down Third Street as far as Bramble Lane and then took a right, past all the big Victorians with their gracious décor, through the park and behind the library and the courthouse, on the neat trail that followed the curve of the Marietta River, back down Court Street as far as Church, where he took a right...

...and found Tully Morgan, in LA celebrity jogging gear, running toward him.

He stopped.

Which was tactless and dumb, because if he'd kept running they could have just smiled and waved at each other and gone past in a few seconds with no awkwardness.

But he was so surprised to see her, and so knocked for a loop by those slinky, sheeny black Lycra leggings and the indigo-blue hoodie with the white tank top peeking between the open three inches of zipper at the top, and the way her neat breasts bounced a little, despite the sports bra...

Yeah.

He stopped, which meant she had to stop, too. She'd been running for longer than he had, or else she wasn't as fit, because she was puffing like a train, and had to bend over to nurse a stitch in her side, with her palms pressed to her knees.

"Tully," he said.

"Hi," she panted.

"How far did you run?"

"Not as far as I should have, to get this out of breath. I've only just started doing it in a regular way. In LA, I went to the gym and did treadmill for ten minutes. This is... much harder."

"Your lungs hurt in the cold, don't they?"

"Like they're frozen."

"So we're crazy, clearly."

"I am. From boredom. I am going nuts. That's why I'm doing it."

"From boredom."

She straightened, her breathing beginning to ease. His was fine. He tried not to show off about it, but he probably could have tried harder.

"Mom was getting exhausted looking after Sugar on her own," she said, "which is why I came home. But with two of us there's actually not enough to keep us both busy. Sugar's showering and dressing herself, still, and she takes lots of naps. I'm... homesick for deadlines and work pressure and horrible colleagues and difficult meetings." She smiled, quirking up the corner of her mouth. "It sounds stupid, but it's true."

"I can understand," Ren told her. He would miss his

own work routine, he knew, if he ever took a long break from it.

And he would miss the sense of peace and well-earned quiet that came, since his separation, when he went upstairs at the end of the day and looked ahead to an evening all his own.

Tully rubbed at her calves and began lifting her knees to keep her legs from stiffening up. He did the same. There was something very pleasant about it. The street was deserted and they stood right on the asphalt, which made gritty sounds beneath their feet as they moved. He'd been officially divorced for about three hours, and for the first time, his sense of gray regret began to ease.

"Sugar is determined to go to New York, by the way," Tully said.

"You thought she might not be well enough."

"I still think that. But when she talked to Charlie it just seemed like it was going to take him too long to find a time to come. She was impatient... and scared... and so she's decided to go. I'm going with her. We have our tickets."

"When for?"

"Friday, coming back Tuesday. We're making it a four-day weekend. He has to work for quite a lot of it, but that's okay because I'm sure Sugar will need to rest, and anyhow I imagine it could be pretty uncomfortable seeing him for long stretches at a time when we don't know each other."

"Your mom's not going?"

"She..." Tully shook her head. "Okay, you might as well know. She's pretty angry. Sugar never told her about Charlie, and she hasn't taken it well. It's been the last straw on a long list of fairly shocking secrets spilled at inconvenient times."

"Secrets can be tough," Ren said.

"I guess you'd know, in your profession."

She looked as if she wanted to say something more, but nothing came, and after a moment she broke into a self-mocking smile and went back to what she'd been talking about before. "So yeah, I'm jogging because I need a hobby," she said. "If you have any more ideas in that area..."

I'm changing the subject, was what she really meant.

"Crafts? Charities?"

"Ah, no." She smiled again and shook her head, and the short little ponytail scraped high on her head bobbed a little. It was only just long enough to be a ponytail at all, and the tops of her bare ears were bright pink with cold. "Mom has a solid claim staked out in both areas, and they're not my style, anyhow. I do a little volunteering in LA, but only because it involves handling books, and I like books."

"Sports, then, since you like running. I think there's a women's basketball team that heads into Bozeman every week."

"I've never played basketball. Don't you remember?" She made a wry face. "I was a nerd in high school."

"Right, high school."

The same guarded look flashed between them, the one that had happened three or four times now. Happened every time they met.

High school. Prom. She'd stood him up and he'd never known why.

Something teetered in the air like a tightrope walker.

She might explain, at last.

He might ask.

Should they?

But she took a shaky breath and the moment passed. Passed so thoroughly that Ren wondered if he'd imagined it—if maybe he'd been imagining the looks, too. She'd been home in Marietta for more than four weeks now, and they'd met...what... three times, and talked on the phone a couple of times, too, and he felt awkward every time.

"Last to get picked," she was saying. "Teams and I don't get along, especially when there's a spherical bouncy thing in the mix. I'm a sporting lone wolf, I guess."

Me, too.

The last to get picked thing resonated a lot. He didn't do teams and balls, either.

"Horseback riding," he suggested. "No teams, no balls. Perfect for lone wolves." His own rides out in the wild were often solitary ones, and they did him good, as much as when he rode with Dad for company.

"I have ridden a little, I guess. I used to, as a child." She grinned suddenly. "Horseback riding. I'll think about that." Her limbering up grew more energetic. She was getting ready to start running again.

"My divorce is through," he said. "I don't know why I'm telling you that. Well, I guess I am telling people, all sorts of people."

"And I'm a person," she agreed.

"So it would seem."

Idiot!

"Thanks for... I mean, good luck with everything," she said. "Your new life. Getting your apartment fixed up the way you want it."

"Thanks. Better get going, muscles will get sore," he added, and started off again. Behind him, he heard her bright white jogging shoes pounding away in the opposite direction.

Chapter Fifteen

Patty was still angry.

Sugar was over it, frankly. It was nearly four weeks since they'd first talked about Charlie and there was still a frost in the air that only went away when Patty let herself give in to exhaustion instead. Tully had been great, taking over the running of the household as much as Patty would let her, soothing her down. Sugar was the bad girl in the middle of a mother and daughter sandwich. She *had* a mother and a daughter, and she *was* a mother and a daughter, and she messed up all of it.

That message was clear.

Clear, and... yeah... she didn't disagree with it. Not at all. Patty was right about her.

But this thing with Charlie was meant to be *good*. Why couldn't Patty see it that way?

"How can you be so naïve?" Patty had said.

"I don't think I'm being naïve."

"You think this fixes everything? You've produced this son who might be wonderful and well-adjusted and successful, and that makes up for your not mentioning his existence for thirty years?"

"Doesn't make up for it, but it's a bonus, isn't it? Would be worse if he *wasn't* wonderful and well-adjusted and successful, right?"

"Just because he's a doctor, doesn't mean we're going to love him, or he's going to love us. You've had a couple of phone conversations, but they've been so short. He's barely said a word, or not that you've told me, anyhow. You said he seemed distracted, as if his mind was on other things, or he had someone with him. What's he thinking and feeling? What if he's not really interested in us, or in making this work? It could get nasty and difficult, or just painful—"

"Which is part of the reason I'm going to New York, so the meeting can take place somewhere else, where you won't be affected if it turns sour."

"Where I won't be a part of it if it's good."

"You can't have it both ways, Patty."

"I'm tired. Leave me be."

"We're going to eat some chocolate. Want to join us?" Tully had invited her.

"No, I do not! You and your candy. It's just chocolate, and I'm not that fond of it."

Sugar exchanged a look with Tully whenever Patty got to this point. She *was* tired. They all knew that. Somehow the revelation about Charlie had made her hit a wall she hadn't reached in a long time, if ever. Sugar knew Tully was worried about her, and about leaving her on her own for four days to go to New York.

"I'm seventy-five, not ninety-five," Patty had said. "I'll be fine, if you're insisting on this craziness."

Sugar was the one who felt ninety-five, today. She'd tried so hard to get herself looking good for Charlie. She didn't want him to be embarrassed about her or shocked at her. Patty had done a wonderful job with her hair, three weeks ago, snipping away with her scissors in a sharp, pointed silence until she'd created a layered, feathery cut that looked and felt so good. Last week, Sugar and Tully had browsed the clothing boutique on Main Street for a couple of new outfits that would work for New York in March –

draped, colorful things that hid how skinny she was.

So she might look a little better, yes, but she felt like crap, and never seemed to get warm no matter what she wore, or what she wrapped herself in, or how high the heating was turned up.

Their flight left at a quarter till one, and didn't get in until nine-fifteen in the evening. Even allowing for the time difference, that was more than six hours of travel. The drive to Bozeman, the check-in and wait at the airport, the bad airport food, the narrow, uncomfortable airplane seats, a long journey between gates at Chicago O'Hare where they had to change planes, the transit from La Guardia into the city, to their hotel, an older-style one near the United Nations building.

Tully was paying for their hotel room, which Charlie had booked for them, and Sugar had been feeling proud about that, in a weird way. She had a successful daughter who could afford to fly her to New York and put her up in a hotel so she could meet her successful son, who was taking them for afternoon tea at the Plaza Hotel tomorrow.

As if I can take any credit for either of them.

If anything, the healthy Morgan genes of intelligence and good sense and success had skipped a generation, going direct from Patty and Walter to Tully and Charlie, leaving out the flawed link—Sugar herself—in between.

Dressing herself and putting her toiletries in a plastic bag, Sugar had to sit on her bed and rest more than once before she was done. She just could not seem to get warm, and the cold drained her and dragged her down. But she had to fight it.

"I can do this," she told herself out loud.

More bravado. Tully had kept telling her she couldn't, that it was too much, and as always, when Sugar was told she couldn't do something, she got stubborn and went way too far the other way to prove that she could. Tully had sat at her laptop last week, poised to make the final commitment on the airline tickets and asked, "Are you sure, Sugar?"

"I'm sure. Get off my back! We have to do this. He says he can't get away right now, and I don't want to make this a burden on him."

She hadn't stopped to think things through, honestly. She'd been pigheaded and rebellious, jumped in with her eyes shut the way she would have at thirteen.

Now, she'd begun to have the horrible feeling that Tully might be right. She felt so terrible today—weak and pale and shivery, drowsy and vague from the meds, and as if there wasn't enough blood in her body to even keep her upright, let alone warm. She didn't have the energy to feel excited about meeting Charlie, to wonder if he had a girlfriend and what his apartment would be like and whether they might take a tour of the hospital.

How many times had she sat down in between buttoning her blouse and collecting her toothbrush and all those tiny, easy tasks of self-care? Seven, probably. Eight.

And now she had to get downstairs, and Patty might have food ready for her, but unless it was something that slipped down easily like soup, she didn't think she'd be able to eat. She'd have to take it slowly, but there wasn't much time left before they needed to go. Tully was calling her right now, and they planned to leave in ten minutes.

"Sugar, are you ready? I'm coming up for your suitcase."

"Ready as I'll ever be," she chirped back, and the bravado kicked in again and she managed to pretend she was fine until she'd eaten a cookie and drunk a glass of juice and Tully had loaded their bags in to the trunk and they'd hugged Patty goodbye—she seemed both limp with fatigue and stiff with disapproval at the same time, which should not have been physically possible—and climbed into the car. Tully was driving and would leave her car in the long-term section of the airport parking lot, to save on cab fare or else saving Patty having to make a double trip.

Forty-five minutes or so to the airport. Sugar could regroup enough in that time if she just sat in the passenger seat and drew breath.

"You okay?" Tully asked.

"Fine. Just closing my eyes for a second."

She didn't sleep. She felt too bad for that—like if she let

herself drift off, she might forget how to breathe and never wake up again.

What if this is it? What if I die right here in the car and never see Zack, and never say a real goodbye to Patty because she's so mad at me?

She clung to the idea that if she just kept breathing she would be fine, her strength would come back by the time she had to climb out of the car, and when she felt it slow to a stop and heard Tully say, "Sugar?" she did manage to open her eyes and smile and move.

"Oh, you're dropping me at the concourse, what a great idea."

"Sit, while I park. It's too far for you to walk from the long-term lot."

"I'll guard our bags, if you get them out for me."

"I won't be long," Tully promised, when Sugar was settled with the two bags beside her, on a bench inside the terminal.

Tully left again, and Sugar tried not to slump down too far until Tully was out of sight through the automatic doors, in case she turned around. She did turn around, right at the last moment, and Sugar lifted her hundred-ton-weight of a hand and curled her fingers in a little wave.

Why can't I get warm?

Then she closed her eyes, everything tilted, and the earth's gravity tripled in size. The armrest of the seat punched her in the stomach and the floor came up and hit her in the face.

When she came to, there was a whole bunch of people standing over her, including Tully. "We can't go to New York, Tully," she said weakly.

"Huh. Yeah. Ya think?"

"I'm so sorry. What this has cost you."

"It's okay. I took out travel insurance in case we couldn't make the trip."

"They would cover that?"

"It was pretty expensive, because of your pre-existing condition. There was only one company that would give it to me at all. But I read the fine print and we should get the airfares covered."

Tully had already called an ambulance. Sugar liked that idea quite a lot. She used to hate ambulances and really, really hated paramedics and nurses. They were the people who injected her with stuff that reversed her hit, the three times she'd overdosed. They were the people who saw right through her when she showed up in the ER, trying to come up with a story that would get them to give her good drugs.

Today, she loved the thought of the paramedics and the ambulance. It meant she wouldn't have to walk, not a step. People would carry her, lying flat. Where to, she didn't even care. Somewhere. A hospital. Where they would cover her in warm blankets. Where they could do something for her. Could they do something? "I'm sorry," she told Tully.

"We'll sort it out. Better than it happening on the plane."

"Tell Charlie."

"I will. Later. When we know what's happening next."

"Okay." She closed her eyes again.

♡

By four o'clock, Sugar was home. At the hospital in Bozeman, they'd given her a blood transfusion and warned that she might need them from now on, at intervals that would grow shorter and shorter with time. With the cancer spread to her bone marrow, she wasn't making enough blood on her own.

"Call Charlie," Sugar reminded Tully, once she was in bed. She didn't look quite as pale as before, but still clearly needed to rest.

"This is my punishment for being so angry, these past couple of weeks," Mom said to Tully downstairs.

"Yeah, no, Mom, it's not."

"Feels like it."

"You're punishing yourself. This gave you a scare."

"When you called from the airport..."

Mom had met them at the hospital. Sugar had been lying in a bed in the emergency room and Tully had heard and recognized the rhythm of Mom's footsteps before she appeared around the edge of the dark blue curtain pulled half way around the bed. She had been white and frightened and full of remorse, and though her color was better now, the fear and remorse remained.

"She's okay now," Tully soothed. "She's asleep, or soon will be. The blood transfusion will help her feel stronger."

"Did you call Charlie?"

"I'm just about to."

"I have to sit down." She dropped into a kitchen chair while Tully took out her phone.

This would only be the second time she'd spoken with him, this stranger brother of hers. They'd exchanged a few stilted words last week, after Sugar had called him with details of their plans and their hotel. He'd seemed uncomfortable and distant, which reflected exactly her own feelings. He'd also seemed a little distracted, and he'd said he was at the hospital.

"I'm looking forward to meeting you, Tully," he'd said.

"Yes, me, too," she'd echoed back.

Of course you said that. How could you not say it? She hadn't known if he meant it, or if she meant it herself.

Now, he came on the line after one ring, with an impatient-sounding, "Yeah?"

"It's Tully Morgan, from Montana," she said.

"Oh, hi, Tully."

"Look, this isn't great news. We've had to cancel, Suzanne and I. I'm so sorry. She collapsed at the airport."

"Shoot, is she okay?"

"She needed a blood transfusion, and now she's home in bed and she's fine, but I don't think we should reschedule. It's too big a trip for her. I've thought that all along. I think you'll have to come here. If—I mean, I know it's hard for you to get away. I know we might have to wait a while."

"Yeah, it is hard. But I do want to. I do want us to meet. Especially as it seems there might not be that much time left for it. Listen, I'm at the hospital. Can I think about dates and talk to you soon?"

"Yes, of course."

"Wish her—Tell her—"

"I'll send her your best regards."

"Yes, do that, and I'll send flowers, so she knows this is okay."

"Thanks. That would be nice. It's really thoughtful of you."

"Look, uh, I should go. I'm really sorry."

"It's fine. We'll... talk again."

"We will. Bye for now."

"B'bye."

She ended the call, put the phone on the kitchen table and looked at Mom, who was sitting as frozen as a rock, on about two inches of chair. "That's it?" Mom said.

"He was at the hospital, busy."

"Is he coming here?"

"He's going to look at dates."

"Why doesn't he talk to us?" Mom burst out. "He has the briefest conversations. I don't trust this. You'd think he'd want to talk to us."

"Mom, go watch some TV. C'mon. You're sitting on that chair as if you might have to flee the country at a moment's notice. Nothing more is going to happen today, and I wish I could tell you why he's not talking to us more, but I have no answers. I imagine he's as scared as we are that this might all be a big mistake, us trying to connect. He has his adoptive parents to think of, and he's not married but maybe there's a girlfriend, or someone. This is a big new thing in his life, just the way it is in ours, and he's right in the middle of his surgical training. I'm going for a run before it gets dark, okay?"

Mom pushed herself slowly to her feet, pressing her hand on the table top for leverage. Tully ambushed her with a big hug, long and warm, because they'd been short with each other too often, lately, over this whole thing with Sugar and Charlie, and neither of them wanted that.

"This is not how I thought it was going to be," Mom said into her shoulder, "When you came back, I thought it would be me convincing you and Sugar to get along with each other better. I didn't think we would have this new thing in the mix, and that I'd be the one struggling to handle it, and feeling the anger. I don't know why I am."

"You do. You said it before. Because you're tired. Go watch some TV."

"I guess that's about all I'm good for, right now. Dinner..." She looked vaguely around the kitchen.

"Dinner is takeout," Tully said. "Did I forget to tell you? It's a big bucket of fried chicken," she improvised, "with coleslaw and gravy and mashed potatoes on the side."

"I like the sound of that," Mom said.

"Do you like the sound of cheesecake for dessert, with some of Sage's chocolate?"

"I like the sound of you making all the decisions for me."

"Go watch TV."

When Tully came downstairs several minutes later in her running gear, there was an ancient episode of Bewitched on screen, and she wondered if there was some deep-seated psychology on Mom's part, in making that choice. It would be pretty nice to be able to twitch your nose and have things just... happen. Magic instant travel between here and New York, for example. Men you cared about but had never met face to face being forced to have long, warm, detailed conversations with you on the phone, because you'd put them under a witchy spell.

Tully decided that Samantha's wardrobe had stood the test of time better than most, too, with all those well-cut sixties sheath dresses. Best of all, Mom was actually taking up the whole of the seating space on the couch, instead of perching right on the edge of it.

"I'll see you when I get back," she said, and Mom nodded and smiled at her.

She'd only gone about a hundred yards when she saw Ren Fletcher jogging in her direction. He stopped in front of her. "I heard," he said.

"That we're not on our way to New York at this very moment?"

"Charlie called me right before I set out on this run." As usual, he wasn't out of breath. He wore navy sweat pants and a white polo shirt, and she was in short sleeves, also, so they would both get cold pretty fast if they didn't keep running.

"He must have done that as soon as I'd spoken to him," she answered.

"It wasn't a long call. Two or three minutes. He wanted me to follow up for him, make sure your sister is really okay. I thought I'd take a route past your place on my run and stop in, but now here you are."

"Here I am," she said brightly, and felt like an idiot. She added more seriously, "Look, Sugar is resting and I've convinced Mom to veg out in front of the TV, which she never usually does, and she really needs it. Can we... um...?"

"Run together while we talk? Sure."

Yeah, that wasn't what I was going to suggest.

Make another time.

Not do this today.

Call each other later.

Those were the sentence endings she'd been thinking about.

But he'd already turned around so he could run in the direction she'd started out in, east along Church Avenue. When she reached Fourth Street, she planned to turn south until she hit Bramble Lane, so she could run back that way, past all the pretty Victorian houses that increased in splendor until the pinnacle of achievement, which was the Bramble House Bed and Breakfast Inn, right beside the prettiest bend of the river at Crawford Park.

They ran in silence for the first two blocks, establishing a rhythm together without even thinking about it. It felt strange and nice. She'd never run with somebody else before, and she was aware of how strong he was beside her, pounding away yet light on his feet. He said as they crossed Third Street, "Is she okay? Charlie told me he regretted how he must have sounded on the phone. Too short and in a hurry."

"Yes, he did sound that way a bit. He said he was at the hospital. I just thought he was busy, so it wasn't a problem."

"I think he's worried that there's not much of a window of time for him to make it out here. I didn't know what to tell him about that."

"Predicting the course of terminal illness is not an exact science, we've been told. The doctors think she has a couple more months at least, and maybe longer, but the travel is clearly too much. I've thought that all along. I'm not surprised this happened. Mom and I want to take care of her, not have her pushing herself through an exhausting and emotional trip."

"Charlie thinks he'll have to wait until late April or May before he can get here."

"So, a month or more." It was almost the end of March now, with spring a promise in the form of yellow and purple crocuses scattered on winter-browned front lawns or even peeking from the snow drifts that still lay on the ground in places.

"Yes," Ren answered. "He told me he has a major research project to complete, on top of his regular clinical load, and there's not a lot of give in a program like his. I looked it up, it's prestigious. He's on a good fellowship."

"You've heard more from him than we have, then."

Ren breathed and ran for a moment, then said carefully, "It must be an uncomfortable situation, knowing you have a close blood relationship with each other when you've never met. It's probably easier for him to talk to someone like me."

"You mean because you're male and professional, like he is, and you're a stranger who really *is* a stranger, not a long-lost member of the family?"

"Exactly."

Hm.

"I think you're right, to look at it that way," she said. "Thanks. I'm going to tell Mom what you said. It might help her a little."

They turned onto Fourth Street.

"She's finding it tough?" Ren asked.

"We're all finding it tough, in our different ways. Sugar is impatient and scared she's running out of time. Mom is tired, after a lifetime of dealing with all the crap Sugar pulls."

"Even when it's good crap, like a long-lost son?"

"Even when it's good crap," she agreed. "It's been making her pretty angry, but I think she's starting to get past that. Meanwhile, I'm just trying to fit in the middle and keep it all together."

They ran in silence again, reaching Bramble Lane. No need to decide on a direction, as you could only make the right turn, at this point. A curve in the river lay directly ahead, while the Rec Center and community park and high school were on their left.

High school.

Prom night.

Sugar.

After eighteen years, was there any point in trying to explain?

Patty, Sugar, Tully and Charlie. Grandmother, mother, daughter and son.

The existence of Charlie changed things, brought Sugar's history right into the present and made her secrets relevant and real. The family relationships made a rhythm like two pairs of feet running side by side.

Grandmother, mother, daughter and son. Not mother, daughter, sister and nephew, the way people would think.

They went all the way along Bramble Lane, past the beautiful renovated houses, until it curved and became Court Street, and Tully wondered if Charlie wasn't the only member of the Morgan family who might find Ren good and easy to talk to. Maybe she would find him easy to talk to, also, if she dared to try.

"There are things... that we want... to talk to Charlie... about... in more detail... when he can... make it out here... that we haven't... talked about to you," she began, but she was getting too breathless now. Ren ran faster than she did. The man was fit.

"Want to take a break?" he asked, hearing her effort.

"A break?"

"We could cut up Main."

"Cut up it?" she puffed.

"Instead of going as far as Front Street."

"Ah, should I confess at this point... that I was

planning... to stop as soon as I got back to Church?" Huff, huff.

"You mean around six strides from now?"

"Yeah. Then."

They both slowed and stopped at the corner, grinning at each other a little, and there was her house, just a few doors away, beckoning.

"Except that we haven't finished," Ren said, looking in that direction and then back again. "You were saying something."

"Panting something, more like."

"So come have coffee in my apartment and talk properly. I'll drop you home, afterward."

Maybe he was still looking at her. Tully didn't know, because she wasn't looking at him anymore. She'd dropped her gaze, like spilling a bag of potatoes, accidental and clumsy and helpless.

When was the last time a man had invited her to his place for coffee and she'd accepted? She was way more comfortable with saying no. She'd said no a lot, and was usually glad. She had the whole single urban woman thing down to a fine art. A couple of times when she'd said yes to coffee, she'd been sorry, but those times had been late at night, not at five o'clock in the afternoon.

Not that those relationships had been *terrible*, or anything. They just hadn't been *fabulous*, and they'd limped to an uncomfortable ending, after a few months—endings that each time had involved the words, "This isn't working," or "It's not you, it's me," or "Maybe we should see other people."

"Coffee is a huge commitment," she blurted out, and felt like an idiot for the half second it took before he grinned.

"Massive," he agreed. "Terrifying. My office manager always warns people about it before they make an appointment—that if they accept coffee it creates a legally binding contractual agreement."

"Oh, you meant lawyer coffee, professional coffee, didn't you? I'm sorry, I'm so stupid, I'm—"

Making this worse with every word that comes out of

my mouth.

"No, I didn't mean professional coffee," he said quietly. "I meant catch-up coffee. Personal coffee. But the boundaries are blurred for us, aren't they? We were at high school together. But then there's Suzanne and Charlie."

"The boundaries are more blurred than you know," she blurted again. She still couldn't look at him. Eighteen years in California should have taught her something. She should be more sophisticated than this. But she wasn't, not with Ren Fletcher.

"Then maybe we need to talk about that, too," he said, the low growl of his voice half threat, half invitation. "Talk about all the things I don't know."

Chapter Sixteen

The run back along Main Street felt like a run back in time. Ren kept to Tully's rhythm, making it an easy jog for him. She had a shorter stride, and he didn't want her to feel as if she had to push.

They didn't speak. They were both waiting for the privacy of his apartment, but the closer they got to it the more those high school feelings from eighteen years ago came flooding back.

He was so damned rusty and out of practice at this! With a twelve-year marriage under his belt, he shouldn't feel this way. Problem was, he didn't feel as if he knew *women*, thanks to his marriage, he only knew *one* woman, Ruth, and something told him that Tully was very different from the woman he could now legally call "my ex."

It still felt like a dizzy-making new beginning.

Wiping the slate clean.

Rediscovering who he was.

Maybe even discovering who he was for the *first* time, because his adult self had been so thoroughly shaped by the mistakes of his marriage.

Nina had closed up his office. The place had a shuttered look, no lights or movement. It was after five-thirty, and he'd told her, before setting out on his run past the Morgan house, to close and lock the place when she was ready to leave.

"We'll go around to the side door," he told Tully, and she nodded and kept pace as they rounded the corner of the building into Third Street, before taking the back alley. He fished a key out of the pocket of his sweats while she waited beside him, and he could hear her breathing and see—as long as she didn't catch him looking—the way her chest rose and fell, and the way the sweat gleamed on her collarbone.

His groin stirred. Her sleek body caught at him, setting him on fire with images of all those taut curves. His fingers felt like sausages and all he could think about was how close he was standing to her, and how easy it would be to move even closer and pull her into his arms, and what a desperate mistake that would be, so soon after the ending of his marriage.

The lock was tricky, as always. He pushed too hard and the key wouldn't turn. "Sorry..." He slid it out and in again, more gently this time. "It jams if I force it."

"Mine's the same."

"Yeah?"

"Force never works. You have to *feel* the lock."

Did she know how that sounded? What kind of a double meaning you could read into a discussion of locks and keys? She didn't. She was really talking about locks. That was very cute. He decided he'd better be talking about actual locks, also.

"Like a Prohibition-era safe cracker," he said, "listening to the tumblers dropping."

"Pretty much. And no impatience. Impatience is the worst."

"Is that a hint?" Because it still wasn't turning, and he definitely felt impatient, whether it was about sticky locks or something else. She was still standing closer than he wanted, all dewy and hot from running but still smelling like shampoo, messing with his self-control, keeping him in that time warp he'd entered as they ran.

What did you do when you brought a girl to your room for the first time?

He hadn't done it since college, during one of the times when he and Ruth had been attempting what she called a "trial separation." Those attempts never lasted long. She always called him in tears, saying she missed him and she wanted to try harder. "We could get some relationship counseling, Ren."

At twenty-one, having relationship counseling before you were even married or engaged had sounded like a very mature and sensible thing to do. Now, he wanted to give his younger self a kick in the pants and a good straight talking to about going with your gut.

Even back then, dude, it wasn't working. Couldn't you see?

"I have this mantra I chant," Tully said. "*Feel* the lock, *love* the lock, *be* the lock."

"Be the lock, huh?" He slid it out, slid it in again, trying to do it like a knife through softened butter, and then he remembered the tiny twist to the right that sometimes helped, before the turn to the left. This time it turned freely. "Got it."

"See?" She smiled at him, like a mischievous pixie.

"You sophisticated city woman, you, with your lock mantras," he said, smiling back. Maybe she had been thinking about the double meaning, like he was.

Maybe.

Shoot, he almost kissed her.

Almost!

The fresh, pink scar of his divorce stopped mattering and only Tully mattered. The way she'd been in high school and the way she was now. The rhythm of their footsteps as they ran together, still echoing in his head. The look on her face that said she wanted this as much as he did, and she didn't think it was too soon.

The universe caught its breath and for a second he stood at a crossroads with "Kiss her" pointing in one direction and "Not yet" pointing in the other.

He wrestled a masterful hold over himself and took the road marked "Not Yet." He let the door swing open and regretted it a heartbeat later. He gestured to her to go inside and she let out a breath as she passed him and he was a hundred percent certain now that she'd been thinking about it too—thinking that he would make a move, and then he hadn't, and now it felt temporarily... or even permanently... too late.

They would have to wait, and maybe he'd been wrong about needing more time because of the divorce. Maybe a better moment than this one would never come, and once more he would lose Tully Morgan before he ever really had her, and how old was he, again, just remind him? Seventeen? Did this *really* not get easier with age?

Apparently it didn't. The fact seemed incredibly wrong and unfair.

You will kiss her before she leaves, René Robert Fletcher, and that's a promise.

♡

Ren's apartment had changed a lot since the last time Tully had seen it, five weeks ago. There were bookshelves now, and a thick Turkish carpet on the floor, in a pattern of dark red, blue-black, and white. There were several framed photographs on the walls, showing Montana landscapes in black and white, and a big green and gold painting of a freshly-harvested field in late afternoon light that seemed to make the whole room glow.

The apartment looked like a place Ren had enjoyed working on making attractive, but there was still the exercise bike in front of the TV with gym clothes hanging over it, making the atmosphere very human and familiar to Tully as she entered.

She thought there would probably be leftover takeout containers in the freezer, and evidence of a secret male vice or two, if she cared to look. Beer from a micro-brewery with a weird name like Blue Yak or Stoneyman's Old Contemptible. A freezer crammed with full-fat ice cream. A whole bookshelf dedicated to Terry Pratchett's Discworld novels. She had her own more feminine equivalents to those things.

She felt at home here, and after a minute or so, when her breathing settled after the run down Main Street, her body shifted into that loose, easy feeling that always came after running. Sweats and athletic shoes were so comfortable. They encouraged you to let down your guard.

Should she do that?

Ren had been right about blurred boundaries. Nobody in Marietta knew the truth about herself and Sugar, but maybe Ren was the right person to tell.

Her family lawyer.

Her prom date.

From both angles, he was involved.

"You probably would have showered if you'd gone straight home," he said.

"Not probably, definitely!"

"Let me grab you a towel, so you can at least splash your face and towel off."

"Thanks."

He went to a closet just outside the bathroom and pulled one from a short stack. It was new, thick and fluffy, in the kind of gray-blue that reminded her of storm clouds and matched the white and blue color theme in the bathroom. She disappeared into it and closed the door, leaving herself alone with his grooming products set in a slightly untidy row along a glass shelf.

He kept his bathroom clean.

And his body.

"Okay if I take a turn in there before I fix us that coffee?" he asked after she'd emerged.

"Of course. You'd be showering right now if I wasn't here."

"That can wait." He disappeared into the bathroom for no more than a minute, emerging with the towel still around his neck, his hairline spiky black and wet and a damp patch or two on the shirt. He rubbed the towel through his hair and over his face, then hung it on the exercise bike—until he realized what he'd done, and grabbed it and the gym gear already hanging there and lunged back into the bathroom to drop them in a wicker laundry basket, as if he might get in trouble for leaving a mess.

"Going to change," he told her, heading for the bedroom, and that only took a minute, too. He came back out in jeans and an unbuttoned buckskin-colored shirt with a white tee beneath.

For Tully, there was far too much male body in the room, far too much clean muscle and smooth skin and loose, lazy movement.

"So did you want coffee?" he asked, fastening the shirt.

"Well, you invited me for coffee..."

"I'm a flexible guy. I have soda water, too. Or tequila. Or even apple juice."

"So what you're saying is, I can have wine?"

"You can definitely have wine. Or I'm opening a beer, if that appeals." He went to the fridge and she watched his shoulders moving.

Had he *really* thought about kissing her a few minutes ago, before they came up the stairs? For a fraction of a second, she'd been waiting for it, feeling it in the air along with the throb of blood in her ears and her veins, but then the feeling had gone again, and he'd gestured for her to go through and up the stairs, and she didn't know why he'd changed his mind. The time? The place?

Or something more long-term called *My divorce only came through ten days ago.*

"I have light beer," he said, "or a full strength from an Idaho micro-brewery. It's called Turtleneck Bog, or something." Tully smiled to herself, but not quite *enough* to herself because he caught the smile, and added, "You're right, I may be interpreting the name of it loosely."

"Sorry, it's not that. I was just thinking a few minutes ago about microbrew beers with weird names, thinking you would probably have some in stock."

"Oh, yeah?" He looked at her sideways. "Should I prepare to be stereotyped?"

"It's... sorry..."

"Stop saying you're sorry. You haven't said or done anything to be sorry for."

"Good to know. And I will definitely have wine, if that's okay."

"White or red?"

"White would be great. As for the Turtleneck Bog, it's just... there's something about living alone. Which I've done for quite a while, so I know. Something about the way you have only yourself to please, and so you really, really do."

"Really, really please yourself?"

"Yes. I was thinking about the harmless secret vices people get when they live on their own, and wondering about yours."

"And you came up with strange microbrews."

"And Terry Pratchett Discworld novels. And a freezer full of ice cream, none of it low-fat."

He laughed and shook his head. "You're not too far off."

"I'm only saying it because I have vices, too."

"You have to tell me yours, now that you've guessed about the ice cream."

"Mine aren't that different. I have ice cream, too, except that some of it *is* low fat, although somehow that always makes its way to the back of the freezer and only gets eaten when I've run out of the good stuff. And I have too many books. Chick lit, and historical romance."

"I actually don't have *all* the Terry Pratchetts. I have some, but there has to be room on my bookshelves for Orson Scott Card and Robin Hobb and some crime fiction. But you have to remember, I'm new at this. Don't know if I have the living alone thing down, yet."

"You look to me like you're doing pretty well, although I'd have to actually inspect the ice cream storage facility to make a definitive conclusion." She heard her own teasing tone and re-thought. "I'm sorry, divorce isn't a joke, is it? I hope you don't think..."

"Divorce isn't a joke, you're right." He handed her a glass filled with pale, chilled liquid, mist already forming on the outside. "But I don't think anything. It's fine. If we can't tease each other a little about what it's like to be a professional thirty-something living alone, then we're both taking life way too seriously, don't you think?"

"Yes, but I wasn't sure, suddenly, if you'd see it the same way."

"You mean because it's too soon?"

"Yes."

He hesitated for a moment, then said, "Look, maybe the divorce has only been through for ten days, but the marriage was over long before that. Long before the separation. Sometimes I think the marriage was over before it even started." He tipped a packet of peanuts into a bowl, then reached out for one of the bar stools pushed under the raised section of kitchen countertop and slid it out for her.

"Does Ruth think that?" she asked carefully.

"Ruth..." he echoed reluctantly, then stopped. She sat, while he took the second stool, and she leaned an elbow on the bench and it felt as if they were in a bar together, sitting too close, drinking too fast, and spilling too much personal stuff over the beer and wine. "Oh, shoot, Ruth... the thing is..."

"I'm sorry," she jumped in. "I'm asking you to dish the dirt on your marriage. That's really nasty and unfair."

"That why you're doing it?" he asked, quiet and deceptively light. "To be nasty and unfair? Doesn't seem likely."

He looked at her, and she couldn't look away. He was so close, she could lose herself in the darkness of his eyes, touch his mouth if she wanted, explore the smooth-curved ridge of his lower lip with her fingertip.

She put down her wine glass, already half-empty, and felt a flush rising in her face. "No, not for that reason."

"So?"

"Oh, Ren, tough question!"

"You're doing it because you want to know where we stand," he said, his gaze dropping to her mouth. In his dark eyes, she saw the kiss he hadn't followed through on earlier, saw the awareness of his effect on her. They were both lost in this, holding their breath about it, failing to act because it felt too soon, too strong.

Too soon to be this strong.

Too late to pretend anything.

She nodded slowly. "Yes." She sucked on her lower lip, a complete giveaway.

Still the kiss didn't happen.

"Ruth..." he began again, "...probably wouldn't want to admit that the marriage was over before it started. But she tends to revise history, a little bit, when it makes her feel more comfortable." He shook his head, as if shaking out cobwebs, and said roughly, "I don't want to talk about Ruth. I really don't. Not today." He pressed the flat of his hands on the bench, then picked up his beer again, taking refuge in it. "That's where I stand, since you want to know. I don't want to talk or think about my marriage or my ex. I feel like I've come out of a cave into the light, and I want to be in the light, not keep looking back at the cave. And you—you started to say something while we were running, and you didn't finish."

"Oh, I... no, I..."

"Don't pretend. It was important. I could tell." He shifted, impatient, and his big shoulder bumped her before he moved it quickly away. "About Suzanne and Charlie, right?"

"Yes."

"Something I need to know as a lawyer, if Suzanne wants me to stay involved."

"Partly. But it's personal, too."

"All of this is personal, Tully. That's what I've come to realize, in a profession like the law. Things that can look like the driest, dullest real estate transactions or property settlements in the world, from the outside, are shot through with personal hurts and betrayals like fractured rock. That's why people keep secrets, or one of the reasons, because the personal and financial and legal and practical get so mixed up. There've been times when I've felt more like someone's counselor than their lawyer."

"I don't know whether to talk to you as a lawyer or as a high school friend, that's the problem."

"Don't talk to me as a high school friend. Talk to me as

a friend now. Talk to me like a woman talking to a man. We're grownups, Tully. It's pretty obvious, don't you think?" His mouth looked so serious, barely moving because of how quietly and carefully and intensely he spoke. "High school was a hundred years ago. We were different people. Even if it sometimes doesn't feel that way."

Tully took a breath, picked up her wine, drank some more for courage, put the glass down again. "The thing is... the big thing is... Sugar isn't really my sister."

He frowned. "Not your sister."

"No. Even though it's what everyone thinks."

"Wow. I never would have guessed you weren't related. You look so alike sometimes."

"I didn't say that we're not related."

"You're going to have to explain."

"I know. I am. This is me trying to explain." She closed her eyes for courage, then opened them again. "Ren, she's not my sister, she's my mother."

"Your mother?" She could almost see his mind ticking over. "Your mother. Right. Wow."

"I've never said that. To anyone. Nobody in Marietta knows. Barely anyone in the world knows."

"Suzanne was born in 1964. I've seen her birth certificate. She's only fourteen years older than you are."

"I know. She was pregnant at thirteen."

"Whew!" He pushed back against the bench, and the tension of awareness between them temporarily snapped.

Tully grabbed onto the moment like a lifeline and breathed the safety that she knew wouldn't last. Talking about Sugar meant they weren't looking at each other with such fiercely restrained need. It was scary to want someone as much as she wanted Ren right now, and a part of her knew that if she was going to cut this off, stop it from happening, then this was her last chance, so she'd better make up her mind if she wanted to use it.

"Huh. Whew," Ren repeated. "That's young."

"That's why it was easy for my parents to pretend," she said. "That's why they *wanted* to pretend. They were protecting her. At first. Then they were also protecting me.

They moved here from San Diego as soon as I was born, so that no one would have to know."

"So who does know?"

"Sugar, Patty, David and Rachel, and me. That's been it, for years. Now there's Charlie, in New York, who I've never met and didn't know existed until a couple of weeks ago. He knows, and that's weird, but Sugar thought it was pointless to pretend to him, so we didn't. He knows I'm his half-sister, not his aunt."

"But you didn't always know?"

"No. My whole childhood, I didn't. Sugar was always a mess, the times she was around. She was addicted and off the rails, or trying to get clean and failing in sordid, predictable ways. She would blow into our lives out of the blue and I would *pray* for her to leave again. She was like a vampire, sucking the emotional energy out of Mom and Dad. Their physical energy, too. Their money, which she'd beg, or "borrow", steal if she had to, she wasn't fussy. I never liked her. Often I thought I hated her, and maybe I really did. And then to find out she was my mother..." She closed her eyes again.

When she opened them, Ren seemed watchful. "But you don't seem to hate her now. There's almost a protectiveness."

"That's been hard-won. That's taken a long, *long* time, and it's still fragile. It couldn't have gotten as far as it has if she hadn't cleaned herself up, seven years ago. It took me years to believe she wouldn't relapse. Even when I came back here, six weeks ago, I was still pretty angry with her. Valentine's Day in the candy store when I saw you I was angry."

"I was buying candy for Ruth, that day."

"And I was buying candy for Sugar. Purely because I thought I should arrive with a gift for her. The right thing to do. Not because I really wanted to."

"And now I'm divorced."

"And Sugar and I have bonded over chocolate. But it's definitely still fragile."

"You said you didn't know, as a child. When did you

find out?"

"Huh. Well. This is where you stop being our lawyer and it turns into something else."

"Yeah?" he said softly.

"This is when you turn into my prom date, Ren, because that's why I wasn't there, that night, when you came for me. I so wanted to go to that prom with you. I'd been dreaming about it for weeks, the way you can only dream when you're seventeen or eighteen. And then it was shattered, by this strung-out woman I'd loathed my whole life. I'd found out the truth about who Sugar was, and I just couldn't face the evening, the kids, my friends, you. That afternoon, I'd learned something that changed so much about who I was, I couldn't have pretended nothing had happened and I couldn't have talked about it so soon. Not to you, not to anyone. Even if I'd been waiting there for you when the cars came, even if we'd had our evening together, it would have been ruined by what Sugar spilled that day."

"Your mom... Patty... your grandmother, I guess... told me you weren't home when we came to pick you up."

"I wasn't. I'd left by then. My parents—you see, even now I still call them Mom and Dad, and think of them that way—bought me an airline ticket and Dad drove me to the airport and I went to live with my... the person who's really my uncle. The person I still think of... would rather think of... as my brother, David. It felt as if we were on the same side, he and I, because he'd always hated Sugar, too. Or... not hated her. I don't like saying that now, even though it's what I used to feel. Hated the chaos she caused. I was so upset that David was my uncle, not my brother. Now, learning about Charlie, I actually *do* have a brother after all, a half-brother, and it's all such a mess, and you're involved. You've been involved, really, since I ditched you on prom night all those years ago. So I thought you should know the full story."

"Prom night," he said again. "I said I didn't want to talk about Ruth, but..."

"Are we talking about Ruth? Aren't we talking about—?"

"For a bit, we're talking about Ruth. I have to, now,

after what you've said. I was looking forward to prom night for weeks, too, Tully. I was aching for it, almost sick to my stomach with nerves and anticipation a couple of times."

"But you never asked me out. I thought after you'd asked me to prom and I'd said yes, maybe we'd date before prom night."

"I didn't know why you'd accepted, you see. Thought maybe you'd been scared you might not get a better offer."

"Ah, but I did get one."

"You *did?*"

"Hobey Anderson."

"Hobey..." He laughed. "Oh, jeez!" He added, "He's actually doing okay, now. He's a car mechanic in Livingston, he's married with kids."

"He was a decent guy in high school, too. Just not very..."

"Yeah. Not very. But, seriously..."

"Seriously," she teased him softly, "you think there was a better offer than you, Ren?"

"I thought so then. I thought pretty much anyone would be a better offer. I wasn't a jock. I wasn't a football quarterback or a cowboy. I had weird European manners that I didn't even know how to ditch. I was scared that if I asked you out *before* prom and we had a horrible time, prom would end up the most embarrassing night in the history of the known universe."

"We were so young!"

"I know. When I look back... Ruth and I got together on prom night. She had a big fight with Sam, her date, and we were both feeling pretty bruised. We ended up at River Bend Park, she and I. We were there when Neve Shepherd drowned, and we were pretty much together from then on."

"Yes, I heard about some of that from Ruth."

"Oh, you did?"

"We ran into each other at the pharmacy a few weeks ago and had coffee." She waved her hand as a kind of apology, although she didn't know what she was apologizing for.

Disloyalty, maybe? Who to? Ruth or Ren?

"Bottom line is, Tully, I don't know if Ruth and I... if our whole relationship ever would have happened, if we hadn't been out at River Bend Park when Neve went in the water that night."

"And you wouldn't have been at River Bend Park if I'd been waiting in my prom dress when you came in Andy Pearce's dad's vintage car to pick me up—because we were going to have our after party in my basement."

"Life turns on a dime, sometimes, doesn't it?"

"Too much!"

"So maybe it can turn again..." he said.

Tully discovered that her wine glass was empty, and knew it had gone down too fast. She felt light-headed, and realized she hadn't eaten in too long. She'd promised Mom takeout fried chicken tonight, and Mom liked to eat early. She said without thinking, "I should go."

He looked shocked at the suddenness of it, and she said quickly, "Not because of what we've talked about, Sugar and Ruth. I—I need to get back, see how things are going at home. Mom'll start cooking if I'm not back soon, because she'll think I forgot that I promised her takeout tonight."

"Sure, yes, of course." He slid off the bar stool, and there was a kind of intent to his movement that she didn't dare believe in. "We... covered a few things, though." He still seemed too close. The pull between them was thick in the air, but he didn't follow through on it, and she felt so helpless about it she could barely speak, let alone send the right signals.

Please follow through, Ren.

Did she want that? Really? Now?

Yeah. She did. She wanted her life to turn on a dime, tonight, no matter what it meant down the track. "We did cover a few things," she said. "We covered a lot." It came out thin.

"I'll drive you home," he said.

"You don't have to."

"I do have to. Look at you. You're in running gear and you don't have a coat. It's chilling down out there, and it wasn't warm to begin with. I'm driving you. We'll pick up the takeout on our way. No arguments, okay?"

Right now, he didn't look like the kind of man anyone would argue with, but she tried it anyhow. "You could just lend me a jacket."

"I'm lending you a jacket *and* driving you to pick up dinner. Guess I should have clarified that."

He was already reaching for the bomber jacket on the coat rack over near the door. She recognized it as the same jacket he'd been wearing when she'd seen him on Valentine's Day, in Sage Carrigan's store.

"Suits you," he said, when she'd put it on. She wasn't sure about that, because it was miles too big. The shoulder seams came half way down her arms.

He was still looking at her, and she was looking back at him, lost in the jacket. He stepped close and fixed the collar for her, folding it outward, setting it flat, letting his fingers brush the bare skin on her neck, right by her shoulder. Letting them stay there. Turning this into the moment they'd both been teetering on the brink of for the past half hour. Teetering, re-thinking, teetering again.

They looked at each other, suddenly fearless and brimming with trust. There was so much going on in their lives, but none of it was important right now. The past wasn't important, and neither was the future. Only this. Only the courage they took from standing so close and seeing what was in each other's eyes. Only the trust.

She leaned her cheek against his hand and felt his desire and his body heat and his tenderness. Nothing else mattered.

Chapter Seventeen

Her cheek was so soft, just bare skin.

Ren touched her neck—the curved column that ran down to her shoulder, the softer part at her nape, where her hair brushed his knuckles. After the naked look of trust they'd shared a few seconds ago, she'd closed her eyes, and for a lingering moment he took greedy advantage of the fact that she couldn't see him. He let himself look at her in a way he hadn't dared to before.

This was the first time he'd ever been so close.

Ever.

In eighteen years.

She had beautiful eyelashes, thick and a little crooked in places. Pixie lashes.

Pixie lashes, button nose, big eyes beneath those creamy lids, lush mouth.

Pretty hair, so slippery and shiny and scented. He ran his fingers through it and even though he could happily have just kept looking at her, he bent to kiss her instead, because he knew she was waiting for it, lips slightly parted, jaw angled up to meet him, eyes closed in trust and surrender.

The first touch of her mouth sent his body into overdrive. His pulses kicked up. His nerve endings sparked. He went heavy, then hard, then harder.

And she felt it.

She wound her arms around his neck like a dancer, parted her lips wider, pressed her mouth against his in a luscious, lingering kiss that tasted of sweet grape. She let her hips nestle against his body, right where the evidence of his need for her was strongest, and her neat breasts pushed softly against his chest.

He felt her weight against him and loved the contrast between her graceful lightness and his heavier, muscle-packed build. She was like a willow, all bendy and curvy and supple. In her running clothes, all he could feel was soft female body covered in a coating of stretchy fabric.

She stroked his neck and his back with fluting fingers and the softness of it was pure, heavenly torture. More than once he wanted to grab her hands and guide them, but every time he thought about it, the thought vanished like magic under the spell of what she was already doing. All the unexpected ways she touched him. All the unexpected places.

Curving her hands around his butt, slipping them between his thighs, fluttering her fingers up his sides, finding his skin under his shirt.

They fit together so perfectly. He couldn't believe that. It messed with his head. Different and new *shouldn't* feel familiar and perfect, should it? It made him dizzy. It made him forget everything but the moment, and Tully. He was so lost in the endless sigh of a kiss that he didn't even register when she began whispering something against his mouth.

It... what... sounded like an apology?

"I'm sorry."

It was.

For what.

"I promised Mom I'd get dinner. I really have to. I'm here to help her, and—"

"That's right, you said before. I... forgot." Not really. It just hadn't seemed anywhere near as important as what she was doing to him.

"I don't want to stop." She laced her fingers behind his neck and he felt her weight against him again. She seemed boneless and content and dreamy and he just wanted to keep kissing her and drift further, drift as far as they could go.

"I don't, either," he said. Was that his voice? It sounded different to his ear, deeper and lazier.

"I have to. We have to."

"Yes."

But neither of them moved.

Her mouth met his again, in a soft, sweet, squishy peach of a kiss that held all the trust and fearlessness he'd felt in her before. She was giving herself to this with every cell in her body.

He began to throb and ache even harder, and thought about pulling his jacket off her, and then those soft, stretchy running clothes. Her thighs were amazing, so long and smooth and lean, and her round butt and her flat stomach and her breasts neat and tight and sweet, like squishy cupcakes. He wanted to see her naked. He wanted to touch her naked, every inch of her. He wanted the hot tightness of his own skin against her and inside her.

"We have to," she said again, and she meant it, this time, he could tell. She sighed away from him, pressed her fingertips to his gloriously numbed mouth in a gesture that seemed half promise, half possession. "This isn't the end."

"Please, no, don't even say it!"

"It isn't, but—"

"But I'm driving you home, and we're picking up takeout on the way," he remembered from about a thousand hours ago.

"Yeah, we are." She grinned at him. "Should we pick up enough for you, too? Will you stop in at our place, please, for a takeout fried chicken dinner from the diner?"

"Only if you promise me you'll come back here, afterward."

"I promise," she whispered.

They left it there, and he didn't know if she'd just promised an hour or half the night. He wanted half the night.

He was shocked again at how strange it felt and how right it felt, both at once. That shouldn't be possible. It should be one or the other. Not both.

She snuggled deeper into the jacket and smiled at him again with the trust in her face, and it took all his willpower not to take them right back to the timeless world of that kiss.

Save it, Ren. Save it. It'll keep.

If it had kept for eighteen years…

In a daze he held the apartment door open for her, and she returned the favor at the bottom of the stairs, her eyes twinkling at him. They weren't talking. They seemed to be saving that, too. Or else she was as overwhelmed as he was, just struck dumb, feeling the astonishment of what had happened—the *equality* of it.

What a weird word to choose!

It felt that way, though. He felt a bone-deep kinship that didn't match the opposite directions from which they'd come to this point. His small-town marriage and divorce, her existence as an urban single woman in a glamorous industry in a glamorous city. She seemed more innocent and more gentle and more restrained than she should be, while he felt more cynical and harder and more damaged.

In a strange way, it felt like they were meeting in the middle, mirror images of each other. He might easily have been the one to end up with a fast-paced city career. She might easily have been the one to stay in Marietta and get married.

They'd met in the middle, but where did they take it next?

Walking side by side to his pickup, he realized their feet were in step the same way they'd been when they were running, and they still hadn't said a word to each other since he'd asked her to promise she would come back here tonight, and she had.

"Oh, honey, it smells so good!" Mom said at the kitchen door, inhaling the aroma of oil and salty chicken and hot cardboard. She took the bag of takeout from Tully's hands and put it on the kitchen table, not seeing Ren.

"Mom...?" Tully prompted. She stepped aside and gestured.

"Oh, hello there." A smile quickly followed the surprise.

"I've brought Ren to eat with us, as you can see."

"How wonderful!"

"Mrs. Morgan, hi."

"No, it's Patty, now, please. Mrs. Morgan was okay when you were eighteen."

"Long time ago," Ren said.

"Right now it seems like yesterday."

And Mom was right. It did.

"How's Sugar?" Tully asked.

"Oh, sleeping, still. I took a look a little while ago, crept right up to the bed and she was almost snoring. It was good to see her looking so peaceful and relaxed. Today really took it out of her. Can't even imagine how much more exhausted she would have been if you'd actually got on that flight." She suppressed a sigh. "But I guess we should wake her. She should eat."

"We'll save some. I know it doesn't re-heat as well, but if she's so peacefully asleep... we should let her body do what it wants, don't you think?"

"You're right."

"I know you're a mother bird wanting to feed her."

"I slept, myself," Mom confessed. "Through at least three episodes of Bewitched. Then I woke up and you still weren't back from your run. I would have been worried if you hadn't called a couple minutes after that, from the diner."

"I'm sorry we were so long. I ran into Ren while I was jogging and we got talking and ended up at his place for a bit. He'd had a call from Charlie because Charlie wanted more detail on us canceling the trip. There was a lot for Ren and me to cover, it turned out."

She saw Ren flick her a look. He was wondering what he was supposed to know about her real relationship to Sugar. Mom would probably be shocked to know that Tully had told him. She wasn't going to admit to spilling such a huge family secret now. In fact, she wasn't sure how or when she would manage to do it.

They set the meal out on the dining table and Mom offered water or sparkling apple juice. They were just about to eat when they heard Sugar coming slowly down the stairs. Tully jumped up from the table and went to meet her in case she needed help—or in case Mom thought she needed help and rushed over.

"Something smells good." She still sounded creaky from sleep.

"We brought fried chicken from the diner. Are you hungry?"

"No, but I'll try to be."

"Good."

Sugar saw Ren. "Oh, hi."

"Hi, Suzanne."

"You can call me Sugar. Everyone does. You here to laugh at the dumb cancer patient who thought she could handle a four-day weekend in New York and two six-hour flights?"

"Yep, that's why I'm here."

"Go right ahead, then. I can take it. Hit me."

"You probably shouldn't have thought you could handle a four-day weekend in New York sandwiched by two six-hour flights, Miz Morgan."

"Thanks for that, Mr. Fletcher. A professional legal opinion is worth a lot."

"You'll receive an invoice for it next week."

Tully felt an odd warmth bloom inside her. Sugar and Ren got along together. There was respect between them. This might just turn out to be a nice meal, for the four of them. She caught Ren's eye and he smiled at her as if he thought so, too.

And they were right, it was nice, and it ended with

chocolate from Sage's store—spheres of dark chocolate truffle cream with espresso, crumbly and rich and almost smoky in flavor—which made it just about perfect. Mom gave her piece to Ren.

"Ren will you stay and sit with us for a while?" she invited him a little later, when everything was cleared away. "We're only having some hot tea and watching TV, but you're more than welcome to stay longer."

"Thanks, that's very nice of you, but Tully and I are going back to my place," he said. He put his arm around her as he spoke, and the words and the gesture and her instant blush and helpless smile turned it into an announcement. She found she was happy about that.

"Should I wait up?" Mom asked. When you'd once had a daughter who couldn't tell you the father of her coming baby at the age of thirteen, two single, consenting thirty-six year-olds planning an evening together didn't come as much of a shock, even if this was Ren, Tully's prom date, and the announcement was eighteen years late.

Sugar didn't seem shocked, either. She had a little smile on her face and a suspicious shine in her eyes, and she was nodding silently as if to say, *Go for it!*

Tully didn't need encouragement from her birth mother, or from anyone else.

"No, don't wait up, Mom" she said to the woman who was really her grandmother. "I'll let myself in. I'll be very quiet, if it's late."

All four of them knew it was going to be late.

"That went well," Ren commented mildly as they left the house a few minutes later.

"Because you handled it well."

"Oh, you liked that? The upfront? The arm around you? The not asking, just telling."

"I did."

"Good. I liked it, too." He put his arm around her again, and squeezed her so close they had no choice but to walk in step. They seemed to be good at that, no matter what speed they were moving. Tully felt like they were floating in step, flying in step. She was so happy, her heart was a helium balloon, lifting both of them off the ground and into the clouds.

She laughed about the balloon and he laughed, too, even though he probably didn't know what he was laughing about. Maybe he had a helium balloon in his chest, too, to match hers. He must. Otherwise how could they walk so well in step together?

By his pickup, he stopped her in her tracks, squeezed her tight and kissed her, an exuberant smack of a kiss this time, a little clumsy and goofy and over-eager, like the way he might have kissed her at eighteen. Her heart felt even lighter at the thought that maybe they would get a few precious chances like this to be eighteen together after all.

"Let's go," he said, after a moment.

"Am I stopping you?" She kissed him some more.

"Yes, you witch," he muttered against her lips. "Your mouth is stopping me."

"My mouth is coming to your place, too, don't forget."

"So it is," he murmured. "And it's probably getting cold, out here."

"Not when your mouth is there to warm it up."

"Stop. Get in the car. I won't be fit to drive in a minute."

Somehow, they made the trip, managed his tricky lock at the bottom of the stairs, tumbled into his living space, and fell against each other without even bothering to turn on the light.

Here it was again, the fearlessness and the total trust. She let him strip her, first the jacket he'd lent her, then the running clothes she'd forgotten to change out of at home. "I like these," he said.

"Why?"

"They peel easily."

"So I'm like a banana."

"No, that's me. I'm like a banana."

"You peel easily, too?"

"Try it and find out."

She did.

Naked in the dim, bluish lighting that spilled from Main Street through the parted drapes, his body was amazing, beautiful. Sculpted with hard muscle and covered in hot, satiny skin that was dusted in places with dark hair. She traced its contours in a kind of disbelief.

This? This body is for me? This is real?

"It's warm in here," she murmured. His skin was warm, and so was hers. His hands heated her up every place they touched.

"Because I turned the heating up before we left."

"So we could do this?"

"Yes."

"I like a man who thinks ahead."

"On that subject, I have protection, when we get to that."

"Good to know."

"Thought you might think so." He bent to kiss her neck, teasing her with the light, warm brush of his breath and the whisper of his lips. Every tiny hair on her body stood on end, and nerve impulses chased each other out to her fingertips and her nipples and down the insides of her thighs.

She felt lush beneath his touch, aware of her femaleness, proud of it. Proud of her breasts and the way he wanted to press his hot mouth to them, proud of the way they responded, with nipples furled tight and throbbing.

"You're beautiful," he whispered.

"So are you." She dropped her hand to his groin and felt the thrusting weight of him, loving the way it couldn't lie. He wanted this. He wanted her. She loved knowing that, feeling it, making it stronger for him with her touch.

He groaned and rocked his hips against her, squashing her hand between their two bodies. "Don't stop." His fingers splayed against her back and they arched away from each other for a moment, then sank close again, panting for breath.

"I want the bed," she said, and before she could breathe again, he'd scooped her up in his arms and carried her through to the bedroom, pausing beside the bed with her still off the ground.

"I'll be back." He lowered her onto the smooth dark cotton of the quilt then folded it over her. She watched him turn on the light in the bathroom and reach into a drawer, the curve of his bare spine a narrow, shadowed channel between the muscles of his back.

For one long moment she wondered if she was crazy to be letting this happen, to be sleeping with this gorgeous man she'd known for so long. It made her vulnerable in a way she hadn't been in a long time. Had she *ever* been this vulnerable?

Well, no, Tully, because this is the first time you've ever slept with a man in your home town, she realized. Your prom date. The man who married and divorced one of your high school friends.

It ran close to the bone, and if she got hurt, that would go close to the bone, too. It would be very different from the handful of relationships that had blossomed and ended in Los Angeles, where two adults could avoid each other very successfully after a failed relationship, and manage never to meet again.

For as long as she stayed in Marietta, there'd be no avoiding Ren. And when she left Marietta, she would be leaving because the saga of Sugar's illness would be over, and that was too hard to think about right now, when she and Sugar were just starting to find something together.

All of it was too hard to think about.

And Ren was back.

He peeled the quilt away from her, then stretched beside her on his stomach, his weight on his forearms and his hip pressing against her side. "This okay?"

"Yes." She let go of the doubt, and as soon as he touched her the fearlessness and trust came back. This was Ren, and right now he filled her whole world.

Filled her whole body.

Filled it with need and sensation and demand.

He rolled her on top of him and curved his hands over her backside while she bent to kiss him, letting her breasts graze his chest. They took an aching, delectable age to reach the point of no return, and by then she was swollen and hungry and desperate, and sensed the same in him.

When he filled her at last, they both shuddered and

moaned and clawed at each other. He would have scratches on his back in the morning, while she would have sore nipples and aching thighs, and they both wanted that. Or they couldn't stop themselves. If they marked each other, they weren't even feeling it right now.

Oh, please. Oh, yes!

He said her name and she fell against him. He buried his face in her neck and rocked into her, pushing forward and back, over and over, dragging her swollen core up, up and over the brink until she flew. Felt like she was flying in space, arching higher and higher, while the world rolled and tumbled and finally settled and was still.

After a long, breathless silence, he asked creakily, "You still here?"

"Maybe."

He let out a lazy laugh. "Where might you be, if you're not here?"

"In another dimension."

"Me, too."

"So I guess that means I am still here, if *here* means being with you, no matter what dimension we're in."

"You are yummy."

"Yummy?"

"And funny and delicious and sweet and I think I want you again."

"Right now?"

"Give me two minutes."

"Clock's ticking," she warned.

It didn't have to tick for long. The second time, they fell asleep in each other's arms, and when she woke again, his bedside clock read nine minutes after one. She didn't arrive home until after two.

♡

Tully had said she would let herself in quietly, and she did, but Sugar was awake anyhow, and so was Patty, Sugar thought. She'd heard her in the bathroom a few minutes ago.

Tully didn't come up the stairs right away. She went into the kitchen, and Sugar heard the pipes clunk as if Tully was washing her hands or getting a glass of water, or maybe boiling the kettle for some hot tea.

Her bones ached dully, the pain meds she'd had before bed several hours ago not quite coping. There was another kind she was allowed to take at night when this happened, but she didn't have the pills by her bed, and she needed water to swallow them with anyhow. Better, juice.

She could ring her bell, and Patty or Tully would come, but she didn't want to do that. She wanted to get out of bed and move for a bit, pace the corridor, because that sometimes helped. She shifted position slowly, sitting up, swiveling her legs to the floor, reaching for the robe she kept laid across the foot of the bed.

Ah, that felt better already. The ache in her hips had eased with movement and a new position. She stood and fumbled with her feet for her sheepskin-lined slippers. Ah, now that felt *really* good.

The old Sugar, twenty, thirty, thirty-five years ago, would have scorned such a simple pleasure, but this Sugar knew better. The soft, thick brush of the wool closing around her bare feet felt like a glimpse of the heaven she believed in, the heaven she might *just* be allowed into, if God was forgiving and good.

Out in the hall she found Patty coming to check on her. "I heard you getting up."

"I think Tully's home."

"Yes, I heard her, too. She's downstairs."

"Why are we whispering?"

"Because I want to talk to you."

"Now? Two-thirty in the morning?"

"Come back in your room. Sit in your rocking chair."

Sugar obediently did. She liked the rocking chair. It was another thing that could often soothe her pain or sleeplessness. It was the glider kind, silent and effortless and smooth, with padded cushions on the seat and chair-back in a velvety fabric—old enough, she remembered, that Patty used to nag her to sit in it and give Tully a bottle when she was six months old, just a few months after they'd moved here.

That nagging had led to Sugar leaving home around then in an act of petty, cruel, and thoughtless defiance, for a jagged, strung-out, three-month trip to Chicago with a carload full of out of control kids—an episode punctuated by screaming phone calls to her mother. "You wanted to take her from me and pretend she was yours, so you take care of her. I have other things to do. I'll come back when I'm ready. Maybe I won't come back. Get the cops on it if it's so important to you. I'm an illegal underage runaway, I bet you'd love that. You have David and Tully. You're okay."

"I wish she'd stayed the whole night," Patty said, perching on the edge of the bed. She would so rarely let herself sit comfortably.

"Oh, you do?"

"I want this to be something good for her. Ren Fletcher is a good man. And don't you remember prom night?"

"Tully said something about that. I don't know anything about prom night."

"You must. You were there. You spilled coffee on her prom dress."

"Did I? Shoot, *did* I?"

"Yes," Patty answered patiently. "And you let slip that she was your baby girl, not your sister, and that was when she left to live with David. Don't you remember? You stayed out half the night. You knew you were not the flavor of the month at home, and I was so angry with you. Tully missed her prom and stood Ren up."

"I don't remember at all. It's just gone."

"You were a mess."

"I was always a mess."

"And now Ren is divorced and it seems like there's been something there between him and Tully all along. Something that hadn't even got going before prom night and that they missed out on all those years ago, but somehow it's still there, and so help me, Sugar..."

"If I mess it up again."

"If *anything* messes it up again."

"Might just be a fling. He's only just divorced. She lives in LA."

"If it's a fling, I don't want that messed up, either. I want her to have something good. Something for her heart. I think her life in LA is lonelier than she wants, sometimes. They work her so hard at that studio, I don't care how good the money is."

"Is this a warning? I really wouldn't mess it up, Patty. I care about her, too. She's my daughter. Even though you're the one who made her the wonderful woman she is. Even though I've done nothing to deserve her. I know both those things are true, but she's mine all the same." Her bones were aching. Ouch. Ouch. "You made her. And I've done nothing."

"I'm not lecturing you, honey, I'm just sharing with you. Don't tell her I said anything."

"I think that's her coming up now."

"Did you want something? Is that why you got up?"

"Yes, my other medication, and some juice to wash it down."

"I'll get it."

"Okay." Sugar wanted to protest, but her body wouldn't let her. She was supposed to be in New York right now, and she got exhausted all over again even thinking about it. The thought of going all the way down the stairs for the juice and then back up again was too much. Twelve hours ago, she'd been in the hospital.

So Patty went out into the hall and met Tully at the top of the stairs, and Sugar heard them having a short conversation, then she could tell by the footsteps that it was Tully going down for the juice, while Mom went back into her room, to bed.

Chapter Eighteen

"Honey, we won't miss hockey practice, I promise you. We have another twenty minutes before we have to leave. Go watch TV." Kira Shepherd squeezed her ten-year-old son's shoulder. He seemed like a good kind of kid, with a mess of dark hair and some freckles on his nose, stocky build, a bit quiet and shy, and very obviously anxious about being late for practice.

"Coach gets mad when kids are late," he said. "He says it's letting down the whole team."

Kira gave him a cookie from the piled plate on the coffee table then shooed him out of the room with a smile and flicking fingers. "I'll call you when we need to get going," she said. "We're not going to be late."

She turned to Tully. "He's crazy about hockey. I have to take him to the rink in Bozeman three times a week for practice." With dark hair tumbling half way down her back and a sweet, heart-shaped face, she didn't look old enough to be the mother of a ten-year-old. But she'd married young, at just twenty, Mom had said, although her ex-husband had already been forty-two, and Jake had been born just over a year later.

"But you're living back here in Marietta now?" Tully asked.

"Yes, in one of the new developments southwest of the river. When the job came up at the Haraldsen Foundation it was too good to turn down. I debated staying in Bozeman and trying to commute, but the Haraldsen ranch is another twenty minutes farther up the valley, which is tough in winter, and with the divorce I thought it would be nice for Jake and me to be close to Mom and Dad."

Kira Shepherd Blair was thirty-two, four years younger than Tully, and that had been a big gap back in high school. Kira hadn't even started at Marietta High when Tully was in her senior year. She'd been in her final year of junior high, neat and polite and crazy about horses, and Tully had only ever thought of her as horrible Neve's not nearly so horrible baby sister.

Now, four years wasn't much of a gap at all, and she sensed the possibility of a friendship—for the remainder of her time in Marietta and maybe beyond. It would be good to have friends here. Tully had let all of hers go, after she'd left, wanting a complete break from her life here, the way there had seemed to be a complete break between her old self, the one who thought she was Sugar's younger sister, and her new self, Sugar's daughter.

Mom always got along well with Annette, even though the two women were very different. Sixty-two-year-old Annette was a former model, with the kind of rodeo queen looks that had meant she'd often been featured in western clothing catalogs in the seventies, while Gary ran a small local construction company. They'd never been quite the same after Neve's death, either of them. What parent would be? Like other people in town, Mom had done what she could to help them through it.

Kira loved her new job as an administrator at the renowned Haraldsen architectural foundation that had lured her home. "We have an exhibition of Scandinavian furniture about to open," she said to Tully. "No Ikea jokes, please!"

Tully laughed. "Well, I was tempted for a moment there."

"Seriously, though, the furniture we have on display is so beautiful. Cabinets and sideboards and dining tables with the most perfect craftsmanship, simple and elegant. And we have some art and pottery by local craftspeople, too, to enhance the experience. Paintings by Stephen Birdsell, the most gorgeous ceramic bowls by Jennifer Gooch, three weavings by Pascale Deslongchamps."

"Oh, Ren Fletcher's mother, you mean?"

"Yes. She goes by her maiden name for her work, and it's so beautiful."

"I've seen a little of it." Tully's heart and pulses kicked. She would be seeing more of it this weekend. She was going horseback riding with Ren on his parents' ranch. It was April now, usually a month of spring rain or late snow in Montana, but the forecast for Saturday showed the promise of sunshine and temperatures creeping into the mid-fifties.

She and Ren had been seeing each other for four weeks. Classic new relationship. Hot and fun and for Tully, scarily intense. They'd have dinner or a movie or just a rendezvous at his place, where they always ended up in bed. Sometimes she stayed the night. More often, she got dressed and came home.

Mom interpreted those creeping entrances in the early hours of the morning as generosity on Tully's part—that she wanted to be home to help Sugar get up and shower and dress in the mornings, help with her breakfast and her medication. And it was true, that was a large part of the reason, but there was another reason, too.

She left because she thought... knew... that Ren wanted her to go. He wanted to wake up on his own in the morning, like a man with only himself to please.

But they all pretended it was for Sugar. Last week, for example, Tully had barely seen him, because she'd been too busy taking care of Sugar. She'd known Mom had needed a solid break, not just a couple of snatched hours for a nap, or reading. As hoped, she'd been able to collect on travel insurance for the airfares for the canceled trip to New York, so she'd bought a flight for Mom to California, instead, to spend a few days with David and Rachel and the kids. Mom had come home looking better—a little color in her face, some stories about Hannah and Mitchell that had made her eyes light up when she recounted them.

"David says he'll come to meet Charlie, if we give him enough advance notice of the visit," she reported. "But he won't bring Rachel or the kids, and I can't move him on that. I don't blame him."

"No. And we still don't have dates for Charlie, so who knows…"

Now that Mom had had her break, she was insisting on the same thing for Tully. "Even if it's just twenty-four hours when you're not on call to help. I want you to, Tully."

So she'd promised, and Saturday was her fulfilment of that promise. She and Ren were spending the whole day together.

And the night.

Maybe after the ride they could drive further up the valley and see the furniture exhibition Kira was so excited about. Then maybe some dinner in town at Rocco's Italian. Then back to Ren's. Oh, definitely back to Ren's…

"I can give you a flyer if you're interested," Kira was saying.

"Oh, I am! I'd love to see it." She couldn't resist adding, "But do I need to bring my own Allen wrench?"

"So! You *had* to go there, didn't you?" Kira said in mock anger, putting her hands on her hips, and her mother—who hadn't heard the rest of the conversation—looked across at her and frowned. "We're joking, Mom," Kira quickly said.

"I was getting nervous," Annette Shepherd said. "It sounded as if you were fighting. Sugar, can I pour you more coffee?"

"No, I'm fine, thanks. These cookies are so good. Did you make them?"

"I did, thank you." Annette was taking very good care of Sugar, jumping up at one point to find a mohair blanket for her knees because she looked cold, concerned that she might be sitting in a draft.

She and Mom would be linked, someday soon, by the shared tragedy of having lost a daughter, and you could tell that they were both aware of it. There was a beautifully framed photo of Neve on the mantelpiece with a vase of glowing yellow daffodils beside it. There was something so poignant about the fact that Annette still kept fresh flowers beside her daughter's picture after all this time, and the photo itself was poignant, too.

Neve looked absurdly young in the head-and-shoulders shot, and the glimpse of shocking pink at the neckline told Tully that the picture had been taken on prom night, in a mood of preening and celebration that had come just hours before Neve's death. She'd heard about that backless pink dress.

This was the last picture her parents had of Neve, and that was why they had chosen it. It was how they remembered her, and how they wanted to remember her, beautiful and happy and a success. This was very different from the way Tully remembered her, because Neve could be bitchy and manipulative in school. She'd given the impression of being sexually sophisticated, but Tully had never been so sure about that. Had some of it been a front? She wondered about Kira's memories of her sister. Where did they fit? Did they match this glowing photo?

We must get family pictures, Tully found herself thinking. Lots of them. While Sugar's hair still looks so pretty after Mom's cut and color. With all of us. Mom and me and David. I wish he'd change his mind about Rachel and the kids. Charlie, if we really can get him to come. All of us! I want pictures of Sugar with all of us!

Had she unconsciously glanced again at the photo of Neve? Was this why Kira was looking at it now, too, with a frown on her face?

The atmosphere in the room had taken on an undercurrent of sadness that hadn't been so obvious before.

"I'll definitely come to the exhibition," Tully said quickly. "And I hope you'll come next door for coffee, Kira, next time you're over this way. I know you're busy so I'll understand if you can't manage it, but I'd love to catch up a little more."

"I will. I'd love it, too. And now I'd better go get Jake, so we can brave the ice rink."

Annette heard this and said, "Oh, will *she* be there?"

"Almost certainly. The figure skaters have ice time right before the hockey team on Thursdays. We'll overlap."

"Just keep your head high, honey."

"I usually do the opposite, and pretend to be rummaging through my purse," Kira said. She sounded self-mocking about it. "That seems to work better for me."

"You have nothing to be ashamed of," Annette coached her. "You have never put a foot wrong. It's all her." In explanation to Patty, Sugar and Tully she added, "Kira's ex's *ex* is a figure skating coach at the rink, and I'm just going to come right out and say it. The B word is too good for that woman."

"Don't start, Mom," Kira said. She reached out and patted Annette's hand to soften the words. To Tully she said, "It's complicated. She's twenty years older than I am, I've known her for twelve years and she has the most incredible ability to put me in the wrong no matter how hard I try to ignore her." She lifted her hands. "None of which is very interesting for you to hear about, I'm sorry."

"Corinne and Stu had been divorced for six years before he even met Kira," Annette said indignantly. "She has *no call* to behave that way toward my daughter."

Kira stood up. "Hockey practice. Let's do this." She went through to the next room and called out, "Jake, time to grab your stuff."

♡

"That was nice," Mom said when they were back home.

Sugar had gone upstairs to rest, the effort of being social with people she didn't know very well having taken a predictable toll on her energy. Tully had had to help her manage the stairs, and she'd wanted a hot water bottle to hug in bed, even though the house was warm and her down comforter thick and cozy.

She seemed to be feeling the cold more and more. Did that indicate the need for another blood transfusion so soon, or was it because she'd lost more weight, despite all of Mom and Tully's efforts in the kitchen?

Maybe Sugar should have stayed at home.

But Mom was right. It had been good to catch up with the Shepherds, especially Kira.

"Are you staying for dinner?" Mom asked Tully now.

"I'm staying to cook, but I'm not staying to eat."

"How 'bout breakfast?"

"I can be home in time to cook that, too, if you want," Tully drawled.

But she was blushing.

"So Annette said Kira's ex had been divorced for six years before they met," Mom mused with deceptive innocence as she took out an onion from the bag of them that she kept in the pantry.

"Yes, I heard that."

Tully could hear Mom's subtext, too. In the silence that followed, she might as well have spoken it out loud. Ren was a good man, but was it wise to date anyone... to get *serious* about anyone... who'd still been living with his wife as recently as two months ago, and whose divorce papers still practically had wet ink?

No, it wasn't wise.

Tully knew that.

Ren probably knew it, too.

But if there was a list of unlooked-for joys that Tully had discovered since she'd come home to Marietta, the thing... the *fling*... with Ren would be at the very top if it—above the blossoming warmth in her relationship with Sugar, above the scary possibility of someday having a new brother to love, above even the magical mysteries of Copper Mountain Chocolates—although admittedly that last one was close.

She couldn't turn her back on what was happening with Ren just because it wasn't *wise*. There was nothing *wise* about the way she felt and she couldn't pretend. It was giddy and crazy and dangerous and wonderful, and Mom could probably see it, which was why she was getting cold feet on Tully's behalf.

Tully didn't care. She wanted to rush through helping Mom cook an Irish stew so that she could meet Ren in his office right before he closed up, and go straight upstairs with him.

Mom knew it, too. "Go on," she said, when Tully had cut up the meat.

"No, let me—"

"Go on. She's asleep. We had a nice afternoon. I'm not feeling tired. He'll be waiting for you."

"He might still be with a client."

"So you'll be waiting for him."

"Well, if you're sure you're okay."

"Go."

She went, like a nine year old off to the circus, or a star actress about to step on stage.

♡

Tully arrived earlier than Ren was expecting. He didn't have a client with him, but he still had work to do, finishing the draft of a complicated will, containing several provisions he'd attempted to talk the client out of, without success.

If you couldn't force your children and grandchildren to do what you wanted them to do when you were alive, trying to force them from beyond the grave didn't work, either. He understood the temptation, but it was a mistake to yield to it. The client wouldn't listen, so he was trying to come up with some compromises in wording that just might stop three generations from clawing at each other's throats once the old man died.

Cheerful stuff, Ren.

And now here was Tully, distracting him. He could hear her footsteps on the ceiling of his office as she moved to and fro in the apartment upstairs. It was more than four weeks since their first night together, and just a few days after that, he'd given her a key.

"I have a spare. You might as well take it," he'd told her. "Then if you come over after work and I'm running late, you're not waiting for me and you can make yourself at home."

"Shouldn't Nina have the spare?"

"She has the other spare."

"Well, then, given the luxury of *two* spares, I would be honored to accept a key," she'd said with exaggerated courtesy, and they'd both laughed.

But he regretted it now. It bothered him.

No, shoot, why?

He had this gorgeous woman in his life. He was dizzy about it, happy in a way he'd never known before. The key was practical. It made sense.

And at the same time, it didn't.

This was Marietta, not the big city. A lot of people still didn't lock their houses in this town. If it hadn't been for a couple of valuable items such as his mother's weaving and the gym equipment, Ren wouldn't have been all that serious about locking up, either, and Tully could have come and gone as she wanted, key or no key.

And that would have bothered him, too.

It was the coming and going, not the actual key.

The will, Ren. Finish the will.

"...in the event of any marriage of the above-named parties ending in annulment, dissolution or divorce, notwithstanding the foregoing provision for..."

He heard her footsteps again. It sounded as if she was tidying up. He'd left the place in a level of mess that Ruth would never have tolerated, and he wished he'd found time to put a few things away this morning.

He'd known Tully was coming over. He should have ducked up there at lunch-time, but when he was grabbing a sandwich lunch from the diner, he'd run into Evie and Jerome, his little niece and nephew, under the eagle eye of their British nanny, Emma, and he'd impulsively invited the three of them for hot chocolate at Sage Carrigan's store.

The footsteps passed back the other way, over his head.

"Leave it, Tully," he muttered out loud.

"...shall be revoked, unless the marriage..."

It was no good. He couldn't concentrate.

She was in his space, and he wanted her there, and yet he felt the pressure of her presence at the same time.

He *wanted* her there.

He wanted her in his bed, and he'd had his wish eight nights out of the past fourteen. She was amazing in his bed, amazing when they went out, amazing when they ate together, talking about a million different things, laughing a lot, learning about each other.

Problem was, he realized, you couldn't have a woman in your bed and in your life without having her in your space, too, and it was the space he needed.

He needed it *his* way, with dirty mugs in the sink, and gym clothes hanging on the exercise bike, and papers spread all over the coffee table, if he'd taken work home.

He'd taken work home last night, he remembered, and it might look like a mess on the coffee table, but it was actually a very well organized mess that had taken him a good hour to achieve, with sticky notes and paper clips in all sorts of very deliberate places, and if she'd piled it all up to make it look tidy...

He picked up his phone. The damned will would have to wait. He called Tully and heard her footsteps again as she crossed the room to where she must have left her purse. "Hi, it's me," he said, as soon as she picked up. "Please tell me you're not tidying those papers on the coffee table."

"No, they looked as if they were in some kind of order, so I left them as they were."

"You are brilliant."

"Thanks, but I knew that already," she drawled. "What makes you think I'm tidying?"

"I can hear your footsteps going to and fro over my head."

"Ouch, sorry, that must be really distracting."

"Yeah, a bit."

"I'm not tidying, I just grabbed a couple of dirty mugs off the coffee table and then I was looking for something to borrow to read."

"Oh. Right." He felt a rush of relief. She wasn't tidying. His space was suddenly his own again, and it felt good.

It felt *too* good, and that was bad.

How could he be doing this? He'd jumped into a full-on relationship mere heartbeats after his divorce was through, and there was a part of him that was so far from being ready for it, he was a ticking time bomb, on a hair trigger.

Yeah, horrible mix of metaphors, but it was how he felt.

If Tully had tidied those papers, he would have charged up there, furious with her. And even though she hadn't tidied them—or tidied anything, apparently, except two dirty coffee mugs—he still felt uncomfortable thinking about her being in his space when he wasn't there.

That made it partly *her* space, and when it came to his apartment, he was like a three-year-old with a sandbox full of toys who wasn't ready to learn to share.

♡

"Tully?" It was Ren again, on the phone, which she'd only put back in her purse about two minutes ago. "Shall I come down to your office?" she teased him. "Or maybe I could do Morse code on the ceiling with my feet?"

"Look, would you mind if I canceled for tonight? I have this complicated will, and the client is coming back in tomorrow to go through it and I really need to get it done."

"Of course I don't mind if you cancel. Well, I mind, because I want to see you, and I do have this candle thing going on up here, which was supposed to be a surprise, but we can do it another time."

"That was more of the footsteps? You were setting out candles?"

"Too girlie for you?"

"I like girls. I like you. I very much like the idea of you naked in candlelight."

"That was the idea. All golden and warm and scented, with lots of skin. There was even a chance I would have been naked by the time you got up here."

"You're messing with me, now."

"Little bit." Because yes, she was disappointed, horribly disappointed, so she was punishing him, by letting him know what he'd be missing. She probably shouldn't do that, even if the punishment was mild, and more erotic than vengeful. This wasn't his fault. She knew all about late evenings at work. Sometimes you couldn't avoid them.

"It sounds..." He seemed to be wrestling with himself. "Look, I don't know. Maybe if I can have another half hour, I'll get through the will and—"

"Doesn't sound like something you should rush."

"No, not really."

"I'll go. We can do the candles another time. I'm seeing you Saturday, to go horseback riding. If I'm not concussed from falling off, we can hang out together until candle time."

"Might turn out that candle time lasts the whole night," he suggested.

"Might, yes."

"Hope so."

Those last two words helped a little. Trying to walk quietly so that her footsteps didn't distract him—she hadn't realized he could hear, down there—she put the strawberries back in the fridge next to the champagne, put the matches for lighting the candles in a drawer, picked up her purse, and let herself out of the apartment, to go home and have Irish stew with Sugar and Mom.

They were in such different places in their lives, she and Ren. She'd been single for too long. He'd barely been single at all. They were coming to this fragile new relationship from opposite directions, and maybe it would turn out not like a perfect coming together, or even like ships passing in the night, but like comets on a collision course.

At some point a month or two down the track there would be a massive impact, and Ren would shoot off on a new course, arrowing through the stratosphere, while Tully shattered into pieces and fell into the ocean. It hurt even to think about, and she knew she was already in way too deep. She'd told herself from the beginning that it was only a fling, but that was just a label, just a word. No matter how often she repeated it to herself, she didn't know if she could make it true.

She couldn't blame Ren. She couldn't be angry, because it so clearly wasn't his fault. But she had no idea how to get through this.

Chapter Nineteen

"I'm so sorry about the other night," Ren said, as soon as Tully opened the front door to him on Saturday morning.

"That's fine." She gave a quick, efficient smile. "You had to work. I've been there. I have a career, too, remember?" She began to turn, going to grab her jacket and purse, he guessed, and so he spoke quickly, to stop her.

"You sound mad," he said.

"I'm not. Really."

"No?" He felt stupid about it, on shaky ground.

He'd lived for more than twelve years with a woman who said, "I'm not mad," all the time, and who then spent the next five or six hours—five or six days, a couple of times—communicating in several imaginative ways that she actually *was* mad, quite a lot mad, and that he was clueless not to have known.

"No, Ren," Tully said. "If I was mad, I'd tell you. Or show you."

"What, beat my chest with your fists?"

"Something like that." She forgot about her jacket and

purse, and came out onto the porch to put her arms sweetly around him. She kissed him in soft, slow smooches on his cheekbone and the corner of his lips, then full on his mouth, cupping his jaw and holding him just where she wanted him. "Does this feel like I'm mad?" she whispered.

"No," he said into her shampoo-scented hair, and was swept by a wave of desire and happiness so huge that he couldn't say another word for a long while. Finally, "I'm sorry."

"Now you're apologizing again?"

"For thinking you were mad."

"Tiny misunderstanding. Cleared up now. For future reference, I never pretend not to be mad when I really am, okay? I'm good with just letting it all out. Sugar will tell you."

"I probably don't need to ask Sugar," Ren said. "I can just believe you right from the start. Saves time."

"Saves time, which we need to do, because we have a lot to accomplish today. Horses, Scandinavian furniture, naked candle stuff. I'll grab my things. Wait here?"

He waited, hands in his pockets, looking out into the street and grinning. She was back in a moment, and they thumped down the steps together into the chilly April sunshine.

♡

Pascale heard Ren's pickup from her studio and came out to meet him and the woman he was bringing here for a ride, Tully Morgan, the same girl who'd stood him up at prom eighteen years ago. Pascale still didn't know why.

But she still remembered how Ren had looked that evening when Pascale herself had been waiting out front at the high school with a clutch of other parents, cameras in hand. It was a milestone moment on the road to adulthood for so many young people. It might be the first time they wore a tuxedo or a long gown, the first time the girls had their hair professionally styled, the first time the boys were willing to put a flower in their buttonhole. For some of them, their first kiss.

Ren had been so shy and secretive about his life back then. Pascale had known he wasn't one of the popular kids, the jocks. She hadn't cared about that. She'd just wanted him to be happy in himself, confident about who he was. Since she'd kept herself a little apart from the closest-knit circles of Marietta parents, she'd never even met Tully, and she'd been looking forward to it.

The black and white photo in their junior yearbook that she'd sneaked a secretive look at hadn't been flattering, but Tully was bound to be prettier tonight. It didn't seem as if she and Ren were actually dating, they were just pairing up for the evening.

You never knew, though. If she was a nice girl...

Pascale had said to him at one point a few weeks before, "You have to at least tell me who you are taking to prom!"

He'd growled at her, red-faced and not meeting her eye, "Tully Morgan, okay?"

And that was it. That was all she knew.

But when he climbed out of the beautiful polished car, he'd had no girl with him. Ruth had been with Ren's friend Sam, and there'd been another couple she couldn't even remember now. They'd formed two pairs, leaving Ren on his own, and with the camera poised in her hand, Pascale had asked him in a voice which had carried all too clearly, "But where is Tully?"

She wished Robert had been there with his scissors, because he could have cut her tongue out on the spot and she would have thanked him for it. All the other parents had heard her, and were looking. Ren might not have seen. She only hoped he hadn't seen. He had his head down, walking in the direction of the gym as fast as he decently could.

"Oh, dear..." she heard one mother murmur behind her. "No date..."

"Poor honey, that has to hurt..."

"Who is it? Oh, Ren Fletcher," said someone else, in a tone that said if it was Ren, it didn't matter much.

Pascale turned, found that it was Annette Shepherd who'd spoken, and looked daggers at her. The woman at least had the grace to blush. "I think we've come too early," she murmured. "Neve said they were planning to get here late..."

"I'm not just taking pictures of my own child," said another mother Pascale didn't know. "I think they *all* look beautiful." She sounded self-righteous about it, and Pascale realized she was making a dig at Annette, who had kept her looks and her figure too well to be popular amongst some of the other parents.

Pascale had left the group at that point, irritated by the gossip and unhappy about her son. Ren had disappeared now, hopefully still unaware of the damage she'd caused him in unwittingly signaling to all the other parents that he'd been stood up for prom.

I will never do it again, she'd vowed. *I will hold my tongue, no matter what.*

She'd never imagined, back then, how much she would need that vow, over the years, when it came to Ren and Ruth's marriage.

And now this was Tully, at last.

♥

"This is my mother," Ren said.

They'd already met his dad out in the yard, cutting back a dead tree. He'd shaken Tully's hand in a big, bear-like grip, told her it was a great day for a ride and then apologized for wanting to get back to work. "I want to get this taken care of before I go check on Coco. She has the foaling alarm in place and she doesn't even notice it, it's just a headstall with a transmitter that'll go off if she lies down in foaling position for the right amount of time. I think she's showing some signs. It could be any time now. Her croup muscles have been spongy for a few days, and she's leaking milk." His enthusiasm had been comical and rather cute.

"Tully..." Pascale Fletcher stepped forward and kissed her, left cheek, then right cheek, then left again, very French. She was wearing black leggings and a bright, chunky sweater, and her thick, iron gray hair had a chic cut currently scraped back into a ponytail, as if she was impatient about it getting in the way. "You will call me Pascale, won't you?" She had a strong and very attractive accent.

"Yes, of course." They let each other go and smiled, a little tentative but ready to like each other, Tully thought.

"Are you coming in for coffee before you ride, Ren?"

"No, I think we'll—at least... Tully? Coffee?"

"Can we ride first? I'm a little nervous about the whole thing, and that's only going to get worse if I have more time to think about it."

"Don't be nervous." Pascale touched her arm again. "We have an old mare, Lucette, who is so quiet we put the children on her, even Jerome and he's only two."

"She's not the one who's in foal?"

"No, that's Coco, and she is *not* quiet! She is a little minx. Ren did your father tell you about the stallion?"

"No, last time we talked about it, he was going to call the sellers and see what they could tell him, but he hasn't told me what they said, and I keep forgetting to ask him."

"He's a thoroughbred, he was only on the property for a few weeks, for spelling from the racetrack, and he wasn't supposed to get into her yard. He jumped a six foot fence to reach her."

"Wow, she must have smelled pretty good to him."

"They didn't realize he'd been in there long enough to... well... take any action, so to speak. They thought they'd found him right away, which is why they never mentioned it when your father bought her. But obviously he'd been there longer than they thought, and she was in foal to him."

"Yeah, two or three minutes longer, at least! She must be due any day. Dad seems to think so, anyhow."

"Oh, we have that foaling alarm all set up, believe me, with the receiver in our bedroom! I am tired of hearing about it, and I can't wait until it goes off and something happens, and then I don't have to hear about it anymore."

"You know Dad and his new toys."

"Yes, I do. I know them very well. Do you want him to help you saddle the horses? He's brought them in for you."

"He didn't have to do that. We could have caught them

ourselves, and we'll be fine with saddling them. See you later on?"

"I'll be in my studio. If you're here for lunch, it'll only be what we can find." She spread her hands in a very French kind of apology. "I haven't shopped."

"Should have told me," Ren said. "I would have picked something up."

"I thought you might be going out for a meal."

"We might." He grinned at Tully.

Pascale went back into the house and Tully followed Ren to the barn, behind which there were several day yards, two of them containing horses. One of them was a paint mare whose back looked reassuringly not too far from the ground, and the other was a brownish-black animal about a mile high. Tully assumed this one was not Lucette.

"His name's Lance," Ren said.

"Lance?"

"After a fallen hero. Lance and Lucette. I thought it kind of worked."

"It kind of does." Tully wondered if Lance liked to bite. It really was a long time since she'd been on a horse, and the ones she remembered were trail riding mounts who knew their routines by heart and could be a little bad-tempered at times.

"Want to come get a saddle?" Ren invited her.

In a store room in a corner of the barn, he loaded her up with saddle, saddlecloth, girth, bridle, and helmet. She was a little surprised, although relieved, about the last item. "Oh, we do helmets, not cowboy hats?"

"I'm a lawyer. I have the word *liability* tattooed on the inside of my skull. My brother doesn't let the kids anywhere near the horses without their helmets on, and if we take care of their safety, I don't see why we wouldn't take care of our own."

"I'm putting it on now, so there's one less thing to carry."

"Can you manage?"

"Yep, got it all now."

Some of those long-ago riding lessons came back to her

as they saddled up, and she wasn't as clumsy and bad at it as she'd feared she might be. Ren brought out a sturdy plastic mounting block, which was a lot easier than putting one foot in the near-side stirrup and hauling herself up the side of the mare until she could swing her other leg over the top.

They spent twenty minutes in a circular corral while he demonstrated stop and go and left and right, a little bit like reminding her how to drive a stick-shift car when she'd been driving an automatic for twenty years. Again, it came back to her. A nudge with her legs, a squeeze of the reins, sitting deep in the saddle and keeping her heels low. Ren was right about Lucette, she was endlessly tolerant, if occasionally lazy.

"Want to head out in the open?" he asked.

"If you don't think I'm an accident waiting to happen."

"You're good. Just relax, because she can feel you're a little tense, I think." He leaned down to open the gate of the corral, while Lance examined a handful of spilled hay on the ground, to see if it was edible. Just when he decided it was, Ren got the gate open and pushed him through it, and Lance broke into an aggrieved trot until Ren slowed him back to a walk. "Didn't tell you to do that, buddy."

It was a gorgeous ride, in the end, a real Montana ride, full of sky and air and mountain and grass. They needed jackets because it wasn't warm, but there was no wind and when the sun shone on their backs it felt so good, after the long winter. Ren took her along the fence line between two big meadows, where the laneway that also divided them was planted with young trees and bushes.

"Another one of Dad's enthusiasms," he said. "Sustainable agriculture and biodiversity. When these grow up a little more, they'll act as a wind break, help keep the soil in place, protect the stock, encourage native birds and all. Not that he's gotten as far as having stock yet, but it's in the plan."

"Sounds as if he's loving his retirement."

"Oh, he's having a blast. Going on family history, he's likely to live till around a hundred and three, so he says he's got to keep himself busy or he'll be bored twenty years too soon."

"I liked him, just now." Should she say this? Did it sound too eager?

"He's a hard man not to like. Kind of shy in a big gathering, but fun to be around when he's with the people he cares about."

They were walking the horses side by side. Ren had asked her if she wanted to go any faster, but she thought a walk was good enough for today. "You go faster, though, if you want."

"When we get to the hill I'll take him for a gallop up it."

"Lucette won't decide she has to keep up with him, will she?"

"She'll be only too happy to wander along at the bottom of the hill and watch."

"Lucette and I have a lot in common, then."

They reached the end of the line of trees and Ren leaned down to open another gate. This time he kept Lance's head up. "No snacks right now, bud." They followed another fence line at a right angle to the first and there was the hill in front of them, a long slope where the grass was just beginning to grow again after winter. "If you just keep walking her along the fence, I'm going to turn up the hill. Don't worry when you see me disappear over the top. I'll get to the fence on the far side, out of sight, and walk him back down that side and around, and we'll meet up."

"Sounds good."

She watched him and it looked glorious, something to aspire to if she kept riding while she was here in Montana. Lance seemed to love the speed, and his hooves thundered across the ground, the steepness of the hillside only just holding him in check. Near the top, she heard a yell and realized it was Ren.

Not "Yee-ha," surely?

Yes, "Yee-ha."

He did it again, a huge whoop of sheer exuberance that carried back to her in the clear, windless air.

She grinned at him, even though he was five hundred yards away and couldn't see. She grinned *for* him, and for herself, because it was such a happy, joyous, life-filled sound, coming from a thirty-six year old man wearing boots and riding chaps, and she thought she could take at least a little credit for the happiness.

They were both still grinning when they met up again. "That looked amazing," Tully said.

"He's fast, when he's told to be. He loves a good gallop."

The horse had a new kind of contentment to him now. They turned to head back to the barn and his walk seemed looser. Ren let out the reins and Lance dropped his head and stretched his neck and ambled along like an athlete warming down after a race.

"Did you like it?" Ren asked, as they unsaddled and brushed the horses.

"I loved it. I'd forgotten. I had a pony craze as a child, the way a lot of girls do, but after you've had riding lessons for a while, the next step is getting your own horse and that wasn't practical for us. The trail riding place I used to go to changed hands and the new people weren't as nice, and I just stopped at around twelve."

"Riding is one of the things—" He stopped suddenly.

"Keep going."

But he shook his head. He'd frozen in place, one hand resting on Lance's glossy brown side, one hand holding the brush that was now thick and dark with hair from the horse's winter coat, beginning to shed for spring. Tully stood beside Lucette in a similar position, with her own brush, but the mare's back was low enough that she could see over it to Ren on the far side. He shook his head slowly once more. "I shouldn't say it."

"That's okay, if you don't want to" she said, careful and quiet, as if he was a nervous horse she didn't want to spook.

"When I wanted to get out of the house, to escape, riding was always a good way. Riding, running, cycling, the gym." He made an impatient sound. "I shouldn't dish on my marriage like that."

She suggested carefully, "I think maybe I should hear some of it."

"Well, that's your piece for today." He didn't look at her,

just leaned forward and rested his forehead against the horse's shoulder for a moment. "Riding and fitness were my escape."

"Don't knock it," she joked. "You have a pretty good body, thanks to all of that."

"Yeah... Ruth used to take that personally."

"How do you mean?"

Personal slavish gratitude, Tully would have thought. She loved Ren's body. Dangerously much. Loved its densely packed muscle, loved its weight on top of her, loved its heat and its smoothness and everything about it.

But apparently that wasn't what Ren had meant.

"Like I was doing it to show her up and make her look bad. "People will start to think you're out of my league, Ren," she said to me once."

"Ruth wanted you to be a schlump so you'd stay at her level? So she didn't have to worry about other women, or her own appearance?"

"Pretty much," he said reluctantly. "I guess that's the way to put it. If I invited her for a ride or a run, she'd say I was only doing it to imply she was lazy, so pretty soon I stopped asking." He fell silent again, then added abruptly, after a moment, "Okay, that's enough."

"It makes you really uncomfortable, doesn't it?"

"Yeah."

"Why?"

"All sorts of reasons. Honor, I guess."

"Honor."

"It's over. It went bad. I don't want to spill the detail all over town. Or even to—to whoever you are. The next woman in my life. The next woman I'm sleeping with." He looked even more uncomfortable now. "To *you* specifically, it seems dirty somehow, to talk this way about Ruth. I just want to draw a line under it and move on and not think about it anymore. I just want space between my marriage and my future."

"I understand that," Tully said.

Because she did.

Possibly too well.

And he'd spoken pretty plainly just now. That was good. She wouldn't want him lying or pretending or softening things because he thought she couldn't handle the truth.

Space between my marriage and my future.

Of course he wanted and needed space. That was healthy and good, yet here she was crowding him, not on purpose but just because of the timing.

The timing was all wrong, and she knew it as well as he did.

Better than he did, maybe.

Relationships broke and failed because of bad timing every day. She didn't even want to think about it, and spoil this beautiful day together, but it hurt in her gut anyway, a dull, fierce kind of ache like the one Sugar described when her meds weren't doing their job.

His hands were moving over the horse's body again, his strokes with the brush firm and smooth and easy. She kept watching him, too churned up to get back to her own task of brushing Lucette.

I want to keep him, but I don't see how I can. I don't want to lose this when it's so good, but we're coming from such different places, what choice do we have? I'm scared.

Scared about how much it would hurt when she went back to LA. Scared about how much she was waiting for him to ask her to stay.

He brushed beneath Lance's belly where the girth had pushed the thick coat of hair the wrong way, then bent down and picked out the horse's hooves, before straightening to turn to her and ask, "How are you getting along, there? Done?"

"Uh, not quite."

Because I've been watching you, the way you move, drinking you in because I'm greedy for you, and I know I can't have you for long. Do I have you at all? Is it just sex and some fun? How much have I touched your heart, Ren? Anything like as much as you've touched mine?

"Want some help?" he asked, jolting her out of the bleak direction of her thoughts.

"Maybe with picking out the hooves. I'm not sure

Lucette would let me lift her legs up like that."

"Sure. There's a bit of a knack to it. I'll show you next time. You've probably had enough to re-learn and absorb for today."

"There's going to be a next time?"

"Only if you want."

"Only if *you* want, Ren." It was her way of telling him he had the space he needed, she wasn't going to crowd him and deny him that. She hoped he'd say something good and reassuring like, "Of course I want," but he didn't, he just nodded, so she was left not quite knowing.

Were they riding together again?

What else might be short-lived, or a one-off, or temporary between them?

Everything, maybe.

Chapter Twenty

Back at the house, Pascale was making open-faced grilled cheese sandwiches, with slices of fresh tomato and bits of black olive and Parma ham and a sprinkling of chopped capers on top. Her idea of "nothing in the house for lunch" seemed very French.

"In case you want to stay," she told them. "But if you're leaving, that's fine, too."

"Tully?" Ren asked.

"They look delicious. I'd love to stay," she answered, hoping she'd opted for the choice that would crowd him the least.

Was she going to find herself thinking like this every time there was a decision to be made about spending time together? That didn't sound good.

And was she only trying so hard not to crowd him in the hope that this would help him move on?

On... to me.

Pascale immediately took out four more slices of bread and began to cut more cheese and tomato, and when Tully offered to help, she said, "Don't be silly, it's so easy. I have everything arranged."

"Can I show her your studio?" Ren asked.

"Of course. If you would like to see it, Tully. It's a mess."

"I like mess, sometimes."

"We're heading out to the exhibition at the Haraldsen Foundation this afternoon," Ren said. "Apparently they have some of your work on show, Mom."

"Yes, they didn't want just the furniture, you know? Even though it's made by some of the top craftspeople in Scandinavia, real artists. They wanted it to look like it was in someone's home. I was so pleased they wanted some of my pieces. Benno Haraldsen was an amazing architect. His younger brother Lars is the one keeping his legacy alive, since Benno's death. He is tireless, that man! He's eighty-four."

"Of course they wanted some of your pieces."

"Well, not everyone likes my work. It's not... you know...*pretty*. Show Tully the studio, or this will be ready to eat and you won't have time."

Ren took Tully down the hall to the big room at the end where his mother worked. It was full of light and color and, yes, mess. Tubs containing hanks of wool and silk and other fibers in countless different colors and textures. Boxes of more unusual materials such as cane and wire and even the plastic strapping that went around heavy boxes for shipping.

Some of Pascale's weaving was conventional, done on her big loom. These pieces were like paintings made of textile. Other pieces were more like sculpture than fabric, and to Tully they showed a hauntingly beautiful sense of the Montana landscape. Ren's artist mother was right in saying her work wasn't "pretty" but it was striking and wonderful, and she could understand why Pascale Deslongchamps was a respected name in the art world.

"What are those birds that decorate their nests with any bright little object that catches their eye?" Ren said. "I think my mother was one of those in a previous life."

"Does she collect all these unconventional materials herself?"

"No, Dad finds things for her, sometimes. He'll go to

yard sales or factory closeouts and come home with stuff that anyone else would think was trash, and Mom goes into raptures. Sometimes he gets it wrong and she can't understand how he could possibly have thought she would want such a thing. To an innocent bystander, there's no clear way of telling what's going to be precious and what's going to be junk, in Mom's view. It makes life interesting."

"Both of your parents seem pretty interesting."

"Which is a recipe for their two sons being driven nuts, sometimes, but yeah, they're good. I'll probably keep them."

She laughed. "Oh, you will?"

"On balance, yeah."

"A considered decision, then."

"Hey, lunch will be ready."

They didn't linger over it. Pascale seemed eager to send them off to the exhibition. "It's so good that you both want to go to it."

She could simply have been grateful for their interest in her work, but Tully wondered if it was a subtle statement about Ren's marriage, too—that he and Ruth wouldn't have enjoyed something like this together.

She and Ren enjoyed it a lot. She'd never been to the Haraldsen Foundation's extensive property before. A large piece of former ranch land, it had been set up after Benno Haraldsen's death in 1999 by his younger brother, who had expanded on the original fairly modest but architecturally significant house and attached studio that Benno had designed and lived in, by building what was virtually a museum.

Lars Haraldsen had used one of Benno Haraldsen's own designs, a building that had existed only on paper in the form of detailed scale drawings and more evocative water color sketches. The whole project was mapped out in one of the museum's displays, and Tully looked at it before she went into the main exhibition room because she wanted to know how this gorgeous place could be here, without her having ever really known about it.

Mom had vaguely mentioned it, and of course she'd discovered that Kira Shepherd Blair worked here, but she'd had no idea it was so prestigious and so well set up.

And when she saw the exhibition itself, she was embarrassed about the Allen wrench joke she'd made to a very patient and tolerant Kira the other day. This was not flat-pack furniture, no matter how high a quality the Scandinavian version of flat-pack usually was. This was incredible craftsmanship, and Ren's mother's weavings looked as if they totally belonged in this setting.

Outside, there was still a lot of work to be done on the grounds, but Tully and Ren could both see that the plan was ambitious. The whole property was set high on a slope above a valley tucked into the side of the Absaroka Range, with vistas that went all the way to the Crazy Mountains and the Bridger Range to the north, and the Tobacco Root Mountains to the west.

There must be days during winter when the roads were closed by snow and ice and the place was cut off, but with the snow almost gone and May's burgeoning warmth just around the corner, Tully felt that Benno Haraldsen hadn't been such a crazy visionary to build here. It would be worth it for the views alone.

"Seen enough?" Ren said, when they'd wandered through the exhibition rooms and the sections of the grounds that were open.

"I'd like to come back when the landscaping is finished, but for today, yes. You?"

For an answer, he didn't speak, he just ran a hand down her back and gave her butt a possessive squeeze. Certain places in her body had been kicking a lot lately, and they kicked again, on cue, at Ren's touch. "Ah," she said.

"Give you an idea?" he said in a slow drawl.

"Gives me a very good idea."

"Like that idea?"

"I do."

There was something very delicious about going to bed in the late afternoon. Something illicit and secret and wicked, because most people were doing much more public and constructive things at four thirty-five on a Saturday afternoon.

Fixing leaky faucets.

Watching sports.

Stocking up on laundry detergent and canned goods.

Tully, on the other hand, was stretched out naked on Ren's bed with one corner of a sheet covering not very much of her, watching him undress and making no secret of her interest. He really did have an amazing body, and what was it about the way men pulled off their shirts? That rough, impatient movement that made everything look so stretchy and strong, that showed off their biceps and their pecs...

Yum.

"So," he said, sending her a sideways smile, "You wanted two exhibitions today, huh?"

"I think this one's my favorite, even if I'm not going to spend as long looking at it."

"Oh, you're not?"

"Going to close my eyes in a minute, see what happens next."

What happened next was predictable, and amazing. He pulled the corner of the sheet aside and slid on top of her, holding her hips in place and then moving higher up her body, very slowly, deliberately letting her feel the full length of him. Her skin flamed and her pulses beat, and by the time he arrived level with her lips, they were parted and eager.

He teased her, brushing her mouth with the tiniest wisp of a kiss then taking himself away. He did it again, and again, until she began to whimper and reached to pin his face between her hands so she could keep him where she wanted him.

"Mine," she said against his mouth. "All mine."

"Same back at you."

"Want more."

"It's yours. Anything. Tell me. This...?" He began to work his way down again, a long way down, making a trail with his mouth, lingering at her breasts and her belly, then going lower.

He made her writhe and cry out, and then while she was still panting for breath, he pushed inside her and filled her, and she held onto him for life and breath and sanity, and even though he was bucking wildly, he felt like the only steady thing in her universe, the only thing she wanted.

They lay without speaking for quite a long time afterward, Tully on her back and Ren beside her on his stomach, his head turned to one side. Tully thought he was dozing, but she wasn't completely sure. His eyes were closed and his breathing was very steady, but so was hers. It was the breathing of complete relaxation and contentment, and she could have stayed in this moment forever. If time decided to freeze, it should freeze right now.

She would *make* it freeze, by savoring it, storing it away in her memory, making sure she remembered every detail. The weight of his arm flung across her stomach, just below her breasts, the press of his side against hers, the tiny tickle of his nose and mouth and breath against her cheek, the smooth dip of his spine and the rise of his backside, with the hem of the sheet resting on his thighs.

He was definitely dozing. He hadn't moved. She watched him some more, and could see the way his back moved as he breathed. She laid her hand across the forearm that rested against her stomach and learned its texture by heart—the hard ropiness of the muscle, the warmth of his skin, the little silky scratchings of hair, the jutting knob of his wrist.

He was wonderful and beautiful, and in this moment he was completely hers. She didn't have to share him with anything or anyone. She didn't have to pick up her clothes and put them on so she could go home and give him space, because they had a dinner reservation later at Rocco's, and he'd already said he wanted her back here after that, also.

To have all those hours unfolding ahead of her felt like the most luxurious thing in the world, but it scared her, too, because she knew she wanted fifty hours like this. A hundred. A thousand.

What if she couldn't hold back? What if his need for space and solitude was just too different from what she needed? She'd had more space and solitude than she knew what to do with, over the years. She'd been living alone since she'd moved out of David's apartment after she'd finished college at the age of twenty-four. She was ready to share her life with someone else, while he was in the exact opposite frame of mind. He'd done too much sharing, and how long might it be before he was ready to share again?

"You're frowning," Ren said.

"You woke up."

"Wasn't asleep."

"You were."

"We'll have to agree to disagree on that one. Although I have to admit, I was having a pretty good dream."

"A dream, even though you weren't asleep."

"It's possible," he insisted, aggrieved—pretending to be—about her lack of faith. "So, you busy?" he said.

"What did you have in mind?"

"Couple of things." He closed his hand lightly over her breast, and whatever his need for space and solitude in the broader sense, he didn't seem to be feeling it now.

Or after dinner, either.

It was eleven o'clock by the time they fell asleep in each other's arms again, happy and complete.

Chapter Twenty-One

"That's my phone," Ren mumbled, his voice thick with sleep. There was a rocking country music riff repeating itself somewhere.

He lunged out of the bed, his movement jolting Tully out of a dream that immediately vanished from her mind. By the time Ren had reached the phone he'd left on the coffee table in the other room, she still felt more asleep than awake, even though her heart was pounding.

What was the time? Almost two in the morning. No wonder waking up felt like being dragged up from the abyss. Who could possibly be calling at this hour, and why?

"Oh, you think so?" Ren was saying groggily into his phone. "So it went off?" He paused. "Oh, you do?" He paused again. "Yeah, I guess you're right. I do want to come out. You're crazy, Dad, do you know that? Yeah, and apparently I'm crazy, too. See you in a bit."

He put down the phone and came back to the bed, sat down on it, then jumped half a mile in the air when Tully spoke to him creakily. "What was that about, Ren?"

"Shoot, you're still here. My heart nearly stopped!

Whew!" He sat back down on the edge of the bed and began to relax again.

"Uh, yes," she said.

"I'm sorry. Sometimes you—often you—"

"Often I'm gone in the morning, and you're alone," she filled in for him.

"Yeah." He stood up again and swiped his hand across the back of his neck.

"Not this time. I was sound asleep."

"You awake now, you think?"

"Not very," she said, still creaky.

"But you heard the phone?"

"Yes."

"It was Dad. The mare is in labor and he thinks she's going to deliver pretty soon. He thought I'd want to be there for it."

"He has rocks in his head."

"Well, yeah, but I'm going." He'd begun looking for his clothes.

"You have rocks in your head, too," she said. "I guess it's hereditary."

He laughed. "So *I'm* guessing that means you don't want to come. Or do you?"

She thought about it for a moment, thought about the way he'd reacted when he'd discovered she was still in the bed—startled and a little uncomfortable, as if he'd wanted the bed empty.

"I should go home," she said slowly, then waited for him to argue.

He might say she should roll over and go back to sleep until morning. She imagined him waking her slowly with the touch of his hand and his mouth, at around dawn. That would be very nice.

Or he might lean over and kiss her in an attempt to convince her that she would enjoy watching a foal come into the world in the middle of the night much, much more than she expected to, and she would dress warmly and go with him and stand beside him in the barn and they'd create a memory that would last for years.

But he didn't say or do either of those things. He just said, "Yeah, okay. You do that, beautiful. It makes sense. I'm sorry you were woken up."

And the "beautiful" was nice, the "beautiful" helped, but not enough.

She rolled stiffly out of the bed and he turned on the light to help both of them find their clothes. It hurt her eyes for too long before she grew accustomed to it, and he was already half-dressed by the time she'd found her underwear.

He waited for her, car keys in hand, and she remembered that he'd picked her up this morning... yesterday morning, really, by now... to take her out for the ride on Lance and Lucette. She didn't have her own car here at his place, and even in a town like Marietta she wouldn't much like walking home on her own at this hour. He didn't expect her to, and was waiting to drive her, and then he would head straight out to his parents' ranch to huddle in a barn full of sneezy hay particles, watching the miracle of equine birth.

She would have loved to watch with him. The only reason she wasn't going to was because she knew he didn't really want her to. He wanted some space, and he wanted his bed to be empty when he came back to it a few hours from now.

It was such a short journey from his place to hers that she was in and out of the car before it even had time to warm up.

"I'll wait until you're inside," he offered.

But she shook her head. "Don't. I'm fine." She showed him the front door key already in her hand. "You might miss the birth."

"I'll let you know how it goes, shall I?"

"Yes, please!"

He drove off and she thought he might slow and wave when he reached the corner, but he didn't.

The moon was out, just a few days past full. The night was so cold and clear and the stars so bright, with the clean smell of dew on grass filling the air. It smelled like home, suddenly—like childhood, like love and happiness.

It *was* home, even after so long. The air in Los Angeles smelled nothing like this. In less than two months, Tully was scheduled to go back there, and her heart ached with sudden, painful heaviness when she thought about it.

Making her peace with Sugar had changed something inside her. For the first time in her adult life, Marietta seemed like a place she wanted to be. The need for exile had ebbed and gone, and she remembered how much she loved it here—loved how real and grounded it was, loved that the mountains and rangelands were so close you felt like you could reach out and touch them, standing in Main Street.

She loved the way you kept in touch, here, with the rhythm of the seasons and the rhythm of the cattle and crops.

"It's not home anymore," she whispered out loud, trying to remind herself of the fact. "It can't be."

But if Ren asked...

No. Impossible. Unfair. She couldn't do it to him, or to herself. There was an end date to this and it was time to be strong about that. She was leaving. What she felt for Ren couldn't last.

♡

"Here it comes, this is it, I don't think she's going to need our help," Dad said. He clutched Ren's arm in excitement, then talked to the mare. "That's right, clever girl, that's it, that's the way. We're going to have a brand-new foal on Easter morning!"

The mare lay on her side as the contraction came, releasing rhythmic gushes of fluid and then two tiny hooves. The burst of pressure eased and she shifted a little, lifting her head and shoulders. With another bout of effort, she pushed and rocked and squeezed and the foal's head appeared behind the two forelegs, coated in membrane.

With the next burst of work and discomfort the long back and second set of crooked, slimy legs arrived on the clean straw of the stall. As always with foals, there looked to be way too much leg and not quite enough of everything else.

Dad came forward to pull the membrane back from the foal's head, then both mare and newborn rest for a few minutes on the straw, panting. The mare peered around at the foal with increasing interest as the moments passed.

Ren and his dad waited.

"Is it going to get up?" Dad muttered.

"Is it supposed to?" Ren asked.

"Within half an hour of birth, I read. And if it doesn't start to feed within two hours, we should worry, too."

"So we have another hour and forty-seven minutes, roughly."

"'Bout that, yeah."

They watched some more.

The mare nuzzled her newborn and began to lick it clean, and a little later the foal began trying to stand. How did they both understand their roles so well, Ren wondered. How did the foal know that those ridiculously long, skinny, uncontrollable stilts were for standing on and walking?

"I can't see, is it a colt or a filly?" Dad whispered.

"Colt, I think."

"What did you see?"

"Might have been just shadow."

Dad peered at the foal for a moment. It was standing now, its limbs splayed out like tent poles or spider legs. It looked as if the straw covered floor of the stall was a high wire it was balancing on, in fifty mile-an-hour winds. "No, I think you're right," Dad decided. "It's a colt."

The mare nuzzled and licked some more. She seemed very pleased with her little package of legs and extra bits, and if she was aware of Ren and his father peering at her from beyond the stall, she didn't show it. The foal lost its balance and flopped onto the straw, before managing to rise again, just as wobbly as before.

"Mom didn't want to watch this?" Ren asked.

"She thought it was invading Coco's privacy."

"Which might be a valid point."

"I didn't get that foaling alarm so I could sleep through this. Besides, this is her first foal. She might have needed help. She doesn't care that we're here."

Dad seemed to be right about that. Her new foal was filling the mare's whole awareness.

"No," Dad went on after a moment, "your mother is tucked up in bed, keeping it warm for me. Which is good, because this has gone fast. It's only just three-thirty."

More minutes ticked by. The mare had finished licking the foal clean now, and already he looked steadier on his legs. He seemed to feel totally secure beside his mother, and was beginning to smell something he instinctively wanted—her milk. Soon he was nuzzling and then drinking, lifting his little head into the shadow beneath her belly and hind legs, his short, fluffy flag of a tail twitching to and fro.

Dad said, "I'm going to go grab a few more hours of sleep in a minute. Hasn't she done good, my Coco? Hasn't she done great? A little colt. We have to find a good name for him, but I'm not going to think about that now. If you have any ideas, tell me."

"Nothing yet. I might head off. More sleep sounds good."

Dad slapped him on the arms and into a bear hug, as if this was a human birth and Ren was the father. "Good to have someone to share this with. Thanks for coming out. I'm glad you did."

"Me, too, Dad."

"Want to come in the house for a hot drink, or something?"

"No, I'll head back, or it won't be worth going back to bed."

"Bring that girl Tully out to see him, whenever you want. He's such a beauty!"

"I will."

They parted company outside the barn and Ren drove away in the cold and dark, back to a bed that no one was keeping warm for him. He was noisy going up the stairs and letting himself into the apartment. He turned on the lights, heated up a can of soup because he was suddenly hungry, watched a little weird four-in-the-morning TV, and didn't have to worry about disturbing anyone or leaving the unwashed soup can and his dirty bowl in the kitchen sink.

It felt good, and even though he missed Tully's warm and fragrant body when he finally crawled into his bed, he was still glad to be alone. He felt mean about it, like he was short-changing her, but he didn't know how he could do anything else.

♡

"Dad can't pick a name for him," Ren said, several days later. "People have suggested a million possibilities, and he's come up with a million more himself, but he just can't settle on anything. Mom's started calling him Fripon for convenience. It means Little Rascal. The other day I heard Dad shorten it to Frip."

"You watch," Tully answered. "That'll stick. That's what happens when you can't decide on a real name. The just-for-now name settles in and won't leave. I know a movie that got its title that way."

He laughed. "I bet you're right."

They were running together, in step as usual. Tully had grown fitter. There was less of a contrast than there used to be, between Ren's easy breathing and her own effort. It was almost the end of April now.

"How did you get Tully for a name?" Ren asked. "It's unusual."

"Sugar came up with it. Tully Lou-Anne. I have no idea why, and she doesn't remember."

"It sounds pretty with the two together. Tully is pretty on its own, too."

"Thanks. One of the nicer things Sugar did for me, in the early days. Although I didn't always feel that way. I used to wonder why Mom and Dad let my druggy sister pick my name."

"Took you a long time to find out."

"It did."

"But things are going well, there?"

"They've had to up her pain meds again, and we're finding it harder and harder to tempt her appetite. So the stuff with her illness isn't great. But she and I... I never would have thought. We sit and watch old movies... and work our way slowly through the entire range of Sage Carrigan's chocolate varieties... and it's good. Really good." Tully had begun to lose her breath. "Stop making me talk. You're just trying... to prove that... you're still fitter.... than I am. And it's working."

He laughed. "Rest? We have a long way to run back."

"Rest for a minute."

They slowed to a walk and then to a stop. They'd reached the playing fields beside the high school, where the grass was thick and soft under their feet, a good place to walk in slow circles or lift their knees to keep their legs warmed up while Tully recovered her breath. It was lunch break at the school, and there were kids lazing in groups under a gray sky, kicking a ball around or just talking.

A car swung out of the teachers' parking lot, and then slowed as it neared them on its way out. There was a woman at the wheel. She slid her window down and waved. Ren recognized her and walked over. "Hi Gemma."

Tully looked more closely at the driver. Was it...? Yes, Gemma Clayton, one of the girls she'd barely had anything to do with at school, because they'd been so different. Gemma looked so respectable now, driving a modest compact and wearing neat, conservative teacher clothes.

"Ren, I wanted to thank you again for coming to our careers day," she said, leaning toward her open window.

"No problem. As I said to Kate Pearce, I enjoyed it."

"Bree was really interested. Several of the kids, actually. Their idea of what lawyers do comes way too much from what they see on TV. Bree hasn't made up her mind about a career yet, but I think law is on the list, now. So I'm grateful as a parent, not just as a teacher."

"Happy to do it next year, too."

"I'll make sure to pass that on."

"Oh, you won't be organizing it next year?"

She smiled. "Not sure. Kate likes to shuffle things around so we don't get in a rut. Anyhow, just wanted to make sure you knew we really appreciated your time." She flicked a quick look and an uncertain smile at Tully, and Ren picked up on it.

"No problem," he said again. "You remember Tully, here, don't you?"

"Yes, of course," Gemma said—more warmly than she should have, really, given how very, very much they'd *not* been friends in high school. "Hi, Tully. I heard you were back in town for a while, helping out your mom and sister."

"That's right," she nodded.

"We should catch up." It sounded uncertain at first, but then Gemma added, more firm and more sincere, "We really should."

"Yes." But Tully wasn't sure if she wanted to, and that might have come across. She smiled, a little too late, hoping it would smooth the moment over.

"I have errands to run," Gemma said quickly. "I'll see you."

Ren said a brief goodbye and Gemma drove off. "Ready to run again?" he said as soon as the car had turned into the street.

"Yes, we'd better, because I think it's about to rain."

"Surprised how much Gemma's changed?"

"Well, haven't we all done that? And I'd heard she settled down pretty fast after high school. I guess becoming a parent so young was a big factor. Her daughter is, what, a junior?"

"Senior."

"Wow, already!"

"She's very bright. Gemma started her in kindergarten before she'd turned five, I think, because she was already reading at eight or nine year old level."

"So you've really kept in touch with her."

"No, but I used to hear updates from Ruth."

He didn't often mention Ruth, and whenever he did, it seemed to kill the conversation cold. No surprise, maybe. The same thing happened now. They both ran and breathed, as if running and breathing were all they could manage.

Timing, Tully thought. *I really hate the timing. Everything else I love, but the timing sucks lemons. Question is, what do I do about it?*

But she knew in her heart, as she'd known from the beginning, that there was only one choice within her own power, and it was a choice she didn't remotely want to make.

They ran in silence until they reached her house, where she peeled off to leave Ren running further, back to his apartment and his office.

♡

Sugar waited until she was alone in the house before she picked up the phone, because she didn't want Patty or Tully to hear. And since Patty and Tully didn't very often leave her alone in the house unless she was sleeping, it meant she was waiting for days.

Finally, though, they went for coffee together with one of Patty's old friends, and Sugar told them she didn't want to come, thanks, if that was okay, and that she'd be fine watching TV with things like tissues and snacks and a glass of juice within reach—and anyhow, if she needed something else, like the bathroom, she could actually get there herself, even if she was slow. The doctor said it was good for her to move around. It eased the pain, usually, too.

She waited five minutes to make sure they were really gone, then she found the piece of paper where she'd written David's work phone number—she'd discovered it by sneaking a look at Tully's phone—and she called him.

Like Tully, he was an accountant. It was as if both he and Tully had chosen the most boring, rigid careers you could possibly imagine as an antidote to Sugar's own chaos and destructive choices. Like Tully, he was successful at it— the way you could, if you wanted, consider that Sugar had been successful in her former career choice of whacked-out druggy street hooker.

He had his own practice, with a receptionist to answer the phone—which she did—but then she wouldn't put Sugar through.

"I'm his sister," Sugar explained.

"So let me go ahead and take your number," said a voice of truly sickening youth and perkiness, "and I'll have him call you back."

"That might not be convenient. I'm—I'm ill, you see, and I was—"

"Well, I'll go ahead and tell him you called," the girl cooed, "and he'll call you back just as soon as he possibly can."

Sugar had no idea that perkiness could be so powerful, over the phone. "Okay, then," she said, defeated. "Please tell him it's important."

"I'll certainly do that, ma'am. Thank you for your call. You have a nice day, now."

Well, I will, after I throw up in my mouth a little bit.

But David did call back, sooner than Sugar had dared to hope for, and somehow she wasn't prepared for it, after the setback and the sickening perkiness, and she stammered and stumbled and it didn't go well.

"I would—I would just really like, if, if you could bring Rachel and the kids, while, while Charlie is here. I—I have the dates for his visit, now, and—"

"I've already told you, Sugar, I'm not bringing them," he cut in. "I'll come myself, and we can talk about those dates now, if you want, see if I can coordinate it with your son's visit, but I will not expose Hannah and Mitchell, or Rachel for that matter, to whatever you're dishing out now—"

"I'm not dishing—"

"—nor to the sight of someone who's spent her whole life taking care of herself worse than a piece of rag."

"You know what, David," she answered, angry suddenly, although she didn't know if she had any right to be. "Maybe that's exactly why they should come. To see what I did to myself. To see that I look sixty-five instead of fifty. You can make sure they know that's from the drugs and the rest of it, not from the cancer. Maybe it'll help them make the right choices in their own lives. Maybe it'll be good for them. Maybe they might even like me, and that might teach them something, too. That love isn't just for clean, decent, flawless people. Maybe it's possible to love messed up, failed people, too."

Silence, then, "I'm at work, Sugar."

"I know. Miss Perkiness got that through to me loud and clear."

"I'll call you."

"You're talking to me now."

"I need to think. Stop while you're still ahead, okay?"

He disconnected the call without another word, and she said out loud to the phone in her hand, with tears in her eyes, "I'm *ahead*? You mean that, David? I got through to you, even a little bit?"

She slumped back against the couch, exhausted by what had happened, and by her tiny little hope that maybe he might change his mind about bringing his family.

Charlie was arriving for a three-night visit on the ninth of May.

♡

The meeting that Ren had been waiting for all these weeks finally happened in early May. He was running on his own in the early evening, enjoying the extended light and the milder weather, and without thinking too much about it, he ran down his old street, past the house he'd shared for nearly eight years with Ruth, and there she was.

They couldn't pretend they hadn't seen each other. He was running along the sidewalk and she was standing by the mailbox with some junk mail in her hand, bending to pull a couple of weeds that threatened to spoil the front yard's manicured curb appeal. There was a For Sale sign out front, which Ren knew had been there for a month now, and she must be working hard to keep the place looking this perfect.

"Hi." He stopped in front of her.

"Hi, Ren."

She looked good. Happier, younger, comfortable in her own skin. "How've you been?" he blurted out, discovering that he really wanted to know. A proper answer, from the heart, not just the polite front or the bravado. How was she *really*?

He didn't expect her to understand this, or respond to it, but somehow she did. "I've been good," she answered slowly. She stood rather stiffly, but then so did he. "There's an offer on the house."

"Oh, there is?"

"Not quite as good as I wanted. Tod Styles called about it yesterday, and I'm still thinking. We might get them to go a little higher, he says, but probably not as far as the full asking price. But I don't know. Maybe it's worth holding out for that."

"You should probably listen to Tod. He knows the market in this town." Ren knew the real estate man quite well, since they often met up over the exchange of contracts. They weren't friends, but as professionals, they respected each other. Tod had engineered the sale on the old rail depot, which Texas oil cowboy Jasper Flint had turned into a micro-brewery. There'd been somewhat of an outcry over this from some quarters, but on the whole Ren thought a micro-brewery would be better for the town than the museum that Annabeth Collier had wanted.

Change happened in a town, its buildings and its businesses and its citizens.

Ruth and Ren, for example.

"I'm thinking about it," Ruth said. "I don't want to lose the sale."

"So you've obviously decided to make the move to California."

She broke into a smile. "I can't wait! I've been down there to look around, and I had a couple of job interviews. I love it! The ocean and the sun."

"I'm glad it's working out."

"Me, too." They looked at each other in awkward silence for a moment, then she spoke again. "You know what, Ren? I've discovered I'm not a people person."

"Yeah?"

"I'm so enjoying being on my own, having my space to myself, I can't tell you."

"Maybe that's temporary. Maybe you just need the space for a while." It was what he told himself about Tully—what he told himself about all the times when he wanted her so much and yet needed to be alone, too, and when he knew he was hurting her with his attitude, but didn't know what to do about it.

"I'm not so sure about that," Ruth said. "Maybe I'm kind of selfish. Not in a bad way," she quickly added. "But, you know, I like things to be just so, and when they're not, it gets on my nerves and I get stressed and I can't put up with things and I get... bitchy. Permanently pre-menstrual, or something."

"I can understand that."

"You're different."

"I'm enjoying being on my own, too."

"No, you're different," she insisted. "We were bad for each other. I used to think we weren't, that we really needed each other, and maybe we did, at first, but that stopped. You know what we were like, I've decided?"

"Tell me."

"We were like in one of those old black and white movies when someone was poisoning their husband or their wife with a tiny, tiny dose of arsenic, every day, day after day. We were poisoning each other."

"And now we've stopped."

"I think so." She smiled again, and he smiled back.

"I think you shouldn't push too high on the house, if you want to make the move to California soon," he said. "It's stupid to put it off, just for the sake of an extra few thousand dollars. If you lose this offer and the place takes another six months or more to sell..."

She gave him a look full of sly humor. "You mean you *can* put a price on happiness?"

"When it's real estate, yes."

They both laughed a little, and said goodbye, and Ren kept running, thinking it was the best conversation they'd had together since he couldn't remember when.

♡

I must have been crazy, Sugar decided.

Though she could hardly believe it, her outburst to David over the phone had paid off, and he was bringing Rachel and the kids for a visit—the same weekend that Charlie was coming, just as she'd asked for. When David had first called to tell her, she'd burst into tears. "Thank you, David. Thank you so much. I promise you won't regret this."

Now, a week before the visit, she was the one regretting it.

Her little fantasy of a poignant and loving family reunion had paled with the approach of reality and she was gloomy and superstitious about it, torturing herself with endless scenarios of conflict and tension when the pain kept her awake at night.

She'd asked Charlie, during one of their stilted phone conversations, if he had any photos he could send, or anything else from his childhood. Copies would be fine. Originals—she promised to mail them back, or Tully would do it for her, if she couldn't get to the post office.

Three days ago, a whole package had arrived and she'd pored over every item, tracing Charlie's growth from the little boy whose image was burned on her heart to the man she'd seen on Ren Fletcher's office computer that very first day. There were class photos and football team photos, a handful of merit certificates and even a couple of cuttings from local newspapers. "Crestwood student wins national junior science award." "High School band tours China."

He'd had a poem in the school yearbook when he was ten. At fifteen, he'd earned a certificate for ocean lifesaving that included swimming a mile in open water. He must have traveled out of the USA not that long ago, because there was a spare passport photo in which he looked about the same age as he did in the photo on the hospital website. In the cover letter, he'd told her, "Keep all of this. I have other copies."

She'd put the passport photo in her purse, because it was the only one that would fit, and because it was clear and easy to see. With its serious purpose and without any kind of atmospheric pose or backdrop, the photo showed what he actually looked like. She'd tried to commit his face to heart, tried to write it onto the scrambled hard drive of her shaky memory, but that wasn't easy when you remembered a three-year-old from real life, and when all the pictures actually in front of you were only in two dimensions.

Oh, dear Lord, she was so scared and jittery now!

Tully wasn't all that happy about the coming weekend, either. She'd arranged with Ren that they would take the kids out to his parents' ranch on Saturday afternoon to ride horses, as a Montana cowboy treat, and on Saturday evening they were all going out to dinner at Rocco's Italian, just down the block. "But I hope we can keep everyone busy the rest of the time," Tully had said. "Because how do we just sit around and talk? It could be so awkward."

Mom ended a five-minute monologue on the subject of what grocery shopping would need to be done and what rooms she would put everyone in, by rushing out of the room to check the linen closet in case they didn't have enough sets of spare sheets, and Tully took advantage of her absence, blocking Sugar's view of the TV and saying at once, with her voice dropped, "Sugar, I can understand why you wanted this, and I guess I'm glad it's happening. I mean, of course I am. We have things scheduled, thank goodness, and I know we'll all try our best, but it's going to be exhausting for Mom."

"You'll be here to help," Sugar reminded her. It was a reminder for herself, just as much. "And Charlie is staying at the Graff Hotel, not with us."

"He'll be here for most meals, and there'll be seven of us actually sleeping here."

"David and his family won't expect it to be five star service, like the Graff." She didn't want to admit that she was even more worried than Tully, if apparently about different things.

Patty would cope with the practicalities. She would plan meals and make lists and Tully would go buy groceries and new sheets and all of that would be fine. But would Patty cope with the emotions? Would Sugar? And Tully? Charlie?

David? Rachel? The kids? What if they all hated each other?

Sugar felt like an upside down kind of bride—the center of attention, the one responsible for bringing everyone together—but she was so unsuited for a starring role. She knew she was going to be exhausted, too, even more exhausted than Patty.

The other thing that kept her awake at night was trying to think of a gift for the kids—not something easy and impersonal like a gift certificate, but something that showed effort and care. She had so little energy to put into it, so little money, so few skills. She'd had one idea, but were Hannah and Mitchell too old for it, now?

"We can keep everything simple," she said, because she could see her own anxiety still mirrored in Tully's face. "Get deli food and takeout. Send the kids to a movie or the park on Friday or Sunday. We have Saturday pretty much taken care of, with the horseback riding. I'm so glad Ren suggested it."

Tully sat beside her on the couch and held out their latest box of candy. Sugar took what she now recognized as a vanilla mango truffle, while Tully picked up a pear and ginger swirl. "You know that's not what I'm talking about," she said gently.

"Oh. No?"

"You know it, Sugar. It's not the practicalities. It'll be the family stuff that wipes her out."

For a moment, Sugar thought about bluffing her way through, but then she just didn't have the strength. "I know," she admitted. "That's just what I was thinking. It's what I sweat about, at night. It could be a really ugly weekend, couldn't it?"

"Yeah, it could." Tully put the piece of candy in her mouth, and Sugar did the same. They let them melt, tasting the flavors as they unfolded, but they didn't talk about what they were tasting, today. They didn't talk at all, until both pieces of chocolate were gone.

"You'll try for me, though, won't you Tully?" Sugar begged.

"Of course I will! Do you really think you need to ask?"

"No, I guess not. Thank you. I'm so glad to have you here. You'll... smooth things. The kids love you. David and Rachel trust you."

"It's Charlie," Tully said. "He's the unknown."

"Yes."

There wasn't a lot more to say.

♡

"Can you buy a few things for me?" Sugar held out a written list for Tully, who was about to go grocery shopping ready for the big weekend. David and Rachel and Mitchell and Hannah were arriving Thursday—tomorrow afternoon.

"Sure." She took it, expecting personal care items like deodorant or breath mints or cotton balls.

But there was candy on the list. Gummy bears and licorice strings and about six other things. Watching her read through it, Sugar looked embarrassed and apologetic. "Maybe it's stupid," she said. She folded her thin hands together.

"If you feel like eating these, of course it's not stupid. I can get them." Tully and Mom were still keeping up the relentless roster of healthy meals, but if Sugar wanted the between meals indulgence, let her have it.

"They're not for me," Sugar said. "I—I wanted to make something for the kids. Candy bugs, like for Halloween."

"Even though it's not Halloween?"

"Six years ago for Halloween, I was in California. I took a vacation for a few days, thought I might try to see you, but it turned out you were away."

"I never knew that." Tully knew she might have shut the door in Sugar's face, anyhow, back then. Six years ago, she hadn't remotely begun to believe in her birth mother's new start.

Sugar knew it, too. "I—I was too scared to let you know in advance. I thought if I'd spring it on you, just show up at your door, you might invite me in for coffee before you had time to think."

"But I wasn't there?"

"I came three times. Finally called Patty and she said you were on a trip to Alaska." But this was a distraction, and Sugar waved it away quickly. "Anyhow, I wanted to see David and the kids, too, while I was there. They were little then, six and four. I made them candy bugs, a box for each of them with ten or twelve chocolate beetles, and spiders with licorice legs, and stuff. They looked so cute and colorful and just right for Halloween. I called—didn't want any more knocking on doors with no one home—and David said I could come over. I was shocked, really. I think I just took him by surprise and he didn't think to say no. I took the candy, but then he met me at the door and said Rachel didn't want me in the house, didn't want me near the kids. He'd told her enough about me, over the years. I don't blame her. I really don't."

"No..." murmured Tully, because she knew it was true. Sugar had accepted a huge amount about her own past, now.

"But he said they could have the candy bugs, and he would tell them the gifts were from me, their Aunt Suzanne."

"Did they like them? Did you ever hear?"

"Mitchell wrote a thank you card, on his and Hannah's behalf. She wrote her name, it was the cutest thing, these big wobbly letters in purple pencil tilting down to the corner of the card. I still have it somewhere."

"Rachel would be pleased to know you kept it. It's important to her that the kids have good manners."

"I know maybe they're getting too old for that kind of thing now, candy bugs, but I thought they might remember that other time. It's stupid." She flapped her hands. "It's the only thing I can think of. I want to do something to show that I'm their aunt and I care about them, and it was the only thing I could come up with."

Tully wanted to cry.

Save it for the weekend. You know you'll be crying then.

"Of course it's not stupid," she said. "Of course I'll buy these. And maybe gift boxes to put the candy in? You're making a box full for each of them?"

"You really don't think it's stupid?"

"No, I don't." She wasn't sure what David and Rachel would think, whether they might imagine it was payback, or emotional blackmail, but she wasn't going to turn Sugar away from the idea on that account. She knew Sugar didn't intend it that way. She seemed hopeful and fragile and helpless and wistful and scared, and it touched Tully's heart.

"Is Ren coming to the airport with us?" Sugar suddenly asked.

"To the airport? David and Rachel are renting a car."

"No. For Charlie. Friday afternoon. When we go to pick up Charlie."

"I don't know. We haven't asked him."

"I want him. We need him. I want him there."

Tully did, too. Different reasons. Scary reasons. She wanted him anywhere she could have him. "I'll tell him," she said.

"You're seeing him tonight?"

"No, but I'll call him for you."

Sugar nodded and closed her eyes. "Thank you. You have no idea, Tully..."

"No idea about what?" she prompted gently after a few seconds, when Sugar didn't continue.

"No idea how much I love my beautiful daughter."

Chapter Twenty-Two

"Charlie," Sugar said, in tears. "Zachary Charles..."

"Oh, wow! Oh, wow!" He was crying, too, pinching the bridge of his nose and wiping the back of his hand across his eyes. He came forward, a tall, strong, good-looking man with a grin on his face and those tears streaming down it, despite the pinching and wiping.

He hugged Sugar, his arms light and gentle around her because he could see at a glance how fragile she was. They stood there, locked together, not speaking, not moving, while more arrivals from the flight came through, parting around them like river water spilling around a rock and moving on to find their baggage or their loved ones.

They weren't exactly standing in the most practical spot, the three of them, right in the middle of the flow.

Tully tried not to sob but she couldn't help herself. Her shoulders shook and her throat closed and her temples ached with trying to force the emotion back. She didn't want to lose it so completely in front of Ren, but control was impossible. Just impossible.

This is my brother. My little brother. My big, grown-

up, strange and familiar little brother.

She pressed her fingers tight against her mouth and then she just wept and wept, because she was so happy and so sad. Happy about now, sad about all the missing years and the reasons for them. Ren stepped close again and turned her into his arms. "Hey…"

"I'm sorry I'm such a mess." She breathed him in, felt the warm weight of his hand against her back and smelled the familiar male scent of him, tangy and fresh. "I'm sorry."

"No…" he said. "Don't be." He held her tighter, and pressed his lips into her hair and against her temple. "You don't ever need to say that you're sorry, Tully, about anything."

"No?"

"Why do you think you would?"

Because our lives are in such different places, and it matters.

But she didn't have time for any of that now.

"Charlie, this is your sister," Sugar said in a cracked voice. "This is Tully, your sister."

Tully turned away from Ren and laughed through her tears as Charlie took his first look at her stained and swollen face. "Your sister, the complete mess, I'm afraid."

"It's okay. We're all that." He engulfed her in a harder, stronger hug than the one he'd been able to give his birth mother. "It's good to be here. It's so good to meet you."

"And this is Ren. You know him. He was your first contact," Sugar explained, unnecessarily, and the two men stepped closer to shake hands.

"Good to finally meet you, Ren."

"I'm glad I could help make this happen." In fact, he'd been the one to drive here, an offer he'd made that Tully had been grateful for. She'd known she would be emotional and distracted. Far better to have Ren at the wheel of his roomy pickup.

"I—I can't think," she said. "What are we even doing? We're just standing here, crying. Do you have checked bags, Charlie?"

"No, just carry-on."

"So we don't have to wait. We can go."

"Whatever you want. I'm... here, that's all." He spread his hands and grinned.

He was so familiar, and yet not. He looked like Dad when he smiled, and he had Sugar's eyes. Like Sugar, Tully had pored over the pictures he'd sent, and she'd mulled over every detail Sugar had given her about the years when she'd had him with her. His moments of toddler mischief, his times of shrinking back and being too quiet because he saw too much, the handful of songs she'd taught him.

He'd loved fire trucks, Sugar said. That was about the only solid detail she could remember. Charlie, aged three, had loved fire trucks. This Charlie, hefting a carry-on bag by its webbed shoulder strap, had probably outgrown fire trucks quite some time ago. Tully almost laughed out loud, thinking about it, and felt such a rush of confidence and happiness. The once-vulnerable little boy was now a successful man.

Ren held her back for a moment, after Charlie began to walk forward. Sugar was leading the way to the short-term parking lot. She'd stopped crying now, and she was beaming, her body language proud and possessive, but her face was still red and tear-stained and her walk painfully slow. "This way, to Ren's truck," she was saying.

"Is it settled where we're going?" Ren asked Tully quietly. "Better decide on that. Does he want to check into the hotel and freshen up a little, have some time to catch his breath, or are we taking him direct to your place? You have your brother and his family there, and the big dinner planned. Is it going to be too much?"

"You mean we need to make sure we all have the same expectations?"

"Yes. The hugging and greeting is the easy part, I would think."

"You're right. I'm glad you're here for this stuff, because Sugar and I are..."

"Of course you are. Too emotional to think. Of course you are. That's why I offered to drive."

"I'll just ask." She caught up to Charlie and Sugar,

which wasn't very difficult. Sugar set a slow pace, and Charlie patiently kept to it, with the bag weighing his shoulder down.

After those first moments, his face had... gone quiet, somehow. Tully wasn't sure about what he was feeling, or what it meant. She stuck to Ren's sensible and practical script. "Charlie, we're wondering if you want to check in to the hotel before we head home." She saw his focus shift back from wherever it had been. "Do you need some time on your own, after the flight?"

He looked tired, she realized. Frayed around the edges from the relentless work of his final year of residency in a demanding medical field. This probably hadn't been the best timing, for reconnecting with the mother he hadn't seen in twenty-seven years. It was good of him, generous of him, to have made room for it. They all knew there wasn't a lot of time.

"Check in to the hotel, definitely," he said. "Get rid of this bag. Time on my own? No, it's fine. Thanks for asking, though."

"Are you sure?" The pretty Queen Anne house had seemed a lot smaller, last night and today, with David and his family there. Hannah and Mitchell were sleeping on camp beds in the family room, while David and Rachel were on the sofa bed in the room that had once been Dad's study. The kids were good... great... but they were siblings and they fought and yelled and thumped up and down the stairs, couldn't agree on a movie to see, or whether they wanted to go to the park.

Sugar had presented them with her wistful little gift of candy bugs, and they'd remembered the ones from before, and made her happy by eating a couple right away and joking about biting off spider legs. Rachel had been very watchful, so far. She was a willowy, graceful, brown-eyed blonde but she was a lot tougher than she looked, and she and David both had firm opinions on how to raise their kids. Neither one was going to let Sugar do or say the wrong thing, or get too close. It wouldn't take much for things to get tense.

"I'm sure," Charlie answered firmly. "I'm here to see

you guys, aren't I?" But he still looked tired.

"Let us know if you do need a break," Tully insisted. "Don't be polite about it, okay? We're family."

"We are," he said seriously.

"Tell him what we have planned, Tully," Sugar said eagerly.

"You can tell him."

"No, you," she insisted, and Tully realized she was struggling. She didn't have the energy and breath to walk and talk at the same time. Their progress toward the parking lot had slowed even further, but it was too late to suggest that Sugar wait while they brought the truck around.

"Well, you know we have the whole family here, Charlie. Patty, your grandmother, and David, your uncle, and his wife Rachel and the kids Mitchell and Hannah. There's a turkey in the oven for tonight. Tomorrow I think Rachel wants to take the kids for a look around Marietta and some shopping in the morning, but then Ren has arranged for us to take them horse-back riding at his parents' ranch in the afternoon. The weather is supposed to be beautiful, so we're lucky."

"It seems so light here, too," Charlie said. "Lighter than it would be in New York, for the time of day. What is it, nearly six, now?"

"It won't be fully dark until after nine."

"Or maybe it's just that there's so much more sky."

"Well, we're known for that in Montana!"

"Sorry, you were telling me about tomorrow."

"Think I already covered most of it. We're having dinner out, in town, and then we'll just let Sunday take care of itself."

"Come for brunch at my hotel," he suggested. "I checked on their website. It looks pretty amazing. Since we never managed our afternoon tea at the Plaza in New York."

Sugar clasped her hands together, over her heart. "Oh, Charlie, that would be great!"

Her eyes were still shining with tears, but she was beaming, too, lit up from inside like a child having ten Christmases at the same time. She was so proud of him and so thankful, the emotion dripped off her like jewels dripping off a spoiled heiress. She glowed and shone. Like sun against a rainbow. Like freshly cleaned window panes.

The comparisons just kept coming, none of them strong enough to fully cover Tully's sense of Sugar's mood. She got a little scared again, suddenly. How wiped would her birth mother be, by the end of the weekend? Even happiness could be exhausting.

They reached Ren's pickup and made the forty-five minute drive to Marietta, going direct to the Graff Hotel. Charlie jumped out, saying he'd be as quick as he could, and Tully thought that it wasn't ideal. With three of them waiting for him in the truck, Ren seated behind the wheel and the engine idling in case he had to pull away from the drop-off in front of the hotel, Charlie was not going to linger in his room long enough to regroup and catch his breath.

He didn't. He was back in less than five minutes, and just a few minutes after that Ren had pulled into the driveway at Mom's, and there she was in the open doorway. She'd been watching for them, waiting.

She launched into speech before Tully even put her foot on the first step. "The turkey's out of the oven and the vegetables are done. David's going to carve. Rachel is making gravy. We used her stuffing recipe, you know the one with the mushrooms and bacon and herbs. It's so mild tonight, maybe we should have done barbecue. I have Hannah and Mitchell setting the table, so do we want to eat right away? I mean, I can keep everything warm in the oven—"

Tully reached her and gave her a hug. "Slow down, Mom. Stop fretting about the food."

"I'm nervous."

"I know."

Charlie had climbed out of the pickup. He was holding the front passenger door for Sugar, and he took her elbow. She moved very slowly. Mom began to mutter under her breath. Praying, Tully thought, seeking divine coaching through this first meeting with her eldest grandson, the total stranger. "He's helping her," she said.

"He's been great, so far."

He threw an unsmiling glance toward the porch where they stood, and Mom did the predictable Morgan female thing and began to cry, just as Sugar and Tully had, at the airport. "Oh, what's he going to think of this?" she sniffed, dabbing at her eyes with a cotton handkerchief. "Of us?"

"Same as he thought at the airport. He was crying, too."

"Oh, he was?"

He came up the steps, leaving Sugar to be helped by Ren. "Hey, my grandmother?" he said.

"Yes. Yes, I am," Mom said.

They hugged, and for a long moment no one spoke.

Inside the house, there were four more sets of greetings, for David and Rachel and the kids, and Tully tried to think when there'd ever been this much family here, and couldn't. Eight of them. Nine, if you counted Ren.

Could she count Ren?

She didn't think so.

Don't think about that, now.

The last time there'd been eight members of the family in this house was probably around twenty-five or thirty years ago, when Dad's brother and his family had come from San Diego for Thanksgiving.

Tonight's dinner was chaos. And wonderful. And exhausting.

They sat down to eat at seven-fifteen, and there were more questions and explanations and potted biographies flying around the table than there'd been at the speed-dating evening Tully had rashly attended in Santa Monica three years ago.

Sugar barely spoke. She was just too tired. She sat there, picking at her food, putting down her fork so she could smile at everyone around the big table—which hadn't been extended to its full length in so long that Mom had forgotten how. Earlier, she and Tully had had to spend ten minutes puzzling it out together. Extended, it was almost too big for the room, so they were crowded in here.

Sugar kept forgetting to pick up her fork again to eat, and Tully kept prompting her, but in the end she gave up on that and leaned across the table to say quietly instead, "Do you want to bail, Sugar?" She looked gray with fatigue, and didn't even have the energy to smile any more.

She nodded, and mouthed back, "Yes, please."

"I'll help you upstairs."

She made no protest that she could do it on her own, just said, "Thank you," which made Tully worry. Might Sugar literally die of happiness, this weekend?

It would be a good way to go.

But I'm not ready. It's too soon.

"You're taking her up?" Mom said.

"Yes."

"I'm sorry," Sugar apologized. She looked as if she wanted to go hug Charlie, but he had David on one side of him and Hannah on the other, and to reach him she would have had to squeeze behind Rachel's chair...

Rachel was a good mother and a good person, but she was strict. Straight. Hard-line. Protective, and determined to raise her kids well. She would be incredibly watchful for any sign that Sugar's presence and the evidence of her bad choices might have a negative effect on her children in any way.

Sugar didn't try to squeeze behind Rachel. "I'll see you tomorrow, Charlie? Sorry about this."

"Hey... no."

At the table, as Tully and Sugar left the room, Hannah said to Ren, "Can you please tell me about my pony I'm going to ride tomorrow, Mr. Fletcher? What's her name? Is she cute? I can't wait to ride her!"

By the time Tully came back downstairs, Hannah's questions had been thoroughly answered and the clearing up was in full swing. Ren was gone. Putting leftover turkey into a plastic container in the kitchen, Mom said quietly to Tully, "He said to tell you he had an hour or so of work to do, to prepare for a client appointment tomorrow morning, but he says to call him or come over later, if you want."

"Thanks." She didn't know if she would. It was already after eight-thirty. Ren hadn't mentioned the hour of work when he'd come to pick her and Sugar up to take them to the airport at just before five, but she realized that if he hadn't been meeting Charlie's flight with them he would have stayed on in his office to finish the preparation then. They'd messed up his schedule, and he hadn't said a word.

"I have the kettle on for coffee or tea," Mom said. "Do you want to ask who'd like some?"

"Where are David and Charlie?"

"I told David to take him outside and show him the garden. It's too crowded in here. They didn't need to help."

Tully found the two men standing at the edge of the brick paving, talking about sports. They had a similar height and build, but Charlie was darker in coloring and was all lean muscle, while forty-four-year-old David had gray running through his mid-brown hair and some thickening around his waistline.

They both said they'd have a decaf, then David added, "But let me do it, Tully. I can bring yours out here, if you want. Sit for a while!" He pulled out one of the wrought iron chairs that matched the round, white-painted table which no one sat at nearly as often as they should, considering how inviting it was.

"That would be nice," Tully said. "It's still so mild. Charlie?"

"I'd love to sit out here," he said. "I spend way too much time under artificial lighting, in New York."

"It was so good of you to do this, Charlie," Tully said to him as David left.

"Hey, how could I not? Of course I was going to come out here."

"It must risk being overwhelming for you."

"It's noisier than I'm used to, with family," he answered. "I ended up as an only child, I think you know that already. Mom and Dad looked at adopting again, but decided against it. We went on vacation with cousins, so I always associate that kind of family noise with August and the beach."

They both sat. The rather obsessive cleaning that Mom and Tully had done before the big visit had included a good wipe of the table and chairs, and they looked pretty and fresh beneath the unfurling new leaves of the catalpa tree that shaded this patio in summer.

"I know how hard it must have been for you to get away, too," Tully said. "Ren says you have a major research project?"

"Yes, I'm examining the correlation between—" He stopped. Gave an upside down, defiant grin. "Nope. Not going to talk about it. Not thinking about work, this weekend."

"But the research project is on top of your regular workload? As a final-year resident, you're supervising junior doctors now, right? You're taking the lead in surgery, a lot of the time..."

"Yeah, all of that." He sighed and wiped his eyes with a thumb and forefinger. "In one way or another, it's been a big year."

"I bet."

"Too big. Crap timing, in a few areas."

"Timing counts, doesn't it? Timing makes a huge difference. Sugar's timing has never been that great."

And neither is mine, with Ren...

"Yeah," Charlie said again, then he fell silent for a few moments. "You know what, though? When the timing is bad, you have to fight back. You can't give into it."

"No?"

"I fought to come here this weekend. I had to call in favors, squeeze my schedule for weeks, do without sleep."

"We appreciate it, Charlie, we really do." Was he pressing for more gratitude? That seemed odd, but she gave it to him, anyhow. "Patty, your grandmother, might not manage to say so. She's feeling pretty overwhelmed right now, and I know that's going to mean she obsesses over the domestic stuff and gets distracted and doesn't get to what's important. But we do understand, as I said, that this hasn't been easy for you."

"It's fine. It was the right thing to do. I wasn't going to let the timing or the geography defeat me. I don't believe in that, you know?"

"Oh, you don't?"

"I really don't. I've thought about it a lot lately, in relation to a few things. And the more I've thought about it, the clearer it's become for me. If someone lets the timing and the geography get in the way of something that could be important, then it's because that thing is not what they really want. If you want something enough, timing and geography don't matter. Seriously. They can only be deal-breakers if you let them be. Deal-breakers are a *choice*."

He sounded angry and upset, and she wasn't sure why. He sounded as if he wasn't actually talking to her about his own visit here at all, but was making an argument about something else entirely.

She didn't know what to say, and ended up giving an uncertain, "I—I guess."

Timing and geography made her think of Ren. What Charlie was thinking about, she couldn't know.

He seemed to realize he'd come on too strong. "Sorry, Tully, this isn't about you."

"I'd begun to work that out."

"It's... something that was happening back in New York, but... yeah... it ended. We broke up." He swallowed suddenly, then clamped his jaw shut on what looked like a powerful surge of emotion. He took a breath and tried to speak lightly. "Something else I didn't have time for this year, but it happened anyhow. Just like I didn't have time for connecting with..." He stopped and changed tack again. "You don't call her Mom, I've noticed. You call her Sugar. Patty's the one you call Mom."

So they had to talk about all of that—about why Patty was still "Mom" to Tully, about how things were getting so much better than they'd been for all those years before Sugar got clean. They talked about Mom's anger when she'd learned of Charlie's existence, how she was over that now, thank heaven, and how it had felt to discover so much family stuff, in good and painful ways.

David arrived with their two mugs of coffee on a tray, along with milk and sugar. He saw that they were in the middle of something, a brother-and-sister heart-to heart, and didn't linger.

"It sounds as if you've had a lot to forgive," Charlie said, after they'd gone.

"That's true," she answered. "And I think I have forgiven her, now. It's been strange, though. Forgiveness doesn't always come in a blinding flash, I've discovered. Sometimes it creeps up on you, very quietly, and one day you notice it's just *there* and you're not quite sure when it arrived."

"I can understand that."

"You mentioned your parents. I'd love to hear more about them, Charlie."

"Oh, they're great. They're the best. They've been a little concerned about this whole thing, coming out here and reconnecting, but they knew I needed to do it. I sent them a text a little while ago, telling them everything was going great."

"Oh, you did? I'm glad. I can understand why they'd have concerns."

The dregs of coffee in the bottom of the mugs were stone cold by the time Charlie and Tully had finished talking, and Tully was getting cold, too, with a night-time chill falling in the garden and the sky fully dark overhead.

"We should go in," Charlie said.

"I should run you back to the hotel. It would be nearly midnight in New York by now. You must be past ready to crash."

"A bed sounds good," he admitted.

"In the morning, don't rush to get over here. Just call when you're ready for me to come pick you up."

"I might walk here. It didn't seem like it's that far, when we drove."

"It's not. Just a few blocks. Walk or call me, whatever works for you."

"I will. Thanks. This has been great tonight, better than I dared to hope for."

"Same for me, Charlie. It's been amazing."

She dropped him back at the Graff, and then sat in her car and called Ren. "Mom said you'd had some work to do?"

"Done, half an hour ago. Are you coming over?" He

sounded relaxed and warm and welcoming, and her stomach kicked.

Of course she was coming over. Her willingness had begun to torment her more and more as her return to LA loomed closer. Wasn't every hour she spent with Ren going to make it harder to let him go?

"On my way," she said brightly.

Would she start to hate herself soon? She couldn't stop thinking about what Charlie had said tonight, as they sat out on the back patio—that timing and geography could only break the deal in a relationship if you let them, that deal-breakers were a choice.

Whose choice, though?

Hers, or Ren's?

Mine, she suddenly knew. I'm the one who has to decide what's happening here.

Chapter Twenty-Three

He was waiting for her, shirtless.

He must have just finished on the exercise bike because there was a T-shirt hanging over it and his upper body was still a little damp in places where he'd obviously had a quick splash and toweled himself off.

When he pulled her close, she felt the damp and the heat, and her whole body prickled and sang with wanting him, and ached and stung with the fear of losing him.

"Did I interrupt your cycling, when I called?" she asked, hiding it.

"It's fine. I was just finishing up."

"Pre-warmed." She ran her hands over this back. "I like that."

"You do feel a little cold." He rubbed his cheek against hers.

"Charlie and I were sitting outside talking, and it got chilly out there before we thought to go in. The drive over to the Graff and then back here wasn't quite long enough to warm me up."

"So maybe I need to help with that..." He nuzzled her

cheek, warming it with his mouth while he cupped her jaw.

She turned into his kiss and closed her eyes, giving herself completely to the moment, the warmth, the familiar bliss. Beneath her hands his body was a package of pure muscle, dense and hard and springy. She felt small against him, but her body fit with his like a hand fitting into a glove.

How much longer?

"Do you want coffee or anything?" he muttered.

"Nope. Nothing. Just..."

You.

This.

Don't need to talk about it.

"Mm," he said, as if he'd heard her thoughts, and agreed.

"I'm glad you're not wearing a shirt."

"I'll try to remember that for next time."

Another kick in her stomach. How many more times would there be? Should she even have let this one happen?

But then they both forgot about next time, and thought only about this time—this kiss, this sweetness, this fire. He cupped her backside and locked himself against her and she melted as fast as always. His touch stripped her of her strength and filled her with aching need instead. She was boneless with it, throbbing with it, blind and hungry and dizzy.

No one else in the world had his hands or his mouth or the taste of his skin. Her clothes came off in a tangle, falling to the floor on their way across the living room and staying where they dropped. The two of them fell into the bedroom, fell onto the bed, rolled together. He painted every curve of her body with heat, whispered her halfway to heaven with the trail of his fingers.

She gave him everything she had. Her nakedness, her cries. For her, tonight, it was emotion way more than body, love way more than sex, connection way more than climax. He turned her inside out, and made her so vulnerable with the strength of what she felt that she would have cried if she hadn't cried enough today already, at the airport.

When he fell asleep in her arms afterward, she wished

time would slow for a while, linger here in this moment for a week or a month, so she could have her fill of it, enough to last forever.

Not possible, Tully, you know that.

All she could do was to savor it right now—listen to his deepened breathing, smell the clean scent of his hair, feel the warmth of his stomach and thigh pressed against her, give herself up to sleep while she was still in his arms, feeling perfectly happy and perfectly right.

When she woke up again, it was one o'clock and he still hadn't stirred. Her mouth felt dry with thirst, so she eased herself away from him and slid out of the bed as gently as she could, to make sure she didn't disturb him. She wasn't sure why it seemed so important to do that, it just did.

Because disturbing him would shatter what had happened before? All that peace and contentment and perfectly poised time?

This didn't make sense.

But she tried for it, anyhow.

First, find the robe hanging on a hook behind the open bedroom door, then tiptoe through and across to the kitchen, grab a glass of water then creep back to the bed, discard the robe and fold herself under the crooked spread of the covers without him even knowing she'd been absent.

That was the plan.

But he woke up, and she heard his voice thick and scratchy from sleep as she reached for the robe. "You heading home?"

"No, just thirsty, getting some water."

"Oh, okay."

He didn't say anything more, and didn't move. If he was looking at her, she couldn't see from here. His cheek was pressed deep into the pillow, and she thought his eyes were closed. She slid her arms into the heavy, chilly satin of the robe and wrapped it around her, watching the shape in the bed. With only some pale light spilling from the street, the room was stripped of color. His body beneath the covers looked like a bare hill in a black and white photo, and if she really concentrated, she could see the rise and fall of his breathing.

"Or maybe I should go, after all," she said after a few moments, needing something stronger from him, more of a signal that he still wanted her here. "Oh, okay," didn't cut it at all.

But he didn't answer. He was asleep.

Really, Ren?

Yes, really. She watched him for another minute. No movement, no sound. He'd slipped away, back into dream or oblivion, and didn't know or care if she was beside him.

Well, she *should* go, she realized. She didn't want to, but she should. She didn't want to be absent in the morning, when the crowded Morgan household awoke. She needed to be home, helping Mom and Sugar, making sure Rachel didn't feel she should be preparing breakfast for everyone.

She took off the robe and hung it back on the hook, then tracked her discarded clothes like a hunter tracking game, following the trail from underwear to jeans to top to boots. She dressed in the living area, and couldn't stop herself from glancing toward the bedroom door and listening for the sound of the covers being folded back or Ren's bare feet plopping onto the hardwood floor.

She wanted him to come to her, wrap his bare, warm arms around her and beg her not to leave.

But still he didn't wake up, and when she let herself out of the apartment she knew he wouldn't be surprised or disappointed to find himself alone in the morning. It was what they so often did. It was what he wanted. She hardly ever stayed. She'd accepted from the beginning that Ren needed his space, and she thought that if he reached a point where he *didn't* need it, then he would tell her so.

But what if that never happened?

Time to be realistic. Time to stop kidding herself. She'd said "fling" to herself many times, but had she ever really meant it? It was easy to say at the beginning, when everything still lay ahead, but when most of it was already behind her, the word "fling" had become so much harder. Would go on becoming harder until one day... night... it would be impossible.

Charlie had talked about timing, tonight. Timing and geography and deal-breakers. He'd been pretty clear in what he thought. Those things only counted if you let them. The deal only broke you if you let it. If you wanted to make something work, you made it work, even when the timing and the geography sucked.

"Am I making this too easy for you, Ren?" she said out loud, under her breath, as she went down his stairs. "Am I making it too hard for *me*?"

If she spent too much emotional energy on respecting what he wanted, would she end up with nothing left for herself?

Sugar didn't have a lot more time. They'd all begun to sense it. David was pushing Tully to lock in her return date with the studio. "Sugar will need hospice care pretty soon," he'd said. "And Mom won't need you so much. Maybe you shouldn't even wait until June. You can fly back and forth, if you need to."

Employment opportunities had tightened, she knew. Did she really want to back herself into a corner on that front? She'd lived in Southern California for eighteen years, and it still didn't feel like home the way Montana did. But the only reason she would consider coming back here, long-term, would be if—

If Ren asked.

And since he so rarely even asked her to spend the night, asking her to change her life for his sake seemed unlikely. It was too soon for him, after Ruth.

Tully knew that she and Mom had been letting things drift with Sugar. On that front, what else could they do?

But she hadn't realized until now, letting herself out into the alley behind Ren's office where she'd parked her car, just how much she was letting things drift with Ren.

"I can't do it anymore," she whispered to the deserted street. "I really can't."

The knowledge hit her hard, as she climbed into the car, the way Sugar's death was going to hit her hard, a few weeks or a few months from now. She couldn't afford to mix those two things up—losing Sugar, and losing Ren. It wasn't right or healthy or fair. Not fair to Sugar. Not fair to Patty. Not fair to Ren.

She'd told him a while ago that she never pretended to be mad when she wasn't, but she'd begun to pretend other things now—to pretend she cared less than she really did—and that wasn't healthy or fun.

When Sugar was ready to let go of this world, Tully couldn't keep on willing her to stay here so that she herself could remain in this special place and time, this interlude of unexpected love.

Sugar, Ren, and Charlie.

Three people she hadn't expected to love, back in February, on Valentine's Day.

Sugar, the sister-mother she'd been so angry about.

Ren, the prom date she'd stood up and hadn't seen in eighteen years.

Charlie, the half-brother she hadn't known existed.

Oh, shoot, she was going to start crying again!

She sat at the wheel of her car without starting the engine and just let the tears come, because she thought they probably needed to, and they might help.

She hadn't expected to love *anyone* new, when she came back to Marietta, and now there were three people, three precious people, and all she could think, right now, was that she was going to lose two of them, and it would be unbearable and unfair to everyone if she let herself lose them together, both at the same time.

She had to lose Ren first.

She had to lose Ren *now*.

In fact, she'd never really had him, she knew in her heart. This was nice, so good, all these half-nights at his place, the meals together, the jogging, the laughs, the sense of connection and of putting right a miss-step from long ago, but it was temporary, convenient, good timing for both of them.

Terrible timing.

Charlie was wrong, Tully decided. She opened the glove compartment and pulled a sheaf of tissues from the box inside, to wipe her swollen nose and eyes.

Sometimes, the timing and the geography called the shots. Sometimes, those things were deal-breakers not from choice, but because they had to be. How could she ask for anything different from Ren, when she knew he was in the wrong place for it, after his divorce?

She was seeing him tomorrow afternoon, when they were meeting out at his parents' ranch to take Hannah and Mitchell for a ride. She would have to tell him then that she couldn't see him anymore.

The fling was over.

♡

The side of the bed where Tully had been was cold and empty. Ren reached out for her, and found she wasn't there. He had the vague memory that she'd gotten up in the night to grab a glass of water, and he'd thought she was coming back, but maybe that had just been a dream.

Disappointment kicked at him.

He wanted her here. It was like an ache or a craving, selfishly making its own demands, right from his gut. He had that mean feeling again. Mean and dirty and underhanded. He was taking more from Tully than he could give back and… yeah… it felt dirty, dishonest.

He'd awakened early. It wasn't even seven yet, so he didn't have to get up for another hour or more. His Saturday office hours didn't start until nine. If she'd still been here, they could have made sleepy, lazy love then drifted back to sleep for a final doze, while Main Street Marietta began to get busy outside.

But he'd dropped back asleep and…

Yeah, it was a pity. Because now he ached.

He almost sent her a text, expressing his regret, but thought better of it. Something often held him back from things like that. What did they call it in the corporate world?

Managing expectations.

He thought that was one of his biggest failures with Ruth, and hers with him. They hadn't managed each other's expectations. They'd disappointed each other. Over and over.

He wasn't falling into that same trap again. He cared about Tully too much to mess up or jerk her around with poorly thought assumptions, or shallow promises, or words that meant something different to her than what they meant to him. He had no idea what he was really offering her, beyond what they had right now, and if he couldn't put his money where his mouth was, then he'd better stay quiet. Anything else was too unfair.

And *managing expectations* wasn't anywhere near as good as she deserved.

Chapter Twenty-Four

"Can we really *all* go to the Fletchers' ranch?" Mom asked Tully anxiously on Saturday morning. "That's a lot of people. I'd thought maybe Sugar and Charlie wouldn't want to come. Or that Rachel would take some time out for herself, but then as soon as Sugar said she was coming, I knew Rachel would want to be there to keep an eye on everything."

"You can't really blame Rachel for her vigilance."

"I'm not blaming her. I do understand. But I'm thinking of the Fletchers. I know Pascale and Robert a little, of course. We say hello at the rodeo, and that kind of thing. This isn't a big town. They're lovely, but we're acquaintances, we're not—"

"Mom, it's okay. Ren specifically told them there might be quite a few of us, and that his mother is *not* to feel we're expecting food and drink, or anything beyond the ride. That's why we've made it two o'clock—too late for lunch, and too early for drinks. We're not even meeting him at the house, we're parking over by the barn. It's fine."

It wasn't fine, but she managed to hide the fact.

As far as Mom, Sugar, David, Rachel, Charlie, and the kids were concerned, it was fine, but she was dreading the afternoon on her own behalf, dreading seeing Ren. She'd folded herself into a cold bed in her old room at home at almost two in the morning and hadn't slept again until nearly five.

Those were always the darkest hours of the night, when you had something on your mind. Over and over, she'd rehearsed what she would say to Ren today. Over and over, she'd imagined his replies. She couldn't stop herself, and even though she told herself what a mistake it was to try to rehearse *any* kind of conversation, let alone a breakup talk, the self-scolding hadn't done any good.

When sheer exhaustion had finally let her mind settle, she'd only managed a couple of hours of uneasy sleep before morning came and the crowded household woke her again. There was someone in the shower, and someone else on the stairs, and Rachel whispering to Hannah to please be quiet because adults were still sleeping.

Charlie came over at eight-thirty, walking here from the hotel as he'd said he might. Mom and Sugar both wanted to feed him. Rachel had made pancakes, but there were only a couple left. He insisted he'd already eaten. "My body's on New York time. I was awake before five."

So was I, Tully thought.

"I had breakfast at six, as soon as the hotel restaurant opened."

"So you must be ready for mid-morning snack," Mom said.

"Just coffee would be great."

They sat talking over it for nearly an hour. Sugar brought out the package he'd sent, wanting to know more of the stories behind his childhood achievements, the photos and merit certificates. "Do you remember how much you used to love fire trucks?" she asked with wistful eagerness.

"Did I?" He smiled, but shook his head. "No, I don't remember. But, hey, I do remember playing with a hose, on some grass in a front yard. Was that with you? It was. It must have been."

"I—I think so," Sugar said. Tully thought she probably couldn't really remember, but hadn't wanted to admit it. Sugar was embarrassed about all the blanks, and the reason for them.

"It was with you, I'm sure," Charlie said. "It was a really hot day, baking summer heat, and the earth was almost bare, there really wasn't much grass. And I loved that hose. I squirted it everywhere, and there was so much water the yard turned to mud and I played with that. I remember the earthy smell of it, and getting it all over me, all gritty and cool. It was so nice in the heat. And I drank from the hose, and I can still practically taste the rubbery, metallic flavor of the water. Oh, and there were these bright flowers swarming over a wall, pinky-purple. Where was that?"

"Would have been San Diego," Sugar said. "I went back there. That's where you were born, where we lived. I had a friend, Sheree. She had a huge magenta-flowered bougainvillea on her house. I remember that. I remember the day when you played with the hose. Oh, that's wonderful! Wonderful that we both remember!"

And for Sugar, Tully knew, it was especially wonderful that Charlie's memory was a happy one. She'd been so afraid he wouldn't have any happy memories of his time with her.

Rachel came downstairs in a pretty skirt and top, with the kids just behind her and her purse slung over her arm. "We're going shopping," she said. "I told the kids they could each have something from Montana. Hannah says she wants cowgirl boots. Mitchell isn't sure."

They were gone all morning, while David and Mom and Sugar and Tully and Charlie sat around talking, with a candy box on the coffee table and an old movie running in the background. Tully had seen so many movies with Sugar over the past few months. *Love Actually* and *Groundhog Day* and *Mickey Blue Eyes* and *Speed*. Sugar had especially loved *Clueless* and *Roxanne*. Today it was *Sleepless in Seattle,* which she peeked at occasionally from her position stretched out on the couch.

The pain meds were making her sleepy, so she dozed on and off, but she had a smile on her face even while she slept, and Tully thought she was probably listening more than she seemed to be, while her brother and mother and daughter and son sat talking. Tully almost fell asleep herself, but then she thought about photos and it jolted her awake again. They should take some pictures while they were all together.

Sugar woke up and they had a little photo shoot with phone cameras as well as Mom's digital point-and-click. Sugar made a joke or two about her tired looks and the glass cracking in the photo frame, but it was obvious she thought this was precious and wonderful and would treasure the pictures... they all would... even if none of them looked model perfect.

Rachel, Mitchell, and Hannah arrived back just before lunch. They'd had iced chocolate at Copper Mountain Chocolates, and found the perfect pair of pink cowboy boots for Hannah. Mitchell had wanted a computer game, but there was no game store nearby so he'd decided on cowboy boots also—a slick pair in brown leather, tooled with stylized black flames.

"We're going to wear these when we're riding," Hannah announced.

Tully's heart flipped like a pancake. All morning, she'd been trying not to think about going out to the Fletchers' ranch this afternoon. What would it be like to see Ren, knowing what she planned to say to him about the future?

She busied herself setting out the cold cuts and salads and bread rolls, and they had another rather noisy and chaotic Morgan family meal, which she cleaned up, also, because it was better to keep busy when she was feeling like this.

David had always encouraged her to be strong and decisive, had always told her that she was smart and capable and in control. Time to act on that. Now that she'd made a decision for herself, she gritted her teeth over it, felt it like armor around her.

They headed out to the Fletcher ranch, as planned, at just before two, and she was grateful that the people who knew her best—Mom and David—were too preoccupied with the complicated layering of family feelings and relationships to notice that she had something different on her own mind.

Ren was already at the barn, waiting for them.

He grinned at her, and touched her fingers briefly with his. "Going well?"

"Really well." But the habitual intimacy between them was painful today. She couldn't hide the fact, and she was sure he'd seen.

He seemed a little strained as he told her, "I didn't saddle the horses, because I thought the kids would like to do that."

"You're putting one of them on Lucette?"

"Mitchell will have Lucette, and Dad borrowed a pony from our neighbor for Hannah. His name's Buddy and he's pretty much bomb-proof."

"That's so nice of your dad! I thought they might have to take turns."

"We'll see how their confidence is, and if it looks like they're up for a trail ride, I'll saddle up Lance and take them out. We have some chairs set up in the shade for anyone who doesn't want to walk with us, and there are cold drinks."

"You weren't supposed to go to any trouble."

"Took me all morning to freeze those ice-cubes and pack that store-bought lemonade into a cooler bag."

She laughed, and the laughter hurt because he was being so good. She knew she needed to harden herself up, or she was only going to hurt more. Worst of all, she might weaken... "Can we grab some time afterward?" she said quickly.

"My place?"

"No, I mean here, before we leave." She knew she was frowning. "I—I need to talk to you."

"Sure." But he looked distinctly wary now. Alarmed, even. He'd seen the frown, seen something more in her body language, or heard something more in her tone. "Let's get the riding done first," he added.

"Of course. Definitely." She nodded with too much energy, and hugged her arms around herself as if she was cold, which must have looked a little strange, because it was perfect and warm and sunny this afternoon.

"We'll have a look at Frip, too," Ren said.

She kicked her attention back to the riding plan and poured enthusiasm into her tone. "Oh, Hannah will love that! A foal!"

"And if we can't grab some time here, we'll work something else out."

She nodded. "That would be good."

Mom and David helped Sugar to get comfortable in the shade of the cottonwood trees that edged the small field where the kids would go through their ponies' paces, while Rachel and Charlie and Tully went with Ren and the kids to meet Coco and her foal. As predicted, the name Frip had stuck and Ren's dad had given up trying to think of anything else.

"Oh, he is so cute!" Hannah cooed, and Mitchell laughed at how long his legs were, and the way his little tail quivered when he drank from his mom.

Then they went into the barn to get Lucette and Buddy saddled and ready.

"Helmets," Rachel said.

"Right here," Ren answered.

He flashed another glance at Tully, the way he'd done a couple of times now. She tried not to meet his eye. Tried not to look at him at all, in fact, but it was hard. He looked good, and familiar, and she'd grown used to looking at him and feeling the wanting and the happiness. Now she had to squash all of that, force it away.

She felt sick about what she was about to do. It was going to be like cutting off her own hand, or stepping off a cliff—deliberately doing something she knew would hurt like a knife.

I don't want to do it.

Easier to wait, but this reminded her too much of the old Sugar finding excuse after excuse to keep on using.

The foal and the ride were both a huge success, and the kids were beaming as they came back to earth after a wonderful hour in the saddle. Over in the shade, Mom and Sugar were smiling, too, as they finished their tall glasses of iced lemonade. "I think he's a keeper, Tully," Sugar whispered to her, about Ren, on the way back to the car.

But then she tripped and Tully had to take her arm in a stronger grip, and the distraction of the near-fall saved her from having to give a reply.

"You want to grab a minute now?" Ren muttered to her.

Tully looked ahead of her. Rachel and the kids were already climbing into Mom's car. Mom was reaching into her purse for her keys. Tully would take David, Sugar and Charlie in her own car. The two men had almost reached it and had turned to see if she and Sugar needed any help.

How could she and Ren talk now? But they had to, or she knew she'd despise herself. He'd stopped dead, planting his feet on the ground like a cowboy standing at the rail of a corral. He wasn't happy, Tully could feel it like a cold blast of air on her neck. He wasn't happy at all.

"Give me a minute, can you?" she said to Sugar, Charlie and David.

"Go for it," Sugar said, and Charlie and David both nodded and said it was fine.

They helped Sugar sit in the front passenger seat and David said, "Toss me your keys, Tully, then I can open the windows for some air. Go talk to Ren. We're fine here."

She lobbed her keys at him, he caught them neatly and she turned away, back to Ren, who was still watching and waiting. "Say it," he said, as soon as she reached him. "Your face has been like a shuttered window all morning and you're spooking me."

"Ren, I think we have to—" Stop seeing each other. She struggled to get the words out, and he cut in before they would come.

"You mean... This is our break-up talk, isn't it?"

"Yes," she answered, miserable.

"Why?"

"Because we both knew it was only an interlude. It had to be. It could only be. I knew. In my heart. The timing is wrong. The geography is wrong." She used Charlie's words from last night, because they seemed to fit. "David's been telling me I have to firm up my return date, and he's right. I can't extend it. The studio won't go for that. I'll lose my job.

I wish I could stay longer, but what would it achieve, really? Between us, I mean. The timing. Ren, the timing is—"

"—is wrong. Yeah. I know."

"Are you saying that's not true?"

Silence. She could probably have counted the length of it in heartbeats. Six or seven or ten. "No, it is true. You're right. I just... hadn't thought that far ahead. Hadn't wanted to."

"To me going back to LA?"

"To us needing to have this conversation," he corrected her.

"But we do need to have it," she said. "I thought I could just keep seeing you until I left, just let it ride along, but I can't. I have to stop it now, or we'll make too much of a mess."

And he didn't argue. He said, "I hate it," but that wasn't the same thing.

"Me, too. I hate it, too." Miserable. Heavy inside.

He wasn't fighting her, and all the words he *didn't* say gathered like thick fog in the air, muffling her ears.

"I really hate it," he repeated.

If that was all he had for her, then there was no point in continuing this. "Ren, I have to go. Sugar can't sit in the car forever while we go round and round on this."

"No," he agreed. "Look, I'm supposed to be coming to dinner with all of you tonight. Sugar has mentioned it a few times. But I can bail if you want me to."

"You'd better come. Unless you *want* to bail."

"Would probably cause some comment if I do," he said.

"It would."

"Look, I'll be there. I've come to really respect Sugar, and to care for her..."

"Oh, you have?"

"She's come a long way, and I can see that. I want to be there for her, since she's asked."

"Then I'll see you tonight." She turned and walked to the car, because at this point there was nothing else to do.

♡

From the dining room window, if she pretended to be dusting the window sills, Pascale could see the extended Morgan clan getting ready to leave.

Earlier, she'd helped Ren take the refreshments out to the table and chairs placed under the cottonwood tree and he'd introduced her to everyone. Patty's older daughter Suzanne who looked so frail and ill, her son and his family visiting from California, Charlie the grandson whom Pascale was a little surprised about.

There was a mystery going on there that Ren hadn't explained. Charlie was Suzanne's son, and Pascale could see the resemblance, but Suzanne must have been quite young when she'd had him, only around twenty.

Well, the mystery wasn't important.

What *was* important was Tully, and the way she looked today.

Tully had been trying to do everything right, appearing cheerful and upbeat, but from Pascale's position on the edge of the family group before she went back to the house, she hadn't been fooled. She'd seen the unhappy glances that Ren and Tully kept sneaking at each other when they thought no one was looking. She'd noted the way they found excuses not to talk. Tully fussed too much over setting out the glasses for the lemonade. Ren spoke too heartily to Charlie and David.

Something was wrong.

Now, the Morgans were leaving and she could see the final unhappy exchange between Ren and Tully before Tully turned, walked away and climbed into her car. Pascale had spent so many years watching Ren look unhappy that she could recognize the mood in her firstborn son through double-glazed windows and across fifty yards of garden.

Her heart sank into her stomach. It had been so wonderful to feel the change in him, over the past few months. First the separation, then the divorce, and then having Tully in his life. Even when he and Ruth had first been going out together, so many years ago, Ren had never looked that way—so glowing and energetic and alive, so dreamy and distant sometimes, with a secret smile on his face that he... for some incomprehensible reason... thought that no one could see.

Pascale loved it. She gloated to Robert about it, wished she dared invite Tully over for family meals so she could see the same feelings mirrored in her, but she was trying to be careful about that, trying not to jump the gun, as that odd English saying went.

And now...

Ren came slowly inside, and she went to the kitchen because that was probably where he'd go first. By the time he arrived there, he'd put a mask of cheerfulness on his face that gave him the keep-your-distance look Pascale knew of old.

"That went well," he said. "Kids had fun, I think. Rachel's very protective, but she relaxed by the end."

Pascale started thinking about scissors—the ones she'd so often begged Robert to use. *Cut out my tongue.* Well, he might have to cut it out today, because she couldn't help herself. She wasn't even going to try. "Did you and Tully have a fight?"

There was a beat of silence. "Not a fight, no."

"I saw you talking, just before they left."

"It wasn't a fight." He sighed, reached for a clean glass in the dish rack, and poured himself some tap water. "Just a decision."

"A decision?"

"Not going to see each other anymore."

"Oh, Ren, why?" she cried, abandoning even the tiniest pretense of neutrality on the issue.

"Timing. Geography. She has to go back to LA pretty soon. She doesn't want to drag it out, and I have nothing to offer her, to encourage her to stay."

"You have nothing?" she cried again.

"It'd be crazy to think that I did. Divorced, what, two months? Less."

"So?"

"So I'm still in recovery. Still damaged. Still working things out."

"But you and Tully are happy together! Won't that heal

your damage? Won't that let you work things out?"

"Don't, Mom," he said, in a voice she knew she shouldn't ignore.

"Well, I already did, but okay, I won't anymore." She gave a shrug that was mostly apology.

"Good girl," he told her absently, as if she was a puppy who'd just learned not to eat shoes.

Poor Robert would have to listen, tonight, to all the things she was forcing herself not to say to Ren.

Chapter Twenty-Five

Rachel cornered Tully at the top of the stairs. There was a shampoo-scented steam still coming out of the bathroom, and both women were dressed up for the evening, Tully in a chic little black dress and Rachel in splashes of spring color. They were due to leave for the restaurant in just a couple of minutes.

"Tully, I have to tell you, I was dreading this weekend," Rachel said.

"I know, and I don't blame you."

"I came so close to telling David we wouldn't do it. But it's been great so far. Thank you so much!" For a moment, they hugged awkwardly.

"I'm not sure that I deserve any credit for it," Tully said.

"Well, you do," Rachel answered firmly. "Hannah is in heaven over those ponies this afternoon. And Sugar has been—you've shown me, the way you act toward her, that it's possible to forget and let go of the past. I've been so angry on David's behalf, over the years."

"You don't have to tell me about anger," Tully said. "I've had my share."

"And I really haven't wanted her anywhere near the kids."

"I understand that, too."

"But there's a quietness to her now, a carefulness, that goes beyond the fact that she's so frail. I—I find myself wishing we had more time. I never, ever thought that I would feel that."

"Me, too."

"We'll have a great dinner. We'll take some more pictures. Hannah and Mitchell will remember her with fondness, I really want that."

"Is that why you're letting her give them all that candy?" Tully joked.

Rachel laughed, "Pretty much. It goes against the grain, trust me."

"Tully, Rachel, are you ready?" Mom called from downstairs.

"Coming," Tully called back.

"David and Charlie have just left, with the kids. I'm going to drive Sugar," Mom said. Even though the restaurant was just down the block, the walk would be a challenge for her now, after a tiring day. "Are you walking, or coming in the car?"

Rachel and Tully looked at each other. "We'll walk," they decided.

"We might catch up to the kids," Rachel added. "I wonder if it would be possible for Hannah to have riding lessons when we get home. The way her face lit up today..."

"There are several places on Riverside Drive, in Burbank, just north of the Ventura Freeway. That would be doable for you, distance-wise."

"I'm going to talk to David about it, and see what he thinks."

It was clear that Rachel's focus had returned to her children, and Tully wasn't sorry. She carried a lump of misery inside her like a ball of soggy dough. It was heavy and sour and it weighed on her stomach and she couldn't get rid of it and didn't know what to do.

You lived with it. Intuitively, she knew that. It was like

grief and bereavement.

No, it *was* grief and bereavement, as much of a loss as the one the Morgan family would soon experience when they lost Sugar.

She cradled the feeling all the way down the stairs and along to the restaurant, schooling herself not to let it show. Not to her family, and especially not to Ren himself.

Just get through the evening, Tully, get through tomorrow, and then Monday morning when everyone has gone, bite the bullet, do what you've been avoiding for weeks, call your office and tell them you're coming back as planned, in the middle of June.

♡

I'm the only one who's noticed, Sugar decided, sneaking another look at Tully.

Rocco's was noisy tonight, and the Morgan family group wasn't the only large table of diners. There were two other big groups, as well as couples and foursomes, and the noise level rose as the evening went on.

It was exhausting, to be honest.

Sugar just didn't have a lot of stamina any more, and she had to work to keep a smile plastered on her face so that Patty wouldn't start to badger her about going home early. She wanted to be here, with all of them. The family that had once seemed so boring and pointless and ordinary and an interfering nuisance, she now knew was everything to her, the *only* thing.

There were seven of them gathered here, seven precious people, eight if you counted Ren, but Sugar was the only one who'd noticed how much Tully was pretending.

Patty, looking the way Sugar felt—tired but happy.

Rachel, with her attention on Hannah and Mitchell.

The kids themselves, old enough now to sit at a meal like this without getting too restless. How many bread rolls had Mitchell eaten? He must have a hollow leg.

David talking to Charlie, getting on with him so well. That brought tears to Sugar's eyes. Of everyone, David had been the most hostile toward her, over the years, and she didn't blame him for that. She deserved every bit of whatever he wanted to dish. Now, Charlie was like a gift she'd given her little brother, and it was such a wonderful feeling when someone loved a gift you'd given them.

Hang on, wow, she'd just remembered something—and that was a victory in itself!

Christmas. She would have been nine or ten, and David three or four. Mom had encouraged her to give him a gift, paying for it out of her own allowance, and she'd chosen a little motorized train set that you wound up with a key, and David had loved it best of all his gifts that year.

Sugar remembered him tearing off the paper and howling with delight, not wanting to play with any of his other gifts for ages, while he wound and rewound that key, over and over. And she'd felt so special and important and wise and wonderful, because *she* was the one whose gift he'd loved.

She blinked back tears. Just a couple of years after that, she'd really started to go off track, and from then on all her memories were so patchy and skewed.

"What's up?" Tully said quietly.

"Just remembered something. A good something."

"Tell me."

"Christmas, when David and I were kids, and he loved the gift I gave him."

"What was it?"

"A train set. That's not important. Just remembering how nice it felt."

"Are you enjoying your meal? You're not eating much."

"Oh, it's okay. It's fine. Tully, I'm so sorry I don't remember messing up on your prom night. I wish I could. I wish I could remember what I did, so I could apologize to you properly. It's not the same, apologizing for something I can't even recall, not the slightest bit."

"You know what? I'm *not* sorry you can't remember. I'm glad."

"Oh, you are?"

"Because that wasn't you, back then. That was a

different person. You don't need to own those memories any more, and I'm glad you can't."

"You're saying I'm not responsible? No, I was, Tully. I've had to accept it. I did those things. All those things."

"Yeah, you did, and I guess you were responsible for the choices that led to them, but... I don't know. I don't want to think of it that way. Not now. You had an illness, the illness of addiction, and it hurts me more to blame you than it hurts me to forgive you, I've discovered."

A short silence fell, then Sugar dared to break it. "You seem like you're hurting tonight, though. It's Ren, isn't it?"

Alarm appeared in Tully's face. "What—? Oh, is it so obvious?" She darted a hunted glance around the table, but there was no one looking at her.

"Shh, no, it's fine," Sugar soothed her. "I'm staying pretty quiet, while everyone else is busy talking and eating, so I can see. No one else has. Not even Ren can see, because he's feeling just the same as you are. Miserable. What's happened, honey? Or don't I need to even ask? I don't, I can tell."

"Hey, we had the whole conversation and I didn't have to say a word," Tully joked, but her voice was tight in her throat, Sugar could hear it.

"Ah, sweetie, ah, shoot!" she said, helpless to know how to make any of it better. She felt the bitter inadequacy of herself as a mother all over again.

"It had to happen," Tully said. "It was there from the beginning. Takes time to get over a bad marriage and a divorce, and we just want different things at this point in our lives."

"What does he want, do you think?"

"To be a bachelor for a good long while, with only himself to please, and lots of time on his own. Probably a fling or two while he's on vacation in the Caribbean, or somewhere. Or maybe he never wants to get serious about a woman again. He knew from the beginning that I wasn't in Marietta long-term. It gave him an out. It made this safe."

"And what do you want, Tully?"

"What he's just come out of. Marriage. And I'd love a

baby, if it's not getting too late. I'm already thirty-six. I want someone to sleep with every night. I want our laundry to go in the same machine, and to call each other five times a day about who needs to stop in at the store, and whether we have plans for the weekend."

"And that's not where he is, in his own life," Sugar knew.

"No, it's not."

"Even though you are wonderful, and he knows it."

"Problem, huh?" Tully said.

The waitress came to take away their plates. Patty looked worried because Sugar's was still loaded down with the pasta primavera she probably shouldn't have ordered. Patty's eyes were fixed on the plate, not on Tully's face. Charlie was asking Ren a question. Rachel poured more iced water for the kids.

No one had noticed the short, infinitely precious heart-to-heart between Sugar and her daughter.

Sugar had only done four good things in her life. She'd gotten clean, she'd gone off the game, she'd given her son away, and now she'd found him again.

She was running out of time, at this point, but was there a chance that she could fit in a fifth good thing? Could she help Ren and Tully find their way back to each other, and to a future together? She didn't believe, just did not believe for one second, that they should let each other go when they seemed so happy, no matter how much they were coming from different directions. But could she convince them of that?

Well, she'd always been a stubborn *bee-yatch* of a creature, so she was sure as heck going to try.

The fifth good thing.

The last good thing. The last, sweetest thing.

As if she would even *think* of letting this go.

Chapter Twenty-Six

Sugar looked dangerously close to a collapse. Wilting visibly at the restaurant table, she'd asked if Ren could bring her and Tully home and he'd raced down Main Street on foot to collect his car and bring it right to the restaurant door.

"But I want the rest of you to stay," she'd said weakly. "Don't spoil your meal. Please."

Now, she left the restaurant with Ren and Tully on either side of her taking much of her weight, and Ren caught the look of fear in Tully's eyes. "Is this okay, Sugar?" she asked quietly, so that none of the family still at the table could hear her. "Or should we be thinking about the hospital?"

Sugar was silent for a moment. "The hospital is such a clinical setting," she muttered, half under her breath.

"Well, uh, yeah, but they have better medication, and people to take care of you."

"The lighting is so harsh there..."

"Sugar, I don't think that's what you should be thinking about, right now."

"Take me home," she answered, decisive about it even though her voice came out on a feeble breath.

"Okay, but if you don't bounce back a little..."

"I'll bounce back," she said.

They helped her into the car, and covered the short distance in seconds. Ren pulled into the driveway, right up to the side door that opened into the mud room. Sugar seemed to need both of them for support as she went slowly into the house.

"Upstairs?" Tully asked.

"No, just the couch. With the dimmers down low. And no TV."

"Are you sure?"

"Yes, but could you go upstairs and find my... my lip balm, and my, yeah, my night pills."

"I didn't think you were still having those. You have the intravenous now."

"I just want to check something on the label. Can you bring them down?"

"Sure, but—"

"Can you, please?" she quavered.

"Is there anything you want me to do before I head off?" Ren offered, and he felt Sugar's grip tighten on his arm.

"Yes. Stay," she said, her voice suddenly stronger. "Don't head off yet. Please don't head off."

Tully hurried up the stairs, and Ren had to fight to drag his gaze away from the sight of her taut, rounded butt rocking as she moved, beneath the silky fabric of her dress. He missed her like breathing, even when they'd been sitting at the same table for the past hour and a half.

He felt so helpless about what she'd said to him this afternoon. He wanted to argue, but then that seemed unfair and his sense of honor kicked in. If he didn't respect what she said, then what was he worth?

For weeks he'd been feeling mean and dirty and underhanded every time he stopped to think about what he was doing, but he had excused it on the grounds that Tully seemed happy, Tully seemed to know the deal, Tully understood, and respected his boundaries.

That was crap. She'd spoken now, and he had to listen.

"Help me sit," Sugar said, still gripping him tightly. "I'm no good at this anymore," she muttered, half to herself. "I've forgotten how."

"Forgotten...?" He didn't understand.

She looked up at him as he helped her lower herself into the couch's embrace, and met his eyes squarely. "How to fake my way into what I want," she said bluntly. "How to manipulate people and get them to give me stuff."

"Oh, I—" He was uncomfortable now.

"Ren, honey..." He heard the huskiness of fatigue in her voice. "I don't have a lot of time. We all know that. I can see that you and Tully are messing things up, and I can't let you do it. I can't. I just won't. There's not much I have left to give, not much time to do something good, but I have this. This one thing left. Call it the gift of plain speaking. She *loves* you. And you love her. I can see it. Sure, yes, the timing is bad, it's cruddy, but does that matter? You can't *let* it matter! It's such a tiny thing. I'm dying, Ren, so I know."

"I—It was her choice," he answered helplessly. "She said she had to go back to LA."

"Yeah, and you were supposed to grab ahold of her and tell her she couldn't, because you wanted her here. Don't you know that? Don't you know how scared she was... how scared she *is*... that she'd be asking too much of you, if she asked for a commitment? She's never going to push you into anything, when you've just come through a divorce. She'll do all the hard yards herself, instead. She's too good, my beautiful daughter. Don't you know that by now?"

"I know she's amazing. I know she's fabulous."

Sugar swore, "Then why the *hell* are you letting her do this, when she doesn't want it, and you don't either? Take me upstairs. I need to sleep. And if I wake up in the morning..."

"Sugar, of course you're going to wake up in the morning."

She glared at him for interrupting. "If I wake up in the morning and Tully is still miserable because you haven't said the right things, I am going to be so mad at you, so damned mad, I swear, I don't know what I'll do!"

"Oh. Right," he said, astonished at the force in her.

He heard Tully's footsteps coming back down the stairs.

♡

Sugar seemed to have lost interest in the lip balm and the bottle of pills. She waved them away. "I'm too tired, Tully. Can you take me up?"

"Do you want...?"

"I just want to go upstairs. And for you to turn the lighting down a little. It's too bright right now."

"But if you're going upstairs..."

"And maybe some soft music?" she said, although it wasn't clear who she was talking to, now.

"Music in your room?"

"Uh, yeah, the radio, or something. I'll leave it up to you, okay?"

"Goodnight, Sugar," Ren said. Tully thought he might have sighed.

She spent fifteen minutes helping Sugar with her night routine, and when she went back down, the lighting was low and there was music playing, just as Sugar had asked for. Wasn't the music playing in the wrong room?

Ren was standing there. "I'm acting on orders," he said, stepping forward.

"Whose?"

"Your mother's. And she's right. She's so damned right, I'm going to do exactly what she wants." He stepped closer. He put his arms around her, and she felt their warm, familiar weight and couldn't push him away. "Tully, stay. Please stay." He bent toward her, his mouth just a few inches from hers, his voice barely more than a whisper. "Please don't go back to LA. Tell the movie studio that you're not coming back. Start up an accounting business here. Stay here and be with me. Please don't end this." She couldn't drag her gaze from his mouth, so close. "Please forget what you said this afternoon, and forget that I didn't argue against it when I should have. That was wrong. I want you. In my life. Here.

Forever. I can't lose you. I *refuse* to lose you, just because of some stupid idea that the timing is wrong."

"But it is wrong," she said shakily. "It's always been wrong."

"We're stronger than timing, don't you think? Stronger than we could have imagined, the way your mother has been stronger than so many unimaginable things, in the end. We're stronger than mess and mistakes. We're stronger than the past." The music changed, went loud and driving, instead of soft and slow. Ren said, "Damn! Wrong kind of CD," under his breath.

"Damn?" Then Tully understood, suddenly. "Sugar put you up to this, not just what you're saying, but the whole thing, the background." She laughed, delighted about it in a way that almost made her cry. "The music, the lights... all Sugar's idea."

"I guess she thought there should be some atmosphere," Ren said softly. "And she has a point. But I picked the wrong CD. And you haven't given me an answer, yet. Please don't go back to LA. Please stay."

"The music changed. We got distracted." But she was leaning her whole weight against him. Her eyes must be shining with the happiness she felt, by this time. He must understand. Still, if he wanted it in words... "Of course I'll stay, Ren. If you want me."

"I want you so much, you have no idea."

"Even if Sugar did put you up to it."

"She couldn't have succeeded at that, if she hadn't been right about how much we both wanted it."

Tully was grinning broadly now. "My mother got pushy and made my boyfriend step up and do the right thing."

"She said it was a gift to us, one of the few good things she still had time for. The last good thing."

Tully blinked back more tears. "I guess she's right."

"I know she is," he whispered. His mouth brushed hers, and then they lost themselves in a long, perfect kiss.

"So how will we do this, Ren?" Tully said, after a while. "We'll work around the bad timing, but how? I don't want to crowd you. I don't want to push the pace."

"We'll take it slow," he said softly, his voice steady and calm. "We'll take it at the pace that feels right. We'll trust and believe that we can make it work, and we'll go from there. We'll keep it simple, and we'll keep it honest."

They heard a noise at the top of the stairs. Sugar had climbed out of bed and made her slow way to the landing, too impatient to wait. She wanted to see for herself if her gift had been well-received. She had her hands clasped together and the smile on her face was a mile wide. "If you want to kiss her again, Ren, don't let me stop you."

He didn't. He bent lower, and Tully closed her eyes.

Chapter Twenty-Seven

Sugar Morgan had only done five good things in her life, but they were five pretty important and satisfying things, when you stopped to think about it.

She'd gotten clean and off the game, she'd given away her son and found him again, and she'd brought two soul mates together when they'd both decided, foolish young things, that it wasn't possible.

She died on June 20, peacefully at home, with her family around her, and a box of Copper Mountain Chocolates right beside her on the coffee table, not yet empty.

LILIAN DARCY

The End

The Sweetest Thing

Thank you for reading! If you enjoyed this story, you will also love these other books by Lilian Darcy.

lilian darcy
late last night
mb
montana born
a river bend novel

An excerpt from

late last night

Lilian Darcy
Copyright © 2014

March, 1996

Really, rock music wasn't what it used to be.

Kate fumbled for the tuning knob on the pickup truck radio and came up with a country station. She liked country, but not today when she was late and tired and stressed after a long day of teaching. The meeting after school with Neve Shepherd's parents had gone on much longer than she had thought it would, and then she'd had several more tasks to complete after that.

"We're worried that her boyfriend is a bad influence," Neve's father Gary had said at one point.

"Jay Brown," Annette Shepherd had put in. "Do you teach him, too?"

"Yes, I do." Kate already knew that Neve and Jay were dating, and she'd resisted blurting out her instant response—Jay a bad influence on Neve? No, it was the other way around. Neve was getting seriously out of control.

Careful with the speed limit, Kate.

She needed rock, and she needed it LOUD, and the Smashing Pumpkins and Foo Fighters just weren't the same as the bands she'd loved in her teens. Blondie, the Eagles, the Police, the Stones. Those were bands.

I sound as if I'm forty.

Which she wouldn't be for ages. Not until three years into the next millennium. She was only thirty-two, for heaven's sake. Meanwhile, if she didn't find a song she liked, she might start screaming instead.

She twiddled the tuning knob once more, finally found

a halfway decent song, started singing with no style and no tune at the top of her voice—it worked a little, as a stress release—then saw the flashing red and blue lights in her rear-view mirror and her heart sank into the pit of her stomach.

Please, no! Not again.

She slowed and pulled over, pressed her forehead against the hard curve of the steering wheel and groaned while she waited for the long arm of the law to step out of his vehicle and arrive beside her.

This couldn't be happening. And yet it was.

A minute later, he appeared in his dark uniform at her window and she wound it down, the battered pickup not being a recent enough model to have push-button windows. It was the sheriff himself, not a mere junior deputy, and not the highway patrol. Sheriff Harrison Pearce had been with the county for just over a year, and had now pulled her over four times in less than three months for traffic violations. She'd run one stop light in town, and was caught speeding twice out here on the highway, but this time she didn't even *know* what she'd done wrong.

"I wasn't speeding," she said, before he could open his mouth. He loomed beyond the open window, big and unmoving, the uniform clinging to strong shoulders and well-worked thighs. "I *wasn't*."

"You know, Miz MacCreadie," he said in a slow Montana drawl, "we gotta stop meeting like this."

"I know we do. Why is it always you? Between the police department and the sheriff's office and the highway patrol, there have to be other officers on the roads, you would *think*." She shut her mouth quickly, before she began to sound completely hysterical.

"I mean that." He wore a sober, serious expression that made the planes of his face look as if they'd been carved by a sculptor in a thoughtful mood. He had dark eyes and dark hair and the kind of short, neat haircut that looked terrible on any man who had a badly shaped head.

Sheriff Pearce's head was very well-shaped indeed.

Almost as well-shaped as his body.

Unfortunately.

"I wasn't speeding," Kate said.

"That is a plus," he agreed. He sounded calm, and almost kind. "But your tail-light is out." He put a hand on the roof of the pickup and leaned in a little.

"One tail-light?" she said.

"I'm sorry, Ma'am. It's still a violation."

"I—I'm sorry, too, but I really didn't know it was out, and I'm late getting home."

"Step out of the vehicle, and I'll show you."

She stepped. Well, she opened the door with a slightly shaky hand, and stumbled out on tired, impatient legs. Every minute she was delayed here would only increase the likely chaos when she arrived home.

Sheriff Pearce walked her around to the back of the pickup, his stride even and long. "See, it's your left light, and these roads are pitch black at night. What if someone thinks you're a motorcycle when they try to pass you?"

"It's not pitch black yet." It was a plea, not an argument.

"Will be, soon," he pointed out, still sounding kind rather than stern. The last fiery edge of the western sun had dipped below the jagged and snow-capped horizon of the distant Tobacco Root Mountains some minutes ago.

She shivered, standing in the cold. There were still thick patches of snow in the ditches, and she wasn't wearing a coat. "Could I get the tail light fixed, and then bring the vehicle in and show you?"

He was silent for a moment, and she breathed in the calm of him. She'd met him a couple of times *outside* the context of her shocking and heinous driving record, and she'd never seen a ruffle or a chink in the aura of strength and peace he gave off.

It was amazing. It was wonderful. If he could bottle it, she would be in the market for a steady supply. Her own life and state of being was anything but calm, and that was why this kept happening, this traffic violation stuff. Really, it wasn't like her. She was a schoolteacher for heck's sake! A role model.

"Bring it tomorrow," he said. "Get the light fixed first

thing. Can you undertake to do that?" He flicked her a narrow-eyed look, and spoke in the voice of the law.

"I—I will. And if there's any delay, I'll call you."

"Here's my card."

I have his card!

Buy *Late Last Night* now on Amazon!

About the Author

Lilian Darcy was born on Valentine's Day. This auspicious date, as well as a love of reading, set her destiny as a writer of romance and women's fiction from an early age. She has written more than eighty novels for Harlequin, Silhouette, Mira Australia, Mills & Boon and The Tule Group, and has also written for Australian theatre and television, under another name. She has made many appearances on the Waldenbooks Romance Bestsellers list, and has received five nominations for the Romance Writers of America's prestigious Rita Award. Her plays have been professionally performed by some of Australia's best-known theatre companies, while in 1990 she was the co-recipient of an Australian Film Institute award for best TV mini-series. Lilian is married with four children, and lives in Canberra, Australia.

lilian darcy

after the rain

a river bend novel

Coming Soon

after the rain
a River Bend novel

How do you stop being angry at someone when they're gone?

Kira Blair's sister drowned eighteen years ago at River Bend Park, on the night of the 1996 Marietta High School senior prom, and Kira is still mired in feelings she can't resolve. So much of her life has been shadowed by Neve – by her vivid presence as they were growing up, and by her death.

Eighteen years later, Kira and her ten-year-old son Jake are finally getting on track after a difficult divorce from Jake's dad, when Neve's high school boyfriend Casey "Jay" Brown comes back to Marietta and turns everything upside down.

Casey has never known in his heart how much he was to blame for what happened to Neve that night, nor what their fraught and frustrating teen relationship was really about, but when he and Kira are forced to work together, she leaves him in no doubt as to her opinion.

That's how you stop being angry at someone when they're gone. You channel your anger onto the man you hold responsible, the man who's right here, right now, and you don't let up, no matter how heart-stoppingly gorgeous he is.

After the Rain: June 2014

Coming Soon

long walk home
a River Bend novel

Nobody knows what Gemma Clayton went through on the night of the 1996 Marietta High School senior prom, between the moment she ran after Judd and Garth Newell's car as it left River Bend Park and when she limped into her friend Neve Shepherd's street more than two hours later.

Soon, though, she's planning to reveal the truth. When her wonderful daughter Bree reaches her eighteenth birthday, it'll be time for Gemma to turn herself in to the police and confess her involvement in what happened that night. She's always intended to do it, but she couldn't bear the idea of her little girl growing up with a mom in prison, so she's made herself this promise: when Bree turns eighteen.

What Gemma hasn't counted on, though, is a man entering her life after all this time–a gorgeous, generous, honorable man living just over her back fence, a man named Dylan Saddler with a dark past and a wonderful daughter of his own.

Long Walk Home: October 2014

TULE
PUBLISHING

Made in the USA
Lexington, KY
06 August 2014